REAPER REBORN

BOOK 3 OF THE REAPERS TRILOGY

REAPER
REBORN

A NOVEL BY

BRYAN DAVIS

BOOKS BY BRYAN DAVIS

The Reapers Trilogy
Reapers
Beyond the Gateway
Reaper Reborn

Time Echoes Trilogy
Time Echoes
Interfinity
Fatal Convergence

Dragons in our Midst
Raising Dragons
The Candlestone
Circles of Seven
Tears of a Dragon

Oracles of Fire
Eye of the Oracle
Enoch's Ghost
Last of the Nephilim
The Bones of Makaidos

Reaper Reborn

Book 3 of The Reapers Trilogy

Copyright © 2017 by Bryan Davis

Published by Scrub Jay Journeys
P. O. Box 512
Middleton, TN 38052
www.scrubjayjourneys.com
email: info@scrubjayjourneys.com

ISBN: 978-1-946253-42-2

First Printing – April 2017

Printed in the U.S.A.

Library of Congress Control Number: 2017901691

CHAPTER ONE

"WAKE UP, PHOENIX. You need to see this."

I opened my eyes. Shanghai slept with her head against my shoulder and her legs curled in my lap. My limbs tingled under her weight. Numbness reigned in mind and body.

Sing paced in front of my chair. Wearing a Sancta's red cloak with a raised hood, she looked like a floating wave of scarlet. She held a sheet of creased yellow paper, her brow wrinkled with creases of its own as she studied the page.

I shifted to ease the tingles. "What is it?"

She stopped and looked at me. The whites of her eyes provided a stark contrast to her darker skin, a hue generated from the blended genetics of a Ghanaian father and a Japanese mother. Wearing forest green Reaper trousers and a black shirt under her cloak, she looked more like a woman ready for battle than did Sarah, the first Sancta I met.

"A coded message." Sing turned the page toward me, revealing an unreadable string of dark letters. "Someone slipped it under the door during the night. I'm trying to decipher it."

"Any progress?"

"It's from the Resistance. A warning of some kind. We should get ready to leave."

"Will do." I patted Shanghai's arm. "Wake up."

"Hmmm?" She opened her eyes and smiled. "What's going on?"

"Sing found a warning message from the Resistance. She's decoding it now."

Shanghai, also dressed in Reaper garb, climbed out of my lap and stretched her slender, toned body. Light from the window illuminated her taut face and intense eyes, accented by the slant bestowed by her Asian ancestors. "I guess the Resistance is still active."

Sing lowered her hood, releasing her dark curly locks. "Since the Gatekeeper died, I'm sure they've been discussing their next step, maybe to stage insurrections and topple any leader still loyal to him. Or to prepare for whatever Alex might do next." She continued reading the note. "Just a couple of more minutes."

Shanghai grasped my wrist and pulled me to my feet. As blood rushed to my legs, I lifted and lowered them in turn. After five days of lying in bed unconscious, they felt lifeless. They needed a good workout.

While Shanghai took the first turn in the bathroom, Sing folded the note and slipped it under her cloak. "The Resistance leaders are meeting in a secret location in Chicago. They want you to know that Alex is back in town, and her movements seem to be trained on you. She was seen near the Fife building right before the fire and then only a block away from this apartment. The leaders think you should go to a secure location."

"Suits me. If we can find a place. Though I don't like the idea of running from Alex."

Sing gave me a firm nod. "Good attitude. No retreat. We should shift to full attack mode. We could even set an ambush."

I drew my head back. "An ambush? What made you so warlike all of a sudden?"

"This *is* a war." She looked straight at me. "It's time to train your mind, but not with what we learned during Reaper school. We were taught how to escape bandits, how to protect the souls in our care. Our purpose was to defend, not to attack. You need a new mindset."

"Okay," I said with a prompting tone. "Go on."

"In the past, whenever you faced Alex, you always put yourself in protection mode. You know, trying to save people like the Fitzpatricks, Misty, Shanghai, and me. Normally, that's a good strategy for typical Reaper duties, but when dealing with Alex, it always puts you at a disadvantage. All she has to do is threaten someone you love, and she immediately cripples you. You have no choice but to play by her rules."

"So you want me to change that strategy?"

Sing nodded. "You have to kill Alex."

"Okay. I get that. But, like you said, what if she's threatening someone I love? That's her number one strategy. She's bound to do it again."

"No doubt she will." Sing narrowed an eye. "Focus only on the goal. If Alex lives, many will die, probably including anyone you try to save by hesitating to go on the offensive. Think about how many are already dead because of her — Misty, Colm, Kwame, camp prisoners. Not to mention the countless people who'll die once Alex begins her murderous march to control the world."

I let out a sigh. "Right. She's a murderer, and we have to stop her, but it'll be hard ignoring one of her threats to kill someone."

Sing cracked a smile. "Saving the world is never easy, hero boy."

When Shanghai came out of the bathroom, I took my turn. The water pressure was barely high enough to allow for a quick wash of hands and face and a swallow or two to quench my thirst. Yet, it sufficed.

While Sing looked out the apartment's window, Shanghai and I whipped on our weapons belts and fastened them. "I restocked your belt," Shanghai said. "Smoke capsules, lighter, two sharp knives, flashlight with fresh batteries, two spool lines, and the radiation-level band you got from the checkpoint guard. It's in your pouch."

I touched the pouch and felt for the band. "Got it."

"Kwame's watch is in there, too. I kept Alex's watch. Timepieces might come in handy."

I scanned the belt and spotted an empty pouch. "Have you seen my camera?"

"Um ..." She offered a sheepish smile. "I lost mine weeks ago, so I borrowed yours while you were recovering. I left it at the condo. I guess it got destroyed."

"No problem, but what did you need it for?"

"I was practicing ... a ... a speech, I guess. I made a recording with your camera." She touched her pants pocket. "I have the photo stick. Remind me to show it to you later."

I smiled. "Okay, mystery woman, but I'm going to be wondering what you're up to."

Someone pounded on the door. "Phoenix! Open up!"

I rushed to the peephole and looked out. A man with gray hair stood in the corridor, his head low, concealing his face. I called, "Who is it?"

"Bill. From the depot." He lifted his head, revealing his familiar bushy gray hair and eyebrows, but his face was raw, red, and peeling. Blood covered his throat and dampened his white sweatshirt.

I unlocked the door and threw it open. When Bill staggered in, I grabbed his wrist and guided him toward my reading chair while Sing closed the door and relocked it.

Shanghai ran toward the bathroom. "I'll get something to stop the bleeding."

By the time I helped Bill sit, Shanghai rushed back with a damp cloth. She stretched his sweatshirt at the shoulder, revealing a series of deep cuts, one of which bled profusely over a thin leather cord around his neck. She covered the deepest cut with the cloth and applied pressure. "Just sit still."

"What happened?" I asked.

Bill spoke with wheezing breaths. "We ... the Resistance leaders ... were meeting a few blocks away to discuss our plans. After a few minutes, clouds of radiant gas came from the ventilation system and covered us. It burned like crazy. When we tried to escape, intruders broke through the door and started beating us. They were invisible. Like ghosts. And they packed a punch." He angled his head and looked at the blood-drenched cloth. "I think they were metallic with sharp edges."

I glanced at Shanghai and Sing. "Illuminaries."

"Poison gas from the ventilation system," Shanghai said. "That's new."

Bill winced tightly. "Testing an efficient way to kill people, I suppose."

"Why did you come here?" I asked.

Bill's face turned pale, and he blinked several times, as if losing consciousness. "To warn you. Our top spy said your apartment will be bombed."

"Bombed? When? Who?"

"I don't know. I ..." His eyes rolled upward, and his head lolled to the side.

Sing ran to the door, unlocked it, and set a hand on the knob. "We have to find a doctor. Let's go."

"Got him." I gathered Bill into my arms and carried his limp body while Shanghai braced his head, the cloth still in place. "Maybe Dr. Rubenstein will help us."

Sing opened the door. Five paces away, two illuminaries stood in the hallway side by side. A slight purr proved that their engines were running, but no flashes emanated. The new models, far more deadly than the older ones, could probably turn that function on and off.

"They're just standing there," Shanghai said. "Like they're waiting for something."

"The bomb." I nodded toward the window. "That way. You two first. I'll pass Bill to you."

Shanghai ran to the window and lifted the sash, letting in a chilly breeze. After she and Shanghai climbed out to the fire escape, I passed Bill through the opening and joined them on the metal platform. The dawning sunlight illuminating the alley made it look like about seven or eight in the morning.

"I'll carry him firefighter style," I said. "Better for taking the stairs."

After Shanghai and Sing helped me lift Bill over my shoulder, Shanghai looked back through the window. "No one's coming."

"That's what worries me." I nodded toward the stairs. "You two first. I'll be right behind you."

Just as Shanghai and Sing began tromping down the metal steps, an explosion erupted behind me. The force sent Bill and me flying over the railing. With my free hand, I grabbed my spool claw and threw it toward the fire escape. When it hooked on the railing, I set the spool's brake and held on. The spool screamed. The line tightened, slowing my plunge.

I landed on my feet and rolled with Bill on the alley floor. When we stopped, I lay on my back with him on my chest. Above, smoke spewed through a gaping hole that was once my window. Brick fragments and glass shards rained in a wide circle, a few striking the ground near my feet. The fire-escape frame swayed, its fastening brackets torn from the bricks, and my claw lay on the ground.

Shanghai and Sing ran to my side and knelt. "Are you all right?" Shanghai asked as they lifted Bill.

"I think so." I rolled out from under him, and the three of us carried him to the side of the building. His eyes were still open, giving me hope.

Once we laid him down, I knelt and checked for a pulse at his neck. Nothing. I set my ear against his chest and listened. No heartbeat. No respiration.

I straightened and looked at Shanghai and Sing as they settled on their knees next to me. "He's dead."

Tears gleaming, Shanghai closed Bill's eyelids. Her voice squeaked as she said, "What should we do with him?"

"Can you reap him?" I asked.

She shook her head. "Tokyo taught me how to reap a ghost, not a soul who's still attached. Without energy, I can't dematerialize my hand and push it into his brain."

Sing ran her fingers through Bill's hair. "We'll have to leave him here and let him self-detach. Maybe you can collect him later."

I gazed at Bill's red, peeling face. In spite of its ravaged state, it seemed noble, virtuous. I had no idea how well connected he was with the higher levels of the Resistance. "I guess since the Resistance leaders are dead, the followers won't know what to do."

"True." Sing's shoulders sagged. "It looks like we're on our own."

Something thudded from my apartment, though nothing appeared at the blown-out window. "We should go," I said as I reeled in my spool line. "The illuminaries are bound to search for us in the damage. When they don't find us, they might come down here."

Shanghai watched my line's claw drag toward me. "That move you made while falling was incredible. I guess you already have your reflexes back. Maybe better than ever."

"Just instinct." I hooked the claw to my belt and looked at the window again. Still no sign of the illuminaries. "Let's bolt."

"Just a second." Sing lifted the leather cord around Bill's neck and drew it over his head. A roughly cut wooden cross dangled at the bottom of a worn boot lace tied to make a necklace. Sing laid the cross in her palm and gazed at it. Stained with blood, it covered most of her hand.

After whispering quietly for a moment, she pushed the cross into her pants pocket and said, "I'm ready."

We hurried from the alley in silence. My legs feeling surprisingly strong, I led Shanghai and Sing along a sidewalk void of any other pedestrians, an odd sight at this time of the morning. The cracked concrete path skirted a row of brick-walled apartment buildings, many vandalized by vulgar graffiti and rude drawings scrawled by local wielders of paint or chalk. Their words and art reflected the sorry state of their existence — dark and hopeless.

Adding to the dismal thoughts, Bill's death weighed heavily on my mind. The poor old man had stationed himself at the depot for years, dutifully warning Reapers about the evils taking place at the Gateway. I had always thought he was just a crackpot, a crazed conspiracy theorist who had nothing better to do than to bother real-world people with his loony ideas.

Now I knew better. He was a soldier for a just cause, not minding his menial task or the ridicule that pelted him on a daily basis. He was doing his part. He was a hero.

I shook my head to cast off the gloom. With Alex and her illuminaries on the march, we had to hurry. I picked up the pace. "Let's head to Eggs & Stuff and see if anyone knows where Liam is. We have to gather whatever allies we have."

My two companions matched my gait. When we turned onto a sidewalk next to a main road, we jogged parallel to a line of nearly bumper-to-bumper cars, inching along in a haze of exhaust smoke. A fear-stoked evacuation was in progress.

A ghost approached from the opposite direction, a man wearing an orange prison jumpsuit, probably a recent execution victim. His semitransparent body and glowing eyes gave away his dead status, and his menacing scowl revealed a violent streak.

Shanghai grimaced. "I don't want to reap that thug, especially with no energy."

"Let him go," I said. "We don't want to attract attention. Besides, he's just a level one, not experienced enough to hurt anyone yet."

When the ghost drew near, he turned and crossed the street, passing through a car before hurrying on. Farther down the walkway, several other ghosts came into view, most huddled under canopies or building overhangs, demonstrating a desire to be covered by something, typical for many low-level ghosts.

Shanghai's eyes darted. "The ghost population is soaring. I see one … two … three level ones. No. More than that. Pretty much everyone around here is a ghost."

On the walkway ahead, a phantom young woman wearing overalls and a baseball cap crept past a liquor store, bending low as if trying not to be seen. A man and a boy chatted as they walked with an umbrella over their heads, like a father escorting a son to school, both apparently unaware of their dead status.

As we passed them, I looked each ghost over. "They're too young for natural causes."

"And they're not the type we normally see at executions," Shanghai said. "Last night's fire at the Fife building, maybe?"

"Or they're executing everyone in the prisons and corrections camps and tossing them into the cremation ovens."

Shanghai nodded. "Fire makes souls jump out in a hurry."

A gust of cold air prompted me to raise my hood. "Alex is spreading fear. A panicked city is vulnerable. Chicago's about to burn, and a lot of people know it. That's why they're trying to leave town."

Still jogging at my side, Sing glanced around, her brow bent low. "You're right. We should ignore the ghosts and get ready for Alex."

"Any idea what our next step should be?" I asked Sing.

"Well, I have been waiting for —"

A siren blared a short blast.

Sing nodded. "There it is."

A second blast followed, then a third and a fourth — the signal for a video bulletin.

"Strange timing," Shanghai said. "The Gatekeeper's dead. The government's in chaos. Why signal an announcement?" She looked at Sing. "And how did you know it was coming?"

"Actually I thought it would come sooner. Alex has always stayed a step ahead of us, so I'm trying to predict her moves. By now she knows that you two survived the bomb and can tell the world the truth about what she did at the Gateway. She needs to neutralize you in the public eye. My guess is she'll use the announcement to do that."

My legs still stronger than expected, I pushed on. "That sounds like her style, a personal message that starts a new chess match."

"I agree," Shanghai said. "But bombing the apartment and setting fire to the Fife building aren't like her. She flaunts her power. She wants to be in your face, not hiding and killing in secret."

"True, but the illuminaries were there. Alex controls them."

"Maybe she has someone working with her." Shanghai shrugged. "I can't imagine who, though."

Bartholomew the depot attendant came to mind. Since he was probably behind my parents' murders, he might be trying to make me his next victim, guessing that I had talked to my father's soul by now. But with no evidence beyond my father's word, it was better to delay airing my suspicions. "I'll keep thinking about it. Let's just see what Alex has to say. Eggs & Stuff will show the broadcast."

Shanghai nodded toward the line of cars, still snaking along at a slow pace. "Looks like some people aren't going to bother watching. Maybe they'll pick it up on their car radios."

After zigzagging from one side street to another, we arrived at the restaurant, pulled the front of our hoods down over our eyes, and entered the main door. More than fifty people sat or stood watching a television mounted at a ceiling corner. Most wore coats and hats to ward off the chill that the restaurant's fireplace had not been able to quell.

A short, bearded man wearing a baseball cap looked our way and nudged a taller man next to him. As every head turned toward us, the word *Reapers* passed across the eating area in a cascade of gasps and murmurs from faces bent in anger.

Shanghai leaned close to me and whispered, "I don't think we're welcome here."

CHAPTER TWO

CROSS THE DINING area, Liam rose from a chair. His towering height and impressive build, along with his clean-shaven face and short hair, made him look like the ideal soldier. He called out with a thick Irish accent, "These two Reapers are here for the announcement just like you are. Be polite and mind your own business."

Standing next to me, Sing fixed her stare on the television. Since Liam didn't mention her, she was probably invisible to everyone but Shanghai and me.

Liam looked my way. "Everyone is jumpy. We have no fire fighters, no food distribution. The only time police come around is to harass people. Ghosts are popping up all over town and scaring folks. Tell us what you know while we wait for the announcement."

Shanghai nudged my ribs. "This is your chance to explain before Alex sets her claws. We might not get another one."

"You're right." I walked to the television's corner and climbed onto a chair. Near the entry door, Shanghai kept a hand on her weapons belt while Sing wore a pensive frown. They knew I would be facing a hostile crowd.

I cleared my throat and spoke in a loud tone. "Here is the short version of the story. The Gatekeeper is dead. At his headquarters, we found hundreds of souls who were being tortured, and we rescued them. Now they have traveled beyond the Gateway, so you can set your minds at ease about any family or friends you might have lost recently."

Another wave of murmurs rolled across the room. I waited for it to subside before continuing. "Regarding the increase in the ghost sightings, we Reapers will soon train to collect and deliver them to the Gateway with a new method. The depots no longer work, but our goal is to get them up and running and make sure the energy lines terminate under an expanded hole in the sky instead of inside the Gatekeeper's headquarters. Until that time, expect to see more ghosts than usual. We'll do our best to round up any aggressive ones."

A woman waved her hand. "What about services? My water got turned off, and all the government offices are closed. I have to drag a bucket to and from a faucet in the park, and I have to wait an hour in line when I get there. Sometimes people fight, and I haven't seen a policeman in three days."

I gave her an affirming nod. "The situation is terrible, I know, and we all have to make sacrifices. The government is in chaos. Until we can hold elections and get new leadership in place, we'll have to make do on our own."

A man called out, "You should have thought about that before you assassinated the leader of the world. At least we had law and order under him."

As sharp whispers volleyed back and forth, I searched for the source of the call. No luck. His voice sounded familiar, but I couldn't place it.

I spread my hands. "I didn't kill the Gatekeeper. Alex, one of the Council members, killed him so she could take control. I saw it all. He was trying to kill me, so I threw him over a —"

"Of course he tried to kill you. You were an intruder in his home."

I spotted the man standing in the middle of the pack — Bartholomew. Wearing jeans and a zip-up jacket instead of his depot robes, he looked like a normal Chicagoan, though his neatly trimmed white beard and hawkish nose made him easy to identify. His white hair, however, was shorter than usual — closely cropped instead of long and flowing.

"Bartholomew," I said in what I hoped was a placating tone, "I know you lost your job because of what happened, but I'm sure you wouldn't want to earn money from a process that tortured souls. The Gatekeeper was holding them captive and draining their energy for his benefit. He was an insane tyrant who was literally making souls suffer for eternity. He had to be stopped. He deserved to die. And I'm glad I was there to see it happen. Now we just have to clean up the mess and start over."

A smattering of applause broke out, though it was short-lived. Bartholomew kept his stare on me and said nothing more.

The television speaker emitted a beep. I dismounted the chair and rejoined Shanghai and Sing. The restaurant manager handed Shanghai and me each a glass of water, an unexpected kindness. Apparently the kitchen's supply had not been shut off.

After thanking him, I took a long drink. The coolness soothed my dry throat, and a renewed sensation of strength coursed through my body. In spite of my lost energy valve, I felt better than I had in a long time.

While the Gatekeeper's anthem played from the television, I whispered, "Strange choice of music, considering he's dead."

Shanghai took a sip of water and nodded. "Something sinister is happening. You can bet Alex is behind it."

An image appeared on the screen, the Gatekeeper standing next to Alex.

I swallowed hard. How could this be? He was dead. We saw his corpse.

New murmurs rose from the restaurant customers. A few glanced at us with curious expressions, though most kept their stares locked on the screen.

The Gatekeeper smiled. His dark curly hair and youthful face made him look as vibrant as he did in any of his propaganda posters. "To quote a clever writer from long ago," he said, his tone lively, "reports of my death have been greatly exaggerated. As you can see, I am alive and well, though monumental damage has been done. Alexandria, here ..." He nodded toward Alex as she stood with her leather-jacketed arms crossed, her blonde hair tied back in a ponytail. "Is the only surviving member of my Council. The other five were murdered by a pair of Reapers — Phoenix and Shanghai from Chicago. They invaded my headquarters and destroyed the Gateway-delivery mechanisms, thereby shipwrecking all hope that the souls of your loved ones will travel safely to the afterlife. Fortunately, Alexandria, as a Reaper herself, was able to drive the rogue Reapers away with her extraordinary skills."

As the Gatekeeper paused, apparently letting his words sink in, the murmurs grew louder. More faces turned toward us, their expressions shocked and angry.

Shanghai shouted, "He's lying. He can't be the real Gatekeeper. I reached into his corpse's brain to reap his soul, but it was gone. Alex must've ..." She turned to me, her eyes wide. "It's his ghost."

"A level three," I said. "He had so much soul energy, he advanced right away."

Sing touched my arm and whispered, "They're not going to believe you. Keep listening, but back toward the door slowly. Our battle is not with these people. They are victims of cruelty."

"So what we must do," the Gatekeeper continued, his tone stern, "is rebuild what has been destroyed. Now that everyone knows I am alive, most government functions will begin to come to order. The only segment that cannot be repaired quickly is the soul-delivery system. Reapers no longer have access to the energy they need to do their jobs, which means that, unless they have surgery to remove their energy valves, they will die. We will have to round them up for their own good."

Shanghai, Sing, and I stepped back. This announcement was going from bad to worse.

The Gatekeeper raised three fingers. "Therefore, I am issuing three new orders. One, a group of new reaping units will be sent to each major city. Not only will they reap souls and transport them to the Gateway, they will also keep the peace. We call them Peace Patrollers, and I trust that you will all learn to respect their mission.

"Two, all former Reapers will be collected and taken to facilities where they will undergo life-saving surgery so they can safely take their places in society. Even those who have already had the surgery must be examined to make sure the procedure was done in keeping with the highest medical standards. We have already heard reports of quick, back-alley operations that resulted in infection, permanent injury, and even death.

"As you might expect, some Reapers will be hesitant to voluntarily turn themselves in. Therefore, every citizen who provides information that leads to a Reaper's detainment will be given free access to medical care for his or her family for a year."

We took several more steps back. Now we had bounties on our heads. That medical examination would be nothing more than a summary execution.

"In addition, we are searching for Chicago's Phoenix and Shanghai. Take a good look at them." Side-by-side photos of Shanghai and me filled the screen. The close-up shots were recent and clear. No one would have a problem identifying us.

Again people turned toward us, this time nodding as they matched the photos to our faces.

When Alex and the Gatekeeper returned to the screen, the Gatekeeper continued. "Anyone who captures or provides information leading to their capture will be given free *lifetime* access to medical care for themselves and their families. They are extremely dangerous, so be careful about approaching them.

"And, finally, edict number three. In order to conduct a search for these two Reapers, we must clear the streets of Chicago. Those who are fleeing the city and listening by radio, turn around and go home. Once the streets are clear, all non-government vehicles will be banned from travel within the city limits until further notice. I am declaring a city holiday until we find these two criminals. Therefore, if you want to go back to work and earn a living, I am sure you will do your part in apprehending Phoenix and Shanghai. Thank you for your attention."

The video display went blank. While the anthem played, every face turned toward us. Some bore hungry eyes.

Shanghai hissed, "We'd better run."

I shook my head. "I'm not running. We haven't done anything wrong."

"Then you'd better talk fast. The sharks smell blood in the water."

I called out, "Who are you going to believe? The Gatekeeper who sucks the life energy out of your departed loved ones? Or me, a Reaper who has lived among you and served you faithfully?"

A tall, hefty man stepped toward us and stroked his full beard. "Belief's got nothing to do with it. I want the free medical care. And besides, I have to go to work. We all do." He looked back at the others in the crowd. "Who's with me? You'll be new members of my family."

Seven more men joined him, all of substantial size, their cold-weather clothing adding bulk to their girths.

Liam walked toward us. "Bastian, don't do this. Phoenix and Shanghai are our friends."

"Friends don't destroy our lives." Bastian picked up a chair. "I'll say it again. Who's with me?"

I raised my fists and set my feet for battle. "We don't want to fight you, but we will if you force us to defend ourselves."

Shanghai copied my pose and growled, "If you attack, you'll be sorry."

"What?" Bastian laughed. "A boy and a girl against all of us?"

Liam stood next to me and folded his muscular arms over his chest. "I stand with the Reapers."

"You're a formidable man, Liam, but you're still —"

"Don't be fools!" Bartholomew squeezed through the crowd and stood in front of me, breathless as he faced Bastian. "These Reapers are highly skilled fighting machines. They could cripple and maim ten of you without batting an eye. Fifty if they put some effort into it. You don't stand a chance."

Bastian set the chair down and pointed at Bartholomew. "Weren't you the one calling him out a few minutes ago?"

Bartholomew nodded. "I was. I was. But I'm being realistic. I've seen these two in action, and I don't want anyone to get hurt. If you want the reward, you'd better come up with another way to turn them in."

"Like what?"

Bartholomew shifted his weight from foot to foot. "There are ways. I am a former demolitions expert, and I have access to bombs, incendiary devices, and the like. We just have to catch the Reapers off guard."

I fumed. He *was* the one who bombed my apartment, and intentionally spilling that information was his way of letting me know he was on my tail and plotting my capture.

Shanghai grabbed Bartholomew's arm and spun him toward her. "Listen you glorified death clerk, you executed my friend without a trial. You sucked the life right out of him without mercy. So don't go around pretending you're the good guy trying to catch a couple of wayward Reapers. You're a murderer."

Bartholomew raised his hands and backed away. "I executed a drug smuggler, which is my right and duty as a depot attendant."

"Liar!" Shanghai punched him in the nose. Blood sprayed. He staggered backwards and slumped into Bastian's arms.

Bastian lowered Bartholomew to the floor, picked up the chair again, and growled to the others, "Let's take them!"

Several men rushed at us. Liam grabbed Bastian's chair and wrenched it away. Shanghai leaped and kicked Bastian across the jaw, flattening him. I threw a right cross at the closest attacker and sent him flying. When Shanghai and I reset our stances and Liam lifted the chair, ready to swing it, the others slowly backed away.

"I told you," Bartholomew said from the floor, holding a hand over his nose while blood flowed between his fingers. "Don't underestimate them. They're dangerous."

I grasped Shanghai's arm. "Let's go."

We hurried outside with Sing and Liam trailing. Once on the sidewalk, we looked back. Several men glared at us through the window. A man with a scarred cheek brandished a knife. Another man shouted an obscenity, muffled by the glass.

"We'd better hit the trail," I said. "Get away from this area before Bartholomew gathers more allies."

Liam pointed toward the street. "My van is around the corner. I will drive wherever you need to go."

I nodded. "Lead the way."

Liam took off at a trot on the sidewalk. Shanghai, Sing, and I followed. The line of traffic moved at about ten miles per hour, an improvement. People were already heeding the travel edict. When we turned at a corner, we found Liam's van parked alongside the curb, its "Mayfield Transport" insignia making it easy to identify.

Shanghai climbed into the front passenger seat, while Sing and I entered the side door and sat on the floor in the rear cargo area, surrounded by small boxes, bags that smelled like coffee, and various tools, including a tire iron, several kinds of screwdrivers, and a sledge hammer.

The aroma raised a reminder of another time Shanghai, Sing, and I rode in Liam's van, the morning we sneaked into the corrections camp and spiked the guards' coffee, hoping to knock them out so we could rescue the Fitzpatricks, including Fiona and her daughters, Anne and Betsy.

When Liam started the engine and its usual clatter filled the compartment, I asked, "Do you know where Fiona is?"

"I do." Liam lowered his window, propped an elbow on the frame, and drove to the intersection where he watched for a gap in the stream of vehicles. "She left town with her girls earlier this morning. She hopes to live with Colleen for a while, but she might have trouble getting out if all the roads are jammed like this one."

Sing lowered her hood. "The Gatekeeper's announcement will probably slow the exodus. Once people hear that their services are coming back, they'll choose security over the unknown."

Liam pulled the van into the flow of traffic and glanced at me in the rearview mirror. "Where do you want to go?"

"The bandits' park?" Sing asked. "That's an unlikely place for us to go."

"Sing's right," I said. "Let's head for the park."

Liam's brow lifted high. "Sing? Do you mean the little squirrel?"

"Yes, Liam," Sing said, laughing. "Look again. You can see me now."

He adjusted the rearview mirror and smiled. "How did you get there? I thought you were dead."

"I was. I mean, I am. It's a long story."

"Liam," I said, "let's go to the park near the train station, and I'll tell you Sing's story on the way. When we get there, drive onto the grass and out of sight in the trees. We want to make sure we're alone to plan our strategy."

"I will."

While Liam drove, I told him about the Sanctae and how Sing became one of them. He had heard much of our story from Shanghai, but that was before Sing showed up at my apartment wearing the red cloak of her new office.

Soon after I finished the tale, he drove the van over a curb and into the park. After pulling it under a thick tree canopy, he cut the engine and looked out his window. "They say this park is a haunt for bandits."

"Don't worry," I said. "If they see Shanghai and me, they'll scatter in a hurry."

"If you say so." Liam plugged a thin cable into his van's radio and inserted buds into his ears. "I'll keep watch and listen to the news while you plan."

"Good. Thanks."

Shanghai climbed into the back, and the three of us sat cross-legged in a tight circle. I glanced between Shanghai and Sing. "First topic. The Peace Patrollers. I'm sure they're Alex's illuminaries, like the one we fought in the energy storage tank."

Shanghai blew out a breathy whistle. "That was one tough hombre. It killed Tokyo by itself. Imagine what an army of them could do."

"Massive damage. Alex will strike hard and fast. We won't last long unless we come up with a way to stop those machines."

Sing raised a finger. "She must have a weakness. The reward they offered for your capture means that she sees you two as a threat. If she's so invincible, she wouldn't worry about you at all."

"Good point," I said, "but what could the weakness be?"

"The illuminaries need soul energy," Sing said. "If they can't get it, they're useless."

Shanghai clenched a fist. "So that's why she's killing people and filling the streets with ghosts. The illuminaries will come in and collect them for fuel."

"And if Chicago burns," I said, "she'll have enough fuel to subdue the rest of the world."

Liam withdrew his earbuds. "It's happening. The government is turning people back at the city limits. No one can leave Chicago."

I nodded toward the radio. "They're building a fence around the slaughterhouse. They want people in their homes, like turkeys in the oven waiting for the heat to be turned on."

"True," Shanghai said, "but all this talk about killing people and getting soul energy doesn't explain the price on our heads. Just because we know what she's up to doesn't mean we can stop it. Why target two Reapers?"

Sing forked her fingers at us. "Maybe she wants something from one of you. Once she has you in custody, she'll try to force you to do something."

"Like when she wanted Phoenix to be the ruler of the world?" Shanghai huffed. "She's got to know that's not happening. Nothing could make him cozy up to that witch."

"Well," Sing said, "there is an old saying — keep your friends close and your enemies closer. We might have to do some spying to figure out why she wants you."

Shanghai slid her hand into mine. "I get that, but I'm staying close to my future husband, and I'm keeping that scheming she-devil as far away as possible."

Sing let out a sigh. "I can't blame you for that."

I peered into Sing's eyes. They seemed conflicted about something. "What's wrong?"

She smiled. "Going to heaven didn't give me the power to hide my emotions, did it?"

"Nope. You're exposed." I prodded her arm. "Spill it."

"All right. Here goes." She inhaled deeply. "Now that I am a Sancta, I learned a lot about what has led to these troubled times."

"Troubled is an understatement. I'm sure it's never been worse than this."

"Not so, Phoenix. More than two hundred years ago, the world was in much more danger. The tragedies of that time would take too long to describe, but ancestors of yours did what was necessary to save the world."

I scrunched my brow. "My ancestors saved the world?"

Sing nodded. "You are a direct descendant of a couple who suffered horrific torture and nearly died to rescue billions of people from annihilation. They were your age at the time and later married and enjoyed many years of peace and happiness."

Shanghai and I locked stares. She whispered, "So we don't have it so bad."

"Bad enough," Sing said, "but maybe their faith and courage will be an inspiration to you."

I firmed my lips and nodded. "I'm getting the picture. You understand why we want to steer clear of Alex, but you're hoping we'll charge ahead instead of retreating like scared rabbits."

"I didn't mean it like that. I meant —"

"No worries. I know what you meant. And you're right, absolutely right." I tightened my grip on Shanghai's hand. "I just wish those ancestors could be here to give us some advice."

"Well, not that I'm a perfect substitute," Sing said, "but you have me here to advise you. Your ancestors were helped many times by the first Sancta, a girl named Scarlet. That, too, is a long story, but she helped them through the use of a —"

"We have company," Liam said as he started the engine. "It's Alex."

I rose to my knees and looked through the windshield. A line of black-cloaked figures walked toward us from the opening to the wooded area. I shuffled to the back and peeked out that window. The line extended around the van. We were surrounded.

CHAPTER THREE

"LIAM," I SAID, "try to break through them."

"Them? What do you mean? Alex is alone."

"Just drive forward as fast as you can."

"I will." The van lunged. When it reached the line, two illuminaries thrust out their hands, caught the fender, and lifted the front of the van off the ground. The back tires spun in the turf and threw dirt to the rear while the engine rattled and whined.

"Something's trying to flip us!" Liam shouted.

"Keep pushing the gas," I said. "We'll take care of it."

Shanghai pulled a couple of feet of line from her belt spool. "Sweep their legs?"

"Right. Let's go." We threw the side door open and leaped out. Shanghai gave me her line's anchor hook, ducked under the raised wheels, and ran forward. Holding the line low, I ran as well. We tripped the two illuminaries and kept running forward, dodging two others that reached to grab us.

The van's front wheels hit the ground. After a quick spin of its tires, it took off over the fallen robots. When it drew close enough, we leaped onto the hood and scrambled up the windshield to the roof, the line slack between us.

Another line whipped around Shanghai, pinning her arms to her sides. Something jerked her off the top of the van toward the rear. I held to our line, but whoever anchored the other end of the line around Shanghai pulled me off the roof along with her.

I dropped to the ground and landed on my back. When I tried to rise, something dragged me. I slid on my bottom feet first. At the other end of Shanghai's line, two illuminaries pulled her toward them, my line still attached to her. I dug in my heels. Shanghai did the same, but we couldn't compete with the robots' power as they drew us closer and closer.

I jumped up, released my line, and charged toward them, grabbing a dagger from my belt as I ran. When I reached Shanghai, I cut their line, but as I tried to free her from the loop around her body, an illuminary jerked me up by my collar and suspended me a foot off the ground. Another did the same to Shanghai. Her arms still bound, she kicked and thrashed as she swayed.

I slung the dagger into the illuminary's shadowed face. The point embedded somewhere in the dim recesses. It dropped me and staggered back. I popped three smoke capsules from my belt and threw them to the ground. When the smoke erupted, I lunged for Shanghai, wrapped my arms around her, and wrestled her away from the illuminary.

It latched on to my arm with a vise grip. I released Shanghai, hooked my free arm around its neck, and, straining with all my might, ripped its head from its shoulders. I backpedaled, taking the head and cloak with me.

Now just a naked metal frame, the illuminary collapsed. The head, still in the crook of my arm, let out a sharp squeal that faded and died away.

I threw the head and cloak to the ground. Crouching, I withdrew Shanghai's dagger, cut the line around her, and hustled with her toward the sound of the van's motor.

When we passed the edge of the smoke, the van appeared, wheeling our way. A call came from behind us. "Phoenix!"

Alex's familiar voice made me cringe. I tried to continue running, but Shanghai faltered and dropped to her knees. She clutched her throat and gasped, "I ... I can't breathe."

I knelt with her. "What's wrong?"

She let out a rasping gurgle. Her eyes rolled upward, and she toppled to the side.

"Shanghai!" I braced her head, opened her mouth, and peered inside. Nothing seemed to be blocking her airway.

Liam parked next to me and called from the window. "Put her in the van. We'll find help somewhere."

"If you take her, she will die." Alex strutted out of the smoke with several illuminaries marching behind her, one of them carrying the fallen illuminary's metallic skull. She wore her usual black leather jacket and pants along with a white band around her head and a Reaper-style weapons belt at her waist. "She has less than three minutes to live."

I balled a fist. "What did you do to her?"

Alex walked closer, smirking. "The illuminary injected her with a drug that constricted her airway. If she doesn't get an antidote soon, she will die."

I spat out, "What do you want from me? Tell me now!"

Alex hummed through a soft laugh. "You know me all too well, don't you?"

I growled as I spoke through clenched teeth. "Just tell me."

"I want Shanghai. Let me take her with me, and I will give her the antidote."

Sing called from the van. "Phoenix, this is your chance. Alex won't expect an attack. Just break her neck and be done with her."

I imagined my hands grasping Alex's head and snapping her neck with a quick turn, but then how would I get the antidote for Shanghai? Alex probably had it hidden somewhere.

"Decide quickly," Alex said. "She is dying as we speak."

"All right. All right." I slid Shanghai's dagger into her belt's sheath, lifted her into my arms, and rose. One of the illuminaries stepped forward and took her from me.

"Hurry to the truck," Alex said to the illuminary. "Give her the antidote and wait for me there."

With two other illuminaries at its side, it marched toward the street that bordered the park, visible through the clearing smoke. A truck-and-trailer combo sat at the curb, likely the vehicle that brought the robots here.

I glared at Alex. "What else do you want from me?"

"Your cooperation." She set a hand on my cheek, but I slapped it away. Letting out a mock gasp, she backpedaled a step. "You've changed, Phoenix."

"If you mean that I'll never trust a syllable that slides off your serpent tongue, then, yes, I have changed."

"Tsk, tsk. You should be kinder to the woman who holds your fellow Reaper captive."

"Look. I saw your broadcast. You want people to turn us in. Now you have Shanghai. Stop playing mind games and tell me what you want."

"Very well." As a breeze blew the rest of the smoke away, Alex unclipped a computer tablet from her belt.

"First, tell your driver to move. I don't want him to hear our conversation."

I gave Liam a nod. "Just drive somewhere out of sight. I'll look for you when I'm done."

His jaw tight as he stared at Alex, he nodded in return and drove toward the street, leaving Sing behind. As she walked toward me, she pressed a shushing finger to her lips. Apparently she was invisible to Alex and didn't want her to know she was there. When she arrived, she stood at my side without a word.

Alex watched the van drive out of sight before refocusing on me. "Phoenix, as I am sure you have guessed, I have taken control of the Gatekeeper's operations. I reaped his soul, and now I have his ghost in a shielded room. He is available when I need to assert his authority. He does what I tell him, of course, because I am able to cast him into the abyss."

"So you turned the abyss machines back on."

She nodded. "As you might expect, my charade with the Gatekeeper won't last long. I have to move quickly to establish myself as a respected authority. The people don't know me yet, so I need fast exposure that demonstrates my benevolence."

Sing spoke from somewhere behind me. "You have a second chance, Phoenix. Alex expects you to obey her because she's threatening Shanghai. Attack her. Kill her. Take her by surprise while you can."

I swallowed hard. Sing's command rang true and followed her plan to shift from defense to offense, but since Alex held Shanghai in her clutches, it seemed impossible to obey. I couldn't let the illuminaries kill her.

Resisting the urge to glance at Sing, I rolled my eyes at Alex. "Benevolence? How can you possibly show benevolence when you don't have a drop of it in you?"

"Considering that I could have ordered my illuminaries to kill you, Shanghai, and your ogreish driver, you should view me as a merciful adversary. But I will ignore your continued insults and simply ask again for your aid. You are the perfect person to help me convince the people to acquiesce to my authority willingly."

"By burning Chicago?" I laughed under my breath. "Good luck with that."

Alex smiled. "So you've already guessed my plan."

"It wasn't too hard. You're more predictable than you think."

"Perhaps, but maybe you failed to predict how I would do it. You see, I don't want to burn Chicago myself. I need someone to do it for me, someone to take the blame for the disaster. In short, I need a scapegoat."

I pointed at myself. "And you want me to be the scapegoat. You want me to burn Chicago."

"Exactly." She showed me her computer tablet. "This device is set to recognize your thumbprint, which will enable you to use it. By the end of the day, I will send you an address where you will begin your work tomorrow morning. When you arrive at the address, you will find a cadre of illuminaries to help you. Your goal is to make it look as if they are trying to stop your activities and apprehend you when all the while they are actually your allies. While you miraculously escape, the illuminaries will collect the poor, wandering souls of the victims you murdered."

I concealed a tight swallow by huffing in a confident manner. "Do you seriously think I would kill innocent people just because you're holding Shanghai hostage? She's a Reaper. She knows her job is dangerous."

"Come now, Phoenix. Do you expect me to believe that Shanghai is merely another Reaper to you? I know she's your fiancée. Did you think you could hide that from me?"

My hand trembled, but I couldn't help it. "How did you find out?"

"I learned it through another source, an additional incentive, you might call them."

"Them?" I tightened my jaw. "The Fitzpatricks?"

An image appeared on the tablet's screen — Fiona and her two daughters huddled in the corner of a cinder-block lined room. Alex spoke in singsong as she extended the tablet. "Don't worry. They are quite comfortable … for now."

I inhaled deeply, both to settle my shakes and regain a steady voice. I had to at least make her believe I was acquiescing. "Okay, okay. You win." I took the tablet and hooked it to my belt. "I'll do it."

"I knew you would come to your senses." Alex's face turned stony. "As I said, I want you to begin destroying Chicago tomorrow morning. Your quota will be one hundred souls the first day, more in future days. Since you're a Reaper, you should be accustomed to meeting, if you'll pardon the expression, deadlines."

Ignoring her macabre sense of humor, I raised a finger. "How will I know Shanghai is safe? And how can I be sure you'll let her go when I'm finished? You could keep holding her and make me destroy city after city whenever you need more energy for your killer robots."

A hint of a smile broke her countenance, as if she expected my question and had a response ready. "To address your first question, I will set up a camera in the place I plan to hold Shanghai. Sometime this afternoon, I will broadcast a video feed to the tablet I gave you. Regarding proof that I will release her when you finish your work in Chicago, you'll just have to trust me."

My voice spiked unbidden. "Trust you? I would rather trust a rabid dog."

Alex's lips twitched. "No need to get dramatic about this, Phoenix. You simply don't have a choice. Either do what I say, or Shanghai, Fiona, and two lovely little Irish girls will suffer."

My cheeks turned hot. I pointed a shaking finger at the severed head in the illuminary's grip and shouted, "Do you know who ripped that monster's head off? I did. And if you harm one hair on Shanghai or on any of the Fitzpatricks, I'll do the same to you."

Alex glanced at the illuminary's head. "You did that?"

My face still hot, I raised my hands. "With these. Maybe your robots aren't as invincible as you think."

When she refocused on me, fear glimmered in her eyes. For that moment, she was actually afraid of what I might do.

Sing hissed. "Now, Phoenix! Now!"

I rolled a hand into a fist, but my feet refused to move. Alex was doing exactly what Sing described, threatening a loved one, and I was paralyzed in my usual defensive mode.

Alex blinked away the fear and gazed at me, her expression curious. "Your eyes are darting, as if you're listening to someone other than me, and your anxiety has spiked. What stalking spirit is raising conflicts in your mind?"

"Don't play those Owl games with me, Alex. You're the demon who stalks me. And anxiety? You kidnapped Shanghai. Isn't that enough cause?"

"Interesting response. Defensive. Dodging the central point. I think my suspicions might be true after all." She pivoted and walked toward the truck. As the remaining illuminaries followed, I counted them, ten in all.

When I was sure Alex had walked out of earshot, I turned to Sing, but I couldn't bear to look her in the eye. "I know. I know. Just ... just don't give me a hard time."

"I won't." Sing grasped my forearm gently. "Let's find a place to sit. You look shaken."

We walked together out of the wooded area and sat on a nearby park bench. Alex's illuminaries marched single file into their trailer, a black rig large enough to hold at least fifty of her robots. Soon, they disappeared inside, and the truck hauled the trailer away.

Guilt rode my back like a ten-ton elephant. Sing was kind enough to stay quiet while I stabbed myself with shame. Alex played her threatening fiddle, and I danced like a marionette.

From beyond the edge of the woods, Liam drove the van to the bench and set his arm on the driver's side window. "I figured out that she has invisible soldiers, but you can see them."

"They're called illuminaries." I patted a space on the bench. "Join us, and I'll tell you what I know about them."

When he sat, I described Alex's army, their powers of invisibility, soul carrying, and incredible strength, as well as the grim task she had given me. I finished with a mention of her other hostages.

Liam's face turned pale. "What are you going to do?"

"I'm not sure yet. Like always, Alex is a step ahead of me. She knew I was in the park, and she knew exactly how to hit me where it hurts. It's like she can read my mind, like she has magical powers."

Sing set a hand on my shoulder. "Alex isn't performing magic, Phoenix. If you'll rest your mind, you'll be able to figure out how she does it."

I gazed into her calming brown eyes. "Do you already know?"

"I have some guesses, but I am not infallible. I'm here to help you think clearly, to plant seeds for you to cultivate, not to hand you my conjectures. I'm afraid you'll trust in them when they might not even be right."

"What do you mean by planting seeds?"

"Probing your mind with questions. Questions are seeds. They sprout into answers that provide knowledge. For example, how did Alex know you were in this park? Think about how she has discovered your location in the past."

I touched my chest where a tracking medallion once hung from a chain. I wasn't wearing it anymore, so Alex couldn't have located me that way. I looked at the van. Alex saw it when Liam drove through the corrections camp gate. "Could she have put a tracking device in Liam's van?"

"Maybe." Sing turned toward Liam. "Is that possible?"

His lips firm, he nodded. "I couldn't keep my eye on my van while I was in the restaurant."

I gazed at his sincere face. He had been so helpful, so loyal, but the danger level was increasing dramatically. He had a wife and two little boys. I couldn't let him take any further risks. "You should go home to your family, Liam. Since Alex saw you helping us, you never know what she might do to retaliate. She wouldn't hesitate to kill your wife and sons."

A fearful expression tightened his features. "I will. But if you need more help, let me know."

"Thank you." I shook his hand. "We would have been dead a long time ago without you."

He stood and looked at me, his countenance grim. "Good luck to you, Phoenix." He shifted his gaze to Sing. "And to you, lass."

She smiled. "Until next time, Liam."

"Until next time." He climbed into his van and drove away. Seconds later, all was quiet.

Sing touched my arm. "Are you sure about sending Liam away?"

"Not sure at all. Just being cautious for his family's sake." I buried my face in my hands, though I peered at her between my fingers. "I'm not sure what to think except that I have to save Shanghai and Fiona and her girls, and I don't know how to do it."

Sing massaged my shoulder through a long moment of silence. When she pulled her hand away, her expression turned serious. "Phoenix, it's all right to lament for a moment, but you need to stay on track."

I lowered my hands. "*Stay* on track? I *jumped* the track when I refused to try to kill Alex. But she has me cornered. I can't let her hurt Shanghai or the other hostages. I have to figure out —"

"No, Phoenix, that's exactly the wrong way to think. You *can* let her hurt the hostages, even kill them if their deaths allow you to kill Alex. If you don't stop her, thousands of Fionas and Annes and Betsys will suffer. Alex is your one and only target. You have to focus on this single objective and not let her dictate your strategy."

I looked Sing in the eye. "So you're saying to ignore the fact that she has hostages."

"That's exactly what I'm saying. Her strategy depends on how you react to what she does. She relies on an awareness of your principles, that you would never violate them no matter what. She believes you won't directly attack her if she's threatening someone you love, and that makes her vulnerable."

I hardened my stare. "Are you saying I should abandon my principles?"

"If they keep you from doing the right thing, then yes."

"The right thing?" I shook a finger. "Listen, you can talk all you want about other families Alex might kill, but it's all theoretical. They're faceless people who someday *might* get hurt. Alex has four real, living, innocent people in her clutches who will die if I don't figure out how to rescue them."

"All right, Phoenix. All right. You make a good point." Sing let out a long sigh. "We disagree on the best strategy, but you have to do what *you* think is right, not what I think. It's your call."

I gave her a conciliatory nod. "We can still work the principles angle. She knows I would never try to burn Chicago, kill innocent people, and send their souls to her to be tortured."

"That's logical. Where does it lead you?"

I let the idea filter in for a moment. "Alex *expects* me to turn her down. She *wants* me to refuse."

Sing nodded. "Go on."

"But why would she want me to refuse? What will she gain? What will be her next move?"

"That's the big question. We have to figure out a way to tip her hand."

"She's too smart. Too careful." I scanned the city, letting my gaze wander across the apartment dwellings to the high-rise skyline beyond them. "Alex must have a hideout close by. If I could discover where she is, I could rescue Shanghai and the others. Then her plans to make me a scapegoat wouldn't matter anymore."

"That's proactive. Aggressive. I like it. But I'm sure she's already anticipated it. Rescuing your loved ones fits your normal thinking pattern perfectly."

"Right." I heaved a sigh. "So I have to come up with something she couldn't possibly think I would do, something that at least looks like a violation of my principles."

"But that doesn't actually violate them."

I lifted my brow. "Any ideas besides directly attacking her?"

"Not at the moment." Sing rolled her eyes upward. "You need to ask yourself, 'What is something I wouldn't do?' "

I laughed under my breath. "Well, I wouldn't trust Alex."

Sing smiled. "That goes without saying. But is there someone else you wouldn't normally trust who might be able to help you?"

"Bartholomew, maybe."

Sing tightened her lips and nodded. "Since he killed Mex, he's an unlikely helper."

"Not just Mex. He was probably behind the murder of my parents."

Sing's eyes widened. "Oh, Phoenix. I didn't know they died. I'm so sorry."

"Yeah, I didn't mention it. I thought maybe you already knew. You know, since you've been in heaven."

"When I got there, I was transferred to the Sanctae right away, so I had no contact with anyone besides other Sanctae. I learned about their origins and how to be a Sancta but not much more."

I withdrew a photo stick from my pocket and showed it to her. "Shanghai helped my parents make this hologram message while they were ghosts. They said Bartholomew wanted to take over the death industry and was worried that my father could stop him with some damaging information. They had no proof, but knowing Bartholomew, I believe it." I slid the stick back into my pocket. "The way he killed Mex makes me think he wouldn't hesitate to kill anyone who crosses him."

Sing stroked my arm. "Can you use this information somehow?"

I tried to ignore the affectionate gesture, but it was distracting. "I suppose I could use his desire to control the death industry. Alex's takeover probably ruined his chances to climb higher on the corporate ladder. He might be willing to help me stop her."

Sing cocked her head. "Assuming the bomb in your apartment was from him, any idea why he wants to kill you?"

"Because I might know the same information my father does?" I shrugged. "Just a guess. Even if it was him, the presence of the illuminaries means he was probably working with Alex."

"Maybe you should investigate. Talk to him before you decide to trust him."

"So now I have to find a man who wants me dead and figure out how to make him my ally." I looked in the direction of the restaurant where we had recently seen Bartholomew. "And I'm running out of time. Not only are Shanghai and the others in danger, I'm supposed to start murdering people in the morning."

CHAPTER FOUR

WITH MY HOOD raised to shadow my face and my cloak fastened high to hide my valve-removal scar, I walked into Eggs & Stuff and looked around. Since the breakfast crowd had dispersed, only a handful of people remained — two men at a booth and three people perched on barstools, two more men and a woman.

As I walked to an empty stool and sat, they all stared at me, probably thinking about the reward for information leading to the capture of a Reaper. They likely wouldn't take me on themselves, but they might tell a DEO where to find me. I would have to keep my time here short.

An attendant behind the counter wearing a white T-shirt and dirty jeans shuffled close and said, "Whaddaya want?"

I raised my voice to a squeaky tone. "Roast beef sandwich, large coffee, and information."

Middle-aged and sporting short, uneven whiskers, he wiped his large hairy hands with a towel. "Roast beef and coffee I got, that is, if you have money or your Reaper code still works. And information? Depends on what you're looking for."

I slid the identification machine close and punched in my Reaper number. It beeped, signaling acceptance. When the screen displayed my name, I turned the machine to prevent him from seeing it. "I need to find Bartholomew, the Gateway depot attendant."

The man snorted. "*Former* attendant, you mean. He's really ticked off about losing his job. You should've seen the brawl we had here this morning when those two Reapers they're looking for strutted in like they owned the place." He whistled. "Old Bartholomew got his nose busted. I thought we'd have a riot for sure. Didn't happen, though. Both Reapers escaped."

"Does anyone know where they went?"

"Into hiding is my guess. Gotta admit, I'd like to catch them myself. The reward's pretty sweet, even for other Reapers like you. But I don't want to get my skull cracked, if you know what I mean."

I touched my chest. "Well, *I* know where Phoenix and Shanghai are. That's why I want to find Bartholomew."

"He can't give you the reward. Like I said, he's out of a job."

I feigned a disappointed grimace, though the shadow from my hood kept my face hidden. "And I'm out of luck. I really wanted that reward."

The man narrowed an eye. "Why would you want it? Don't you Reapers already get free medical care?"

"True, but I won't be a Reaper much longer." I laid a hand over my shirt where my valve used to be. "Besides, I don't trust the Gatekeeper's doctors. I want to get my own surgeon to remove my valve."

"You still might be in luck. Bartholomew talked big about having connections. He might be able to get a doctor for you."

"So maybe a trade. A good doctor in exchange for my help finding those Reapers."

"Worth a try. I know he wants to find them. He left me a way to contact him in case they show up again."

"Can you give that information to me?"

He set an elbow on the bar and lowered his voice. "You got anything to trade? You Reapers always carry some valuable stuff, right?"

I pushed my cloak to the side, revealing my empty weapons belt. Leaving everything behind with Sing, including the tablet so she could watch for a broadcast from Shanghai, proved to be a good idea. "Already traded everything I have. I'm losing my energy supply. Haven't been able to reap in a while."

He drew back. "Then I guess you really are out of luck."

Just as he turned, I called, "Wait."

When he rotated back, a triumphant grin ran across his face. "Change your mind?"

"How about getting my sandwich and coffee? I'll try to think of something to trade."

"You got it." He turned and walked toward the kitchen. "I'll be right back."

The two men at the bar rose and left together, along with the men in the booth. Not a good sign. I would have to hurry.

One customer remained, a wrinkled woman sitting on a nearby stool. She rose and sat on the one next to me, then reached under her scraggly gray hair, pulled off her earrings, and set them on the counter. "They belonged to my great-grandma. Not worth a whole lot, but there's a small diamond in 'em. Can make a sharp knife if nothing else." She nodded toward the kitchen. "I think Ronald'll take 'em."

Maintaining my high-pitched voice, I said, "I can't. They're heirlooms. They must be important to your family."

"No one but me left to care." She picked them up and pushed them into my palm. "Take 'em. I want those two Reaper scoundrels caught before they mess up anything else."

I closed my hand around the earrings. "Thank you."

When Ronald returned with my food, he accepted the earrings in exchange for an address written on a scrap of paper. I used the restroom and rushed out to the sidewalk. The four men who had left the restaurant were nowhere in sight. I hurried back to my apartment building, eating the sandwich and drinking the coffee along the way.

After climbing the steps to my floor, I crept to my bombed-out apartment and looked inside. Only one corner still had flooring remnants — scorched laminate that spread across about twenty-five square feet. Bare support beams spanned the rest of the floor, and my reading chair, nearly split in half, balanced precariously on one of the beams.

With the tablet on her lap, Sing sat close to the center of the room, perched on an exposed beam, her legs and red cloak dangling into the vacant apartment below.

"Any broadcasts from Alex?" I asked.

She shook her head. "And no one came by. The illuminaries must've searched the place already."

"No surprise." I walked to her on the beam and showed her the address. "It's not far. We can get there on foot without a problem, probably before noon."

"Then let's go." She set a hand on the beam and vaulted to her feet. "By the way, I noticed the plumbing still works. Living here is possible."

I grinned. "You checked the plumbing? Do Sanctae need to use the toilet?"

She handed me the tablet. "No. Just trying to make sure you're comfortable. We Sanctae are nosy like that."

"Then this'll be my hideout. Knowing my building manager, she won't bother to repair it for weeks, if ever." I looked the tablet over, found the volume control, and turned it to silent mode. "We'd better leave it in case it has a locator. I don't want Alex to know where I'm going."

After I hid the tablet in my reading chair's torn-open cushion and reloaded my weapons belt, we left the building and walked the few miles to the address, a row house in one of the nicer neighborhoods in Sing's former district. I climbed the front stoop's three steps and knocked on the door.

A moment later, Bartholomew called from within, his voice alarmed. "Phoenix, I don't want any trouble from you."

"I'm not here to give you any trouble."

"Then what do you want?"

"I have a proposal. I think we can work together for a common cause."

He opened the door a crack and peered out, protected by a chain that held the door in place. "What common cause?"

"I suspect that you aren't happy with the changes regarding the Gatekeeper and Alex."

He stared at me for a moment, then said, "Go on."

"Alex is an obstacle to your goals. My guess is that you had a friend on the Council who was helping you, but now that person's dead, so you no longer have any influence at high levels."

He kept his stare locked on me. "What exactly do you see as our common cause?"

"Removing Alex from power."

He blinked. "What makes you think Alex is in power instead of the Gatekeeper? Are you still claiming he's dead?"

"I saw Alex kill him. In this morning's broadcast, she showed us his ghost. She has control over him. He has to do what she says."

"The Gatekeeper, a ghost? Are you off your rocker? I've seen lots of ghosts. No one gets to level three that fast."

"He was loaded with soul energy, so he jumped to level three in a hurry. Trust me. I saw his dead body. What you saw on the broadcast was a ghost. Alex told me so herself this morning."

Again he stared at me, skepticism in his eyes. "Give me one good reason to trust you."

"I took a huge risk coming here. I know you want to turn me in."

"True. I'll give you that. But what's worth so much risk?"

"Simple. You might be the only person who can help me take Alex down."

He chuckled in a dismissive way. "You take Alex down? That's a laugh."

"Go ahead and laugh. Maybe I can't take her down by myself, but if we work together, it might be possible."

After staring at me for another moment, he said, "All right, suppose I do help you. What's in it for me?"

"We still need a soul-transport system. If everything works out, I'll do what I can to make sure you're in charge of it."

"Good, but not good enough."

"What is good enough?"

He inhaled and rolled his eyes upward for a few seconds before looking at me again. "Let's say we can do the impossible and take Alex down. Who will be in charge of the government? The population is accustomed to being under a controlling thumb. Someone has to lead this bleating flock of sheep."

"Are you suggesting that *you* want to be the ruler of the world?"

"No, Phoenix. I don't want to be the target of a thousand assassination attempts. I'm satisfied with being head of the soul-transport system. I just want to know who'll be above me. I'm sick of overstuffed prima donnas telling me what to do."

I hesitated for a moment, long enough for him to draw a conclusion.

"You haven't thought that far, have you?" Bartholomew huffed. "You want me to join you in a conspiracy to depose the ruler of the world, a powerful Owl you can't figure out how to defeat, and you haven't bothered to consider how to replace the authority structure."

I shifted uneasily. "I guess I thought we could have elections. One vote for each citizen."

He shook his head. "Won't work. At least not unless a powerful force puts an organized system in place. The people have no idea how to do it themselves. Rebels and anarchists would disrupt your efforts."

"Do you have a suggestion?"

"Perhaps." He slid the chain and opened the door fully. "Come in. I want to show you something."

I entered, careful to walk slowly enough for Sing to creep in behind me. Bartholomew led us down a hallway, past a master bedroom and a kitchen. His home was not as richly appointed as I had expected but certainly better than the slums most of my district dwellers lived in.

We arrived at a den at the back of the house where a desk covered with scattered papers sat against a wall to the right. A partially open rear window faced an alley that separated his row of houses from another similar row. Weeds infested his tiny backyard, surrounded by a fence with a board missing here and there.

Bartholomew gestured toward a wooden straight-back chair to the left. "Have a seat."

I sat while he took a rolling chair next to the desk. Sing settled at a spot on the floor near the window, crossed her legs, and eyed Bartholomew closely.

He leaned back in a casual manner. "Before I reveal some critical information, tell me more about why you want to take Alex down. I know you don't trust me, but if you want my help, you're going to have to."

"You're right. I don't trust you." I curled my hands into fists and took on an intentionally angry tone. "Alex kidnapped Shanghai along with a mother and her two young daughters. She threatened to kill them if I don't burn Chicago and take the blame for it while she gets credit for trying to stop me. I also have to supply her with a hundred souls tomorrow, which means I have to kill that many people."

Bartholomew cocked his head. "Whatever for? You can't possibly reap more than what? Twenty at a time?"

"More like fifteen. Anyway, Alex has robots called illuminaries to do the soul collecting. Do you know anything about them?"

He nodded. "Quite a lot. I helped in their early stages and planned their upgrades, but the Council transferred me out when the robots became more powerful. They wanted the circle of people who knew about the progress to be as small as possible. By now I assume the illuminaries are nearly invincible."

"They are. And when they collect the souls I'm supposed to kill, Alex will drain their energy and use it to fuel more illuminaries. Once they're all energized, she'll probably send them out to finish the job I started." I shrugged. "So I'm stuck. I don't know what to do to stop her. I can't kill innocent people and send their souls to be tortured, but I can't let Alex kill my friends either."

Bartholomew stroked his chin. After a lengthy pause, he said, "You have quite a dilemma. Since Alex already ruined your reputation, no one will believe you if you try to publicize her cruelty."

I leaned closer to him. "Do *you* believe me?"

"Of course I do. One truth I have discerned is that you are the most altruistic young man I have ever met. When you tried to take the blame for Mexico City's possession of contraband, you sealed my opinion."

I stayed silent without so much as a nod. The syringe he found on Mex was mine, and I did claim ownership, but reaffirming my claim would work against me at this point.

I cast a stealthy glance at Sing. She studied Bartholomew with a skeptical stare. I would have to ask her about her concerns later. "All right," I said to Bartholomew, "I'm glad I have your trust. What did you want to show me?"

He set a hand on a short stack of paper on the desk. "These documents contain information on every living Reaper in the world — their genealogy, places they've lived, their relative prowess at reaping, even where their birthmarks are. Just about anything vital you can imagine."

I peered at the stack but couldn't see any writing from where I sat. "Why have you been gathering that information?"

He focused on me, a hint of fear in his eyes. "If I tell you the entire truth, you have to promise to restrain yourself and not beat me to a bloody pulp."

"Okay," I said, stretching out the word. "I promise."

He cleared his throat. "I collected these facts in order to determine which family lines to eliminate."

Heat surged into my cheeks. "Eliminate? Why?"

"As a death industry veteran, I know that Reapers are the most vulnerable link in processing and delivering souls. They are often temperamental, stubborn, and certainly independent, and it is clear that the most powerful Reapers are also the most difficult to keep in line."

I nodded. "Okay. I can't argue with that."

"Nor should you." He pointed at me. "You and your friend Shanghai, as the best of the best, are in that unruly category. My goal has been to cull the herd, so to speak, to eliminate the genetic lines that create Reapers who might rebel against the system. We prefer obedient soul carriers who won't be likely to shake things up, and we hoped to propagate soul-collecting illuminaries to replace the human Reapers we might lose because of the culling."

The casual way he spoke about *culling*, as if we were a herd of cattle, raised my hackles. I had to force myself to stay calm. "But my parents probably weren't going to have any more children. Why did you kill them?"

He shifted in his chair. "What makes you think I killed them?"

"Don't play games. Just tell me. Like I promised, I'm not going to hurt you."

"I suppose it wouldn't do much good to defend my actions."

"Defend murder? Not likely."

"Especially since I would have to tell you the truth about your father. He was not the moral, upstanding gentleman he appeared to be."

My ears flamed hot. My father was no angel, but criticism from Bartholomew's lips felt like acid. He was the worst of hypocrites. I suppressed a growl and said, "Just tell me why you killed them."

"Well, my motivation wasn't because your parents might produce another Reaper like you. Your father knew that my research wasn't sanctioned by the Gatekeeper. A different high-level person in the death enforcement division authorized my activities with a promise to promote me if I succeeded in our culling efforts."

"A different person? Let me guess. Alex."

"Correct. Alex was in charge of making sure soul collection carried on without interruption, but now that she has wrested control of the Gatekeeper's throne and cast me to the gutter, so to speak, I have no loyalty to her."

His confession rang true to a point. He probably had no loyalty to Alex, but he still might be working with her. My next question seemed to rise from my belly like a gushing fountain, but I managed to speak it in a calm tone. "Did you kill Shanghai's parents?"

Shifting again, Bartholomew nodded. "Her mother was pregnant. Genetic tests indicated that she would likely have a son with Reaper traits similar to Shanghai's."

I balled a fist. It took every fragment of self-restraint to keep me from flattening his face. After swallowing to quell the rage, I again spoke calmly. "I suppose you planned to kill Shanghai and me as well."

"At some point, if it seemed that you might procreate." His own calm tone seemed inappropriate, irrational. "Or earlier if you became too rebellious as a Reaper."

I let his veiled threat fly by without a retort. "Well, someone's still trying to cull the herd. My apartment got bombed this morning."

Bartholomew's brow lifted. "Really? I heard no news about a fire in your area."

"No fire. Just a blow out. Tore up the floor, like it came from below. The walls are still pretty much intact. Just a big hole where my window used to be. I barely made it out in time."

He stroked his chin again. "No incendiary fuel, but since it blew out the floor, the concussive shock should have killed you."

"You're right. It caused a lot of damage."

"Then how did you escape? If the explosion originated below, you couldn't have seen the bomb."

"I … I mean, we. Shanghai was with me. We were out on the fire-escape platform when the bomb exploded. We got lucky, I guess." I gave him a steady stare, hoping my clumsy reply didn't reveal that I left out an important fact, that Bill had given us a warning.

"Interesting," Bartholomew said, "but I had nothing to do with it. As I told you, my plans are no longer valid. The soul-carrying train has been derailed. No one cares about controlling rebellious Reapers anymore. Certainly not I."

I kept my stare trained on him. Since I had no evidence of his involvement in the bombing, I had to move on. "So will you help me?"

"Maybe. Alex is strong and smart. Knowing her, she's probably thought of every possible way to halt her march toward world domination and has already plugged any potential holes in her defenses. We need a mode of attack she can't predict, a weapon she is unaware of."

"Is there such a weapon?"

"Perhaps." Bartholomew opened a desk drawer and withdrew a mirror, a simple square of glass with bare edges.

Sing gasped. I resisted the urge to glance at her, knowing Bartholomew couldn't hear her reaction.

"During my research into your family history," he said, "I came across this relic along with a journal your ancestors kept of their activities. They used this mirror to accomplish extraordinary feats more than two centuries ago. The journal is fragile, rotting with age, so I keep it in an airtight container off site. In any case, I couldn't figure out how your ancestors made the mirror work, only that it was powered by a mystical being called a Sancta."

Hearing the name spill from his lips sounded odd, sacrilegious, as if a devil had uttered a holy word.

"I've heard legends about the Sanctae," he continued, "but the journal is the only first-person account I have read that affirms their actual existence." He extended the mirror toward me. "Do you know anything about this or the Sanctae?"

As if receiving a fragile museum artifact, I took the six-inch square with both hands and looked it over. It appeared to be a normal mirror with a polished reflective surface and rough edges, not sharp enough to cut into my skin.

Sing whispered, "Tell him you have also heard about the Sanctae, and you might be able to learn how the mirror works, that you will research it and let him know what you find out."

I repeated Sing's reply almost word for word.

Bartholomew nodded. "Since this is the only weapon I know that Alex can't possibly prepare for, I will help you only if you learn its secrets. Come back to me with a report. If we can use it effectively, then we can wrest power from Alex, take control of the illuminaries, and use them to facilitate proper elections."

Sing whispered again. "You should know by evening."

"I'll try to have the information by evening."

"That will be fine," Bartholomew said. "While I am waiting —"

A siren blared somewhere in the distance. It repeated three times, signaling another video bulletin.

I squinted out the window as if able to see the sound waves. "Two general announcements in one day?"

"Most unusual." Bartholomew pulled a DEO tablet from under a pile of papers and turned it on. "Let's see what fresh devilry Alex is hatching."

I nodded toward the tablet. "If you can watch a bulletin here, why did you go to the restaurant this morning?"

"Breakfast is good there. A man has to eat. And I am no cook." He propped the tablet where I could see it. "Speaking of which, have you had anything to eat lately?"

"Yeah. A sandwich and some coffee. My Reaper code still works."

"Of course it does. Every time you use it, Alex will know where you are."

The idea raised a mental image of Alex peeking around the door, prompting a nauseating stir in my stomach. "Good point. I'll have to be more careful."

"What about energy? Are you low?"

"Why? Do you keep a supply here?"

"When the depot shut down, I brought some of the left-over energy home with me." He nodded toward a scuba-style tank standing in a corner at the back wall. "I thought a Reaper might need some while waiting to get the valve-removal surgery. Just a way to thank them for their service."

"That's generous." I avoided eye contact, hoping he couldn't sense my doubt. Bartholomew's gesture seemed out of character. He probably had other reasons for keeping the gas on site, maybe as a way to bribe a Reaper. I touched my sternum. "I already had the surgery. Thanks for asking."

While we waited for the bulletin to begin, Bartholomew told me about his rise in the death industry from the ranks of a clerk like Albert Crandyke to the watchman of the Gateway depot used by the Reapers in our region. He was furious when the Gatekeeper promoted Erin, the gate attendant, to be his personal assistant, but his fury diminished when he learned that they were romantically involved.

Bartholomew laughed. "I am ambitious, but not that ambitious. Imagine kissing that egotistical, pretentious —" The tablet beeped, and the Gatekeeper's anthem played. "Ah. It's time." He angled the tablet to avoid glare from the window. "This tablet provides another advantage over hurrying to a community television site. It automatically records the message so I can view it later if I'm too busy to watch when it broadcasts."

Alex appeared on the screen, standing in a dim, cinder-block room. She crossed her arms and cocked her body in a confident pose. "I apologize for interrupting your day again, but I need to update our progress with regard to the Reapers the Gatekeeper mentioned during the earlier broadcast." The camera panned ninety degrees to the side, revealing Shanghai standing with her hands folded at her waist. A toilet sat behind her, and a sink and mirror hung on the wall above it. Although she looked tired, she seemed uninjured.

"We captured Shanghai," Alex continued. "And she has a message for Phoenix."

The camera zoomed in on Shanghai until her upper body filled the screen. Her eyes sparkling with tears, she spoke in an entreating tone. "Phoenix, I implore you to listen to me. Alex will extend leniency if you'll do what she told you earlier. Don't try to rescue me. It's impossible. For both of our sakes, heed my words."

CHAPTER FIVE

A S THE CAMERA zoomed back, Shanghai mouthed something, but I couldn't make out what she was trying to say.

The camera shifted to Alex. Now wearing a soft expression, she seemed to be looking straight at me. "Phoenix, I expect to hear word about your decision by morning. Don't disappoint me. To everyone else viewing this, if you see Phoenix, do not approach him. He is volatile and dangerous. Report any sightings to a government official and allow the Peace Patrollers to apprehend him. The rewards we offered earlier still apply. I will update you as necessary."

The video turned black, and the Gatekeeper's anthem played again.

I stared at the tablet's blank screen. The Gatekeeper failed to make an appearance. Maybe Alex didn't think she needed his authoritative presence anymore. What might she have done with his soul?

Also, since Bartholomew said that his tablet automatically recorded messages, maybe mine had done so. I could watch it again and try to figure out Shanghai's hidden message.

I rose from my chair, the mirror in hand. "Like I said, I'll figure this out and see you this evening, but let's meet at Eggs & Stuff. I prefer a neutral site."

"That will be fine," Bartholomew said as he got up. "In the meantime, I will see what I can do about finding souls you can deliver to Alex tomorrow. She needs to believe you're cooperating."

I blinked. "But she'll torture any souls I deliver."

"Which is why I need to find some who deserve it."

"Deserve torture? How can you decide —"

"Just go, Phoenix." He set a hand on my back and guided me toward the front door. "We'll discuss it when we meet again. Nothing will happen between now and then."

Sing caught up and walked at my side. "Tell him that you're in charge of this operation, that you'll make the decisions."

"All right, Bartholomew," I said as I opened the door, "but this is all on my head, and Shanghai's. I have to make the final decisions about any plans to take Alex down."

"Of course. Just keep an open mind about what I hope to show you this evening. Let's say seven o'clock."

"I'll do that." I walked out with Sing and hurried to my apartment in silence. When we arrived, I retrieved the tablet from the chair cushion, sat in the intact corner of the floor, and set the mirror to the side. "Did you notice how Shanghai tried to give me a message?"

Sing nodded. "But I couldn't read her lips. It went by too fast."

"I'll see if I can replay that portion." I located the video controls on the screen, turned the volume up, and, after entering my thumbprint, found the broadcast and played it. When Shanghai began speaking, I paused the video and magnified her face until it filled the screen, then let it continue.

"Don't try to rescue me," she said. "It's impossible. For both of our sakes, heed my words." As before, the camera panned back, but her lips were clearer as she mouthed three syllables.

"I'm not a lip reader," I said. "I can't make it out."

Sing nodded at the tablet. "Play it again."

When I restarted the segment, Sing and I leaned closer. Shanghai's lips again moved through the syllables. One appeared to have a letter *p* and another a letter *s*, maybe a letter *t* as well.

Sing whispered, "Poster? Posit?"

"Opposite?" I picked up the mirror and mouthed the word while looking at my reflection. My own lips moved in the same way Shanghai's had. "I think that's it."

"Which means she wants you to do the opposite of what she said. She wants you to rescue her."

I turned the video off and clipped the tablet to my belt. "So it must not be impossible. Maybe she already knows about a weakness in Alex's defenses."

"Right. She wouldn't want you to try to rescue her if it's a suicide mission."

"But how do I figure out the weakness?" I touched the mirror. "Can this help? Bartholomew said it has great powers. What do you know about it?"

Sing ran a finger along the mirror's edge. "I told you about a Sancta named Scarlet, but I didn't get to finish the story. Like Bartholomew said, she helped your ancestors by using a mirror. This might be the one."

"What does it do? How does it work?"

"I know a power it once had." Sing laid her palm on the surface and looked at me. "Tell me, Phoenix, what do you want to see more than anything in the world?"

"That's easy. Shanghai."

"Then concentrate. Think about her."

I closed my eyes and raised a mental image of Shanghai. She stood with her hands folded in front, similar to the pose she took in the broadcast. "Okay. I'm ready."

"Now look," Sing said.

I opened my eyes. When she lifted her hand, the reflection seemed normal, just her and me staring at the mirror.

Sing's lips drew a thin line. "Nothing happened."

"Did we do something wrong?"

"I don't think so, though it's impossible to be sure."

"What is supposed to happen?"

"The mirror was supposed to show the place you were thinking about. Scarlet used it to transport your ancestors away from danger. I didn't really expect it to respond, but I thought I'd give it a try. The Sanctae's use of this device ended two centuries ago. It served its purpose."

"And now it's just a paperweight. We can't use it."

Sing let out a heavy sigh. "Phoenix, I'm sorry I'm not as powerful as Scarlet was, but —"

"No." I waved a hand. "I'm not complaining about you. It's not your fault the mirror doesn't work."

"True. It no longer has the power to transport people, but ..." Sing again laid a palm on the surface. "It *can* reveal stories from the past."

"What stories?"

"Stories that might aid your purpose."

When she lifted her hand, the reflection clouded. After a few seconds, the haze thinned and vanished. A boy, maybe thirteen years old, stood next to a bed in a clean, well-lit room. He gripped the bed's metallic side railing with both hands and gazed at a gray-haired woman lying under a pristine linen sheet. She looked at him with weary eyes, barely visible as they peered from under heavy lids.

Atop a nearby overbed table, a small radio played a soft tune — a blend of violins and piano. Somewhere out of sight, a heart monitor beeped in an unsteady rhythm.

I searched the mirror for speakers, but none were evident. Somehow the reflection had become a vision, complete with sound.

"Don't be scared, Phoenix," the woman said with a wheezing whisper. "I'll see you again. Death is just a doorway to another life."

I drew my head back. Another Phoenix?

A tear rolled down young Phoenix's cheek. "How do you know? No one's ever come back from the dead to tell us about it."

"Oh, really?" She reached with a trembling hand and brushed the tear away. "You're always the logical one. Just because you don't know anyone who came back from the dead, it doesn't mean it hasn't happened."

"True, but I think I'd have heard about it."

"But would you believe it? You've heard my stories, and you don't believe most of them."

"They're great stories, Grandma, but they can't be true. I mean, you and Grandpa jumping through mirrors to alternate worlds? They're like fairy tales."

"Only because you've already decided that the supernatural can't be true." She set a finger close to her eye. "Look. My irises are purple, donated to me by a Sancta, just like I told you. And I am a personal eyewitness to every story. But you decided beforehand to toss away any tale that doesn't fit your preconceived notions about the world. In other words, you think I'm either a liar or a senile old fool, just because my words don't match your narrow-minded view of the world." She let out a huff. "That's not being logical. That's just being stubborn."

I drew the mirror a few inches closer, but I couldn't see the color of the grandmother's eyes. Donated by a Sancta? This vision was getting more and more interesting.

"All right," young Phoenix said, "you busted me on that. Maybe there are alternate realities and invisible portals, but you never saw someone come back from the dead, right?"

"No, but other eyewitnesses did. Jesus Christ rose from the dead, and —"

"Here we go again." He rolled his eyes. "Grandma, we've been over this a hundred times. The church made up the resurrection so it could control people. No one really saw it, because it didn't happen. When you're dead, you're dead. Your brain stops functioning. We all just rot in the ground. What I'm saying isn't comforting, but it's reality."

"Well, Mr. Know-It-All, do you have any scientific proof that there's no eternal soul?"

"Well ..." Phoenix cleared his throat. "I don't really have ... I mean there isn't a way to check ..."

"There." She pointed at him. "You see? It's just like I said. You believe what you want to believe. It's got nothing to do with proof."

He heaved a sigh and slid his hand into hers. "Grandma, can we change the subject? I'm here because I love you. Ever since Grandpa died, you've been my only family. I don't want my last memory of you to be an argument."

"You're right, Phoenix." She pulled his hand close and rested the clasp on her chest. "But allow me these final thoughts." As she gazed at him, a tear coursed down her cheek. "I've been praying for you, that God will open your eyes so you can see beyond your physical senses. Then you will believe that life goes on, even after the grave."

A tear trickled down Phoenix's cheek as well. "No problem, Grandma. Pray for me all you want. I know it means you love me."

"I do, Phoenix. With all my heart."

"I love you, too." He sniffed and brushed away the tear. "And don't worry about me. I'll be fine at the school. I made a lot of friends there, and the headmaster seems to like me, so —"

A voice from the radio broke in. "We interrupt this broadcast for a bulletin. Yesterday's fire at Missouri's Midlands nuclear power plant has been extinguished and the spread of radiation has been contained. Authorities say that the method they used to snuff the flames has resulted in a plume of smoke that is expanding high in the sky. Although the smoke is likely to come as far as our area here in Chicago, local officials tell us there is no need to be alarmed. The smoke is non-radioactive and will disperse in a matter of hours."

The radio fell to silence. Even the music failed to play. The heart monitor broke the stillness, beeping faster and more erratically than before.

"Propaganda," Grandma said. "That's what they want us to believe. You can bet that smoke is deadly. Mark my words."

"Gotta admit, it does sound weird." Phoenix walked toward a window in the background. "I'll check it out."

"That's my boy," Grandma said with a smirk. "Cast all caution to the wind, just like your grandfather."

Young Phoenix looked at her and laughed. "Because it's against the hospital's rules to open the window?"

"No, silly. Because you might poison us with whatever's out there."

"Just a quick check." He lifted the window sash and removed the screen. A breeze tossed his short dark hair and long-sleeved shirt. As he leaned out and looked up, he called with an excited voice, "Smoke's heading this way." He pulled back and gestured with his hands. "It's a huge wave. And it's sparkling, like a fireworks tsunami."

"Then close the window. No use both of us dying."

Before Phoenix could react, radiant smoke burst in. Like a sparkling cyclone, it enveloped his body in a wild spin of coal-like dust and flashing lights. Grandma shouted something too garbled to understand. The cyclone expanded and filled the entire room, shielding everything else from view.

As the flashes diminished, the heart monitor's rhythm slowed. After several more erratic beeps, it stretched into a long squeal.

Like a vacuum, the window sucked most of the smoke from the room, leaving a thin haze. Phoenix lay curled on the floor while Grandma still lay on the bed, her eyes closed.

I whispered, "Are they both dead?"

"Keep watching." Sing brushed a hand across the mirror's surface. "I'll make some time pass."

The image warped for a moment, then returned to clarity. The scene appeared to be the same, except now a glowing ghost that looked like a younger version of Grandma knelt next to Phoenix. Her body remained on the bed.

An aura surrounded Phoenix, bright and pulsing.

"Phoenix," the ghost said as she shook him. "Wake up."

I pointed at the scene. "How can she move him? She's a ghost."

"Good observation," Sing said. "Keep watching."

Young Phoenix stirred and blinked open his eyes. When he saw the ghost, he gasped and sat up. "Who are you?"

She smiled. "What's wrong, Phoenix? Don't you recognize me?"

"Your voice." He glanced at the bed, then squinted at her. "Grandma?"

"Of course." She rose and looked toward the bed. "Is that me?"

"No. I mean, yes." Still radiant, Phoenix climbed to his feet and stared at her. "You look younger. Like you're thirty, maybe."

"I do?" She touched her cheek. "I don't understand. What's going on?"

Phoenix shifted his stare from the ghost to the corpse and back again. "Then ..." He swallowed hard. "You're a ghost?"

Her misty form undulated as if moved by a light breeze. "A ghost? How can that be? Why didn't I go to heaven?"

Again staring, he whispered, "Souls really do exist. And you prayed for me to see it."

She glanced around as if confused. "I think I remember saying something like that."

He grasped her wrist. "If you're a ghost, how can I hold your arm?"

"I have no idea."

He released her and looked at his hand. "And why am I glowing?"

Something banged. Phoenix and his grandmother jerked their heads toward the sound. A man called in a muffled voice, "Take him."

Two huge men dressed in white hazardous-materials coveralls, complete with gloves and gasmask-equipped hoods, rushed past the ghost and grabbed Phoenix by his arms, one at each side. While he struggled to free himself, he shouted, "Who are you? What do you want with me?"

A third similarly dressed man walked in and stood facing Phoenix, his back toward the mirror view. His voice still muffled, he said, "We're from the federal government, and we're here to help you. What's your name?"

Young Phoenix rested and glared at the newcomer. "Phoenix. Phoenix Shepherd."

"And who is she?" He pointed a gloved finger at Grandma's corpse.

"My grandmother. Kelly Shepherd."

Kelly's ghost's eyes darted. "Phoenix, what's going on? Who are these men?"

Ignoring her, the man withdrew from a pocket a short black tube that looked like a portable microphone. He waved it in the air for a moment before looking at something on its side. "Safe enough." He pulled the hood off and set it on the floor. Black curly hair covered most of the collar of his white dress shirt. As he looked around, his identity became clear.

I whispered, "Melchizidek. The Gatekeeper."

"This was a time not long before he became the Gatekeeper," Sing said. "Again, keep watching. There's much more to learn."

Melchizidek set an end of the tube close to Phoenix, then looked at the meter on the side. "The kid's through the roof. No wonder he's glowing."

"How many does that make?" the taller of the two other men asked.

"Six." Melchizidek scanned the room. "Phoenix, did you happen to see something that looks like a ghost, maybe a phantom-like presence that resembles your grandmother? She'd probably look younger. Twenty-five. Maybe thirty."

Phoenix scowled. "Of course not. What are you, some kind of crazy ghost hunter?"

Melchizidek gestured to the two men. "Let him go. You can take your hoods off. Just don't touch him without gloves."

They released him and shed their hoods, revealing crewcuts, clean-shaven cheeks, and square-jawed faces.

"Now, Phoenix," Melchizidek said in a gentler tone, "tell me the truth. Did you see a ghost?"

Phoenix's eyes shifted for a split second toward Grandma Kelly before refocusing on Melchizidek. "I don't believe in ghosts."

Melchizidek smiled. "An interesting way to dodge the question." He strolled to where Kelly stood and waved an arm through her head. "Is she over here somewhere? I saw you look this way."

Kelly's eyes followed his hand's motions as if she were bewildered.

"You have nothing to fear," Melchizidek continued. "Like I said before, I'm here to help you. If you want your grandmother to get to heaven safely, you'll tell me the truth."

Phoenix crossed his arms, his head low. After a moment of silence, he nodded. "I can see her."

"Were you able to touch her?"

Phoenix nodded again, his head still low.

"Good man." Melchizidek patted Phoenix's back with a gloved hand. "Listen carefully. A radioactive cloud shield has covered this area and is spreading across the planet. The force that normally draws souls of the dead into the sky has been blocked, so they're unable to depart to the afterlife. You, however, have an ability to see and touch the souls, which, we believe, will enable you to act as a guide to lead the souls to a place we can hold them until we figure out how to help them get to where they're supposed to go."

One of the other men laughed. "He's a soul shepherd, just like his name. Phoenix Shepherd."

Melchizidek cocked his head. "Actually, that is an excellent metaphor in more ways than one." He turned toward Phoenix. "Did your parents name you after the city or the mythical bird that burns and gets reborn by rising from its ashes?"

Phoenix lifted his head and gave him a defiant stare. "The bird."

"Do you know why?"

"My grandmother suggested it to my parents. She used to say, nothing can kill you, Phoenix. No matter what anyone does to you, even if you get burned at the stake, you will rise again. Take confidence in that. Death is just a doorway to another life."

Melchizidek nodded in a thoughtful manner. "Your grandmother was right. And if you have the abilities I think you have, once we train you, you will be among an elite class. Since you will be ushering souls into heaven,

everyone in the world will honor you as some kind of god."
He looked at the other two men and heaved a sigh. "It's
finally over. We have all six."

Phoenix narrowed his eyes. "You've been looking for
me? Why? And how did you know to find me here?"

"Long story, kid. Let's just say we know about what
your grandparents did, and we believe their genetics
were altered somehow, so we've been keeping an eye on
their descendants."

"Their genetics?" Phoenix said. "Who are the other five?
I don't have any brothers or sisters."

"An aunt. An uncle. Couple of cousins. Don't worry.
You'll see them soon."

"So are you telling me my grandmother's crazy stories
are true?"

Melchizidek chuckled. "I don't know what stories she
told, but what really happened is probably more bizarre
than anything you can imagine." He nodded toward something off screen. "We have to go. Take your grandmother
by the hand and lead her. Our theory is that she is likely
confused, so you'll need to comfort her."

"Yeah. She does seem confused." Phoenix grasped Kelly's
hand. "Come with me, Grandma. I'll take care of you."

CHAPTER SIX

THE SCENE IN the mirror faded and reverted to a reflection of my face, my mouth hanging partially open. I closed my mouth and looked at Sing. "So that's how Reapers got started. Six descendants of Kelly Shepherd and her husband."

Sing nodded. "The first of many."

"But we're not all related. Even in two hundred years you couldn't get that kind of diversity. You and Shanghai have Oriental heritage. Your father was from Africa. And I'm as Caucasian as they come."

"The ability to reap has multiple genetic sources, which Melchizidek and his scientists discovered when they tested the first Phoenix and his relatives. It turned out that all Reapers have a special birthmark that was easily identifiable, so they expanded their search for gifted people beyond Phoenix's close relatives. Yet, only the first six had special abilities that no Reaper has had since then."

"And those abilities are?"

Sing raised a finger. "One, he could touch and move a ghost even when he wasn't in ghost mode." She lifted another finger. "And two, he could survive doses of radiation that would kill anyone else. There was also a prophecy about Phoenix, that when he died he would someday be reborn in another life. Not literally. His soul went to heaven and is still there. But a new Phoenix would be born with the same kind of spirit and powers, just like the mythical bird."

"I assume you're talking about me, but I don't have those powers. I can't move ghosts. I did survive some radiation in the Western Wilds, but it wasn't a deadly amount. Shanghai survived it, too. And I chose the Phoenix name because of the burned city, not the bird."

"True, but I was told to let you know the story. There has to be a reason. We could test the first two powers."

"How? By exposing me to a mega-dose of radiation?" I laughed, though the effort felt shallow. "Not exactly a safe experiment."

"No, but since you had some exposure, maybe you can manipulate ghosts in a minor way." Sing shrugged. "It won't hurt to try. There are plenty of ghosts around."

I touched the stitches where my valve used to be. "The first Phoenix could collect ghosts without energy or a valve connection. How did the valve system get started?"

"Cruel experiments by Melchizidek. You see, the first Phoenix became immensely powerful, as skilled as Tokyo and without the shackles of the energy valve. Melchizidek knew he had to control Phoenix as well as the other Reapers, so they experimented with the souls they collected and discovered that their energy could enhance the capabilities of Reapers who were not as gifted as the original six. As you know, the energy also enslaved them, but the situation was perfect for Melchizidek. Energy drained from the souls kept him alive, gave him more powerful Reapers, and allowed him to control them."

"So he made it mandatory for all Reapers," I said, "including Phoenix and his five relatives."

"Exactly. The energy was Melchizidek's lifeline. He had to keep it coming. So he made sure all Reapers depended on it."

"Then what happened to Phoenix? If he was so powerful, why does everyone say Tokyo was the greatest Reaper who ever lived?"

"Melchizidek feared Phoenix, so he made sure Phoenix met with a fatal accident."

"Let me guess. Fire. Burned to ashes."

Sing shook her head. "Radiation couldn't kill him. Neither could fire. So they invented the sonic gun. No mess. No evidence of foul play. Phoenix died before his twentieth birthday. He never had a chance to establish a legend as great as my mother's."

Feeling a tingle, I massaged the back of my head. "Not even fire could kill him? That's another ability I don't have."

Sing lifted an eyebrow. "Oh, really? Didn't you rescue people from a burning building once?"

"Yeah, but I don't remember much about it. I was running too fast."

"Fast is right. Witnesses said you looked like you were on fire yourself, like you were part of the inferno. One called you a flaming ghost."

I painted a mental picture of myself running through the building while carrying one of the children I rescued. Obviously the witnesses were imagining things. If I had been aflame, the children in my arms would have been burned. "A tragedy can alter perceptions."

"Maybe so, but I'll be watching for signs that you're a Reaper reborn."

I let out a huff. "Right. The Phoenix bird. More wishful thinking."

She raised a finger. "Ah. There's a sign. You're a doubter, just like the first Phoenix. You need more proof."

I set the mirror on the floor. "What I need right now is a way to rescue Shanghai."

"Well, then, just like Grandma Kelly did for the other Phoenix, I'll pray that you'll find one." Sing reached under her cloak and withdrew the cross necklace she had taken from Bill. "In the meantime, I want to talk about this."

At the sight of the bloodstained piece of wood, a renewed sense of grief welled. I swallowed it down and gave her a nod. "Sure. Go ahead."

"It's a symbol of the cross Yeshua died on. I'm sure you heard Kelly mention him. She called him Jesus."

"He had two names?"

"More than two. We Reapers should be used to that. You have two names, and I have three." Sing set the cross on her palm. "Have you heard the stories about him?"

"When I was little. Nights when I was home from training. My mother told me stories at bedtime, but my father made her stop. I guess I was about eight."

"Oh? Why did he make her stop?"

"He said the stories are myths. No one could be that good. Too much evil in the world. It corrupts everyone to some extent. Every heart is a dark heart. We just have to set our own principles and follow them instead of old myths."

Sing shook her head. "All things are unclean to those who are unclean themselves."

I blinked. "What?"

"Never mind. Just ruminating out loud." She gazed into my eyes. "What do you think about what your father said?"

"After all I've seen?" I took in a deep breath and let it out slowly. "I don't know. I really can't prove him wrong, but ... I don't know."

"Well, it's true that many people have dark hearts." Sing set a hand on my knee. "Phoenix, I would love to tell you everything I've learned, explain the light I have seen, but I have only words. You need to see the light yourself, to experience that life is more than dark shadows in a dark world. There is light if you know where to look for it."

"Okay. I'll bite. Where do I look for it? And don't say to follow my principles. I'm sick of hearing about them."

She smiled. "You're right. There's been far too much talk about your principles, but I need to start there to lead you to the true answer. You see, your principles must have had an origin. I think they came from your mother's influence. She implanted them in your heart with her stories."

"I can believe that. Go on. Where does that lead?"

"To this. The light in the world doesn't come from a set of principles. It comes from the one who established them, who declares them to be good." Sing lifted the necklace, letting the cross sway in front of my eyes. "Phoenix, your mother's stories are not myths. They are about the true light, the originator of the principles you follow, the one who died and rose from the dead."

As I watched the cross's motion, a mental image of a bleeding man hanging there tied my tongue. I couldn't say a word.

"My point," Sing continued, "is that after hearing the stories about Yeshua, you followed in his footsteps instinctively. You heal people in spite of laws against it. You are kind to lost souls and lead them to eternal rest. In every way possible, you show love to the oppressed while opposing the hypocritical rulers of this world. In short, you modeled your principles after Yeshua's without even realizing it."

She set the cross closer to my eyes. "My question is, will you now believe the stories and *consciously* follow in Yeshua's footsteps? Will you follow the person and not merely a set of principles?"

Memories of my father's harsh words crashed in. *Don't fill his mind with those fairy tales. He needs to be ready for the real world. It's dog eat dog out there, and that religious talk will make him soft. He'll be torn to pieces.* My throat tightening, I swallowed to relieve the pain. "Yeshua got killed. He couldn't fight back."

"*Wouldn't* fight back. Love for others kept him on that cross." She compressed my knee. "Following Yeshua's footsteps might mean giving your life in sacrifice, but for those who do, death always leads to resurrection. Knowing this makes us strong, courageous, able to face any evil that darkens our doors."

"You mean, Alex."

"She is one of many evils. Worse than most, but she, too, will fall."

I gazed into Sing's soulful eyes, letting her words sink in. She had already followed those footsteps and given her life for the greater good, and she did indeed rise from the dead. Her faith was amazing, something I never really had.

On the contrary, I always relied on my own perception of the world and a vague sense of justice. My self-prodding was often no more than a niggling sensation that I couldn't identify. I tried to give it a label, a reason for my so-called principled behavior — I was too busy as a district hound to get into trouble, I had to stay faithful to Misty, and smuggling medicine to people in need gave me a sense of purpose. Yet none of these reasons really explained my actions. They were merely guesses.

It seemed that I always walked in the darkness, fumbling my way through life as a Reaper, hoping my next step wouldn't send me plunging into a darker pit. Yes, my mother had taught me about "being good," but I lost her long ago. I had no guide. No teacher. No light. Just memories.

Maybe Sing was right. Maybe I was instinctively mimicking the stories, though far from perfectly, like an orphan wandering lost in a violent storm with only a weak lantern glowing vaguely in the distance to guide my staggering steps.

As if reading my mind, Sing whispered, "Love conquers fear. Light dispels darkness. Faith will lead you to a brighter path. Yeshua has already blazed the trail. All you have to do is follow him."

I kept my stare locked on her pleading expression. After years of fending for myself, it would be hard to follow someone else's lead. Yet, the hope of a more certain path seemed attractive, no matter where it eventually led. Still, the transition might prove to be more difficult than the words *follow him* suggested.

"Okay." I gave Sing a confident nod. "I'll do the best I can."

"That's all I can ask." She draped the necklace over my head, guided it down to my neck, and set the cross in front of my chest. "This will help you remember."

I grasped the cross and held it tightly. "Thank you … for everything."

The tablet beeped, like an alarm telling us that our time in another world had ended. I detached the tablet from my belt and propped it on my lap. On the screen, Shanghai appeared in the cinder-block room, pacing quickly from wall to wall, one hand combing through her hair. Her footsteps were audible as was a sigh of exasperation.

Sing flashed a triumphant expression. "Already an answered prayer."

"Don't gloat." I feigned a scowl, but I couldn't make it last as a smile broke through. "All right. Go ahead. You deserve it."

"I'm not gloating. Just celebrating." She scooted close and looked at the screen. "Do you think this is a live broadcast?"

"Most likely, but she probably doesn't know we're watching. Otherwise, she'd try to talk to us. Then again, she might think that Alex is watching every move she makes. Listening to every word. So she can't risk talking to us."

Sing nodded. "We need to look for clues. If we can figure out where she is, I can go to her."

"And since you'll be invisible to Alex, she'll never know." I studied the scene. Shanghai walked into a shaft of muted sunlight and stepped in a puddle. When she pivoted, her cloak swept with her spin. Something small and white appeared on the cape portion.

I focused on it — a feather. "Look. A bird's feather."

Sing squinted. "It's bigger than a songbird's. And the presence of water is odd. It hasn't rained today. The sky is cloudless. Just the usual haze."

"Water must have splashed in somehow. A white feather could be from a seagull."

Sing looked at me. "Do you think she's on a boat?"

"With a room that size lined with cinder blocks, it would have to be a big boat." I squinted at Shanghai's prison, trying to detect any sign of bobbing in water. "It's almost always windy in Chicago, so you'd expect some kind of movement."

"If the boat were moving, the camera would move with it. You wouldn't be able to detect any rocking motion."

"True, but Shanghai doesn't seem to be fighting any motion when she walks. Maybe the boat's dry docked."

"Either way, we know she's in the area. She didn't have time to go very far."

"Here's another odd thing." I pointed at the screen. "In the earlier broadcast I could see a toilet and a sink and a mirror, but not now."

"The camera might be hidden in the wall were the toilet is." Sing looked through the blown-out hole that used to be my window. "Okay. Time to make an educated guess. A big boat probably means she's at Lake Michigan. I'll go there and see if I can find a likely candidate.

"Good. I'll keep watching Shanghai to see if —"

A short-lived buzz emanated from the tablet, followed by Alex's voice. "Are you hungry?"

On the screen, Shanghai halted and faced a metal door as it opened to the right. "I don't want anything from you, you murderous witch."

"Temper, temper," Alex said in singsong as she walked in with an illuminary at her side. "You might be here for a long while."

Clutching the tablet tightly, I whispered, "Come on, Shanghai. Give me a clue. Tell me where you are."

Shanghai set a fist on her hip. "Do you really think Phoenix is going to burn the city and kill innocent people?"

"I suppose it depends on how much he loves you, doesn't it?" Alex glanced toward Sing and me, obviously aware of the camera. "It remains to be seen how well he follows my plan."

"Your plan?" Shanghai scowled. "What devious, evil things are you going to do?"

Alex let out her all-too-familiar humming laugh. "My dear Shanghai, telling you would be counterproductive. If you happen to escape, you could ruin my plan."

"Escape?" She slapped the wall to the left. "It's impossible. A ghost couldn't escape this room."

Sing whispered, "There's a clue. Maybe it has an energy shield around it."

"I've learned," Alex said, "never to underestimate you or Phoenix, so I am taking every precaution. Don't bother to ask again about my plans. I'm not giving away anything." She and the illuminary turned and exited through the doorway, disappearing from view as it closed. "If you decide you're hungry, you know how to signal me." The buzz returned, then fell silent.

Shanghai gestured with wiggling fingers and mimicked Alex in a witchy voice. "If you decide you're hungry, you know how to signal me." She turned toward the wall at the left side of the screen, walked to the shaft of light, and looked up, hands on her hips. After taking a deep breath, she backed away a few steps and ran. She leaped, planted a foot on the wall, and lunged upward.

The top half of her body now above my view, she dangled as if she had grabbed something. She set her toes against the wall and scrambled higher, maybe trying to muscle up to a new perch.

A sharp buzz snapped once again. She let out a loud "Ouch" and dropped to the floor, shaking her finger and whispering, "What a jolt!"

"You were right about the field," I said to Sing. "But maybe you could get in."

"How? She said even ghosts can't escape."

"Maybe not ghosts, but Sarah, the other Sancta who helped me, was able to be absorbed into the Gateway's energy line and travel through it. She did the same through an energy field that surrounded the abyss when she visited me in the machine room underneath. Maybe you can do that to get to Shanghai."

"The way Shanghai reacted, the field might be powered by electricity instead of soul energy, but I'll see what I can do."

On the tablet screen, Shanghai walked to the right, pushed a button on a box mounted on the wall near the door, and said, "Alex, I changed my mind. I'm hungry." A series of electrostatic noises echoed in a cadence similar to her words. "If the food's still available," she continued, "I'd like to have some." Again the noise seemed to repeat her phrases.

After a silent moment, static returned, followed by a voice. "I'll send it down soon."

"Down," I repeated to Sing. "Alex is at a level above Shanghai. Remember that when you go."

"I will."

"Or maybe I should go. I can probably get back to meet with Bartholomew by seven."

"No, Phoenix. If Alex sees you, the plan is ruined. I know the area where the big boats dock. I'm the better choice."

I breathed a resigned sigh. "You're right."

Sing touched my arm. "What are you going to do while I'm gone?"

I nodded toward the hole in the wall. "I guess I'll poke around to see if I can find a clue about who did this. Since Bartholomew's Reaper-reduction plan stopped, he had no reason to try to kill me."

"True. He didn't seem to be lying when he said that."

"Which reminds me. You looked kind of skeptical at one point."

"Oh. Right. It's because of the compliments he was giving you about your principles." Sing rolled her eyes. "Spare me. Pure boot licking. He didn't mean a word of it. The whole speech was rehearsed."

"Rehearsed? Like he knew I was coming?"

"Maybe." She shrugged. "That's just my take. I'm not a mind reader."

"All right. I guess you should get going. And thanks for your help. Especially …" I grasped the cross. As more memories of my father's harshness threatened to punch in, I pushed them back. "You know."

"I do. And you're very welcome." Sing and I rose together. She wrapped her arms around me and laid her head against my chest. Her touch felt wonderful, warm, perfect.

After a quiet moment, she stepped back and looked at me, tears in her eyes. "Just think, Phoenix, we'll be together for years to come. You and Shanghai and me. I'll always be around whenever you need help."

"*Always* around? What do you mean?" My face grew warmer. Sing could probably see my cheeks reddening.

She fidgeted. "Oh. Well, of course I'll respect a married couple's privacy. I won't pop in unless you call for me. What I mean is, I'll always be available, and I hope you'll invite me frequently."

"Sure. Of course we will. It'll take some getting used to, you know, having the spirit of a dead person always popping in, but Reapers are used to having ghosts around."

Sing's brow creased. "Phoenix, I'm not a ghost. I'm a Sancta. And I won't always be popping in. I'll just be ready to come when you *want* me. No more. No less."

"So you'll be with us until ..." I tried to suppress a negative expression, but I doubt I succeeded. "Until we die?"

A hurt look crossed her eyes. "Um ... I suppose so. Or until you ask me not to return." She spun toward the door. "I'd better go."

"Sing. I'm sorry. I didn't mean to upset you. This is all new to me."

She looked back and waved a hand in casual dismissal, though her expression still seemed injured. "Don't worry about it. I understand." She walked along a beam to the door and ran out in a flash of red.

CHAPTER SEVEN

SING'S ABRUPT DEPARTURE felt like a vacuum sucking the air out of the room. I had hurt her feelings, and my unintended jab recoiled and stabbed my own soul. I needed to make it up to her, but how could an earth dweller salve the wound of a heavenly being? The task seemed out of reach.

I returned my focus to the tablet screen. Shanghai sat in the far left corner, her hands covering her face as crying spasms ran across her body.

I extended a hand. If only I could touch her, give her comfort, but I couldn't — so close yet so far.

After a few seconds, the image faded, as if the lights had dimmed. Shanghai was still visible, though not much more than a silhouette against the wall. Maybe Alex decided that I had seen enough for a while.

I reattached the tablet to my belt, picked up the mirror, and slid it into my cloak pocket. My pace slow, I walked across a beam to the ragged hole where my window used to be. The fire-escape landing was still there, though no longer connected to the wall at my level. As the metal stairs swayed in the breeze, the brackets scraped against the bricks.

Inside, the interior walls lacked any scorch marks, though holes pockmarked the plaster, more of them near the floor. Since the explosion failed to ignite a fire, it probably didn't contain any incendiary fuel, like Bartholomew said earlier. His ability to diagnose the type of explosion without seeing the remains seemed too convenient.

As I examined the room, questions gnawed at my mind, some of them familiar. Assuming Sing and I were right about Alex's plot, if she wanted the city to burn, why did she plan for me to refuse to be the culprit? What could she gain? If I were to try to rescue Shanghai, capturing me wouldn't give her anything new.

Or would it?

I reached into my pocket and touched the mirror. Did Alex want it? Did she predict that I would go to Bartholomew to cook up a scheme to defeat her? Had she already conspired with him to give me the mirror, hoping I would figure out how it works and walk right to her doorstep with it and its secrets in hand? If so, that would explain Bartholomew's rehearsed speech about my principles, something that Alex had talked about far too often.

Still, as Sing noted, Bartholomew didn't seem to be lying about not bombing my apartment. Yet, if he didn't do it, then who did? Maybe Alex forced me out as part of her grand scheme. She pushed a button and manipulated me like one of her robots. She anticipated my plan, my hope to outmaneuver her by doing what she would least expect, even visiting that scoundrel Bartholomew. No matter what I did, she was always ... *always* ... a step ahead.

So what should my next step be? I had the mirror, but it didn't work the way it once did. As a relic that merely viewed the past, I couldn't use it as a weapon, which meant that Bartholomew, if he happened to be telling the truth, might not be willing to help me stop Alex.

In any case, if my conspiracy theories were true, to this point I had followed her plan perfectly. Now I had to veer away from it, but how? What could I possibly do that she hadn't already anticipated?

From the window, a weak voice called, "Phoenix?"

I laid the mirror and tablet on a beam, climbed through the hole in the wall, and set a careful foot on the swaying platform. Below, a female figure stood in the alley. Dressed in Reaper garb with her hood raised, she hugged herself while staggering, as if she might fall at any moment.

I leaped from the platform and landed on the alley floor in a roll. When I jumped to my feet and ran to her, she sprawled into my arms. As I held her steady, I pushed back her hood, revealing a thirtyish black woman's face and short afro-textured hair.

"Saigon?" I lowered her to the alley's broken pavement and sat next to her. "What's wrong?"

"No energy." She gasped for breath. "Heard you live here ... Thought you might know ... where to get some."

"Why didn't you get the surgery?"

"Went to ... the clinic." She swallowed and looked at me with bloodshot eyes. "They were ... executing the Reapers. ... All of them."

My throat caught, though I had suspected this might happen. "But you escaped."

She nodded. "I've been ... on the run ever since. No food. No sleep. My energy drained."

The plackets of her shirt lay partially open. As she took in quick, shallow breaths, her chest rose and fell along with her embedded sternum valve. It seemed that it begged for energy, just a sip of sustenance.

She grabbed my shirt and pulled it open. Her eyes widened. Then she lowered her head and wept. "You ... you don't have it ... You don't need energy."

"No." I laid a hand on her back. "But I know where to find some."

"You do?" She lifted her head and looked at me, her eyes hopeful. "Where?"

"It'll be tough. I have to —"

She clutched my arm with trembling hands. "You owe me, Phoenix. I ... I risked my life ... to save yours ... I didn't have to ... but I did."

"I know. I know. Just let me think a minute." My mind reeled with possibilities. Saigon couldn't be part of Alex's schemes, could she? Since the day Saigon saved my life, my relationship with her was no more than a passing glance on the train. That changed with a recent encounter. She reaped my parents' souls and transported them to the Gateway. Bartholomew knew about that, which provided a possible connection to Alex.

Obviously Saigon still had a valve, and her need for energy was undeniable, unless she was faking it. Maybe Bartholomew had already filled her with energy and sent her to find me, to use her heartfelt plea to convince me to do something. But what?

I let out a sigh. My thoughts were really paranoid. Even if she was a fraud, I had to try to help her. After all, I did owe her my life.

"Can you walk?" I asked.

"A little ways, I think."

I climbed to my feet and extended a hand. "I'll help you."

She grasped my wrist. When she rose, I pushed my shoulder under her arm. "Lean on me while we walk. If you get tired, we can rest."

"Thank you, Phoenix."

After deciding the fire-escape ladder was too fragile, I guided her around the building and through the front entrance. When we arrived at the bottom of my apartment building's stairway, she looked at the steep steps doubtfully. "We'll have to take it slow. My legs are like wet noodles."

"Then let's do this." I scooped her into my arms.

She wrapped an arm around my shoulders. "You don't have to carry me."

"I know. And like you said, you didn't have to save my life." As I climbed, my leg muscles once again flexed with more strength than I expected. When we arrived at the top, I set her down. "Just warning you, my apartment is a mess. Someone tried to kill me with a bomb."

"Well, that's comforting."

With my shoulder again under her arm, I walked her to my apartment, then, leading her by the hand, guided her along a beam before settling her in the still-intact corner. "Wait here while I try to get some energy for you."

Saigon scooted to the wall and leaned against it, grimacing. "Thank you. It's good to rest. Catch my breath."

I gathered the mirror and tablet from the beam and, while Saigon wasn't watching, hid them in the chair remains. I then found an apple and a cereal bar in a cabinet and slid them into her cloak's pocket. Just as I turned to leave, she called, "Phoenix. Wait."

I crouched next to her. "Yes?"

She grasped my hand and gazed at me with pain-filled eyes. "You're the real deal, aren't you?"

"What do you mean?"

"The hero type. You're out to save the world. You're not in this game for yourself like other Reapers are."

"Well, I'm not really a hero. I just —"

"Don't be so modest. I talked to your parents. When they were in my cloak, I mean. They told me all about you. Your mother gushed, but I thought it was just a mom being partial to her kid, you know? Most parents have no idea all the garbage that goes on inside their own kids' heads. They imagine that they're perfect angels. Never do anything wrong."

She set a finger on her chest. "But I was the one who was wrong. Ariel Shepherd is a real-life hero."

I whispered the name. I hadn't heard my real first and last names spoken together in years. They sounded good, warm ... and heartbreaking. As a tear welled, I forced my voice to stay steady. "So you really talked to my parents."

"I said I did." She smiled, though her lips trembled as a new grimace emerged. "Thank you again, hero."

"Thank me if I manage to get that energy for you. I'll be back soon."

As I walked along the hall and down the stairs, doubt shadowed every step. It made no sense to trust anyone except Sing, and here I was ready to risk everything for a woman I barely knew.

I shook off the dismal thoughts and hurried toward Bartholomew's house. As I drew near, I made a wide circle around the row of homes and skulked through the back alley. When I arrived at his yard, I bent low and crept toward his window. A scraggly rosebush stood under it, complete with sharp thorns and a smattering of leaves. It likely served as a deterrent to burglars, enough to send them looking for a more easily accessible house.

With my face toward the wall, I squeezed between the bush and the house, glad for my thick cloak as the thorns dug into the material. I straightened until my eyes rose above the windowsill. As before, the window was open a few inches. Bartholomew's den appeared to be vacant, and the door leading to the hallway stood closed.

I slid my hands under the window's sash and lifted. It rose with a grinding noise, forcing me to lift more slowly. The moment the gap grew wide enough for me to climb in, Bartholomew entered the office, his head low as he looked at a sheet of paper in his hand.

I covered my head with the cloak and ducked into the bush. Keeping my respiration quiet, I waited. One minute. Two minutes. Five minutes. No sound came from the window.

I uncovered my head and looked up. The window was still open. I rose slowly and peered inside. Again no one was in the room, but the doorway to the hall now stood ajar.

Staying as quiet as possible, I crawled into the office and lifted the energy tank. Made out of metal, it weighed at least thirty pounds. Yet, since it had wheels, transporting it would be no problem.

Footsteps approached. I set the tank down and ducked low next to the desk on the side closer to the window. Making myself as small as possible, I covered every part of my body with the cloak.

Seconds later, the chair squeaked. A tapping noise commenced. "This is Bartholomew," he said, probably into his tablet's communicator.

"Is everything in order?" a woman asked.

I strained my ears. Although the voice was weak and tinny, it sounded like Alex's.

"Perfect order. I'm meeting him again this evening. I will know more then."

"Good. Keep me informed."

"I will. Everything is proceeding exactly according to your plan. I was doubtful at first, but when he showed up at my house, I had to keep the door closed for a moment to get over the shock. Your ability to predict his behavior is phenomenal."

"People who have integrity are always predictable. That's why I have to keep my eye on you. Your integrity level struggles to rise above zero."

"That's true, I admit. Integrity never put a coin in my pocket, so I chose a different path."

A humming laugh followed, Alex's trademark. "Keep following my plan, and your pockets will be jingling soon enough."

"I will. And you will get what you need from Phoenix."

"Back to your integrity issues, how did you get Phoenix to trust you? Does he suspect anything regarding his parents?"

"He knows that I ordered their executions. I told him a troubling fact or two about his father. My thought was that confessing my part would help him believe me. I think it worked."

"Then he doesn't know the rest. The real reason."

"No," Bartholomew said. "I don't think he would believe it. I decided it was best to reveal only what I knew he would believe. In other words, the truth, but not the whole truth."

"The whole truth might prove to be a valuable weapon in the future. We will keep that sword in its sheath until the proper time."

"Understood. By the way, Phoenix mentioned your bomb. I asked him how he and Shanghai escaped. His story was shaky, at best."

"Phoenix has many skills," Alex said, "but deception is not one of them."

"True. And since his story has a big hole, I think your suspicion that he has a helper might very well be true."

"Excellent. Then we'll assume it's so and act accordingly."

"Got it. Look for another call tonight." A louder tap ended the conversation. The chair squeaked again. He muttered an obscenity followed by, "Did I leave it open that much? Getting too cold for that."

I peeked past the edge of the cloak. Bartholomew leaned out the window and looked around. He shrugged, closed the window, and walked out of the room, shutting the door behind him.

I let out a long breath. That was too close.

Again carrying the tank, I opened the window, leaned over the sill, and set the tank on the ground. After climbing out and lowering myself between the wall and the rosebush, I closed the window and hurried out of the yard.

I draped my cloak over the tank and rolled it at my side. A chilly breeze kicked up. As Bartholomew had said, it was getting cold. A frigid night might be in the offing.

Along the way, Bartholomew's conversation with Alex stirred dozens of thoughts. What had he not told me about my parents' deaths? Apparently it was something I would have a hard time believing, something he and Alex could use against me later. Whatever it was, I had to be ready for a surprise. I couldn't let them catch me off guard.

Also, what had our escape from the bomb revealed? Was Bartholomew referring to Bill when he mentioned a helper? Or did Alex suspect that we had a Sancta helping us? That idea seemed too farfetched to be true, though it wouldn't surprise me if Alex knew about the Sanctae. She seemed to know a lot about everything.

When I returned to my building, I carried the tank up the stairs and walked into my apartment. Saigon lay curled in the corner, her eyes closed and a string of drool stretching to the floor. I rushed in, set the tank down, and rolled her to her back. As I connected the tank's tube to her valve, her chest barely moved. Death was near.

"Hang in there, Saigon." I opened the tank's valve and looked at the meter. Her energy status read two percent. No Reaper could survive at that level for long. She wasn't faking.

As energy hissed through the tube, the meter rose to six percent, then eight, then twelve. When it reached twenty, Saigon sucked in a deep breath. Her eyes opened, and she looked at me, blinking. "Phoenix?"

I nodded. "How are you feeling?"

"Like I got run over by the depot train." She closed her eyes and smiled. "But keep doing what you're doing, and I'll be dancing a jig in no time."

"Glad I can help."

She opened her eyes and looked at the tank. "Where'd you get that?"

"From Bartholomew, the depot attendant. I guess you could say I borrowed it."

Her smile widened. "My lips are sealed."

When her level reached 105%, I shut the tank off. "I overfilled you a bit. You might need the extra boost."

Saigon climbed to her feet and shook her legs one at a time. "Oh, man! I feel fantastic!"

"Trust me," I said as I rose. "I know the feeling."

She stepped close and kissed me on the lips, a quick peck. When she drew back, she shook a finger. "Now don't you go getting notions about that kiss. It was just a thank you, and I'm old enough to be your mother."

My cheeks warming, I nodded. "I won't. I have a … well, I guess you could say a …"

"A girlfriend?" She crossed her arms tightly. "Don't tell me it's Shanghai."

I waved a hand. "I know you and Shanghai got off on the wrong foot, but she's not like she used to be."

"You mean cocky? Full of herself? Never shuts up?" Saigon let out a sigh. "Phoenix, being a district hound is lonely work. I know. I've been at it for almost twenty years. But now that the rules got flushed down the toilet, you don't have to settle for the first pretty girl who catches your eye. Shanghai's gorgeous, but she's not your type."

I firmed my tone. "Listen, if you really want to thank me for shooting you up with energy, don't talk like that about Shanghai. Maybe she used to be all those things you said, but she's changed. And I have to save her life."

Saigon's brow lifted. "Oh? What's going on?"

I gave her a brief summary of recent events, including Shanghai's capture by Alex, the capabilities of the illuminaries, and some of my suspicions about Bartholomew. With each detail I provided, I wondered about the wisdom of revealing secrets, though I kept the presence of the mirror to myself. Whether it could be used as a weapon or not, it seemed to be the key to Alex's plans.

"So," I said, "I need to be two places at once. I have to search for Shanghai, and I have to start burning Chicago and murdering innocent people or Alex will start killing my friends."

Her arms still crossed, Saigon stared at me for a long moment. "What's so special about you that's got Alex riding you like a demon spurring a tired war horse?"

"She thinks she can always predict what I'll do, that she can control me like one of her robots. And so far, it's true. I can't seem to get ahead of her. She always outthinks me."

"Well, you can count me as your ally. I hate that yellow-haired hell cat." Saigon laid a hand over her valve. "We saved each other's lives, Phoenix. We don't owe each other anything. But to take down that self-worshiping, leather-wrapped lizard, I'll do whatever I can to help."

I looked her over. Standing only an inch shorter than me and boasting muscles that filled her sleeves in an impressive fashion, she could pass for me if someone got only a glance. "Could you pretend to be me while I search for Shanghai?"

"What?" Saigon pointed at her face. "Look at me. I'm as black as they come, and you're lily white. My cloak can hide my curves, but it'd take layers of makeup to cover my face and hands."

I gestured toward the window. "It's getting cold out there. You can wear gloves and a ski mask. Do you have those?"

"I can get them. But how am I going to pull this off? I've been in trouble a few times. Mostly pickpocketing. But I'm no murderer. I won't kill innocent people for anyone."

"Let me talk to Bartholomew tonight and see what he has in mind. Maybe I'll get a clue about how to make it work." I lifted the edge of her cloak's cape. "Do you think Bartholomew would recognize you if you weren't wearing Reaper clothes?"

"Not likely. Whenever I unloaded souls at the depot, he hardly ever gave me a glance. Why?"

"You could come to the restaurant and listen in."

She touched her stomach. "And get something else to eat. The energy boost made me hungry."

"Alex is probably monitoring Reaper codes, so pick up your food somewhere else, preferably pretty far away."

"I'm a marked woman. If I punch in my Reaper code anywhere, the executioners will be after me in a hurry."

"Then just come to the restaurant at seven. I'll get some food for you somehow."

"Perfect. In the meantime, I gotta get my stuff. I managed to clear my clothes and a few other things out of my apartment and hide them before some DEO snakes slithered in looking for me. Then I need to find a place to get cleaned up. I haven't showered in days."

I pointed with my thumb at my bathroom alcove. "You can use my shower. The door blew off, so there's no privacy, but I don't think anyone will come in. The water pressure's low, but it works."

She glanced at the alcove. "What are you going to do between now and seven?"

"I'll shower while you're out getting your clothes, then I have to take the tank back to Bartholomew before he misses it. After that, I'm not sure, but I'll see you at Eggs & Stuff at seven."

"That'll work." She slid her hand into mine and shook it. "Glad we're on the same team."

"Me, too."

"See you soon." She walked out of my apartment with a lively gait.

As soon as she was out of sight, I retrieved the tablet and mirror from the chair and looked at the screen. Shanghai still sat against a wall, barely visible in the dimness. Apparently, Sing had not yet arrived. Lake Michigan lay a few miles from my apartment. Not knowing all the means of travel she could employ, I had no way to guess how long it would take her to get there.

After I showered and shaved, I checked the tablet again. Nothing had changed. I attached it to my belt, slid the mirror into my pocket, and left the apartment. I hid the tablet in an alley to avoid the possibility that Alex could track me to Bartholomew's house, then returned the tank without incident, an easier procedure since he didn't appear to be home. When I finished, I retrieved the tablet and exited the alley. A nearby city clock chimed six times. I had an hour left before my meeting.

The wind even colder now, I walked to the restaurant. Remembering that the two-story building across the street had a parapet around the roof, I climbed the fire escape to the top and sat with my back against the parapet, concealed from view. I detached the tablet and propped it against my knees. Shanghai's dim silhouette leaned against the left wall, the room still too dark to distinguish anything else.

Soon, the sun settled below the horizon. As if cued by the sunset, the frigid wind knifed through my cloak, forcing me to duck low to avoid the swirling air. After another minute, the telltale buzz emanated from the tablet. I looked again. The lights had come on. Shanghai walked to the cell's door and crouched, her ear close to the communications box on the wall and her face toward me.

For the next several minutes, her expression remained stoic, as if she were listening to nothing in particular.

The door's buzzer sounded. Shanghai backed away. An illuminary walked in, set a food tray on the floor, and walked out.

Shanghai sat next to the tray and picked up a small sub sandwich. As she bit into it, she looked straight at me for a brief moment, most likely a sign that she knew I was watching. Maybe Sing had spoken to her through the communications box.

I checked the time on the tablet — 6:45 p.m. After looking into my cloak pocket to make sure the mirror was still safely tucked inside, I returned the tablet to my belt. Since Alex already knew I was meeting with Bartholomew, it didn't matter if she could track my location.

I climbed down to the pavement and crossed the street. Eggs & Stuff was open, as expected, but it would probably close at electricity-shutoff hour.

When I walked in, I took note of a digital clock on the wall — 6:52 p.m. I made a quick scan. A fortyish white couple sat at a far table eating soup and bread, both scooping food to their mouths as if someone might snatch it away at any moment. Closer to me, a black man perched on a barstool sipping a large cup of coffee, a baseball cap askew on his head, bald at the sides and maybe all over.

Taking a seat at the table nearest to the bar, I waited. Although Bartholomew would probably arrive at exactly seven, I had hoped Saigon would come earlier. She was cutting it close.

I picked up a menu from a holder near the edge of the table and glanced from it to the clock and back again. Since restaurant workers knew that a Reaper who eats alone always sits at a barstool, no one would come to the table till after my dinner companion arrived.

The manager from the morning shift walked by, glancing at me before entering the kitchen. Since he had shown kindness earlier by offering water to Shanghai and me and had seen my fighting skills, he probably wouldn't try to accost me to win a reward. Still, I hoped to keep a low profile. No use risking a confrontation with him or the other customers.

The moment the clock switched to 6:59, Bartholomew strode in, wearing a thick coat. He spotted me and sat in the chair opposite mine, his elbows propped on the table. "What have you learned?"

I laid the menu down. "Not much. The mirror seems normal so far."

"I guess you'll need this, then." He withdrew a diary-like book from his coat pocket and set it on the table. "This is the journal I mentioned. Much of it is unreadable, but see if it helps."

"Thanks." I picked it up and slid it into my cloak pocket. "I'll keep experimenting with the mirror."

"I'm sure you will, but we should assume that you won't have a weapon you can use against Alex." Bartholomew pulled a folded sheet of paper from another pocket, spread it out on the table, and set his finger on a spot. "This is a good target. A prison filled with murderers, pedophiles, rapists, and the like. Burn that to the ground, and you'll kill the worst of the worst. The planet will be better off without these scum. My contact at the enforcement office says they're all scheduled for execution later this week anyway, so it's perfect."

I studied the map. The area appeared to be only a couple of miles from Lake Michigan. The smoke would be easy to see from Alex's dock. I pointed at a building near the jail. "What's this?"

Bartholomew squinted. "Looks like a strip of businesses you'd normally find near a jail. Bail bondsmen, lawyers, that kind of thing. Why?"

"I just want to know who to evacuate. Anyone close might get hurt."

"Don't worry about that. I have already taken the liberty of warning the guards to evacuate, and I placed explosives in the proper places. The damage will be localized."

"You already placed the explosives?"

"In precise locations to ensure that the jail will burn without harming anyone else. All you have to do is set them off." Bartholomew narrowed his eyes. "What did you expect? You don't know how to make firebombs, do you?"

"No. I just —"

"And you don't have a weapon to defeat Alex, do you?"

"Like I said, I'll keep experimenting."

"Of course you will, but if the mirror's power is nothing but a myth, you have to at least start the burning. You don't want innocent people to die. Let the murderers, rapists, and pedophiles die instead."

"But Alex is supposed to send an address for me to start with. Knowing her, it won't be a prison filled with hardened criminals. It'll be a school or a daycare center."

"As long as you blow up something and she gets souls while you take the blame, it will all work out." He picked up the menu. "Order your food. While we're eating, I'll tell you how to set off the firebombs."

Wanting to get enough for myself and Saigon, I selected my maximum food allowance from the menu — two jumbo sandwiches and a baked potato — and provided my code for payment. Since the manager already knew my identity, giving it away wouldn't make any difference.

While Bartholomew and I ate, he drew a diagram on a napkin that described four firebombs and told me that the remote detonator could be found in a furnace room adjacent to the cafeteria. He warned me not to try to adjust or move the explosives. Only a trained expert could do it safely.

Although I paid attention, Saigon was the person who really needed to see this. I scanned the restaurant every minute or so. No one new came in. The couple at the far table left, while the man at the bar sipped coffee, apparently in no hurry to go anywhere.

After about fifteen minutes, Bartholomew excused himself and went to the restroom. The man at the bar got up and followed him. Another couple of minutes later, they returned and sat where they were before.

When Bartholomew and I finished talking, I packed one sandwich and half of the potato in a brown paper take-home bag. "I guess I'd better go. I have a big day tomorrow."

He half closed one eye. "Do you think you're ready?"

"As ready as I can be. It's hard to imagine killing a bunch of people no matter how evil they are."

"True, but it's necessary." He wrote the target's address on the napkin alongside the diagram and slid it to me. "Are you sure you know how to get there?"

"I don't often go into that part of the city, but I'll find it."

"Do you know where City Center is?"

"The government building with the big grass courtyard?"

"That's it. Your target is about five blocks south and six blocks east."

"Should be easy to find."

"Good. When you figure out how the mirror works, we can talk about where to find Alex and how to attack her. Until then, we'll meet here each evening to plan the next target. But it won't take long for me to run out of targets you won't regret. Eventually, some innocent people will have to die."

"I'm not going to let that happen." I folded the napkin and put it in my cloak pocket. "If you don't hear from me, I'll meet you tomorrow. Same time, same place."

He rose and left. When he opened the door, Sing slipped in and hurried to my table. She sat across from me, breathless as she spoke. "Just like we thought, Shanghai is on a big boat docked at a pier on Lake Michigan, and her prison cell is below the deck."

"Did you go into the cell?" I whispered, moving my lips as little as possible.

Sing shook her head. "The cell door and window are electrified. I tried to enter, but a jolt stopped me. The field has a strange intertwining of multiple electric layers. I can't cross it, but I managed to talk with Shanghai. In fact, we had a fairly lengthy conversation."

"What about Fiona and the girls?"

"I saw them in another cell. They're alive. Tired and scared, though."

"Did you see any guards?"

Sing nodded. "Five illuminaries standing on a deck area at the front. While I watched, they always faced the city, which means they probably aren't expecting someone to approach from the water. The ship has a lower rear deck that can't be seen from the front, maybe a good spot to get on board."

The man at the bar rose and sat in the chair adjacent to mine. He set his cap and coffee cup on the table and pointed at my take-home bag. "Is that for me?"

The voice was a woman's. I looked closer. Saigon had shaved her head and applied dark makeup to her cheeks and chin to provide the shadow of emerging whiskers.

"Yeah." I pushed the bag to her. If Bartholomew happened to be spying on us from outside, it would look like I was feeding a hungry beggar. "It's all yours."

"Thanks. And you'll have to pay for my coffee. I put the manager off three times already."

"No problem. I maxed out on food, but I have some left for coffee." I glanced at Sing. She looked at me in a questioning way. I had to give her a heads up without letting Saigon know about her.

I withdrew the napkin and stealthily gave it to Saigon. "Did you hear the instructions?"

"Every word." She opened the bag and pulled out a sandwich. "I'm sure I can handle it."

"And you heard it's a prison filled with the worst convicts around."

"Sure did." She bit into her sandwich. "Got the ski mask," she said as she chewed, a hand over her mouth. "And the gloves. With my hood up, I'll be your twin."

Sing gave me a knowing nod.

The ceiling lights blinked off. A solitary streetlamp shone through the window, enough for us to see each other.

The manager called from the kitchen. "Time to go, Phoenix, and whoever that is with you."

"On our way. And can you add this man's coffee to my order?"

"Yep. Already guessed he's some kind of vagrant."

Saigon glared at him but said nothing. While she and I slid our chairs back, Sing rose without moving hers. I walked ahead to the door and opened it. As Saigon passed, I whispered, "My apartment in twenty minutes."

CHAPTER EIGHT

WHEN THE THREE of us exited the restaurant, Sing and I walked toward my apartment, and Saigon hurried in the opposite direction, still eating the sandwich.

"Pretty risky," Sing said as we picked up the pace on the streetlamp-illuminated sidewalk. "But it's also pretty brilliant."

"Thanks. I'm kind of sickened by it, though. Killing people, I mean. Bartholomew said they're all supposed to be executed soon, so I guess that helps. That is, if he's telling the truth."

"That's a huge if." Sing gestured with her head back toward the restaurant. "Who's the woman who came to the table?"

"Saigon, a Reaper who still has her energy valve. She carried my parent's souls during my most recent trip to the depot." I lifted my brow. "Did you know her?"

Sing shook her head. "Heard of her. Never met her."

While we hurried on, I told Sing about meeting Saigon in the alley and that the clinics were executing Reapers who showed up for surgery. When I finished relating the tale of borrowing the energy tank from Bartholomew, we slowed as we climbed the stairs to my apartment's floor. With my flashlight now in hand, I set the beam a few steps in front of us.

"Isn't it convenient," Sing said, "that Bartholomew showed you the energy tank not long before Saigon arrived in the alley? Isn't it also convenient that you were able to hide in his office without him noticing?"

"Convenient is an understatement." We halted in front of my door. "I've been wondering if Saigon's a setup. What's your guess?"

"Well, think about it. She got recharged at the depot, right? That was what? A week ago? Unless she sprung a leak, she ran dry really fast."

"She said it's because she was running from the people who were trying to kill her, and she had no food. A week of that would drain any Reaper."

"I suppose so, but I was watching through the window and saw her go to the restroom the same time Bartholomew did. Isn't that suspicious?"

"It is, but she drank a lot of coffee. She probably just had to go." We entered the apartment and walked toward the intact floor, my flashlight beam again leading the way.

Shanghai's battle staff leaned against the corner. A small suitcase lay nearby along with a toiletry bag and a framed photo of a black woman who looked like an older version of Saigon.

After setting the flashlight in the corner with the beam aiming outward, I touched the staff. "Shanghai left this on the train. Saigon must've picked it up. The other stuff belongs to her."

Sing ran a hand along the staff's wood. "Shanghai will be glad to get it back."

We settled on the floor, sitting cross-legged. The flashlight's glow provided just enough light for us to see each other. After electricity cutoff hour, I usually lit my reading lantern, but it was probably destroyed in the bomb blast. I didn't bother looking for it.

"Look," I said, "Saigon is on our side. She shaved her head, for crying out loud. If she's a traitor, she didn't have to go that far to disguise herself. I know Alex is a master at this game of chess, and maybe Saigon showing up at the right time and me being able to get the energy so easily were convenient, but if I keep second and third guessing everything, I'll paralyze myself with paranoia."

Sing grasped my hand. "You're right, Phoenix. I just want to make sure you think everything out. That's why I'm here. I don't want you to be sorry if you don't consider every angle."

I exhaled heavily and nodded. "Thanks. You are helping."

"Then since we're trusting Saigon, we should go all the way."

"What do you mean?"

"When she comes, I'll let her see me."

"Good. I like that." I withdrew the journal from my cloak pocket and opened it. Fragments flaked off the edges of the fragile, yellowed pages. "This is the journal Bartholomew mentioned when we were at his house. I'm supposed to get clues about what the mirror can do."

"But its powers are gone. It's just a history viewer now."

"I know. I just want to see what Bartholomew learned from reading this." In the dim light, I squinted at the faded ink that formed words in the old-fashioned cursive script, abandoned in schools long ago, though I had exposure to it during Reaper training.

After reading the few legible parts, I closed the journal. "If you piece it together, you can figure out that the mirror can transport people from danger, just like you said. And it also mentions a Sancta named Scarlet who powered the mirror."

"So I guess it doesn't give you any new information."

"No." I returned the journal to my pocket. "Except that Bartholomew probably knows more than he's letting on."

"If he does, why would he give you the journal? He had to know you'd figure out he was holding back information."

"True. Maybe it's a signal."

Sing cocked her head. "What kind of signal?"

"That he's on my side. He gave me the only first-hand account that proves what the mirror can do, and pretending he doesn't know might be a way to tell us that he really does know, but he won't tell anyone else."

"Meaning Alex."

"Exactly. I just don't know why he's being so secretive."

Sing shook her head. "Pretty farfetched, Phoenix."

"You're right, but do you have another explanation?"

"Maybe he couldn't piece it together. You already knew what the mirror could do. That made it easier to figure out."

I shook my head. "Trust me. It wasn't that hard. And he's highly intelligent."

"Okay. We'll assume he knows and keep our eyes and ears open."

I patted my pocket. "And the journal in our possession."

Saigon walked in, carrying a lit lantern and wearing Reaper garb. She tiptoed across a beam and set the lantern down near the wall. The glow filled the room with light. "Thought we might need this."

"Good idea. Thanks." I looked at Sing. "Go ahead."

"Go ahead and what?" Saigon jumped back from Sing and gasped. "Who are you?"

Sing rose and offered a head bow. "I was known as Singapore when I was alive."

"But ... you ... how ..." Saigon set a fist on her hip. "What are you? You can't be a ghost. I would've seen you."

"I'm not a ghost. My mother was Tokyo, and —"

"Tokyo?" Saigon's eyes grew wide. "*The* Tokyo?"

"Yes, and when she died, the second time she died, I mean, she ..." Sing shook her head. "Wait. First things first. I committed suicide so I could see what was beyond the Gateway, mainly to learn if my mother made it there, but she was pulled back from the Gateway by a Reaper named Peter who was murdered by his mother."

"Alex was Peter's mother," I said as I rose and retrieved my flashlight.

"Right," Sing continued. "You see, a person who has gone beyond the Gateway can be pulled back by a Reaper, but only by a Reaper, and the soul returns to the body, assuming the body is still viable."

Saigon waved a hand. "Whoa. Slow down. My head's spinning." She pointed at Sing. "So you're dead."

"Yes, I have been sent here to help Phoenix."

"Sent here?" Saigon squinted. "Like an angel?"

"In some ways, but the reality is more complex."

"And Reapers can snatch people right out of heaven?" Saigon touched herself on the chest. "So I have that power?"

Sing nodded. "Like every other Reaper. Most just don't realize it."

"Good to know." Saigon whistled. "So we have an angel among us. Now I feel a lot better about what we're doing, except for one thing." She narrowed her eyes at me. "You and Bart were talking about a mirror and its powers. That sounded like hocus pocus."

After turning the flashlight off and clipping to my belt, I withdrew the mirror from my cloak pocket and showed it to her. I gave her a hurried summary of its past and its supposed abilities before sliding it back to its place.

"That's really spooky stuff," Saigon said, "but it sounds like the mirror's not going to do us much good." She reached under her cloak, unfastened a computer tablet, and extended it toward me. "This might be a lot more helpful."

I took the tablet and looked it over. "Where did you get it?"

Saigon feigned nonchalance. "I just bumped into a grumpy man in the restroom, and it showed up in my hand. Strange, isn't it?"

I smiled at Sing. She returned the smile. Saigon was definitely on our side.

"I didn't show it to you earlier," Saigon said, "because I was worried Bart might be watching. Anyway, I figured we could use it and the one you have to talk to each other. You know, coordinate while we're separated."

"If we can do it without anyone listening in." I turned Bartholomew's tablet on, but it wouldn't allow me to do anything without entering his thumbprint. "I'm stuck. I need his print."

"Oh, I already got that." Saigon pulled a bar of soap from her cloak pocket. "I got his print on this. I'm not sure how to get it from the soap to the screen, but I thought it might be possible."

"Maybe," Sing said. "I can try to draw it on paper and test it until it works."

"Draw it?" Saigon gave her a doubtful look. "That'll take hours. Even for an angel."

"I have plenty of hours. I don't need sleep."

"Well, then," Saigon said as she handed the soap to Sing, "the resident angel has work to do."

I set Bartholomew's tablet on the floor and unfastened my own. "That tablet won't do us any good if I can't secure this one." I pressed my thumb on the identification square. When it beeped, I looked through the options and found one that allowed me to secure a channel so that only a specific tablet could communicate with this one by voice.

While I worked, the unit beeped again, this time with a different tone. A text message from Alex appeared.

Here is the address where you will begin your, shall we say, activities. Be there at 6:00 a.m. Since most everyone will be asleep, you should have no problem killing 100 people. When you escape, several of my illuminaries will arrive to collect the newly released souls. At least one will chase you to make a show of our law-enforcement efforts.

I assume you have seen Shanghai on your tablet. The lights will be off the rest of the night, so you won't be able to see her again until after you finish your first assignment. Rest assured that she and the Fitzpatricks are well.

I read the attached address — not the same as the one Bartholomew provided. I showed it to Saigon. "Know where this is?"

She shook her head. "But the tablets have maps. I can find it."

I handed her my tablet. "Look it up and see how close it is to the address Bartholomew gave me."

"I'm on it."

While Saigon searched the map, I found a sheet of paper and a pencil for Sing. She took them, sat against the wall, and began the meticulous job of copying the soap imprint to paper.

"Here it is." Saigon pointed at a roadmap on the screen. "It's pretty close to the other place. Maybe a mile."

"Let's hope it's close enough to convince Alex." I took the tablet and reset the security so that it no longer needed my thumbprint to operate. "Now you'll be able to use it whenever you want. If it has a location beacon, Alex will think you're me doing the assignment. That'll free me up to try to rescue Shanghai and the Fitzpatricks."

Saigon clipped the tablet to her belt and sat next to Sing, her brow knitted with tight furrows. "I don't know about this, Phoenix. The plan sounds good, but setting off firebombs? Killing people? They're scum, but who are we to put them to death? Sure, they're going to die soon, but pulling the trigger's not our job."

I sat in front of her and Sing. Sing's eyes seemed to pierce mine, carrying an unmistakable message — Saigon had a great point that I couldn't ignore.

"I know what you mean, Saigon. I've been to the executions. I know what it's like to watch convicts die, and I'm always glad I'm not the one on the trigger side of a sonic gun."

Saigon's expression softened. "Same here. Sometimes the souls are like crazed wolverines when I reap them, and I ignore their cussing and all, but some ..." Her chin quivered as she brushed a tear. "Some just cry. They're so sorry. Just so sorry for everything. What they did. Who they hurt. How they wish so bad they could make up for it. But it's all over. It's too late. They can't do anything but ride in my cloak and go on that final journey to the unknown. Then I thank the Lord that I wasn't the one deciding their time was up. I didn't want to pull the trigger then, and I don't want to do it now."

I heaved a deep sigh. "You're right. You shouldn't be the one."

"But you feel the same way, right? You don't want to pull the trigger. And what about the plan?"

I unclipped the flashlight from my belt. "I'll take a look at the site and see what's going on. Maybe I can move the bombs to an abandoned building."

"No way," Saigon said. "You heard Bart. Only a trained expert should —"

"I know. But you nailed me to the wall, and I can't shake loose. I wouldn't want to be a trigger man, so I can't expect you to be one."

"Glad you see it that way." Saigon detached her own flashlight. "But you're not going to the site alone. You heard how Bart described the bombs. It'll probably take two of us to handle them."

Sing showed us her drawing, only about five percent complete. "I want to join you, but I'd have to stop working on this."

"Just keep at it," I said. "If we get blown to bits, you'll need to rescue Shanghai and the Fitzpatricks."

"If I'm allowed to stay on earth." Sing set the page on her lap and stared at it. Her voice fell to a whisper. "Your death might mean the end of my time here."

"Then I'll rescue them as a ghost. One way or another, we have to get it done."

Saigon shoved my knee. "I like your attitude, hero boy." The lines in her brow returned. "But let's try to stay alive.

My mother's been waiting twenty years for my term to be over, and I have three months left. I don't want to go home in a mayonnaise jar."

"We'll try to avoid getting killed," I said, "but if you want your Reaper term to end, we'll have to get a surgeon for your valve removal. The executioners are probably still looking for you."

Saigon blew out a sigh. "Thanks for the reminder."

"Sorry to darken the mood." I looked at Sing. "As soon as you get Bartholomew's tablet unlocked, set it up so that both tablets can see each other's location beacons, but make sure the beacons are switched off for now." I withdrew the mirror from my pocket and gave it to Sing. "Then come find us, and bring the mirror and the tablets with you."

"Sure, but I don't know how long it will take. It depends on how sensitive the thumbprint reader is."

"Just do the best you can." I rose and extended a hand to Saigon. She grabbed it with an interlocking thumb and leaped up. The tremulous smile on her face communicated a blend of excitement and nervousness.

After drawing a map to each location and saying our good-byes to Sing, we raised our hoods and hustled outside to the street. Hoping to stay out of sight, we kept our flashlights off and used light from streetlamps to wind our way through Chicago's neighborhoods.

Each turn brought us into a new breezeway. Cold air funneled through and knifed into our cloaks. Winter's chill always arrived early in Chicago compared to our southern neighbors, but it seemed earlier than usual this year.

The weather, combined with fear of Melchizidek's travel edict, kept residents inside, though ghosts wandered about here and there, mostly level ones, confused and searching. A few tried to communicate with us as we passed, but we couldn't stop to converse. Explaining a new reality to a ghost always took a long time.

At about one a.m., we arrived at the block where Alex wanted me to begin work later in the morning. I turned my flashlight on and walked with Saigon while sweeping the beam across the numbers on the buildings — a series of former office structures that had been converted into low-rent apartments.

When I found the address, I flicked off the flashlight and looked up at the rows of windows lining the ten-story brick structure. This apartment building probably held at least eighty units and maybe a couple of hundred people, assuming it was fully occupied.

A young male ghost, about eight years old, walked out through the building's closed main door. His eyes glowed brightly, likely an early level one. He stopped within a couple of paces of us and stared. "Reapers?" he asked.

I nodded. "What's your name?"

"Evan."

I pointed at the building. "Evan, do you know how many people live here?"

"Lots." He glanced at the door. "I live in two-eighteen."

"Why did you come outside?"

He wrinkled his nose. "I smelled something bad. I tried to wake Mom and my brother, but they wouldn't get up."

Saigon crossed her arms. "That can't be good."

"Let's check it out." I opened the door and stepped in. A choking odor filled the lobby. We would have to get in and out fast. "Saigon, can you reap Evan and bring him with us?"

"No problem." She plugged her clasp into her valve, crouched next to Evan, and wrapped her cloak around his phantom body from his shoulders down. As she whispered into his ear, he filtered into the material and vanished. Sparkles rode along the cloak and gathered at a spot on her back. She rose and strode into the lobby, speaking into her cloak. "Which way to your apartment, Evan?"

Following Evan's instructions, we jogged up the stairs to the second floor. As we hurried down the hall, the fumes grew more and more choking. "We can't stay long," I said, coughing. "This stuff has got to be noxious."

"And maybe flammable." Saigon's coughs echoed mine. "One spark and we're cooked."

When we found apartment 218, I tried the knob. Locked. I slammed my foot against the door and broke it open. Saigon and I walked into a small living area, strewn with dirty dishes, scattered clothes, and death-stroking roaches.

"Keep talking, Evan," Saigon said, still coughing as she led the way toward a bedroom.

At the interior door, Evan lay on his stomach, his fingers pressed against the floor as if he were trying to crawl to safety. Inside, a woman lay sprawled face up on a double bed, a toddler curled in the crook of her arm. I stepped over Evan and checked the woman's pulse. Nothing. I shifted to the little boy in her arm. He, too, was dead.

My heart thumped. My throat nearly closing, I choked out, "We have to move."

We ran out of the apartment, down the stairs, and out to the street. Once safely away from the fumes, we set hands on knees and coughed through a long spell. My ribs aching, I wrapped my arms around my torso and knelt on the sidewalk. Saigon joined me, and we hacked and spat until nearly exhausted.

When our coughing finally eased, I looked at the building. Tears flooded my eyes, both from the gas and the sadness of an apartment complex filled with dead bodies.

I rose and helped Saigon to her feet. While we took in deep breaths, more ghosts filed out the front door — men, women, and children, all with glowing eyes and confused expressions.

At the end of the street, red dots appeared. I grabbed Saigon's arm, pulled her into a nearby alley, and peeked around the corner. The dots clarified — pairs of eyes surrounded by dark cloaks.

I whispered, "Illuminaries. A bunch of them. They've come to reap the souls."

"They're early. You've got, what, four more hours?"

"Alex is making sure no one gets away. She probably didn't know how quickly her victims would die, so she sent the robots now. Or maybe even sooner. No telling how long they've been here."

"First she gasses them, then she rounds them up like cattle." Saigon growled. "That witch is going down."

The illuminaries formed a line from one side of the street to the other, maybe fifty yards away. At about the same distance in the opposite direction, they formed a similar line. "Look," I said. "They're establishing a perimeter to keep the souls from escaping. They probably plan to move in after I burn the place."

Saigon squinted. "One of them has a video camera. Peace Patrol propaganda film coming up."

"Let's get to the other address." I scanned the alley and found the apartment's fire escape. We scaled the ladder to the roof and stood at the front edge. As we looked down, cold wind pummeled us, flapping our cloaks.

At street level, the two lines of about twenty illuminaries each were spreading out, apparently trying to surround the building. "We'll have to go from roof to roof to get past them."

"Which direction?" Saigon asked.

I pointed to our right.

She looked that way. "Well, I'm game, but the third building is a monster, maybe ten floors taller."

I mentally measured the distance to the line of illuminaries and compared it to span between us and the tall building. They were approximately the same. In the light of a haze-covered crescent moon, the building's side looked like a bare wall. "We have to get past it. Let's check it out. See what it looks like."

After backing a few steps, we ran to the side of our building and leaped over the alley to the next roof, one floor lower than the first. When we landed, we ran across the roof again and leaped to another building, which stood at the same level, then walked to its far edge.

At the other side of the next alley, a fire-escape ladder climbed the building's wall. The ladder's only landing below our level lay about eight feet lower than our perch and at least fifteen feet in horizontal distance.

"No way," Saigon said. "Jumping would be suicide."

"You're right." Below, an illuminary stood at the front corner of the alley and another at the back corner, blocking a ground-level escape. I pulled line from a belt spool and threw the claw across the alley to a landing one floor higher. The line wrapped around the railing and held fast.

I spread out an arm. "Let's ride down."

"What is this? Tarzan and Jane?" She batted my hand. "You go first and send the jungle vine back this way."

"Suits me." Holding the line, I jumped from the roof and swung through the swirling wind while reeling line out until I planted my feet on the lower landing, careful to keep the impact quiet.

I unclipped my spool and swung it back to Saigon. Seconds later, she joined me on the landing and handed me the spool. We climbed the fire-escape ladder to the next level where I retrieved the claw, reeled in the line, and clipped the spool to my belt. Then we hustled up to the roof and walked out onto its gravelly surface.

From our new vantage point, the entire area lay in view, though dim and fuzzy in the moon's hazy glow. Boat lights on Lake Michigan's shore bobbed in the distance. In another direction, the City Center Bartholomew mentioned spanned an entire block. Tiny lights dotted the perimeter of its semi-circular courtyard, a huge expanse of grass that attracted children when the weather was good.

I withdrew the map from my pocket and shone the flash-light beam on it. Comparing its symbols to the cityscape, I located Bartholomew's target about eight blocks away, merely a blob in the dimness.

"Do you see it?" I asked, pointing.

"I think so." Saigon set a fist on her hip. "Doesn't make sense to put a prison around here. I think old Bart's telling tales."

"I know what you mean. Too close to apartments and businesses."

"Well, we came this far. We'd better check it out."

I peered down at the street. The illuminaries' perimeter lined the alley we had just swung over, crossed the street, and turned left on the sidewalk on that side. They all faced the interior of the section they guarded. The front door of our building stood outside the line. If we could sneak out quietly, maybe the darkness would cover our escape.

I gestured toward a roof access door. "Let's see if we can get down that way."

After breaking through the door and descending about twenty flights of stairs, we entered the lobby. Bank-teller windows lined one wall, and an open vault dominated another. Scraps of paper littered the cracked marble floor.

I whispered, "An abandoned bank."

"Yeah. I guessed that."

We exited the front door and looked to the left toward Evan's building. The closest illuminaries still faced away. Bending low, we skulked to the right toward our new destination. When we turned a corner, we straightened and picked up the pace.

As before, frigid air buffeted our bodies. Dimness forced us to decelerate at times to avoid lampposts and other obstacles. At one point, we crossed a demolition zone where a huge crane had parked, ready to resume collecting debris at daybreak. Ghosts loitered here and there, as if drawn by the sight of damage. Or maybe the implosion charges caused a massive accident.

A few minutes later, we arrived at the address. Several one-to-two-story buildings populated an expansive yard that included swing sets, a sandbox, and monkey bars. My heart raced. This wasn't a prison. It was —

"A school," Saigon said. "A little kids' school."

I swallowed through a lump in my throat. "Yeah. Bartholomew really pulled a fast one."

Saigon cursed. "I'm gonna stomp that cockroach."

"This is all part of the big scheme," I said. "Alex and Bartholomew working together, I mean. Alex knew he would tell me about this place and that I would check it out, and now of course I have to find the firebombs and move them somewhere else."

"But why?" Saigon asked. "Why wouldn't Bart just put them where Alex hopes you move them to? That would save a lot of time."

"Maybe time is the whole point. Maybe she wants to squeeze me time wise."

"You mean, you couldn't possibly move the bombs fast enough. She expected you to get here later in the morning. But that still doesn't answer the big question. Why?"

The mirror came to mind. Maybe Alex expected me to use it somehow to move the bombs and reveal whatever power she thought it had. If it did have the ability to transport people and things, her scheme might have worked. I would have been sorely tempted to use it. "I'm not sure, but we have to do something about it." I pointed at her cloak. "Have you talked to Evan lately?"

"No. I unplugged just before we ran out of his apartment. Easier to cough without it plugged in." She half closed an eye and nodded. "Oh, right. You're the hero Reaper. You probably chat with the souls all the time, don't you? Try to comfort them."

"The ones who'll listen." I touched the spot on her back where Evan's sparkles had been. "I was just wondering if Evan went to school here. Maybe he can help us."

"Good thought." Saigon plugged in her clasp and asked my question. After a few seconds, she nodded. "Since the beginning of the school year."

"Does he know where the cafeteria is?"

She repeated my query into her cloak. Although I could have listened in by standing closer, I opted to let her handle the conversation. After a few moments of whispering and nodding, she walked into the schoolyard. "Follow me."

When we arrived at a door of a two-story building, I tested the knob, assuming it would be locked, but it opened freely.

"Not a good sign," Saigon said. "It's like we're birds being led into the cat's lair."

"We don't have much choice." I stepped inside. Long tables filled the rectangular room, chairs upside down on their tops. A quick count confirmed that the cafeteria could hold at least 200 students. "Ask Evan if his school serves breakfast and at what time."

Saigon did so and nodded. "Eight a.m."

"Interesting." I scanned the ceiling. Pipes about the width of my arm ran from one end of the room to the other, maybe heating conduits. I followed the pipes to a room at the end of the cafeteria and opened the door. Something beeped at a slow, constant rate.

I aimed my flashlight inside. The beam swept across an old furnace, turned off at the moment. I walked around a toolbox on the floor and followed the sound to the back of the furnace. On its rear panel, duct tape covered an object the size and shape of a television remote control.

I peeled the tape away and pulled the device free. A red light flashed above a label that read "Armed." A tiny screen displayed a digital countdown, showing 06:15:45. The last two digits decreased by one every second, keeping time with the continued beeping. Under the screen, a red button labeled *Detonate* protruded.

Saigon joined me and looked at the controller. "A remote detonator. Looks like it's timed to set the bombs off at eight."

I nodded. "When the kids are here."

"We could dodge some danger by blowing the place up early."

"True, but, knowing Alex, she's already thought of that. We should see if anyone is trapped in the school."

"A hostage who'll die in the explosion?" Saigon shook her head. "You come up with the most morbid possibilities."

"I've been around Alex too long." I pointed the beam toward the furnace room exit. "Let's search for the bombs, then for hostages."

We reentered the cafeteria and began looking under the tables. At the third one, I found a rectangular metallic device affixed to the underside by brackets. It appeared to be about two feet long, a foot wide, and a few inches thick. A rubbery bladder of similar dimensions, probably filled with flammable liquid, was attached to the underside of the device.

I shouted, "I found one!"

"Same here," Saigon called from a table across the room.

"He said there are four. Keep looking."

I checked more tables. At the fifth one, I found the third bomb and called while kneeling, "Number three."

Saigon gasped. "Oh, my God!"

"What?" I leaped up and jogged toward her. She knelt next to a table, her flashlight trained on a human form underneath. I joined my beam with hers. A girl dressed in a jumper and leggings lay on her back with the fourth bomb strapped to her chest.

CHAPTER NINE

M Y HEART RACING, I aimed the beam at the girl's face — Anne Fitzpatrick, Fiona's younger daughter. Trying not to tremble, I whispered, "Her name is Anne. She's nine. No, ten."

Saigon checked her pulse. "She's alive. Probably sedated."

"Let's get the table out of the way." We rose and threw the table to the side, crashing it against another. Kneeling again, I passed the beam slowly across Anne's body. Wires ran from the bomb to her limbs and head. "Do you know anything about bombs?" I asked.

Saigon shook her head. "Only that they destroy things."

"I'm guessing if we move her, it'll explode."

"We'd better assume so." Saigon rolled her hand into a fist. "Looks like you were right about Alex. She's making sure you can't blow this place early."

"Always assume the worst about Alex. She's sadistic to the core."

"But like I asked before, why the two locations? Why did she send you to the apartment building and use Bartholomew to lead you here?"

"I think it's a test to see what the mirror can do."

A new voice broke in. "You're right, Phoenix." Sing walked toward us, a computer tablet in each hand. She set them on the floor and withdrew the mirror from within her cloak. "The power the mirror once had could transport Anne to safety and leave the bomb behind."

Saigon touched the mirror's edge. "That still doesn't explain the two locations. Alex could have tested the mirror here and gotten the answer she wanted."

"Alex always has multiple threads in her plans," I said. "If we used the mirror to get Anne out of here and bombed this place before the students arrived, Alex would still need soul energy for her illuminaries. She also wants a scapegoat. Since everyone's already dead in the other building, I can't save them. When I go there, she'll make a recording of me escaping the Peace Patrollers, and I'll be on the hook for the murders. She'll have everything she wanted, including knowledge that the mirror works."

"But it *doesn't* work," Saigon said, "so what now?"

"We could make her think it does and use it against her."

"How?" Saigon and Sing said at the same time.

"The idea's still formulating." I rose to my feet. "First things first. We have to spring Anne from this trap."

Saigon joined me. "What's the plan?"

"Remember the demolition site we passed? I saw maybe eight ghosts. Probably an accident happened there recently."

Saigon pointed at me. "They're bound to have an explosives expert."

"Exactly. If the accident was from an explosion, their expert might not be the best, but even a ghost expert with a bad record is better than any of us. We'll go there and see if one's around."

"I'll stay with Anne," Sing said as she picked up the tablets. She gave Bartholomew's to Saigon. "The locator's turned off, and no thumbprint is needed now." Sing handed mine to me along with a small battery. "The voice channel is locked on to Saigon's with encryption, so you can talk to her without anyone listening in, and you can still get text messages from Alex."

I pinched the battery and squinted at it. "Why did you take this out?"

"To disable the locator. As soon as you put the battery back in, the beacon will activate. I couldn't deactivate it any other way."

"Makes sense that Alex wouldn't allow it." I gave Sing the remote detonator and clipped the tablet to my belt. After filling her in on what happened at Evan's apartment building, I nodded at Saigon. "Let's go."

Saigon and I exited the cafeteria and jogged toward the demolition site. Once again cold wind buffeted us, and we passed several more wandering ghosts, all level ones. When we arrived at the site, we found a pair of ghosts conversing — a man and a woman sitting on the hood of a pickup truck. The man wore jeans, a long-sleeved flannel shirt, and a baseball cap, likely the outfit he died in. The woman wore denim coveralls over her stout body, and a genial smile graced her middle-aged face.

When we halted in front of them, I nodded. "Either one of you know where I can find your explosives expert?"

The man flicked a thumb between himself and the woman. "That would be us. Me and Tricia are a husband-and-wife team. We're called Bombs Away."

I concealed a wince. What a terrible company name. "Did you have an accident here?"

Tricia patted her husband on the knee. "That's what Ollie and I were just talking about. We're really confused. It's the middle of the day, and no one's walking the streets. The rest of the crew packed up and went home, and we can't find the keys to start the truck. So we're stuck here."

"They think it's the middle of the day," Saigon whispered. "Early level ones. They're in their own world."

"Not real early. They're able to sit on the truck without passing through it. We'll use their status to our advantage." I cleared my throat. "Ollie. Tricia. We have a super important job for you. A little girl's life is at stake."

"A little girl, you say?" Ollie slid to the ground. "Name it. We're there."

"Of course we are." Tricia sank through the hood and landed feet first, her immaterial body melding with the truck's frame. She seemed unaware of the oddness of her position. "What do we do?"

"Follow us." I turned with Saigon and began retracing our steps toward the school. Ollie and Tricia kept up with our quick pace without a problem.

When we arrived, we knelt with Sing around Anne. Saigon and I shone our flashlights on the bomb. The fuel-filled bladder lay on top of it.

Ollie let out a tsking sound. "Who did this to the poor little girl?"

"I'll tell you the whole story later," I said. "Let's just get her out of this mess."

"Right. Right." Ollie leaned close and scanned the bomb. "Good craftsmanship. Someone knows their stuff."

"Look," Tricia said, pointing, "a motion detector."

Ollie nodded. "Series six?"

"Most likely. And a remote control option."

Ollie turned toward me. "Do you happen to know where the remote detonator is?"

"I have it," Sing said. She withdrew the beeping box from her cloak and extended it toward him.

He grasped at it, but his fingers passed through. Blinking, he glanced at Sing and me in turn. "What's going on?"

I let out a sigh. "I'll explain that later, too. Just tell us what to do."

"First, pop open the controller. It should have a seam. But don't pull hard. Wires hold the two halves together. If you break the wrong one, we're all scrambled eggs."

I set the flashlight down, grasped the box with both hands, and pulled it apart. Three wires connected the two halves. "Got it. Now what?"

Tricia pointed. "Do you see a little button on the circuit board?"

I moved the box into the flashlight beam and found a pair of buttons. "I see two."

"Two?" Tricia look at Ollie. "Which one do you think?"

"Two buttons on the circuit board means the detonator can be programmed to control something else, maybe a bomb on a different frequency. If he pushes the wrong one, it won't set off these bombs."

"I think you're right." Tricia looked at me again. "Try either button and hold it down. If the beeping stops, it's the right one. Then let go when I tell you."

I held a button down with a fingertip. A few seconds later, the beeps silenced. As I continued holding it, I looked at Tricia. She nodded, as if counting, while Ollie seemed to be holding his breath.

After several more seconds, she said, "Now."

I released the button. Nothing happened. I exhaled and snapped the box back together.

Ollie brushed his forehead as if wiping sweat. "That was risky, Tricia."

"Risky, yes, but sometimes we have to take —"

The box started beeping again, faster than ever.

Tricia gulped. "Uh-oh."

"What does the timer say?" Ollie asked.

I looked at the box's screen. "Twenty-five seconds."

"Must be a series seven," Tricia said. "Something activated its anti-tampering protocol."

"Twenty-one seconds. What do I do?"

Ollie shrugged. "I never used a series seven. We don't have a reason for anti-tampering."

"I read about it in the manual," Tricia said, tapping her chin. "Let's see if I can remember."

"Think fast," I said. "Fifteen seconds."

"It's something that seems counterintuitive."

I showed her the box. "Twelve seconds."

"Even dangerous."

Saigon grasped my shoulder with a shaking hand. "Phoenix? I don't want to die."

"Then run. Maybe you'll survive."

Saigon leaped up and dashed for the door.

"Eight seconds, Tricia." My own hands trembled. "Give me something."

She snapped her fingers. "I think I remember."

"You think? Five seconds."

"Push the detonate button."

"What? You gotta be kid —"

Tricia stabbed a finger toward the box. "Just do it! And hold it down!"

Wincing, I pushed the button and held it. The timer halted at one second. My heart thumped. Sweat trickled down my forehead. Swallowing hard, I looked at her. "What now?"

"Keep holding it down." Tricia pointed at the wires connecting the bomb to Anne's limbs. "They should be deactivated. Pull them out."

"Should be?" I asked.

"Yes." Tricia bent her brow. "Don't you trust me?"

"I trusted you when I pushed the first button."

"And you're still in one piece." She pointed again. "Now pull the wires."

With a thumb on the detonator button, I used my free hand to pinch one of the wires as I looked at Sing. "Maybe you should leave before I do this."

She smiled. "Why? I'm already dead."

I glanced at the door. Saigon walked in, her hands behind her back. "I see it didn't blow up."

"No, but it still might. I'm about to pull a wire out. You can leave again if you want."

"Nope," Saigon said as she knelt at my side. "I decided to stay on this ship, sinking or sailing. Sorry for abandoning you."

"What's all the fuss?" Tricia said. "Just pull the wire."

"Here goes." I jerked the wire from the bomb. Nothing happened.

Tricia exhaled heavily. "Sometimes being lucky is better than being good."

"Lucky?" I said. "You mean you guessed?"

"An educated guess." She nodded at the box. "You can let go."

I released the button. Again, nothing happened. I pulled the rest of the wires free and unfastened the straps that held the bomb against Anne's chest. "Can I move it? How volatile is it?"

"It's quite volatile," Tricia said. "Move it slowly, and it should be all right. Just don't jerk or jostle it."

I lifted the bomb and laid it carefully on the floor. "Okay, Saigon, we have to detach the others from the tables. I saw a toolbox in the furnace room. We'll need screwdrivers."

"On my way." Saigon leaped up and jogged toward the furnace room, her flashlight in hand.

I gave Ollie and Tricia thankful nods. "I appreciate your help."

"My pleasure," Ollie said, pinching the brim of his cap.

Tricia touched the bomb. "It's still loaded for bear, and the remote will work. The timer's off, but if you press the button again, all four will go kaboom."

"Understood." I looked at Sing. "While Saigon and I detach the bombs, would you mind explaining to Ollie and Tricia about their status? Ask them if they want to keep wandering for a while or if they would rather ride in a cloak."

Sing nodded. "Sure."

Saigon returned with two screwdrivers. We worked together on each remaining bomb, unfastening the brackets and lowering the device while turning it over so that the bladder rested on top. When we finished, we gathered the bombs on a table.

I looked again at Sing as she walked toward us. "How's Anne?" I asked.

"Not a sound or even a wiggle, but she's breathing fine."

"And our ghosts?"

Sing smiled. "They're kind of shaken up, so they went for a walk."

I glanced out a window but saw no one. "I hope we can find them if we need them again."

"It shouldn't be hard. They said they'll probably stay close to the demolition site."

"Good." I placed my hands on the table and looked at the bombs. "All right. Now we transport them to the apartment building, get the illuminaries to come inside, and push the detonate button."

"What if there are survivors?" Sing asked. "It's possible that the gas didn't reach every apartment."

"Good point. We can't risk it." I mentally set myself on the bank's roof and recalled my view of the area. The bank appeared to stand pretty far from the other buildings. "Saigon could bomb the bank instead."

She touched her chest. "Me? Where are you going?"

"Like I mentioned before, you'll be the distraction while I rescue Shanghai, Fiona, and Betsy."

"So you're telling me that I have to draw maybe fifty invincible robots into the bank, then make sure they stick around long enough for me to set the bombs off and get away before the explosions rip me into little pieces of my formerly beautiful self."

I nodded. "Something like that."

Saigon blew out a sigh. "You sure know how to show a girl a good time."

Sing knelt next to Anne and stroked her hair. "I'll take her to Liam while you two get some rest."

"What time is it?" I asked.

Saigon looked at Bartholomew's tablet. "Two fifteen. We can sleep a couple of hours before launching our plan."

"Sounds good. We'll hide the bombs and find somewhere to lie down. I think schools usually have an infirmary with cots."

Saigon walked toward the door. "I'll look for something with wheels to carry the bombs in."

When Saigon left, Sing extended the mirror to me. "Don't forget this. If you can't rescue Shanghai and the Fitzpatricks, you might be able to trade the mirror for their lives."

I took it from her. "What if Alex demands to see it work?"

"Before you leave here, wait for me to come back, and I'll go with you. I can make the mirror look like it's doing something."

After Sing left with Anne in her arms, Saigon returned with a wagon. We loaded the bombs and wheeled them to the school's infirmary where we found two cots. Light from a streetlamp provided the barest of glows through a window, but it was enough to see what we were doing.

Saigon set her tablet's alarm for 5:30, and we laid our weapons belts on the floor along with the tablets, the mirror, and the remote detonator. I surveyed Saigon's belt. It held two knives, a line spool, smoke capsules, a billy club, a flashlight, a pair of gloves, and a sewing kit in a plastic box, all standard items. Many Reapers repaired their torn clothes on the spot. I always waited till I returned home, choosing to carry extra smoke capsules instead of a sewing kit.

When we lay on the cots, separated by the width of the small room, Saigon let out another sigh. "Good night, hero. Like I said, you really know how to show a girl a good time."

"Yeah. Sorry about all the danger. I didn't mean to get you mixed up in —"

"No. No. Don't apologize. I'm having a blast. Reaper life was boring me stiff. For almost twenty years it was collecting souls, kicking a few bandit butts, taking the train to the depot, and coming home to an empty apartment, only to start all over again the next morning."

"Well, the fun's just beginning. I hope you don't have the wrong kind of blast."

"I'll do my best to avoid that." After nearly a minute of silence, she said, "So you've been to the Gateway."

"To the dome that opens to it, yes."

"And Sing's been past it. To heaven, I mean."

"Yeah. Pretty amazing, isn't it?"

Another pause ensued before Shanghai said, "So all that stuff my mother says is true."

"What stuff?"

"Stories hardly anyone talks about anymore. Mostly old folks. You know, about God and faith and stop being a bad girl or God'll burn your butt in hell. Light your toes on fire. Melt your lips off."

I laughed. "Your mother told you all that?"

"Not really. Most of the extra stuff was in my imagination. I guess that means it scared me good. But I guess not good enough."

"What do you mean?"

"I told you before that I did some pickpocketing. And stealing from people is one of the big things that'll get you kicked out of heaven and hung over the roasting pit. At least that's what my mother told me."

"I don't know much about that. My mother sometimes talked about God, but neither of my parents talked about heaven or hell."

"But you know a lot about being good. Word on the street says you risked your life to save people lots of times. Now I've seen it for myself, and I did it, too. It felt good. Real good. Righteous."

"Well, I don't really try to be good, like I'm hoping to punch a ticket to heaven. I just do what comes natural. From the heart. If people are in danger, I have to try to save them. Turning my back on them just isn't possible, no matter what might happen to me. That's just who I am."

After another pause, she said, "So you *do* good, because you *are* good."

"I don't know. Maybe. Or maybe it's more like I can't be someone I'm not." I exhaled heavily. "I don't think I'm explaining it very well."

"Perfectly well, Phoenix. Perfectly well. I just have to think on it awhile."

"All right, Saigon." I let out a stretching yawn. "I'll see you in a few hours."

"See you then, hero boy."

I fell asleep immediately. Shanghai drifted into my dreams. It seemed so long since I had seen her face to face, though it hadn't yet been twenty-four hours. The entire day was filled with constant pressure to figure out how to rescue her. Yet, I hadn't taken time to think much about her personally, what she had been doing all alone in that prison.

Being in rescue mode had narrowed my focus too much. Shanghai was my fiancée. We were getting married in a few weeks. I needed to think about her thoughts and feelings instead of just the task at hand.

My dream persona wandered into her cell on the boat, and I watched as she paced from one wall to the other in a hopeless march. Yet, this despair posture might be an act for the camera. When the lights went off, maybe she was doing something more, figuring out a way to escape. She was too much of a warrior to sit around and wait for me.

After not nearly enough sleep, the tablet alarm beeped. Saigon and I roused ourselves and refastened our weapons belts. I handed her my computer tablet and took Bartholomew's. "When you're ready to let Alex know where you are," I said, "put the battery in and turn it on. Call my tablet by voice to keep me informed. I'll let you know when I'm in position at the boat. Then you'll blow up the bank and distract Alex."

"Got it." She slid the ski mask and gloves on. "And once I put the bombs in place, I'll go to Evan's building and see if anyone survived. The gas might've cleared out by now. Then I'll leave the tablet there and get the illuminaries to chase me into the bank."

"Perfect." I locked wrists with her. "Let's do it."

With the bomb-laden wagon in tow, Saigon left the infirmary and headed toward the bank while I walked to the cafeteria with the mirror in hand.

Sing stood at the door, smiling. "Anne is safe with Liam. He found the tracking device in his van and got rid of it, then he drove me back here and dropped me off."

"That's great." I scanned the street. A few ghosts wandered about, including a jogger who wore only gym shorts. A police cruiser rolled slowly by as the officer conversed with the jogger, but no van was in sight. "Where is Liam?"

"Making deliveries, I suppose. He said he wasn't afraid of the ban." Sing took the mirror and tucked it under her cloak. "It'll be invisible to Alex here."

"Ready in a second." I plucked Bartholomew's tablet from my belt and turned it on. "Let's go."

While we hurried through the cold breezes toward Lake Michigan, I held the tablet close to my ear to listen for Saigon's call. The farther away from her I ran, the more terrible I felt about giving her such a dangerous assignment. We could have switched roles, but that option didn't occur to me earlier. For some reason, rescuing Shanghai had to be my job. Besides, I might have to face Alex, which could be more dangerous than handling a hundred bombs.

I heaved a silent sigh. I hadn't convinced myself of anything. Guilt about Saigon's danger wouldn't go away.

When lights from the pier came into view, Sing touched my shoulder. "We're almost there."

I halted at a street corner and looked around, puffing white vapor that scattered in the wind. About a quarter mile away, several boats bobbed on the water, not yet dry docked for the winter.

Sing pointed to the eleven o'clock position in my viewing range. "Shanghai's boat is that way. While I was there, they put it back in the water, I assume to be ready to leave at a moment's notice."

"So we need to find a boat and sneak up from the back."

"No time like the present."

Our bodies bent and heads low, we hurried toward the lake. When we arrived at the dock, we found a canoe tied to a post. As I untied the rope, a light flashed in my face.

"Who's there?"

I released the rope and blocked the light with a hand, both to be able to see and to try to keep my identity hidden. "I'm a Reaper."

The light angled away. A man in a security guard uniform walked toward me, a hand on a gun in a belt holster. "What's a Reaper doing trying to steal a canoe?"

"It's an emergency," I said, my hand still raised. "I'll bring it back."

"What's the emergency?"

"Souls to collect."

"Where? Out on the lake?"

"Just trust me, sir. It's the best way. And you know what the law says about hindering Reapers who are trying to collect souls."

"Yeah, I know," he said, irritation infecting his tone, "but I heard Reapers are being put out of business by the Peace Police, or whatever they're called. You guys are being phased out."

"Quite true, sir, but we're not phased out yet, and our services are desperately needed. You've probably noticed that there are a lot more ghosts around than usual."

"Like flies on garbage." The guard shifted his beam to the canoe, highlighting a pair of paddles. "All right. Take it. I'm trusting you to bring it back in one piece."

"Thank you." I finished untying the knot and boarded the canoe. With the guard watching my every move, I refrained from guiding Sing as she stepped in.

I grabbed a paddle and eased the canoe away from the dock. When the guard's flashlight flicked off, Sing took the other paddle and helped me navigate into open water.

Waves broke against the canoe's side and sent cold water flying into our faces. We turned toward the wind, cut into the waves, and kept about a hundred feet away from the dock and a line of boats. As we pressed on, Sing looked toward the shore, her eyes narrowed. After several minutes, she pointed and whispered, "That's the one."

As we continued paddling to stay in position, I followed her line of sight to a ship that stretched about sixty feet in length, illuminated by a dock light. Script letters on the hull spelled out "Better than Heaven." Bordered by a metal rail, a wooden deck spanned the middle of three levels. A smaller pilot-navigation level sat at the top. The stern probably held dual propellers, though darkness and foamy water hid any evidence of them.

"Sing," I whispered, "hold us in place while I check in with Saigon."

"Will do." She dug her paddle into the water and pulled through several strokes. "The wind is getting stronger."

"And colder." I unfastened the tablet from my belt and looked at the screen. Saigon's beacon flashed at Evan's apartment building. She had probably already placed the bombs in the bank and was now searching for survivors.

I glanced at the clock at the corner of the screen — 5:51. She had only a few minutes to lead the illuminaries to the bank. "Okay," I said as I fastened the tablet to my belt, "Saigon's lit up. Alex thinks I'm in the apartment building. Let's get closer."

Both of us paddling, we eased toward the ship. Five of Alex's cloaked robots stood near the ship's railing, looking toward the city skyline.

When we drew close enough, I reached out and pushed against the rear deck to keep from bumping into it. Near the dock, the waves were less severe, but they were big enough to make our canoe bob. This deck lay only a couple of feet above the water, most likely to allow easy access to swimmers and sun bathers.

While I bent my knees and rode with the motion, Sing climbed onto the deck. I leaped up and joined her, thrusting the canoe away with the same motion.

I looked back at the canoe. The waves swept it toward the dock. Someone would find it eventually.

A tiny voice emanated from my hip. I whipped the tablet from my belt, lifted it to my lips, and whispered, "Say it again, Saigon. I didn't hear you."

I shifted the tablet to my ear. "I'm at the bank." Nearly breathless, she rushed through her words. "Fire escape. Got a bunch of illuminaries on my tail. Ready to swing to the next building. Detonate from there."

I kept my voice down. "I'm in position. Do it." I turned the volume off and set the tablet to vibrate for notifications.

Staying low, we climbed a short flight of stairs to a middle level, skulked past a door leading to a passenger area in the ship's midsection, and stopped at the rear edge of the bow where the illuminaries lined the deck's perimeter.

We crouched in a dark shadow in front of the passenger area. While we waited, I imagined Saigon swinging from the bank to the lower building. In my mind, she landed, lifted the remote detonator, and pushed the button. I squinted at the city skyline's dim silhouette, waiting for a flash and an accompanying boom. Sing clutched my hand and massaged my knuckles with her thumb.

Something rumbled in the distance. Fire shot up over the skyline. Light flashed around the illuminaries like a strobing halo. They let out a vibrating squeal. Seconds later, Alex strutted onto the deck and watched the fire. The white band still wrapped her head, maybe a bandage protecting the place where she had excised her locator chip.

Bartholomew joined her. "Phoenix did it," he said. "I told you he would. You owe me fifty."

"Not so fast." In the light of a lamp shining from the dock, she turned to the side and looked at a computer tablet. Her lips firm, she shook her head. "Something's not right."

"What?" Bartholomew looked over her shoulder and pointed. "That's his signal, isn't it?"

"It is, but look." She set a finger on the screen. "My illuminaries' signals are going out. I have only one ... two ... three ... four left."

"Only four?" He looked toward the skyline. "Does Phoenix have a weapon we don't know about? Or maybe the mirror is as powerful as you suspected."

"Find out. Take these units with you. When you get there, report your findings to me."

Bartholomew shifted on his feet. "I ... uh ... lost my tablet."

"What?" Alex pivoted toward him. "When? Where?"

"At the restaurant where I met Phoenix. I bumped into a guy in the restroom. I think he might have plucked it from me."

She slapped his face. "Fool! Don't you have sensitive files on that unit?"

"They're password protected," he said, rubbing his cheek. "Without the password, they're double encrypted."

Her voice calmed. "Well, we still have a communications problem. I can't get a report on the illuminaries' progress."

"Don't you have remote voice communications with them?"

"I can speak to them through the tablet. Why do you ask?"

Bartholomew pointed at his jaw. "I designed a microphone in the headpiece just below the cheek. Is that still in this model?"

"Yes, they can speak to me in their robotic tongue, but their vocabulary is limited. I prefer having a human in the field."

"Then I can report by speaking to you through one of these units you send with me."

"Good. If you can figure out what Phoenix is doing with the mirror, I want that information first." The dock's light flickered, then went dark. Barely visible now, Alex cursed and waved a hand. "Go. Hurry."

Bartholomew and the illuminaries crossed a ramp that spanned the gap between the ship and the dock. After another moment, they blended into the darkness of Chicago's streets.

Alex, now a silhouette in the dimness, tapped on her screen with her thumbs as if typing a message.

"Phoenix," Sing said in a low tone, "you have another chance. Alex is alone. You have the element of surprise. Attack and kill her, and it will all be over. She'll be dead, and you can rescue everyone."

I whispered in return. "She's not stupid. She always has a failsafe. If she goes down, it'll set something terrible into motion."

"You're imagining things. If she's dead, what could she possibly gain by ..." Sing shook her head. "I shouldn't be so adamant. It's not my place. But you have my counsel. Kill her while you can."

"I'll keep it in mind."

My tablet vibrated, and a text notification appeared. I silently read the note against the backlit screen while Sing looked on.

Phoenix, I gather that you have Bartholomew's tablet. Well played.

After Alex typed again, another message popped up.

I assume that you have a surrogate who has your tablet. Once more, well played. Your scheming skills have advanced considerably.

Still typing, she walked slowly along the deck. The next message said:

I also assume you saved Anne, but I have a similar bomb strapped to Betsy at another location. It is set to auto-detonate at eight a.m.

I pointed at the words, hoping Sing would get my meaning. This was Alex's failsafe.

Alex walked past us and stood next to the railing, again typing. A moment later, a new message arrived.

It's funny that you think a dark shadow can conceal you from my Owl eyes. I only wish they had adjusted in time to see you before I sent my illuminaries away.

She turned toward us and said, "Hello, Phoenix."

CHAPTER TEN

I ROSE AND GLARED at her. "Hello, kid killer."
Her despicable humming laugh burned into my ears.
"Oh, Phoenix, you have such a flair for dramatic appeal.
I am ready to rend my garments and repent in dust
and ashes."

Tightening my fists, I walked onto the deck with Sing
at my side. I growled, "Where's Betsy?"

Alex began a slow strut around us. "Tied to a column
in a warehouse, hugging a bomb. The difference between
her and Anne is that she is twelve years old, so I decided to
leave her wide awake. She knows that the slightest move
will trigger an explosion that will tear the limbs from her
torso and sever her head. Her mental suffering is horrific,
but if the bomb explodes, I think the sudden pain from
having her body parts scattered throughout the warehouse
will be short lived."

I fought hard to keep my voice calm. "You should know
by now that your threats and intimidation don't work on
me. I don't fear you anymore, and you can't make me hate
you more than I already do."

"True, Phoenix, but painting a vivid picture of Betsy's
torment surely inflames your heroic nature. You will do

anything to ease her suffering, including giving in to my demands."

"Which are?"

"First ..." She halted and extended a hand. "Give me the mirror. Considering its value, I'm sure you have it with you."

"Release Betsy, Fiona, and Shanghai first."

Her humming laugh again knifed into my brain, but I resisted the urge to cringe. "Come now, Phoenix. They're my only leverage. And since I dismissed all of my illuminaries, I have nothing to defend myself with. Although I am more than a match for you alone, once you have Shanghai, the two of you could dispatch me in short order."

I tried to ignore her taunt that she could beat me in a fight, but it stabbed my ego all the same. Could she defeat me? In my earlier weakened condition, maybe, but my strength had returned, or so it seemed. "If you release Shanghai and Fiona and let me know where Betsy is, I will give you the mirror and also my word that we will leave without accosting you."

"So you'll trade the mirror for their freedom." Alex smiled in her usual devilish fashion. "But I need more than just the mirror. I need to know how it works. Since you seem willing to give it up so easily, I fear that it might be worthless. I'm not going to trade three valuable hostages for a piece of junk."

I dared not look at Sing. I just had to hope she could do something convincing with the mirror. "I'll give you a demonstration."

Alex glanced around. "Not here. It's too dark. Come below. I have lights in Shanghai's cell."

"Walk straight into the spider's web?" I shook my head. "Not a chance."

"And I'm the stalking spider, I suppose." Alex chuckled. "Phoenix, if the mirror has the power I think it has, you have nothing to worry about." She narrowed her eyes. "Or perhaps it really is worthless, which is the reason for your fear."

"You can try coaxing me into your web all you want, but I won't fall for it. And besides, why do you think it's too dark here? Your Owl eyes were sharp enough to see me in a shadow. Have they suddenly lost their edge?"

"Spotting a hunched-over figure in the darkness is one thing. Evaluating a potentially world-shaking phenomenon is another. For that, I am glad to stand here and wait until dawn. Just remember, every minute that ticks by adds to Betsy's living nightmare and brings her gory death closer. That's your choice. But I'm not setting Shanghai free until I see what the mirror can do."

"And I'm not showing you what the mirror can do until I have proof that Shanghai and Fiona are still alive." I nodded toward the east. "Dawn's almost here. By the time you bring Shanghai and Fiona up, there will be enough light for a demonstration on the deck."

Alex huffed. "Very well. I will bring them up, but only to show you they're alive. I will put them in shackles."

"Before you go, tell me where Betsy is."

"It seems that I am the one giving everything away." She lifted her tablet and typed on the screen with her thumbs. "She is at the old restaurant supply warehouse on Belleview Road. I'm sending the address to Bartholomew's tablet." When she finished, she tapped a button on her screen that opened a trapdoor in the deck. As she descended a steep flight of stairs, she added, "We'll see how trustworthy you are."

I looked at the screen and read the address. After checking the location on the tablet's map and verifying that it was in a warehouse district, I clipped the tablet to my belt. "Sing, where did you put the mirror?"

She reached under her cloak and showed me the mirror's edge. "Just let me know when you want it. I'll figure out a way to give it to you without her knowing I'm here." She pushed the mirror out of sight and stood at my side while we waited.

A moment later, footsteps pounded up the stairway. Alex appeared, her eyes ablaze. "They're gone! Both of them!" She jabbed a finger at me. "You stalled me while they escaped!"

I raised my hands. "I had nothing to do with it. I had no idea."

"Liar!" She slapped my face. "And I trusted you!"

I grabbed her arm and twisted it behind her back, adding torque. "Listen, witch. Don't play me for a fool. What did you do to Shanghai and Fiona?"

Alex flexed and tried to break free, but I held her in place. "Your strength," she said with a gasp, "is surprising. What happened to you?"

"Like I said, I don't fear you anymore." I applied more pressure. "Tell me where they are."

She grunted and nodded at the trap door, now more visible in the dawn's early glow. "They're gone. If you don't believe me, see for yourself."

"Stop playing me!" I shoved her, making her tumble facedown to the deck.

She rolled to her back, rocked up to her feet, and hopped into a battle stance, raising her fists as she blew hair from her eyes. "Phoenix, you bested me this time in a battle of wits, and you might be stronger than I realized, but I'll wager my skills are still better than yours." Blood trickled from a nostril, and a red welt rose on her cheek. "I want that mirror. Show me what it can do, and I'll let you go unharmed."

"Not until Shanghai and Fiona are safely with me."

"Now you're the one playing me. You know they're gone. You planned their escape. It's the only explanation."

Sing whispered, "I'll check the cells and let you know." She hurried down the steps and disappeared from view.

Alex smiled. "She's gone, isn't she?"

I cocked my head. "She? Gone? What are you talking about?"

"Maybe you don't fear me anymore, Phoenix, but you're still a terrible liar." Something buzzed downstairs. Alex lowered her fists, unclipped a small boxlike device from her belt, and pressed a button. When a second buzz rose from the stairway, she said, "I've got you now."

Sing shouted, "Phoenix, I'm trapped!"

I swallowed hard. I couldn't react to her call without giving away her presence. "What was that buzzing noise?"

"The sound of a prison cell closing around your invisible friend." Alex reclipped the device to her belt. "I've read the legends about the mirror, and I know you need a Sancta to make it work. For that and other reasons, I assumed you had one with you. Otherwise, no demonstration would be possible. Therefore, I set up a trap to capture your Sancta, and I assume she was carrying the mirror. If you have it, prove me wrong by showing it to me."

I clenched my fists. Obviously she had read the journal. Bartholomew had been stringing me along. "I'm not biting. I don't have to show you anything."

"Yet you have already shown me everything, Phoenix. You hunger to prove me wrong. You're so embarrassed that I'm always right about you that you would leap at the chance."

I reached into my cloak pocket as if the mirror were really there. "But if I showed it to you, I would be proving *that* prediction of my behavior." I withdrew my hand. "I won't be baited."

Her humming laugh returned. "You already took the bait, and I reeled you in. Judging by the look on your face, I am quite sure I have both your mirror and your Sancta."

I narrowed my eyes, trying to feign confusion. "You keep mentioning my Sancta. What are you talking about?"

"Your ability to lie is getting worse and worse, but I will give you credit for springing Shanghai and Fiona. That was unexpected."

My mind raced. Should I believe Shanghai and Fiona really escaped, or was it part of Alex's scheme to get me to believe a lie and just leave to rescue Betsy? I could shout and ask Sing if she saw them down there, but that would confirm to Alex that she had trapped a Sancta. I could also call for Shanghai, but if Alex had cooked up this scheme, she would have already guessed my move and made sure Shanghai couldn't answer. And if I went down to check for myself, I might be walking right into the spider's web. Then *I* would be trapped, and Betsy would die. I had to figure out another way to confirm the truth.

"I can tell by your hesitation," Alex said, "that you're mentally paralyzed. You're trying to outthink me, but you simply don't have the brainpower." She walked to the trapdoor and shouted, "Oh, Sancta, I know you can hear me. Would you tell Phoenix what you found in the cells? He's listening, though I know you won't allow me to hear your response."

"The cells are empty, Phoenix," Sing called from below.

"Alex," I said, pretending not to hear Sing, "you're out of your mind."

"I couldn't find anyone down here," Sing continued.

I kept talking to Alex while listening. "You believe in some mythical creature called a Sancta."

"But this cell is definitely the same one Shanghai was in," Sing said.

I kept my focus on Alex. "And you expect me to believe Shanghai and Fiona are gone."

"I found a mark only she could have made," Sing added, "but I have no idea how she escaped. It's possible Alex just moved her."

Alex smiled. "Feel free to go down and check, that is, if you have the courage. Then you can talk to your Sancta face to face. No need to fear me. I have what I want. I'll stay right here until you return. But do hurry. Betsy's time is quickly running out."

Anger boiled. Alex had beaten me yet again. And every option was terrible. Go downstairs? Danger. I could get trapped, too, and Betsy would die. Stay upstairs and leave to rescue Betsy? That would prove that Sing was really in the cell, that she had given me the message that the other prisoners were gone. Alex knew I wouldn't leave without certainty that Shanghai was safe.

"Stumped, Phoenix?" Alex wiped her bloody nose on her hand. "Just be on your way, knowing that I have bested you once again. Yes, your two friends escaped, but I don't care spit about them. I now have the power to control the world."

I charged at her, but she deftly spun and kicked my feet out from under me. I sprawled across the deck and banged my chin. I rolled, leaped up, and faced the barrel of a handgun aimed between my eyes.

"At this range, my sonic gun can obliterate your cerebral cortex, but I am showing you mercy because you did, indeed, save my life. We are forever even. If I see your face again, I will surely kill you." Alex waved her free hand. "Be off to the warehouse. Save Betsy if you can. You have fully served my purposes, and I am done with you."

My cheeks burning, I turned and ran across the ramp to the dock like a kicked dog scampering away with my tail between my legs, once again humiliated by Alex.

As I ran, anger stormed within. How could I leave Sing in Alex's clutches? And how could I not? I had to save Betsy, but abandoning Sing was betrayal at its worst. Once again, every option was beyond terrible. Not only that, I failed to listen to Sing's advice. If I had attacked Alex when I had the chance, she might be dead and all of this would be over. I could rescue everyone without any interference.

When I ran out of earshot, I halted and grabbed the tablet. After turning up the volume, I called Saigon's tablet. "Saigon? Can you hear me?"

Her irritated voice erupted from the speaker. "It's about time you answered. I've been trying to call you."

"I had to turn the sound off."

"Where are you?"

"At the docks."

"Same here. When I finished blowing up the bank, I hustled over."

"Stand on something high so I can see you." I scanned the area. With dawn breaking, the entire lake side had brightened. About a hundred yards away, someone stood on a big crate and waved both arms.

"I see you. I'll be right there." I refastened the tablet and ran toward the spot. When I arrived, Saigon, no longer wearing a ski mask, hopped down and embraced me.

"Phoenix, I did it." She drew back and smiled as she chattered. "I must've blown away thirty of those robots. And no one died. I mean no one *else* died. I couldn't find any survivors in Evan's building. Anyway, the fire didn't spread. It stayed inside the bank building, just like we hoped. Four illuminaries chased me, but ..." Her smile wilted. "Uh-oh. Something tells me things didn't go so well for you."

"Not even close." I searched the docks and the nearby water for any sign of Shanghai or Fiona — so far, nothing. "Have you seen Shanghai?"

"No. I thought you were supposed to rescue her."

"I was." I scanned the docks one more time and found no one. "I met a security guard earlier. Help me look for him."

With Saigon at my side, I walked quickly toward the place where I had borrowed the canoe, constantly glancing at the lake. Along the way, I gave her a quick summary of events, including our need to get to the warehouse as soon as possible. She listened without a word, though she winced at some of the details.

Soon, the security guard appeared about a quarter mile away. Bending over, he appeared to be tying something to the dock. "There he is," I said, pointing.

We broke into a run. When he saw us coming, he straightened and called, "So *there* you are!"

"Yeah," I said as we decelerated. "Sorry about the canoe. I thought it would float back to —"

"It's right here. Complete with a different Reaper and another passenger. They're alive, but unconscious. I had to borrow another boat to fetch them."

Inside the canoe he had just tied, Shanghai and Fiona lay curled at the bottom, both with their eyes closed. Puddles had pooled under their saturated, shivering bodies.

Balancing myself against the canoe's rocking motion, I climbed in and patted Shanghai's cheek. "Shanghai, can you hear me?"

She opened her eyes and winced. "Glad you could make it."

"Sorry for the delay. It's a long story but no time to tell it now." I grabbed her wrist. "Let's get you two out of here."

I helped her rise and hobble out of the canoe. When we both stood on the dock, she squinted at Saigon. "Aren't you Saigon?"

She crossed her arms. "Surprised?"

"More like shocked." Shanghai looked at me. "You teamed up with her?"

Saigon frowned. "You got a problem with that?"

I raised a hand. "Hey. We're in this together. Same goals." I curled my arm around Shanghai's. "Like I said, it's a long story. Just trust me."

Shanghai offered a mechanical smile. "Hey. No problem. I'm a team player."

With help from the guard, we hoisted the canoe onto the dock and lifted Fiona from inside. When we set her down, she coughed and spat out a thin stream of water.

Shanghai helped her sit up while I straightened her skirt and covered her legs. "Are you all right?" I asked.

Shivering hard, she replied in a thick Irish brogue. "Oh, never better. Goin' for a swim with Shanghai in an ice-cold lake is a dream come true."

The guard pointed over his shoulder with a thumb. "Heater's on at my station. It's not far." He narrowed his eyes at me. "When I saw you earlier this morning, it was dark, but now I think you look familiar for some reason."

I lowered my head. He had probably seen our photos on Alex's broadcast. "A lot of people think Reapers look alike."

"I'll think on it."

"You do that. In the meantime, let's get this poor woman out of the cold. And hurry."

With Saigon's help, I pulled Fiona to her feet. As we guided her to the station, I whispered to Shanghai, "Big problems. Once we get Fiona settled, we have to haul out of here. I'll tell you my story then."

"And I have a story for you, but I guess it can wait."

"Saigon," I said, "see if you can find Ollie and Tricia at the demolition site. We might need them. Meet us at the warehouse."

"On my way." Saigon took off in a dead run, her cloak flowing in her wake.

"Do you know where Betsy and Anne are?" Fiona asked as we continued toward the guard station.

"Anne's safe with Liam," I said. "We still don't have Betsy, but I know where she is. We'll have her soon."

Fiona leaned her wet head against my shoulder. "Thank you. I know I can count on you."

Her words drove a spike of guilt deep within. I couldn't tell her the truth about Betsy's danger. Not yet.

When we arrived at the station, a one-room edifice with windows all around, we laid Fiona on a cot near the heater. Although her clothes moistened the cot's bedding, the guard didn't seem to mind.

After giving him instructions on how to contact Liam, Shanghai and I left and jogged toward the warehouse. As cold wind beat against us, Shanghai's teeth chattered. "We need to get you some dry clothes," I said.

She forced her teeth to stop chattering. "I'm all right. We trained for situations like this. Just tell me what's going on."

"At least we could trade cloaks."

She shook her head. "Listen. I know you see me as someone to protect, but when we're in warrior mode, you have to let that go. I'll be fine."

"All right. As long as you do the same for me when I risk my life."

"You got it." Shanghai peered at my chest. "Are you wearing Bill's cross?"

I looked down. The cross dangled outside my shirt, bouncing along with my gait. "Sing gave it to me."

"That's cool. When she came to the cell, we talked about it. You know, the faith thing."

"Oh? Any conclusions?"

"I'm thinking about it. I mean, she came from heaven. It would be stupid not to listen." As if shaking off the topic, she shivered and said, "So fill me in. What's happened since Alex took me? And what's the big rush?"

I launched into the story, including Bartholomew's lies, the mysterious mirror's vision from my past, and Alex's schemes. Shanghai stayed quiet, more likely because she had to concentrate on silencing her teeth than a lack of a desire to comment.

When I finished, she said, "So we rescue Betsy first and then Sing."

"Right."

"And you're sure Saigon is on our side."

"She risked her life multiple times." I gave her a firm nod. "I'm sure."

"Okay, then. Here's my story." Shanghai coughed twice before continuing. "I found a way to break through Alex's electric field. My cell had a mirror above a sink. While the lights were off, I pulled the mirror down and used it to block the field in the cell's window. Then I climbed through and pulled the mirror with me.

"I came out just below the deck but still a few feet above the lake. Fiona's cell was a little ways down, so I slid into the water, swam over, and rode the waves until they lifted me enough to kick up and grab the bottom of her window. I blocked the field with the mirror again while I crawled in. Then I boosted her to the window. That was the hard part. She's not as limber as I am. When she finally wiggled through, she jostled the mirror, and the field jolted her pretty hard. Then she splashed into the lake. I leaped up and threw myself out, but I knocked the mirror and got quite a jolt, too.

"When I hit the water, Fiona was floating with her head down. I had to give her mouth-to-mouth while I swam away from the ship. I found a canoe floating out there and heaved her into it, then got in myself. Once I was sure she was breathing, I laid next to her to try to keep her warm, but I guess I passed out."

"So Sing has a way to escape," I said. "She can use a mirror."

Shanghai shook her head. "Not if she's in my cell. The mirror there is gone."

"No, the mirror I told you about. The one that used to have powers. Sing has it in the cell."

"Do you think Alex will take it away from her?"

"Hard to say. Alex might not do anything for a while. She can't see Sing, so she'll be hesitant. Maybe scared. She said she was done with me, but once she realizes Sing's not going to help her, that might change pretty fast."

"Then you can be sure she'll do something to threaten you again, something that'll force you to persuade Sing to use the mirror for her."

"True, but Sing can't do the impossible." I shook my head. "Let's just save Betsy, and we'll work the rest out —"

An explosion rocked the ground. Fire skyrocketed from a tall building less than a block away. Flames shot out the higher windows, sending glass cascading to the street and smoke billowing into the air.

We halted and stared. "Alex again?" I asked.

"Probably." Shanghai ran toward the building, shouting, "You save Betsy. I'll handle this."

I glanced at the tablet at my hip. The time was 7:42. I had to trust Shanghai and hurry to the warehouse.

After sprinting the rest of the way, I arrived at the address. The warehouse filled most of a city block. Truck loading docks lined one side, all with open or dented doors.

I ran through one of the doors and into a dim cavernous area with a grimy concrete floor. Columns stretched from floor to ceiling at regular intervals. Several head-high boxes stood here and there, probably remnants of the warehouse's inventory. I stopped and called, "Saigon?"

"Over here!"

I hurried toward the voice and found Saigon kneeling in front of a column with Ollie and Tricia. Betsy sat with her back against the column, her arms around the same kind of bomb — a rectangular device attached to a filled bladder. Three segments of rope lay on the floor nearby, likely the rope that had fastened her to the column.

Trembling, Betsy looked at me with terrified eyes, tears streaming. A puddle of what smelled like urine spread under her wet dress. "Phoenix?" she whimpered.

"Yes, I'm here." I pushed a strand of hair away from her face and looked at a digital timer on the top of the bomb. It beeped while counting down — 3:18, 3:17. 3:16. "We'll get you out of here."

"But Saigon doesn't know what to do." Betsy wept through her words. "Phoenix, I'm so scared. I don't want to die."

"You won't. I'll save you. I promise." I looked at Saigon. "What's the story?"

She leaned close and whispered, "Ollie and Tricia are stumped. I haven't mentioned them to Betsy. She can't see them, and they don't know how to become visible to normals yet. But she hears some of what they say, so she's confused."

Ollie pointed at Saigon. "She has the detonator, and we tried both buttons inside it, but they didn't work. That means we can't use the same trick to disable this bomb."

"And it has a tripwire," Tricia added. "I'm surprised it hasn't blown the poor girl to bits already. She's a brave one, that's for sure. Staying rock steady."

"There has to be a way to disarm it," I said.

Saigon hissed in my ear. "Don't bet on it. I'm guessing Alex set this up as another mirror test. She's cruel. Heartless. She even had the poor girl blindfolded."

"So no description of the bomber." I read the timer again — 2:24, 2:23, 2:22. "Ollie. Tricia. Think. Are there any options? Can something ruin the bomb and keep it from exploding? Water? Extinguisher foam? Anything?"

"Depends on the kind of bomb," Ollie said. "Water might work on some bombs, but if it doesn't, it could make it blow. You know, the force of the water could trip the wire."

Tricia nodded. "He's right, and extinguisher foam isn't much more likely. Besides, where are you going to get that in two minutes?"

Ollie snapped his fingers. "Could it have a gravity trigger? You know, one of those devices that detects motion by sensing g-forces?"

"Maybe," Tricia said. "They're getting pretty common."

"G-forces?" I asked.

Ollie pointed at Betsy. "If she stands up, while she's rising, g-forces on the bomb increase slightly. If the force goes above a certain level, it'll explode."

I nodded. "And g-forces go down if she lowers herself again, but what good is that to us?"

"Zero gravity will disable the bomb, that is, if it's the right model. If not, you're out of luck."

"Zero gravity?" I looked up. Metal beams crisscrossed high above with gaps between them and the ceiling. As I continued scanning the upper reaches, I said, "How much time left?"

"One forty-one," Saigon replied. "What are you thinking?"

"I'm going to simulate zero gravity. Help Betsy stand. Real slow. Make sure she keeps her arms tight around the bomb." I pulled line from my belt spool and threw the anchor claw over one of the beams. When I reeled it back a bit, the claw caught the beam and held firm.

After testing the line with my weight, I extended a hand toward Betsy. Saigon helped her shuffle slowly toward me. As she drew near, the timer's digits continued their morbid countdown — 0:57, 0:56, 0:55.

I wrapped my arm around Betsy and pushed the spool's auto-retract button. The motor whined, but it wouldn't lift us. "Too much weight. Saigon, tie her to me. Hurry."

Saigon snatched the rope segments, wrapped a knotted pair around our waists, and fastened us together. "Hope it holds."

"No time to test it." I grabbed the line and began a hand-over-hand climb. The spool's motor helped some, but our combined weights made the going slow. I whispered, "Just stay calm, Betsy, and keep your arms steady around the bomb."

She spoke with a quiet whine. "Phoenix, I'm scared."

"Of course you are. So am I. Just stay as still as you can. We're almost there." Although I ached to hurry, I had to climb with slow and steady progress. The slightest jolt or too much speed might trigger an explosion.

From below, Saigon called, "I'll find something for you to land on."

Not bothering to answer, I glanced at the timer, now at 0:22. Based on my rate of ascent, I would probably make it to the ceiling beam at about the five-second mark. Yet, would we be high enough? Could a fall of such a short distance create a suspension of gravity that would disable the bomb, assuming it was the right model?

I sighed. Only one way to find out.

Our slow climb continued, fifteen seconds remaining. Below, Saigon pushed a huge box into place under us, but with the top closed, I couldn't tell what was inside.

Ten seconds left. Just a few more yards to the top. Eight seconds. My guess was off. We wouldn't make it to the beam before zero. Five seconds. I had to separate and pray for the best. I pressed the spool's detach button, and we plunged toward the floor.

CHAPTER ELEVEN

THE TIMER BLARED. We crashed through the box's top and into a mass of paper. My shoulder struck first, minimizing the impact on Betsy. The bomb's bladder burst open and covered us with an oily liquid that smelled like fuel.

As we lay in the soft paper, Betsy hugged me. "We're alive! Phoenix, you did it!"

I returned her sticky embrace. "*You* did it, Betsy. You stayed still enough to keep us both alive." While unstrapping the bomb from her, I looked around. We sat in stacks of paper napkins, surrounded by the box's walls. "We'd better get cleaned up."

"Everyone all right in there?" Saigon called.

"We're fine." I pulled the bomb free, set it to the side, and smiled at Betsy. "Is that better?"

She hugged me again. As she squeezed me and kissed my cheek, the odor of urine and fuel again assaulted my nose. Yet, the joy of being able to breathe air, even smelly air, was heavenly.

A knife sawed through one of the walls and split it open. Saigon appeared at the hole and helped us climb out of the pile of napkins. "Best I could do on short notice," she said. "Lucky I found it. The other option was plastic utensils."

"You did great. Thanks." I grabbed several napkins, gave a few to Betsy, and began working with her to wipe the fuel off her clothes. "This liquid is flammable. We both need to clean up a bit."

Saigon crossed her arms and stared at me. "So you're not just a hero. You're a superhero."

I glanced from her to Betsy and back again as I continued mopping fuel. "What do you mean?"

"The way you shinnied up your spool line. Gripping a thin cord and climbing that steadily with your own weight plus Betsy's. Not to mention that the slightest wiggle could blow you to smithereens." She shook her head. "Impossible."

"The spool's motor helped. I really didn't notice how hard it was. I just had to get it done."

Saigon snorted. "Spoken like a true superhero."

Although I wondered myself how I pulled off that feat, I tried to change the subject. "Can you take Betsy to the guard at the docks?"

"Sure." Saigon picked up a stack of napkins and handed me half. "Where's Shanghai?"

I blotted my shirt and cloak, neither as fuel-soaked as Betsy's clothes. "She took off to save people in a burning building. A firebomb attack."

"Oh, she did?" Saigon looked toward one of the loading dock doors. "I heard the explosion."

"Yeah, it's not far." I blotted one more spot and handed the soiled napkins to her. "I have to get over there and help."

"Two peas in a pod." Saigon shook her head. "Looks like I misjudged Shanghai. I guess people do change. She's a hero, too."

"Without a doubt." I ran a hand across Saigon's bald head and smiled. "We heroes do what we have to do."

She returned the smile. "Get going, before I kick your butt."

"I'll meet you at the docks."

"Wait." She withdrew a small silver cylinder from a pouch on her belt. "I found this near Betsy."

I took the cylinder and studied it. About four inches long and an inch wide, it didn't look like anything I had seen before, just a shaft of silvery metal. "Maybe the bomber dropped it."

"Maybe. I asked Betsy, but she doesn't know how it got there. Like I told you, she was blindfolded."

"I'll hang on to it."

"Speaking of hanging," Saigon said. "Our ghost friends want to hang around Chicago for a while. They don't want to be reaped yet."

"That's fine with me. We're in a hurry anyway." I slid the cylinder into my pants pocket. My hand brushed my belt, reminding me that my spool line still dangled from the beam, but I didn't have time to retrieve it. The extra one Shanghai had supplied would have to do.

After kissing Betsy and thanking Ollie and Tricia, I ran out the door and dashed toward the bombing site. When I arrived, I found about thirty people milling around on a sidewalk a hundred feet from the inferno, some dressed only in underwear or bathrobes. Heat from the flames warmed the area enough to keep them from freezing.

Closer to the building, Shanghai sat on a low brick wall, using her folded cloak as a cushion. Covered with soot and ash, she looked at me with a forlorn gaze. "Did you save Betsy?"

I nodded. "I'll tell you more later. What's the story here?"

"It's an apartment complex. Some people —" She coughed and spat a wad of black mucous onto the sidewalk. "Some people are still inside. I rescued about twelve, and I heard more people screaming. I tried to go back, but I nearly got cooked."

"Any firefighters?"

"Not a sign of one. Probably Alex's doing."

"Right. Maximum casualties." I looked at the building. Tongues of fire shot from windows at the upper floors. I unfastened the tablet and handed it to Shanghai. "I'll see what I can do."

"No, Phoenix." She grabbed my wrist. "It's too hot. Way too hot."

"Maybe the fire's dying down. Watch and listen from outside in case I need help." I jerked away, ran to the building's entrance, and jumped over a pair of broken, charred doors lying on the porch. Smoke veiled the interior, but no flames were in sight on this level.

I found a stairway and ran up, calling, "Can anyone hear me?" I paused at a second-floor doorway. Smoke hovered in the hall but still no flames, though heat made me wish I had left my cloak with Shanghai. Since fuel from Betsy's bomb had made it more flammable than usual, it might be dangerous.

After taking the cloak off and draping it over my arm, I called again. "Hello? Anyone need help?"

From far above, someone cried, "Yes! We're trapped!"

I dashed up the stairs, shouting, "Keep yelling. I'll follow the sound."

"Hurry! It's so hot!" Coughing followed and a choked, "The smoke is … is …"

My own coughs interrupted my reply. "Stay low. If you can't talk, just keep coughing."

I stopped at the third-floor hallway access and listened. Flames crackled close by, maybe the next floor up. Yet, no more calls or even coughing reached my ears. As the smoke grew thicker, I suppressed my own coughs. I had to listen for the slightest sound.

"Up here!" At the next stairway landing, a female teen-ager with glowing eyes waved a hand. "Hurry!"

I raced up the steps and joined her. "Lead the way."

The ghost girl tried to take a step to the stair above, but her foot passed through. "I can't walk. Something's wrong."

I put my cloak on and turned my back toward her. "Try hanging on to my cloak. While you're riding, you can tell me which way to go."

She grasped the cape portion and climbed onto my back, her hands on my shoulders. "Two more floors up. Hurry."

I took off again. As we climbed, the air grew hotter. Flames licked the walls, and smoke filled the air. I pulled the front of my shirt over my face and used the material as a filter, but it wasn't enough. I coughed with nearly every soot-saturated breath.

"What's your name?" I asked.

"Iris."

"I'm Phoenix. Do you understand what happened to you?"

Grief flooded her voice. "I … I don't want to talk about it."

"I heard you coughing. Is the smoke affecting you?"

"Not really. I was coughing so much a little while ago, I guess just seeing the smoke made me cough more."

"All right. Just tell me where to go."

When we reached the top of the next flight, Iris said, "Down the hall to the left."

I grabbed the access door's knob. As I flung the door open, the metal burned my palm. Ducking under a cloud of smoke, I ran down the hall toward a wall of flames where the floor and ceiling had collapsed.

A few feet in front of the wall, a man wearing coveralls lay prostrate on the floor. I turned him over, revealing a soot-covered, bearded face and a gas company logo just below his collar.

"It's my papa!" Iris said.

"What's his name?"

"Cyrus."

"Cyrus and Iris. Nice rhyme." I patted his cheek. "Cyrus? Can you hear me?"

Groaning, he opened his eyes and looked at me. "A Reaper? Am I dead?"

"No, but you will be if you don't get out of here." I helped him rise to a crouch and pointed toward the stairs. "That way. It's clear to the bottom floor."

Sudden terror twisted his expression. "My family! I was trying to get to them."

"Where are they?"

Coughing, he pointed at the wall of fire. "Through there."

"I'll save them." I gave him a more-than-gentle push. "Get out of here."

"But —"

"No buts. If I have to drag you out, I won't be able to save them. Now go!"

"All right. All right." He limped down the hall toward the stairs, coughing all the way.

"He couldn't see me," Iris said, still clutching my cloak. "I must be dead."

"We'll talk about that later. Which apartment is yours?"

Her phantom hand came into view from behind me, a finger extended. "Last door on the left."

I tried to see past the flames. They had chewed a chasm in the hallway floor and continued gnawing at the edges as the blaze roared from below. Beyond the gap, the rest of the floor appeared to be solid. I coughed as I asked, "How many are in there?"

"Four besides me. I think they're all unconscious. Or maybe dead."

"Okay. Hold on tight." After backpedaling a few steps, I ran and leaped over the chasm. When I landed, I checked my cloak. No flames had caught hold, and Iris was still hanging on. With the fuel embedded in the fibers, I felt like a walking bomb, but so far, so good.

The door to the left stood open, smoke veiling the interior. Fire engulfed the apartment to the right. No escape that way. I ran into Iris's apartment. Flames roared along a wall to the left and through a massive hole in the floor. Its tongues lashed at an open window on the far wall.

Sweat poured into my eyes, stinging them. Each breath coated my throat with a dry, scorching film. To the right, five people lay facedown on the floor, all with rags over their mouths. One appeared to be an adult woman, and the other four were children of stair-step ages, two boys, two girls. "Are you the oldest?" I asked Iris as I pulled line from my remaining spool and looked for a place to attach the claw.

"Yes." She pointed at the bodies in turn. "I'm fourteen, Jack's twelve, Polly's ten, and Jimmy's eight. Mama's name is Yvette."

I scanned the room for glowing eyes. No ghosts. Since fire often chased souls out of bodies quickly, maybe the others were still alive. I connected the claw to one of the door hinges, scooped Jimmy, and held him under one arm. He seemed no heavier than a sack of peanuts. His rasping breaths told me the good news. He was alive. "Iris, stay here and listen for any sign of victims in other apartments."

"All right." She climbed off my back and stood wringing her hands. Dressed in jeans and a plain gray sweatshirt that hung on her like clothes on a scarecrow, she appeared to be near starvation. Even her stringy brown hair looked malnourished. "I know I'm dead, but I hope you'll come back for me."

"I will. That's what Reapers do." Dodging the tongues of fire, and holding the spool line with one hand, I stepped backwards through the window and leaned into a narrow alley, another building only a few feet behind me. I rappelled down the exterior brick wall toward the alley floor. "Shanghai," I shouted as I descended. "Can you hear me?"

"I'm here!" She ran into the alley and stationed herself under me, her hands raised. "Keep coming. I've got you."

Jimmy wriggled. The fresh air was reviving him. "Stay calm," I whispered. "You're going to be all right."

When I drew close enough, Shanghai took Jimmy from me. "I'll carry him out front," she said. "A nurse is secretly making the rounds. Someone gave the word that no medical help is allowed for fire victims."

"More of Alex's work. His father's out there by now. Name's Cyrus. See if you can hook them up." I shed my cloak and draped it over Shanghai's shoulder. "I have to go back. Four more to get."

"What? You've got to be —" She cleared her throat. "I mean, of course. Go. I'll be back in a minute."

I engaged the spool's reeling motor and climbed with my feet against the bricks. When I reached the window, flames shot out across the right side. Dodging the fiery tongues, I crawled in and stood on the creaking floor. It felt like it might give way at any moment.

The fire in the hall had breached the door and now engulfed the frame. The hinges would soon break loose, and the claw was probably too hot to grab and relocate. I had to hurry — take two at a time.

After setting the spool's drag to a high level, I gathered Jack and Polly, one in each arm. Iris frowned at the claw-and-hinge connection. "It's going to break."

Coughs punctuated my words. "Pray … that it lasts."

She wrung her thin hands harder. "Okay."

With the two children tucked under my arms, I backed again toward the window. The line tightened, and the spool fought against my pull. Now unable to dodge the flames covering the window, I leaned backwards and plunged through them. The spool's brake engaged with a squeal and slowed my descent. Like Jimmy, both children began squirming. I couldn't hold on much longer.

Shanghai called, "Okay. Take it easy. Five more feet. Let the boy go. I can catch him."

I released Jack. The moment he dropped to Shanghai, the spool line gave way. I pulled Polly to my chest and wrapped both arms around her. I dropped a few feet and landed on my bottom. Something caught my shirt collar, keeping my head from thumping on the pavement.

"Got you," Shanghai said from behind me. "Are you all right?"

"I think so." With Shanghai's help, I laid Polly on the ground next to Jack. They both turned to their sides and coughed violently.

I rose to my feet. "I have two more to get," I said as I reeled the line in. "One alive and one dead."

Shanghai looked up at the window. Fire roared through the opening. "If you say so, Phoenix, but it looks impossible."

When the claw caught on the windowsill, I looked at her. The white in her eyes provided a sharp contrast to her blackened face. "These children need a mother. If there's any chance she's still alive, I have to get her."

"But if she's dead, you'll be risking —"

"Phoenix!"

We both looked up. Iris leaned out the window, her face in anguish. "The fire's getting close to Mama! Please hurry!"

"Is she breathing?"

She sobbed as she replied. "I don't know. Maybe."

"I'm going." I pulled on the line. It held firmly ... for now. "Get those two to the nurse."

"Okay," Shanghai said. "I trust that you know what you're doing."

"I'm glad one of us does." After setting the spool to reel, I again scaled the wall. When I neared the window, I pushed off, spun a 180, and thrust my feet against the other building's wall. With another spin, I jerked on the line and hurtled headfirst through the fire and into the apartment.

I hit the floor in a tumble, rolled through flames, and stopped at the edge of a towering blaze that shot from below. Heat scalded my skin, instantly drying every pore. I rolled back, climbed to all fours, and crawled toward

Yvette. She lay motionless in a fetal position about five feet away. Iris's ghost knelt at her side.

Iris's phantom tears dripped and disappeared. "I think she stopped breathing."

I rolled Yvette to her back. "How long ago?"

"Just a few seconds."

I spoke between rasping coughs. "Iris, jump out the window ... and tell the female Reaper ... to find an oxygen tank ... if they have one."

Her brow shot upward. "Jump out the window?"

"Trust me. You'll be all right."

She trembled as she answered with a weak, "Because I'm a ghost?"

"Right. Now go. We have to save your mother."

"Okay. I'm going." Iris walked to the window, flinching before passing through the flames. After looking down for a brief moment, she climbed over the sill and fell out of sight.

I set my ear close to Yvette's mouth and tried to tune out the crackling flames. No breathing sounds emerged. I hoisted her over my shoulder and rose to my feet. Wearing stitched-together rags, the poor woman weighed little more than her underfed children.

Fire sprang up in front of the window and completely covered it. The flames ate through the windowsill, making my line's claw drop. I pressed the auto-reel button and drew it back. With fire blocking the door and the window, there was no safe escape.

On the floor, fire encircled me, and smoke choked every breath. I couldn't stay another second. I had to burst through the flames one more time and follow Iris out the window.

The moment I took a step, the floor gave way. As we fell through a fire-filled room, I pulled Yvette down and held her close. I struck another floor with my feet and crashed through it as well, breaking boards with loud snaps and slowing our plunge. When my feet struck the next floor below, it held firm. I bent my knees to absorb the impact, and I rolled with Yvette until our momentum eased, her on top of me, chest to chest.

My body aching, I opened my eyes. We lay in a vacant, smoke-filled apartment. Light from its window illuminated scattered trash and piles of wadded clothing on the floor. The odor of urine and feces tore into my senses, but I shook it off. At least I could breathe.

When I flexed to rise, Yvette sucked in a short breath. Her chest expanded, then contracted as she exhaled. When the breath finished, her respiration paused.

"Come on," I whispered. "Breathe!"

She inhaled sharply again, and her respiration continued in a steady rhythm. Exhaling a breath of my own, I rose with her in my cradling arms and limped to the hallway, down the stairs, and out the front exit.

About fifty paces away on the sidewalk, a crowd of at least forty had gathered. I staggered toward them, coughing and spitting. As I passed the alley, Shanghai joined me and braced my shoulder while we walked on. When we drew close to the crowd, a man pointed at me and called, "Look!"

Everyone turned toward us. The crowd divided, revealing Cyrus kneeling while hugging Jack, Polly, and Jimmy. The ghost of Iris stood nearby, looking on and weeping.

I walked into the circle and laid Yvette in Cyrus's arms. "She's alive."

Applause broke out. Tears rolled down Cyrus's dirty cheeks. "Thank you." His voice rasped from his smoke-ravaged throat. "How did you do it? It was so hot. Impossible to breathe."

"I don't know." My legs ready to buckle, I knelt in front of him. "I just don't know."

He looked at the apartment building. "Did you see Iris?"

While stifled sobs rose among men and women alike, I nodded toward Iris's ghost as she laid her hands on her papa's shoulders. "She helped me find her mother and her siblings. She's touching your shoulders."

"She is?" He twisted his neck and stared. "I think ... I think I see her."

More sobs erupted along with a smattering of applause. Although Iris had perished, the sight of her parents and surviving siblings provided soothing relief to this scorched and weary crowd.

I rose and backed away from the family, far enough to get out of earshot. Shanghai gave me my cloak and helped me put it on. After fastening the clasp, she laid a hand over the cross on my chest and looked at me, her soot-smeared brow furrowing. "You don't fear anything, do you?"

"I haven't ..." I coughed to clear my throat. "I haven't really thought about it. I did what I had to do."

"Of course you did." She shifted her gaze to the cross and fingered it. "I was scared spitless. The heat got to me. I thought I was going to fry, so I gave up." She refocused on my eyes. "It was fear, Phoenix. Pure fear."

"Don't worry about it. You did the best you —"

"Don't worry about it? Phoenix, if I hadn't given up, I might have saved Iris. Maybe others. I'm supposed to be the swagger queen, but when the heat turned up, I turned tail. I ran. I can't do that."

"Maybe I just have a gift, an ability to withstand fire. You can't help it if you don't."

"That's not it. I need the gumption that kept you going back into that inferno again and again. You didn't care a lick about yourself, that you might get roasted. You thought only about those kids and their mom. You had no fear."

"Well, I don't know about the fear part, but —

"Hey." One of the men from the crowd walked up to me and whispered, "I recognize you. You're Phoenix, one of the Reapers the government's looking for." He turned to Shanghai. "And you're the other one. But don't worry. Your secret's safe with me."

I pulled my hood up. "Are we that easy to recognize?"

He shook his head. "You're both a mess. It took me a while to figure it out."

"Well, thanks for holding your tongue."

"Only until you leave. As soon as you're safely down the road, I'm telling everyone. I don't trust the Gatekeeper or that blonde witch of his. People need to know you're not criminals."

"Good luck with that." I thanked him again and walked with Shanghai toward the docks. I wanted to run, but my body ached way too much.

"Well, I'm warm and dry now," Shanghai said with a cheery voice.

Her change of subject and tone made me think she no longer wanted to talk about her fears, so I obliged. "I'm toasted. My skin feels like it's going to peel off."

She looked me over. "You have a few superficial burns, but not too bad. Mostly just char and soot. We'll wash when we get to the docks. If you don't mind lake water, you can get hydrated there."

"Sounds good."

After several seconds of silence, Shanghai asked, "How did you save Betsy?"

I coughed a few more times before answering. "Two ghosts helped me disable the bomb. Betsy and I would both be dead without them."

"Where is she now?"

"Saigon is taking her to the guard. I told her we'd meet her at the docks."

"Perfect. Good job." She curled her arm around mine. "You're amazing."

"How about you? Didn't you say you rescued twelve? That's pretty amazing."

"Yeah. Keep trying to prop me up. It's nice, but what you did is way over the top. Maybe you really do have a gift, like you're fireproof."

"I'm not fireproof. I feel the flames. They're hot. They hurt. I know they can kill me."

"Well, whatever it is that keeps you from getting roasted, you might need it again. This is just the start. Alex and Bartholomew are probably going to firebomb the entire city."

"To get robot fuel."

"Right. Did you see all the ghosts who came from that building?"

I shook my head. "I was preoccupied."

"There must have been eighty, and that doesn't include the ones who haven't come out yet. Alex will probably send illuminaries to pick them up, and she'll have more souls to torture."

I scanned the street that we walked alongside. As expected, only parked cars lined the pavement. People were still heeding the travel ban. A few living folks meandered, as if wondering what to do with themselves during this government-mandated holiday. Yet, ghosts wandered aplenty, at least ten within view. "So we have to stop her."

"How? It's just you and me."

"And Saigon."

Shanghai rolled her eyes. "Right. Saigon."

I forced an even tone. "Give her a chance, Shanghai. She already admitted she was wrong about you, and she's proven her courage a bunch of times. She stuck with Betsy and me throughout the bomb ordeal, even though she could've been blown to bits. Don't hold a grudge."

"All right. That's fair. If you trust her, I'll trust her. I'll give her a chance." Shanghai shielded her eyes with a hand and looked toward the lake. "Once we find Saigon, do you have a plan to rescue Sing?"

"Not yet. We'll put our heads together, combine what we know."

"Do you want to pick up the pace?"

Since my muscle pain had eased somewhat, I nodded. "The sooner we get to water, the better."

When we broke into a jog, Shanghai continued talking, her words in cadence with her footfalls. "So we have to spring a Sancta. Do you have any idea why Sing couldn't come into my cell while I was there?"

The jogging loosened my muscles further. Even my face felt better. "She said something about the field around it having layers, like Alex designed the cell specifically to capture a Sancta."

"So that's been part of her plan all along. She used Fiona and me as bait to lure you and Sing to the ship."

"Yeah, I've been kicking myself over it. I thought I had outwitted her. And I did for a while, at least in rescuing Anne and destroying a bunch of illuminaries, but she still got exactly what she wanted."

"Not really. She thinks the mirror works. She traded those illuminaries for a worthless piece of glass."

"And Sing," I said. "She's priceless."

"Don't worry. Sing can take care of herself."

"But Alex might have a way to torture her. She's already proven that she knows a lot about the Sanctae. If she can capture one, maybe she can hurt one."

"I suppose you're right." Shanghai scowled. "Since it's Alex, we should assume the worst."

We jogged in silence for a moment before I spoke again. "When Sing first got trapped, she said she saw a mark on the wall only you could've made, but she didn't get a chance to tell me what it was."

"A mark?" Shanghai glanced upward for a moment. "I saw a mark, but I didn't make it."

"What was it?"

"Just four letters. Shan."

"The beginning of your name. Everyone knows your name. Why would Sing think no one else could've put it there?"

"Everyone knows my city name, but not everyone knows my real name. It's Shan. That's why I chose Shanghai. A lot of people think I'm Chinese, so they assume that's why I chose the city, but they're wrong on both counts."

"I guess Sing knows your real name because she's been to heaven. But even if Alex knows it, she wouldn't have any reason to write it on the wall."

"And it wasn't in the open where it's obvious. It was behind the mirror. I didn't see it until I pulled the mirror off the wall."

"That's really strange. No one would write your real name unless he or she wanted you to see it, but how could that person know you'd remove the mirror?"

"Not to brag on myself," Shanghai said, "but maybe that person knows I'm smart enough to try using it on the electric field."

"You are, but it doesn't feel like Alex's style. You know, baiting you and hiding it at the same time. She seemed genuinely surprised that you escaped, like using the mirror didn't occur to her."

"So all the clues point to someone else doing it," Shanghai said. "Bartholomew maybe?"

"He did a lot of research on our genealogies, so I'm sure he knows your real name, but what's the point? Why would he write your name behind a mirror?"

"Let's just let the mystery simmer awhile." She nodded ahead. "We're almost there."

As we closed in on the docks, Liam's van drove into the area and parked at a curb near the security guard's station. We accelerated and arrived just as Liam began helping Betsy into the side door, Fiona in line behind her.

Fiona threw her arms around me and kissed my cheek. "Oh, Phoenix! Betsy and Saigon told me what you did. You risked your life to save my girls."

"Anything for your family, Fiona." I scanned the area and found Saigon standing at the edge of a dock, staring at the lake as if thinking about something far away.

Fiona stepped back and laughed as she looked at her clothes. "I have a black imprint of you on me."

"Sorry." I brushed a clump of soot from my shirt. "I need to get cleaned up."

"Let me get you something." Fiona opened the van's front passenger door and retrieved a dripping towel and a jar of water. "Here you go."

"Thank you." I downed half of the water and passed the jar to Shanghai. While she drank, I washed my face and hands with the towel. "That helps a lot. Thanks again."

"It's nothing. I owe you everything."

After giving the towel to Shanghai, I clasped Fiona's hand. "It was my pleasure to rescue your girls, but Saigon risked her life, too."

"Yes, I heard. I thanked her, but when I took her hand, it trembled like an earthquake. Then she nodded and walked away. She seemed ... I don't know ... melancholy?"

"She's probably just realizing the hugeness of what she did. Reliving the danger. Saving someone's life. The first couple of times you do it, it takes a while before it hits you. But it hits you hard."

After Fiona and Betsy settled in the van and Shanghai and I had a chance to drink more water and get cleaned up, Liam took me to the side and whispered, "The little squirrel brought Anne to me. Where is she now?"

I kept my voice low as well. "Alex has her." I nodded toward the lake. "She's a hostage in a ship, a big yacht, maybe a couple of hundred yards down."

Liam looked that way. His jaw firmed. "I will find it."

"You will? But you're leaving."

"When I take Fiona and Betsy home, I'll come back. My brother Ian is at my apartment. Everyone will be safe with him."

"What if we're not here? Or if the yacht's gone?"

"Then I'll keep looking. I'm not going to let Sing down."

"I'm glad you're on our side, Liam." I shook his hand. "Thanks for everything."

"You're welcome." His eyes seemed to flash with determination. "Now let's save that little squirrel."

CHAPTER TWELVE

S HANGHAI AND I walked to where Saigon stood, still facing the lake. Shanghai tapped her on the shoulder. When Saigon turned, Shanghai extended a hand. "Welcome to the team. I heard about your heroics, and I'm proud to be your teammate."

As Saigon shook her hand, a trembling smile broke through. "Same to you, Shanghai."

"Let's get going," I said. "We'll travel to the yacht by water again."

We hurried to the canoe, pushed it from the dock back into the lake, and climbed aboard. Now in full daylight, we no longer had the advantage of darkness. We would have to be careful and quiet.

Shanghai and I manned the paddles and battled cold wind and choppy waves. We kept the canoe close to the docks, sneaking in and around boats of various sizes. When we neared Alex's yacht, it began backing out. The propellers churned the water, making a splashing racket.

I hissed, "Hurry! Before it gets away!"

We dug our paddles into the water and cut through the waves. The ship turned, its stern coming toward us as the front angled away. I passed my paddle to Saigon. "Get us close enough for me to jump."

The two women strained at the paddles while I grabbed the rope and stood on the bow. As we closed in, the canoe bucked in the props' turmoil. I bent my knees and rode with the bounces. When I came within reach, the props slowed, probably preparing to shift to forward.

I leaped to the rear deck and tied the canoe to an upper railing that circled the middle deck. I then grabbed the rope and slid back to the canoe, touching down on the bow feet first.

When I settled on the canoe's front bench, the props reversed and churned again, spinning faster than ever. The ship accelerated forward. The rope lifted the canoe's bow and pulled us along. We skimmed the water about twenty feet behind the yacht. Cold water sprayed us. Wind knifed through our dampening clothes. If this trip lasted too long, the elements might kill us before Alex could.

"No time to rest," Shanghai said as she braced herself with a hand on the side of the canoe. "Take a look."

At middle-deck level, an illuminary walked toward the stern, staying near the railing. It appeared to be searching for something on the lake. In seconds, it would see us.

I rose and stood on the bow again. "When I get to the deck, toss me a paddle."

Shanghai picked one up. "Is it a new-model illuminary?"

"It hasn't flashed yet, so probably." I jumped out to the rope, grabbed it halfway to the yacht, and climbed. When I drew within range, I swung to the rear deck, leaped up, grabbed the middle-deck's rail, and vaulted over it.

The illuminary lunged and grabbed me by the throat, too quick to dodge. With one arm, it lifted me into the air, and its robotic fingers cut off my air supply. A beast like this had killed the great Tokyo by crushing her skull. How could I possibly defeat it?

"Catch!" Shanghai threw the paddle. I snatched it out of the air and swung it at the illuminary in one motion. The edge crashed into its neck and broke the paddle in half.

The illuminary dropped me. I landed on my feet, leaped, and kicked it square in the face. It toppled over the railing and splashed into the lake. It flailed amidst the waves, weighed down by its wet cloak and metallic body. The boat zoomed on, leaving it behind.

I massaged my sore throat. If Shanghai hadn't thrown the paddle so perfectly, I would have been dead only seconds later. Yet, I wasn't in the clear yet. Other illuminaries might be on board.

Hunkering low, I waved for Shanghai and Saigon to come aboard. They copied my rope-climbing maneuver and joined me in a crouch on the middle deck.

Shanghai touched my throat. With water noise providing cover, she spoke at a normal volume. "Are you all right?"

I swallowed. The muscles worked. No cramping. "Yeah. I'm fine."

"How did you do that? I mean, whacking the illuminary so hard with your feet off the ground?"

Saigon grinned. "He's a superhero, I'm telling you. The guy's got skills."

"Probably an old model after all," I said. "It went down too easy."

"Too easy?" Saigon gestured with her hands. "It lifted you clean off the ground. You broke the paddle in half." She gave me a light punch on the arm. "That's crazy good."

I smiled. "Thanks for the vote of confidence."

"Need to be careful, though. Could also be more of them below deck or up top with Alex. Maybe like the holy terrors that chased me through the bank. I kicked one of them in the face, but it was like kicking a brick wall. I didn't have super strength or a canoe paddle to fight them with, so I just ran like the devil himself was chasing me."

"Speaking of paddles," Shanghai said, "What should we do about the canoe?"

I turned toward the rear. No longer weighed down, the little boat careened from side to side. Water splashed in, threatening to swamp it, and the bucking had already tossed the other paddle out. "If it capsizes, it'll probably drag like an anchor, but if we cut it loose, Alex might see it when it gets far enough behind."

"Keep it," Saigon said. "We might need it. If it drags, maybe one of Alex's minions will come to check on it, and we can push another guard overboard."

Shanghai glanced up toward the highest deck — the navigation level. "It wouldn't surprise me if she already knows we're here. She's not one to let anything slip past her Owl eyes."

"We should split up," I said. "One will sneak below deck to look for Sing. The other two will head to the navigation level and see what's going on."

"I'll go below," Shanghai said, "I know my way around down there."

"Sounds good. I assume you know where the trapdoor is, but do you know how to open it? Alex used her tablet."

"Yep. It has a manual release." Shanghai skulked toward the front. When she reached the passenger area, she belly crawled the rest of the way to the trap door.

Following Shanghai's path, Saigon and I dropped to our stomachs and crawled single file past the passenger windows, our target a side door leading inside.

When I reached the door, I rose and stood with my back to its windowless panel while Saigon waited on her stomach a few paces back. I turned the knob and opened the door a crack.

Saigon crawled forward and peeked in. When she flashed a thumbs-up sign and began climbing to her feet, I opened the door fully, and we walked in together.

Once inside, I closed the door, muffling the engine and water noise. Leather-like sofas and chairs lined the windows on both sides, and polished wood covered the floor. To our right, a refrigerator and cooking appliances stood at opposite sides with a dining table for six between them. To our left, a short run of four stairs led to the navigation level.

I whispered to Saigon, "Wait here." I skulked to the bottom of the stairs and climbed slowly toward the upper chamber, a room that narrowed in front to a curved end. Windows provided a view of the open expanse of water ahead, and a long control panel stretched across underneath. An empty chair sat in front of the pilot's wheel. A pill bottle on the panel was the only sign of human presence.

I walked in, snatched the bottle, and dropped it into my cloak pocket. Obviously no one was running the yacht. Someone, maybe the illuminary, had set it to cruise at high speed toward the middle of the lake.

I called to Saigon. "The place is empty."

"That's creepy," she said, replying from the passenger cabin.

"As soon as Shanghai comes up, we'd better haul out of here."

"I see her. She's running this way."

I hustled down the stairs. Shanghai burst into the passenger compartment, breathless. "Phoenix, I couldn't find Sing anywhere. Or a mirror. And the electric field was turned off."

I pointed toward the stern. "To the canoe! Hurry!"

We ran outside, sprinted to the rear of the yacht, and slid down the rope, Saigon first, then Shanghai, then me. When Saigon reached the canoe, she flopped backwards into a pool of water that had collected at the floor's center. Shanghai tumbled on top of her, and I fell on my bottom in front of them.

An explosion in the yacht sent a geyser of fire and plumes of smoke shooting into the sky. The yacht slowed but glided on. Wood, plastic, and fiberglass rained on us, many pieces sharp. We raised our hoods to deflect the shower, but some fragments pierced my cloak with painful jabs.

The yacht slowed further. Fire raced toward the stern, and the canoe's momentum sent us closer. I lunged forward, jerked my dagger out, and sliced through the rope. As we continued gliding, the yacht listed and sank lower in the water, lifting the still-spinning propellers above the surface.

We rammed into the stern. One of the propellers sliced into the side of the canoe's bow. I pushed us away, but water leaked in and ran into the floor's slowly expanding pool.

"Get a paddle!" I reached over the side, grabbed a broken board, and drove one end into the lake with a long stroke. Shanghai and Saigon did the same. We turned the canoe toward shore and paddled as fast as we could. As we pulled away from the sinking ship, the pool in the canoe deepened. Since we were at least a couple of miles from shore, we would never make it without sinking.

"Do you see anything we can bail with?" I shouted.

Saigon pointed. "A plastic cup."

Among the hundred other items floating in the water, a cup bobbed nearby. When we paddled to it, Saigon grabbed it, dipped water from the pool, and tossed it over the side. "I got this. You two paddle."

With Shanghai at the rear and me at the front, we paddled hard and fast while Saigon, sitting at the center, bailed at a furious rate, switching the cup from hand to hand every minute or so. Water continued leaking in, but she managed to keep the puddle from growing.

I scanned the shoreline and guided our crippled craft toward the docks. Since our makeshift paddles weren't designed to catch water and drive us forward, our progress was excruciatingly slow. Sweat dampened my clothes. Cold wind bit through them, but the exhausting effort kept me from freezing.

With each stroke, I mentally kicked myself. Once again Alex had played me like a fiddle. I gobbled up every bait in every trap. Shouldn't I have seen that attaching to the yacht with only one illuminary noticing us was too easy? And getting through the trapdoor and inside the passenger compartment? Way too easy. She guessed that my frantic rush to rescue Sing would blind me to her obvious trap.

I shook my head. My ruminations weren't helping. I had to concentrate on the task at hand. "Are you two doing all right?" I asked as I looked back while paddling.

"Cold and wet," Saigon said. "And my arms hurt. But no worries. I can handle it."

Shanghai dug her paddle into the windblown water. A wave slapped the boat, sending spray into her face. "Wet is an understatement. How are you doing?"

I shifted my gaze forward and paddled as I answered. "All right. Just kicking myself. Alex beat me again. I should've seen that trap."

"We all missed it, Phoenix. How could we have guessed she could move Sing without her escaping?" Shanghai thrust her paddle harder. "Alex is just smarter than we are. The sooner we face it, the sooner we'll be able to beat her."

"What do you mean? How can we beat someone who's smarter than we are?"

"Brute force. We outhustle her. Overpower her. Bust her chops with three pairs of fists. Shatter her spine. Light her corpse on fire and cast it into an unmarked grave."

Saigon laughed. "I like your style, girl."

"That's harder than it sounds," I said. "You know how skillful she is. I'm sure she won't get caught three against one. And by now, she's probably gathered a couple of hundred souls and fueled the rest of her new-model illuminaries. They're the brute-force monsters we have to beat, not her."

Shanghai puffed through her words as she continued paddling. "True, but don't get worked up about her skills. I've seen them, and she's good, but not as good as you are. If you have to fight her one on one, don't get intimidated. If you can beat a souped-up illuminary, you can take Alex down."

"Thanks for the boost, but by the time we get to shore, we'll be spent."

"After a little rest, we'll be fine."

"We probably won't have time to rest." I let out a sigh and kept up the work, stroke after stroke after stroke. "I'm not giving in to the idea that she's smarter than we are. She's just willing to torture and kill her way to the top. In war, it can be an advantage to be cruel. We just have to figure out a way to counter her cruelty."

For the rest of the journey, we paddled in silence, though the waves striking the canoe's side, our pitiful paddles hitting the water, and Saigon's sliding cup provided plenty of noise. After about an hour of exhausting effort, we glided into the spot where we had picked up the canoe.

Liam stood on the dock, binoculars dangling at his chest. "I saw the explosion and that you got away. Thought I'd meet you here." He extended a hand. "And I have blankets in the van. Just a couple of blocks down."

"Great. Thanks." I grabbed his wrist and let him pull me to the dock. "Get the blankets. I'll help the women."

While Liam jogged to his van, I hoisted Shanghai and Saigon out of the canoe. At dock level, the bitter wind blew more fiercely and stabbed our wet bodies. While we waited for Liam to return, we huddled close, our arms wrapped around each other, and our noses nearly touching.

Shanghai smiled, her lovely eyes brightening. "Reminds me of survival training. Remember when we got caught in the blizzard? We had to make a snow fort, strip off our —"

"I don't want to hear it," Saigon said, rolling her eyes. "What you two do in the privacy of your own snow fort, that's your business. Keep it to yourselves."

Shanghai laughed. "Saigon, we were seven. And we just took off our cloaks and shirts and hunkered under the cloaks. It was innocent."

"Seven? Oh. Okay. Good to hear you two've known each other so long. No wonder he defends you like a guard dog."

Shanghai's brow lifted. "Defends me?"

"With sharp teeth, girl. When I started trash talking you, he jumped right in and shut me down. I mean, I was wrong. I know that now. But you got a good one, honey. Better hold on to him tight."

"Don't worry." Shanghai slid her hand behind my neck and kissed my forehead. "I will."

When Liam returned with the van, he parked in a tow-away zone next to the dock, emerged with two blankets, and handed one to Shanghai and one to Saigon. The van's familiar rattling engine kept running. "Sorry. I had only two. But my van's warm. I can take you wherever you want to —"

An explosion boomed somewhere close. Fire and smoke erupted from an apartment building only a couple of blocks from us. Another explosion followed farther away, then a third farther still. Bomb after bomb sent thunderous booms rumbling across the city, so many that I stopped counting after the tenth.

"What are we going to do?" Shanghai asked as she shivered under her blanket. "Run to the closest building and rescue people?"

Liam shook his head. "You'll get killed for sure. While you were gone, Alex sent another broadcast. It just showed your photos the entire time. Yours and Phoenix's, I mean. Now she wants you delivered dead. She sweetened the reward to include food and housing for life."

"So we'd better bolt," Shanghai said. "We probably look like a pair of free tickets to a lifelong smorgasbord."

I shook my head hard. "I have to help. I can't just run away like —"

"Hold it right there. Don't move."

I spun toward the voice. The security guard stood a couple of steps out of reach, a handgun aimed at us, a traditional pistol instead of a sonic gun. "I recognize you now. Phoenix and Shanghai." He waved the gun. "Liam and the other Reaper can go."

"Sir," I said, raising my hands. "You're the one who should go. We don't want to have to hurt you."

He laughed in a nervous manner. "What are you talking about? I'm the one with a gun."

"If you fire a shot at one of us Reapers, the other two will cut you down before you can fire another one."

Shanghai and Saigon dropped their blankets and stood in battle-ready stances — legs braced and fists raised. With their wet clothes clinging to their skin, their flexed muscles looked ominous.

As the guard's confident expression melted, his gun hand trembled.

"You'll be dead," I continued. "How will you collect your reward then?"

His hand grew shakier. "I ... I don't believe you. You wouldn't kill me. That would be murder."

"Self-defense, sir. And you won't be around to testify in a courtroom. One of us will reap your soul, and you wouldn't go to the Gateway anytime soon."

"You're lying to save your skin!" He fired. A bullet ripped into my left arm. Shanghai and Saigon lunged at him. Shanghai slapped the gun away while Saigon body slammed him and drove an elbow into his throat. Something snapped, and the man fell limp.

I pressed my hand against the wound and wobbled from side to side. Liam grabbed my good arm and held me up. "Let me see it, Phoenix."

As I lifted my hand, Liam peered under my fingers. Blood oozed through a hole in my sleeve. He felt the other side of my arm. "The bullet went straight through."

"Is that good or bad?"

"Good, most likely." He looked at the fire as it spread from building to building. "Put the guard in my van. People will be heading for the lake to escape. We need to get out while we still can."

Shanghai and Saigon carried the guard and loaded him in the van's cargo area. Compressing my wound, I joined them in the back while Liam hopped into the driver's seat.

From the direction of the fire, dozens of people stampeded toward us, some alive and some dead. Glowing eyes intermixing with terrified ones made the scene look like a horror movie. I longed to stop and help them, but in my condition, what could I do? The best way to help was to find Alex and stop her brutal crusade. "Better punch it, Liam."

CHAPTER THIRTEEN

L IAM LOCKED THE doors and slammed down the gas pedal. Tires squealing, the van shot toward the dock-area exit. When he slowed to turn onto a road, a woman grabbed the driver's door handle and held on. Her muffled scream penetrated. "Help! Let me come with you!"

A running man bumped into her and tore her away from the van. As Liam drove on, shifting lanes to dodge people, he looked at me in his rearview mirror. "I don't think the bullet hit the bone. More than just a flesh wound, though. It likely tore some muscle tissue. You'll definitely need stitches."

I settled in a cross-legged position with my back to the van's front bench. The guard lay face up, his feet in front of my knees and his head near the rear door. Saigon sat at his left and Shanghai at his right. "I guess I could go to Dr. Rubenstein," I said, "but could I get there without bounty hunters chasing me?"

Liam shook his head. "I think not. Even the doctor might turn you in."

Saigon touched my knee. "I can stitch you up."

I gave her a skeptical look. "With your sewing kit?"

"Don't worry. I've done quite a bit of Reaper-skin mending in my time, including my own leg once and my arm twice. I'm not a bad stitcher, if I do say so myself."

I nodded. "Sure. Thanks."

"I have a first-aid kit under the seat," Liam said. "No pain-killers in it, of course, but you can use whatever's there. Got some bandages, I think. Maybe some alcohol."

"That'll help." I looked under the bench, found a white metal box, and slid it next to my hip. "Just get us out of downtown. Once you're clear, let me know. Then we'll decide what to do next."

"I will."

I nodded at the guard. "How is he?"

"Dead," Saigon said. "I didn't mean to kill him. The elbow slam crushed his throat. Maybe broke his neck. I guess I got carried away."

I sighed. Another senseless death. Although I thoroughly warned him, guilt still weighed me down. "Do you mind reaping him?"

"No problem. If your bullet hole can wait."

I glanced at the wound. Blood still oozed but not too badly. The throbbing, however, sent pulses of pain to my fingers and shoulder. "I think it's okay."

"All right. I'll just —"

"Let's do it together," Shanghai said. "I need to teach Phoenix how to collect a ghost without valve energy. You pull him out, and while you're stitching, I'll put him in my cloak."

Saigon blinked at her. "You can do that?"

"I think so. At least I did it when I practiced with a ghost named Crandyke. Tokyo taught me."

"All right. Let's give it a try." Saigon pulled her sleeve over her hand and covered the guard's eyes. Seconds later, the sleeve flattened. She whispered, "Take it easy. You can trust me. ... What's your name? ... Okay, Knox, just relax and let go. ... I know. The darkness is scary, but I'll take care of you. ... Yes, I'm a Reaper. ... The one who killed you?" She glanced at me, then at Shanghai. "The Reaper who'll carry you didn't kill you. You'll be safe with her."

Saigon lifted her arm. Her dematerialized hand clutched a glowing sphere with snaking tentacles. When the sphere fully emerged, it expanded and took the shape of the guard. While most of his semitransparent body still melded with his physical frame, Saigon kept his upper ghostly half raised above his corpse, her nebulous hand around his throat.

Knox's radiant eyes darted in all directions, obviously confused and terrified.

Saigon nodded at Shanghai. "He's all yours."

Looking at me, Shanghai said, "Our genetics are the key. Even though we can't use energy to transform into ghosts, our cloaks can still absorb a soul. Since the energy doesn't run through the fibers anymore, it takes longer, but you can speed it up with your breath."

I drew my head back. "My breath?"

She nodded. "Tokyo said we still have the same energy flowing through us. It's locked up within. Our breath expels small particles that contain tiny bits of the energy. If you breathe on your hands, you can manipulate a ghost. Watch."

Shanghai set her hands close to her mouth and breathed on them for several seconds. She then slid her hand under Saigon's and grasped the guard's ghost by the back of the neck. When Saigon drew her hand away, Shanghai held the ghost in place. "Now I'll pull him into my cloak."

"You work on that," Saigon said as her hand rematerialized, "and I'll stitch hero boy." She unfastened her sewing kit from her belt and touched my cloak. "Strip down to your waist."

While Saigon helped me remove my cloak and shirt, Shanghai spread her cloak with her free hand and slowly eased Knox's soul underneath. When the cloak fully engulfed him, she breathed into the fibers, her lips pursed as she blew gently and shifted her breath from place to place to cover the area. He whimpered softly, not as loud as many ghosts. Being a level one helped ease the pain of the absorption process.

My upper body now bare, Saigon ran her fingers along my left triceps. "Liam's right. The bullet tore some muscle tissue. You won't be able to use this arm for a while." After threading a needle, she opened the first-aid kit. "Alcohol swabs. Perfect."

"Good," I said. "I'll take the burn over an infection any day."

Saigon grinned. "Yep. You're lucky. The last time I did any stitching, it was to myself, and I didn't have anything to sterilize with. Got an infection that lasted for weeks. Fever. Chills. The whole bit." She wiped the needle and thread with a couple of swabs, then the arm wounds with two more. "Ready to go. Grit your teeth and think about hornets stinging your arm. It won't be any worse than that."

While Saigon stitched, I focused on Shanghai as she continued breathing on her cloak. Far from thinking about hornets, I concentrated on her comely lips, her passionate expression, her incredible dedication to any task no matter how dangerous or difficult. Although the needle pricks stung, and the pulling of the thread was worse, the pain seemed minimal compared to the poundings I had taken recently.

Shanghai opened her cloak. "Abracadabra. He's gone."

The slightest of shimmers ran along her shoulder and quickly vanished, Knox's presence in the fibers. Since she could no longer plug the cloak into an energy source, the shimmer couldn't last like it used to. "Thanks for the lesson," I said. "I'll have to give it a try."

Saigon jabbed me with the needle. "Hold still. How do you expect a surgeon to do her job with you wiggling so much?"

"Sorry." I relaxed and tried to stay motionless. "Liam, what's your status?"

"No traffic, but lots of scared folks running around. I think we'll be clear soon. Better start thinking about where you want to go."

I looked at Shanghai. "Any ideas?"

She closed her cloak. "Well, Alex is saying she wants you dead, but that could be deception. In reality, maybe she wants you to lead you into a trap, and she'll drop clues around, like my name behind the mirror."

"I still don't think she's the one who put it there, but speaking of clues ..." Keeping my wounded arm motionless, I reached into my cloak pocket, withdrew the pill bottle, and tossed it to Shanghai. "I found this in the yacht's control room."

She turned the bottle while reading the label. "It's the same stuff we took when we went to the Western Wilds. Protects against radiation poisoning." She shook the bottle, making the pills rattle. "Maybe ten or so left."

"I guess Alex left it behind," I said. "Maybe she's heading that way."

Shanghai put on a skeptical frown. "Or she wants us to think so. The clues must be intentional. Alex doesn't make mistakes."

"Would you two stop it?" Saigon tied off the thread closing the entry wound. "You act like Alex is an all-seeing super genius. Wrong. She set up that yacht bomb to kill you, not to slip you a pill-bottle clue. And she had no idea that I'd help you. If it weren't for Betsy being strapped to a bomb, we probably could've taken her down. She's not unstoppable."

"But that's the point," I said. "Even if we surprise her, she always has a way of escape, a backup plan."

Saigon slid a few inches and began working on the exit wound. "So we mix in enough surprises to make her run out of backup plans."

"Easier said than done." I withdrew the silver cylinder and passed it to Shanghai. "Another clue. Saigon found it near Betsy. Any idea what it is?"

Shanghai looked it over. "No. Never seen anything like it."

"I think I know," Liam said, his eyes visible in the rear-view mirror. "It looks like a fuel cell for an air transport vehicle. I used to pilot one when I worked for the government about ten years ago. I flew a Council member between Chicago and Baltimore. I wasn't much more than a kid, but I could fly that little beast. It was a thrill."

"Why did you stop?" I asked. "And why don't I ever see those vehicles flying around?"

"There were only three in Chicago, as far as I know. When Baltimore burned, the Council member tried to escape by flying it himself, but he crashed and died. After that, the government mothballed every one of them. I know where the local ones are kept, but it's a two-hour drive."

"Erin's is a lot closer," Shanghai said. "A garage in an abandoned mechanic's shop. I pushed it there and covered it with an old tarp. Fortunately, I had already landed when it ran out of fuel." She looked toward the front. "Liam, it's across the street from the big grain mill. Do you know where that is?"

"I do."

I twisted toward him. "Will you take us there?"

Saigon jabbed me again. "If you don't hold still, I'm gonna push the needle all the way through and tie the back stitches to the front."

"All right. All right." I settled in place. "Liam?"

"I'll take you there. It's closer to the city. Traffic isn't a problem, but fire and scared people might be."

"Speaking of fuel," Saigon said as she continued stitching, "all that water bailing lowered my energy level. Not bad yet, but I'm guessing I won't be able to get a recharge for a while, so could we get Bart's tank again?"

"He's probably with Alex," I said, "so it shouldn't be a problem." I twisted again. "Liam, change of plans. First —"

"Phoenix!" Another stab brought me back. "Okay. That does it." Saigon tied off the thread. "If you spring a leak and bleed out, it'll be your own fault."

"Thanks, Saigon." I tried to lift my arm, but ripping pain shot from shoulder to elbow, forcing me to keep it down. "That's not good."

Liam called from the driver's seat. "You were about to tell me something, Phoenix?"

"Right. Let's go to Bartholomew's house." I recited the address. "Do you know where that is?"

"I do. At least the street. I'll find it."

After I put my shirt and cloak back on with Saigon's help, I extended my right hand toward Shanghai. "The fuel cell?"

She laid it in my palm. "Do you have another idea?"

I pinched it and held it close to my eyes. "I don't know if these clues are from Alex or not, but someone is leading us back to the Gateway. Who knows? Maybe the person is on our side. Either way, we'll keep looking for more clues and take every step carefully."

"How could it be someone on our side?" Shanghai asked as I returned the fuel cell to her. "Whoever left them has to be involved with strapping a bomb to Betsy and putting another one on board the yacht."

"True, but maybe he or she is just going along with the bomber while secretly trying to help us."

Saigon huffed. "Wishful thinking. More likely it's just stuff someone dropped. You're reading too much into it. Like I said before, you give Alex way too much credit."

"Well, if it *is* Alex," I said, "then we'll try to guess what the trap is before she springs it on us."

Shanghai rolled her eyes. "Not this subject again. I'm sick of trying to outguess the queen of conceit. I say the first chance we get to take her down, we go straight for her throat."

"I know. You said it before. Brute force. And I get it. But we have to combine strength and smarts. It's the only way, especially with my arm so injured. I don't have much brute force left in me."

"Phoenix ..." Shanghai leaned close. "I'm going to say this only once, so listen carefully. You've got to get over this idea that you can't beat her. You are so much better than she is in every way. Why? Because you're a better person than she is. No contest. She's as evil as hellfire itself. And you?" She kissed me on the cheek, brushing close to my lips. Her warm breath bathed my skin as she continued. "You're the best person I know."

When she drew back, I touched my cheek, anointed by the most amazing girl in the world. Her sparkling eyes begged me to believe her, to let her words sink in, to let them be true. All I had to do was grasp them as a sword and wield it with courage. That was the only way to beat Alex. To believe that I could. To act like I could.

I whispered, "Thanks. That helps. Really."

Everyone quieted, leaving the engine's rattle the only sound in the van. Several minutes later, Liam parked at a curb in front of Bartholomew's row house and killed the engine. "We're here."

We got out and walked silently toward the house. With cold wind still blowing, Shanghai, Saigon, and I lifted our hoods over our heads while Liam zipped his jacket and stuffed his hands into his pockets.

As we neared the door, I scanned the street and nearby houses. No living humans appeared anywhere, though a couple of hundred feet away, a pair of elderly level-one ghosts walked hand in hand across a leaf-strewn lawn dressed only in doctor scrubs.

Liam opened the unlocked door. "That was too easy."

"Just be quiet and careful," I said.

We entered and found the place nearly vacant — no furniture except for a bed and easy chair in the front master bedroom and a sofa in the living room, and no sign of people. The floors had been swept clean, and Bartholomew's desk was gone. Yet, the energy tank still stood where it was before, the only object in the den. "Strange," I said, my voice echoing. "It's like he left it here for us."

"Seems that way." Shanghai bent close and squinted at a meter on the tank's valve. "Nearly full. Too valuable to leave behind."

"Then maybe Bartholomew is our secret helper," I said. "I'm not sure I want to follow his lead."

Shanghai nodded. "It's like tracking the scent of a skunk. At the end of the trail, you find it but you get sprayed."

"Well," Saigon said, touching her sternum valve, "you can decide later if you want to track the skunk, but I'll take the risk that this stuff is safe. Someone shoot me up."

While Shanghai connected the tank's hose to Saigon and began filling her energy supply, I sidled close to them. "You know, Bartholomew could be playing both sides. If Alex is ordering him to lure us into a trap, he wants us to come at full strength. That way, if ... I mean, when we defeat her, he can claim to be our ally."

Shanghai detached the hose. "Finished."

"Thanks." Saigon flexed her biceps. "That stuff has some extra pep. I feel like I could wrestle a gorilla."

"Any dizziness?" I asked.

"Now that you mention it ..." Saigon closed her eyes tightly. "Yeah. I'm feeling kinda woozy."

"Bartholomew must've filled it with the purified energy." I looped my arm around hers. "We'll tell you about it on the way."

"Thanks ... um ..." She blinked at me, and her words slurred. "You know, you're really a handsome dude. When I was sewing you up, I couldn't keep my eyes off your muscles. Are you married?"

Shanghai grinned. "Yep. She's soused. But the extra power might come in handy once the high wears off. I'll help her use the bathroom, and then we'll get out of here."

Liam lifted the energy tank and tucked it under his arm. "We might as well take it with us."

I nodded. "Good idea."

After Shanghai and Saigon finished in the bathroom, I took a turn in there myself. We then hurried to the van as quickly as Saigon's dizzied state would allow. When I opened the side door, I found the elderly couple in the cargo area, both kneeling next to the security guard, one at each side.

"The cause of death is a neck fracture," the woman said, ignoring me and looking at the man. "What do you think, dear?"

The man nodded, his scant hair, bifocals, and narrow wrinkled face making him look like an elderly professor. "Or the collapsed throat. Perhaps he suffocated."

"Oh, you might be right." The woman's face looked like a feminine version of the man's, complete with similar eyeglasses, though her short gray hair was much thicker than his. She patted the guard's hand, her fingers passing through it. "The poor man."

"Hello." I crawled inside and knelt between the guard and the front bench. "Are you doctors?"

"We were," the man said with a grim smile, "but we now appear to be dead."

The woman chuckled. "Leave it to Jasper to diagnose with quick accuracy. He was the best doctor in Chicago."

"Second to you." Jasper blew her a kiss and turned toward me. "Jasmine's only fault is not knowing that she is the best."

Shanghai joined us in the rear while Saigon climbed into the front seat with Liam, muttering something about wanting to sleep off the dizziness.

When Liam adjusted his rearview mirror and saw the phantom passengers, he swallowed hard. "Ghosts?"

I nodded. "After all the ghosts you've seen, I thought you might be used to it."

"Seeing them on the street is one thing. But in my van?" He focused forward, started the engine, and began driving. "Don't mind me. I'll take you to the mechanic's shop. I just hope the ghosts leave when you do."

Shanghai gave Jasmine a tight smile. "Jasmine and Jasper. A cute combination."

"It's a pet name," Jasmine said. "Jasper says my presence is a sweet fragrance. My real name is Vera. You can use that if it will help avoid confusion."

"Who were your patients?" Shanghai asked, her tone spiced with bitterness. "Rich people, I assume. The elite class."

Jasper nodded. "Mostly, though we occasionally donned disguises and ventured into the poorer sections of town. Dangerous business, you know."

"Oh?" Shanghai's tone softened. "Did you smuggle meds to the poor?"

"As often as feasible. The government keeps track of our supplies, so we have to fudge a bit to save leftovers."

"How did you die?" I asked.

"It's hard to say." Jasper clutched his throat. "I remember being unable to breathe. Something in the air was choking me."

"Probably poisonous gas," Vera said. "We were at an apartment building downtown, trying to distribute fever reducers because of flu-like symptoms that were going around. Then a choking gas permeated the area, probably from the heating system. We tried to get out with one of the families, but we collapsed in a hallway. The next thing we knew, we were walking on the street outside. It took a while before we realized we were dead."

Jasper chuckled. "Being able to go through walls was the first clue."

"Did you see any cloaked robots?" I asked.

Vera nodded. "Getting away from those creatures is how we discovered we could pass through walls. They didn't follow."

"But they did catch other souls," Jasper said. "Too many to count. Since they were so busy, it helped us escape. Once we slipped past them, we eventually made our way home."

"In the neighborhood where you found us," Vera added.

"Right." Jasper tugged at the front of his scrubs. "I'm not sure why we're wearing these. We were disguised as maintenance people when we died."

"That's strange," I said, "I guess your souls manifested in the outfits you're most comfortable in. After a while, you'll be able to alter your clothing."

Vera sighed. "It's such a shame. I so enjoyed being a doctor. Helping people. Healing people. And now you Reapers will take us to the Gateway, right?"

"Not anytime soon. The delivery system's messed up, and we're going to a place that could be dangerous."

Shanghai patted my knee. "They could ride in your cloak, Phoenix. It's a perfect chance to practice collecting souls the new way."

"True, but once they're in my cloak, can I talk to them? We could benefit from their knowledge. You never know when we might need a doctor."

Shanghai shook her head. "No sternum valve, no energy link. Tokyo said she tried, but it can't be done."

"Then maybe Saigon should reap them." I looked at the front seat. Saigon leaned against the passenger window, snoring lightly. "Or maybe not."

"Joy juice hangover. Just let her sleep." Shanghai tugged on my cloak's sleeve. "Go ahead and reap them. You need to learn how. When we defeat Alex, you and Saigon and I might be the only Reapers left."

"I guess you're right." I looked at Jasper and Vera in turn. "Is that acceptable?"

Jasper shrugged. "I suppose so. It's the last ticket to punch, if you know what I mean."

"Right," Vera said. "Everyone knows they'll eventually ride with a Reaper, so why object? Our time has come."

"Okay, then." I set my hands close to my mouth and blew on them, taking time to cover every inch. After several seconds, I slid my hand into Vera's. As I made contact, a tingle ran along my skin. "I'm going to pull you into my cloak. It might hurt, but since you're still a level-one ghost, it shouldn't be too bad."

Vera closed her eyes. "I'm ready."

I guided her under my cloak and breathed on the fibers. Vera grunted once, then exhaled. Soon, she thinned out and filtered into the cloak until she disappeared. A shimmer ran along the material and stopped at my left shoulder before disappearing.

Shanghai's mouth dropped open. "That was quick. It took me a lot longer the first time."

"You're a good teacher." I went through the same process with Jasper. Less than a minute later, his shimmer crawled toward where Vera had settled. A moment later, it, too, faded.

A wispy voice filtered into my brain. "Are you all right, Jasper?"

A deeper voice followed. "Fine. Fine. It's a bit stuffy, though."

I whispered to Shanghai, "I can hear them."

"Really?" She scooted close and set her ear next to my shoulder. "See if they can hear you."

I cleared my throat. "Jasper? Vera? Can you hear me?"

"Phoenix?" Vera said. "Is that you?"

"Yes. I guess I can communicate with you after all."

Shanghai smiled. "I can hear them. Just barely. But I'm picking it up."

"I wonder why."

Shanghai drew back and ran a finger along my cloak. "Must be something special about your genetics. Maybe you have more natural energy. You can probably be just as effective at reaping without the valve connection."

I sighed. "Nearly four years of suffering, and I didn't need to go through it."

She clasped my hand. "That suffering shaped you, Phoenix. You're a better man because of it."

I attempted a smile. "And I probably would never have met you if not for the quota system. The train ride would never have happened, and —"

"Oh, please," Saigon said from the front seat. "Can you shut off the syrup faucet? I'm already sick to my stomach without you two lovebirds spraying sugar everywhere."

I laughed. "All right, Saigon. We'll cut it out."

While Saigon slept, Shanghai and I sat hip to hip, holding hands. Our closeness helped ease the pain in my wounded arm. I could definitely get used to the comforts this angel of a woman provided. I just had to show her that I was worthy of her company. Somehow I had to do as she asked, to believe her words, to have faith that I could defeat Alex, even with a nearly lifeless arm.

After several minutes of quiet riding, Liam parked the van in front of a garage with a dented metal front. "Is this the place?"

"Yep." Shanghai opened the side door and got out.

After waking Saigon, I got out as well and joined Shanghai at the garage. When I bent toward the ground to reach the door's handle, she grasped my wrist, stopping me. "Not so fast. You're going to have to count on me for the heavy lifting for a while."

As if responding to her warning, a sharp stab jolted my wound. I straightened and tried to rotate my shoulder, but pain kept me from raising my arm. "You're right. I don't think I could lift a book, much less a door."

"No worries. I got your back." Shanghai grabbed the handle and slid the door upward. When a sizable dent reached the top, the door stopped. She set both hands under the door and shoved. The door sprang loose and reeled the rest of the way up, revealing a dim garage. Inside, a gray tarp covered something the size of a large auto.

"Strange," Shanghai said. "The tarp's been moved. Its label was on the other side. Someone's been here."

CHAPTER FOURTEEN

SHANGHAI PULLED THE tarp away and let it pile up on the concrete floor, revealing a circular craft that looked similar to a storybook drawing I had seen of a flying saucer with wheels. A transparent dome about six feet in diameter protruded from the top, like a 360-degree windshield.

Inside the dome, four black cushioned seats faced a foot-wide pedestal at the center. The pedestal's top angled toward one of the seats, giving whoever might sit there easy access to buttons, levers, and a pilot's yoke that protruded from the surface.

"Does it look like it's been tampered with?" I asked.

Shanghai scanned the craft. "Not that I can see."

When Saigon and Liam joined us, Shanghai pressed a button on the vehicle's side. The dome split at the top, and its two halves receded into the body. "Erin used a computer tablet to fly it, but it also has manual controls. I figured most of them out."

With a high step, Shanghai entered and took a seat behind the yoke. Pinching the fuel cell, she looked at Liam. "Where does it go?"

He reached into the craft and touched a small, circular hole on top of the central pedestal. "Just drop it in here."

"Got it." After doing so, Shanghai pushed a button on the yoke. A second later, the vehicle emitted a humming noise. "All aboard."

I helped Saigon climb in. We sat with Shanghai between us, me on her left. Liam propped the energy tank on the fourth seat and backed away. "This is as far as I go. I have to take the guard's body to the morgue and then look after my wee ones. Fiona and her girls are staying with us as well, and Anne and Betsy were sore afraid when I left."

"After what they went through, it's no wonder." I reached out and shook his hand. "Thanks again, Liam."

"Don't mention it." He unfastened a small canteen from his belt and set it inside. "Clean water. You might need it."

After we said our good-byes and Liam began walking toward his van, Shanghai pushed another button. The dome rose and enclosed us within. She turned the yoke and pressed a pedal at her feet. Moving slowly, the vehicle rotated toward the garage entrance and rolled out. When we reached an open space in the parking lot, Shanghai said, "I couldn't find any seatbelts, so just hold on to anything. I got jostled quite a bit when I flew it here."

I rested my aching arm on my lap and clutched the bottom of my seat with my right hand. "Ready."

"Same here." Saigon groaned as she held her seat with both hands. "I'll try my best not to puke."

"No puking allowed." Shanghai pushed a lever on the yoke. The engine's hum heightened, and the craft lifted off the ground. Outside, Liam stood next to his van and watched, shrinking as we rose.

"I assume you know how to get there," I said.

"This vehicle's computer does. Remember Alex and Erin said some kind of gas would put them to sleep during the ride to make sure they wouldn't know where the Gateway is. It flies itself there. Unfortunately, I couldn't figure out how to get it to guide me home, so I lost my way a few times. I guess that's why I ran out of fuel. Anyway, it probably also ran out of knockout gas. Good thing. Its bad enough flying ignorant. Unconscious would be even worse."

Saigon peered at the control panel. "Then this thing must have an autopilot you can program."

Shanghai nodded. "When I finally figured out how it works, I checked the destinations. The Gateway was the only one programmed into it." She pushed a button. The screen displayed two lines — "The Gateway" and "Warehouse."

"What's the warehouse?" I asked.

"I don't know." Shanghai squinted at the screen. "That option wasn't there last time. Someone's been here and added a destination."

"We're getting more help," Saigon said. "A fuel cell, pills, and now directions."

Shanghai frowned. "More bait, you mean. This is like a *free candy* sign on a kidnapper's van."

"Right," I said. "We're kind of stuck. It's either an obvious trap, or someone's trying to help us. You could argue for the stupidity of following the trail or ignoring it."

"Let's see where the warehouse is." Shanghai pressed the entry. A glowing map appeared on the screen, displaying ground features like rivers and lakes as well as topographic contours. Two dots flashed west of the Boundary River inside the crater left by the explosion that snuffed the nuclear plant's fire. "The Gateway and the warehouse are close together, both inside that crater we were in."

I looked the map over. Based on my memory of the size of the crater, the two locations were about a mile apart. "If the warehouse is where Alex stores and stages the illuminaries, Sing might be a prisoner there. That's where we need to go."

"I agree." Shanghai touched one of the flashing dots. The aircraft swerved and ascended at a sharp angle, making us sink in our seats. "Okay. We're on autopilot. We can sit back and enjoy the sights."

"Enjoy?" Saigon slapped a hand over her mouth and lowered her head between her knees. After a few seconds, she straightened, her face red. "That was close."

Shanghai patted her on the back. "The purified energy's still affecting you. But it's good in the long run. When you recover, you should be able to transform into full ghost mode."

"Full ghost mode?" Saigon blinked. "What's that?"

While Shanghai explained the term and recounted our near-fatal experiences at the Gateway, I looked out through the transparent dome. Below, a patchwork pattern crisscrossed the land — recently harvested farms that grew wheat and corn or whatever the Gatekeeper's Council ordered.

Word on the street said that the farmers' quotas were difficult and strict, regardless of how the weather, radiation levels, insects, or disease affected the crops. A bad harvest resulted in severe penalties, such as loss of food rations or, at worst, confiscation of children until the next planting season.

Yet, if the farmers made their quotas, the Gatekeeper rewarded them handsomely — free healthcare, a vacation to the tropics during the winter, and their choice of new farming equipment. Such was the up-and-down life of the people who supplied food for every person on the planet. The farms zoomed by, a mesmerizing sight. Although I had watched videos of flying experiences, I had never flown before. Huge, nearly deserted airports in every city gave evidence that flying was once a normal way to travel, but airlines shut down more than a century ago. Now, as Liam described, only government officials could take advantage of the few remaining aircraft and the quick transports they offered. Some passengers, however, flew against their will.

My mother was one such passenger. After my Reaper-initiation ceremony, Alex, wearing a mask so that I wouldn't remember her, whisked me away to Chicago's biggest airport to meet my mother. She had been flown there from a secret location where Death Enforcement held her hostage to "encourage" me to accept Reaper service. Alex allowed me five minutes with her. I barely remember the warm embrace, the whispered words of love, the parting tears. Those precious moments flew by far too quickly.

Then Alex took me to my district and settled me in my apartment. At the same time, a DEO drove my mother home and forced my parents to move to a new location, standard procedure to keep Reapers from trying to flee their districts and find their families. To this day, I never learned their new location, only that it was in another city, not that it mattered anymore.

I shook the dark thoughts away and renewed my stare at the ground, letting the experience of floating over vast stretches of land ease my mind. During my daydreaming state, I stayed half aware of Shanghai's activities as she taught Saigon how to switch to ghost mode. Saigon learned quickly. Within an hour she was able to transform from one state to the other in a matter of fifteen seconds or so, though after each transformation, she needed time to recover from the dizziness associated with the change.

Something beeped. I followed the sound to the craft's control panel.

"Radiation warning," Shanghai said. "We're closing in on the Western Wilds. I'll fly lower and see if that helps."

"Speaking of radiation ..." I pulled the detection band from my belt pouch and wrapped it around my wrist. The readout on its face displayed a numeral 5. "Do your instruments show a level?"

She leaned closer to the panel. "Yep. Five point one. I guess it beeps when it rises higher than five."

"Not terrible yet." I showed her the band. "This reads about the same."

"Let's make sure we don't get cooked." Shanghai withdrew the pill bottle from her cloak, poured three pills onto her palm, and handed one each to Saigon and me.

Saigon pinched the pill and stared at it. "Wait. Wait. What's all this about radiation levels and being cooked?"

"We're going into the Western Wilds," I said. "Do you know about that region?"

She glanced at Shanghai, then refocused on me. "Okay, I'm feeling about as low as a moose pellet in a snow trench around you two world travelers. Try to explain without sounding too uppity. All right?"

"I'll do my best, but take the pill first." We each swallowed a pill and washed it down with water from Liam's canteen.

As the beeping continued, I recited the story Salvador told about the nuclear plant meltdown and how the land west of the Boundary River became contaminated with radiation that pooled in pockets. When we had the wrist-bands, we were able to detect if we were entering high-radiation zones, so we tried to avoid them whenever possible.

The beeping grew louder. I checked the band. "I'm showing six. What do you have?"

"Six point nine," Shanghai said as she grasped the steering column. "Must be because we're crossing the river. We're already lower than the flying instructions call for, but I'd better try going down a bit more."

Below, the Boundary River looked like a beige ribbon with snowy flecks — whitecaps whipped up by a low-level breeze. As we descended, the craft rocked to the side as if slapped by an invisible hand.

Shanghai angled toward the wind. "Radiation's dropping. I guess it's better to stay low. I had to shut off the navigation system. I'm going by memory."

I checked the band again — a reading of 5. At ground level, a highway ran east-west. "Shanghai, see that road? I think it's the one we took with the motorbikes. Follow it if you can."

"Will do." Shanghai steered due west, keeping the road to our left. The craft began shaking as if driving over a bumpy road. Her voice bounced with it. "Let's hope she holds together."

Ahead, the hazy shield above ended abruptly, giving way to a huge ring of clear blue sky, at least a hundred times bigger than the old Gateway opening. "We're going in the right direction. Just aim for the center of the new circle."

"Yep. Got it marked." Shanghai glanced at the panel. "Four point seven. That'll rise again soon. We got up to nine point one last time."

Saigon shook her head. "Do you two ever go an hour without risking your lives?"

"Not lately," I said. "But I won't mind breaking the pattern. This death-defying business gets kind of old after a while."

Saigon huffed. "At least wink or grin when you talk like that. I can't help but be gullible when I'm flying blind."

I smiled. "I guess I was half kidding. I am getting tired of us risking our necks. I just want it to be over, either way." I glanced at the Gateway hole as we crossed its outer boundary. "Dying means going to a better place, right?"

"Maybe for you, Mr. Perfect, but I still have some amends to make." Saigon closed her eyes and folded her hands in her lap. "My mother taught me about Jesus, and I ignored her warnings for far too long. I'm going to start praying my sins away." She opened one eye and looked at me. "But with all my sins, it'll take a while, so don't interrupt me till we get to wherever we're going."

While we flew on, still bouncing heavily, Shanghai and I searched for the crater. After a few minutes, the edge rose over the horizon.

I pointed. "There. See it?"

"I do, but I think —" A new beep sounded, this one lower and less shrill. "Yep. Low fuel warning. Whoever gave us that cell knew it was just enough to get us here. No return flight."

"A one-way ticket," I said. "Looks pretty bleak."

"Hush that faithless talk," Saigon said, her eyes still closed. "I'm in touch with the Almighty. I don't want any doubters clogging the communication lines. You'll mess up my soul cleansing."

Heeding Saigon's request, Shanghai and I stayed quiet as we flew toward the tree-filled crater. The radiation alert sounded, blending with the low-fuel alarm. The meter rose quickly past six and headed toward seven while my band changed to six and stayed there.

"I'm switching the navigation system back on." Shanghai pressed a button. "Maybe it can guide us around the high-radiation zones."

The craft swerved to the left and flew in an arc around the edge of the crater, staying about two hundred feet from the ground. "Radiation's back down to six," Shanghai said. "It's working."

"Of course it's working." Saigon opened her eyes, a contented smile on her face. "Everything's going to be just fine."

After another minute, the craft cut sharply toward the center of the crater and began descending into its forested depths. I spotted a small clearing ahead and pointed. "Can you put us down there?"

"We'll find out in a second." Shanghai switched off the navigator. The moment she grabbed the steering column, the craft angled downward. "Uh-oh. Fuel's empty."

"Hang on!" I called.

Saigon kept her hands folded, though more tightly than before. She whisper-chanted, "We're all right. We're all right. We're all right."

The craft brushed across evergreen treetops and sank into their grasp, breaking branches in front and on both sides. One branch speared the protective dome, shot between Shanghai and me, and knifed into the craft's rear section.

With a loud bump, we halted, suspended at least eighty feet off the ground by the piercing branch. The dome was gone, shattered. The engine's hum died along with the alarms.

Saigon blew out a long sigh. "Okay. We made it."

"We still have to get down." As the craft swayed precariously, I crawled out and wrapped my arms around the tree's trunk, in spite of the pain in my wound. The weight release made the branch snap. When it broke away, our vehicle fell with it.

Shanghai lunged and grabbed my ankle. Saigon latched on to hers. The three of us dangled with only my arms around the trunk keeping us from plunging. Mind-numbing pain ripped through my wound, radiated to my fingers, and throbbed in my spine.

"Phoenix," Shanghai called. "Are you all right?"

I grunted. "Not really."

Saigon shouted, "I'm gonna let go. I think I can catch a branch."

"I'll do the same," Shanghai said. "Right after you."

With my cheek pressed against the trunk, I could no longer see what was going on below. The torturous weight swung to my right, then to my left before suddenly decreasing. My arms slid down the trunk. Even worse pain throttled my senses, and numbness tingled in my hands.

More weight released. My arms fell limp, and I dropped, turning headfirst toward the ground. After a quick plunge, my descent slowed, and I eased closer and closer to the forest floor at a safe rate, bumping several thin branches along the way. Something still had a hold on my ankle. I tried to twist to see what was going on above me, but pain and numbness kept me pointing downward.

When I reached the ground near the wrecked aircraft, my head and hands landed softly on a bed of pine needles, and the rest of my body followed as something above set me down easily. I rolled over and looked up. High in the trees, Shanghai and Saigon stood together on a limb, both holding a spool line, the lower end wrapped around my ankle.

"We caught us a big one," Saigon said as she wrapped the line around the limb. "Is he a keeper, or are we doing catch and release?"

"Definitely a keeper." Shanghai put on a pair of gloves, grabbed the line, and slid to the ground. As she helped me sit up, she said, "How's the pain?"

I rotated my shoulder. The bullet wound throbbed but not as badly as I expected. "Not terrible."

While Shanghai untied the line from my ankle, Saigon detached the other end and began climbing down the tree limb to limb, reeling the line in along the way.

Shanghai grabbed my good arm and hoisted me to my feet. "Phoenix, if you keep doing superhero stuff like that, you're going to wear that label forever."

"All I did was hug a tree. No big deal."

"Yeah, right. No big deal." She pulled my cloak down my shoulder and looked at the bullet holes in my shirt sleeve. "Some blood around the exit point." She put my cloak back in place. "Not too bad."

Saigon joined us, staring at me. "What are you? A shaved gorilla? No one can do what you just did."

Shanghai crossed her arms and gazed at me for a moment before shaking her head. "Something's going on with you, Phoenix, but we don't have time to figure it out. Alex must have noticed our noisy arrival."

"She probably already knew we were coming," I said. "We just rang the doorbell."

"So much for a surprise attack." Shanghai kicked a bent piece of metal attached to the aircraft. "It's a goner. Even if we had fuel, we're not going home in this wreck."

I nodded. "Whoever gave us the fuel cell probably calculated exactly how much we needed to fly two passengers here. The extra weight made it run out a few minutes too soon."

"There," Saigon said. "You see? Alex isn't so smart after all. She doesn't know I'm here, so I'm your secret weapon." She lifted the energy tank out of the passenger compartment and looked at the meter. "Empty. The impact must've broken the valve." She tossed it to the side. "Worthless."

I checked my inventory. Bartholomew's tablet, still attached to my belt, was intact. In my cloak pocket, the journal also seemed fine. A quick glance at Saigon's belt told me that my tablet had also survived the crash. I retrieved Liam's canteen from the wreckage and clipped it to my belt.

"Well, secret weapon," I said, "the dose you got will last you quite a while. The purified energy is more potent."

"Speaking of potent ..." Saigon pointed toward my wrist. "Are we getting cooked?"

I looked at the reading. "It's at two. It was low down here the last time we came, but not that low." Although I assumed that the electrified cats were gone, I scanned the area — nothing but trees, underbrush, and fallen leaves. When I leaned to the side to look around a massive tree, something gray caught my attention. "I see something."

With Shanghai and Saigon following, I walked to the object. Near the cliff at the edge of the crater, a long gray hose snaked up a tree, tied to the trunk at regular intervals. At knee level, the hose, about the width of my forearm, dangled loosely, a coupler attached to the end.

I ran my foot along a section of bare ground near the trunk. "Something used to sit here that kept the undergrowth from sprouting." I lifted the hose and examined the coupler. "This connected to whatever the object was. Maybe a collection tank."

"To collect what?" Saigon asked. "Air samples? Checking radiation levels at the top?"

"When we were last here, the area directly above us was still covered by the sky's radiation shield. Now the Gateway opening is wider and extends beyond this point."

"And the tank is gone," Shanghai said. "Maybe because it can't collect what they want anymore."

"Exactly my thinking. Someone was collecting the radiation shield itself. Since it receded, the process won't work."

Shanghai looked up into the tree. "How can the hose reach that high? I didn't see it when we were flying around."

"Maybe an aircraft attaches another hose to the top end and carries it into the shield. Remember, they can fly those things without a pilot."

Shanghai pointed at me. "The attack on the Resistance leaders. The radioactive gas came from here. Alex has probably been collecting it for a while."

"Right. Another deadly weapon in her arsenal."

Saigon whistled. "All right, super sleuths. I kept up with all of that, but I wouldn't have put the puzzle pieces together like you did. What do you do? Just invent the wildest conspiracy theories possible and assume Alex is smart and evil enough to pull them off?"

"Pretty much," I said. "That's a good way to guess her next move."

"If you say so. You two have the experience, not me." Saigon rotated in place. "So where's the warehouse?"

"We've never been there, but on the map it looked like it was about a mile north of the Gateway building." I nodded at the tree we collided with. "We'll just walk in the direction we were heading. At least we won't be attacked by electrified ghost cats."

Saigon sucked in a breath. "Electrified ghost cats? Nobody told me about electrified ghost cats."

"Don't worry. Since the Gateway hole is so much bigger, they were probably sucked right out of the forest."

Her voice trembled. "Probably?"

"Right. No guarantees."

Saigon swallowed, looked to the sky, and whispered for a moment. Then she marched ahead. "Well, let's go, then. What are you waiting for?"

Shanghai and I caught up and walked abreast with her. We kept our footfalls as quiet as possible and watched for the slightest movement. At times we had to split up to avoid trees and ruts, and cold air made us bundle our cloaks close.

My arm still ached, though, again, not as badly as it should have considering everything I had put it through. Shanghai's comment echoed in my mind. *Something's going on with you, Phoenix.* It was true that weird things were happening, especially being able to reap the two doctors so easily, but solving the mysteries would have to wait.

Thinking about the doctors prompted me to check on them. I whispered, "Vera? Jasper? Can you hear me?"

"Sure can, Phoenix," Jasper said. "Is everything all right?"

"Just making sure you can still hear me. We're under the Gateway, so I'll let you out as soon as I can. We're bound to run into danger, though. It might take a little while."

"No hurry," Vera said. "And if danger means injury, call on us. We'll be glad to help."

"I will. Thanks."

After a few more minutes, the white exterior façade of the Gateway building came into view in the midst of the trees. From this distance, the exterior seemed to radiate light, as if the building were glowing, but it was probably just my imagination.

To avoid detection, we turned left and made a wide circle around the building. When we completed the arc, we marched on through the forest. After about fifteen more minutes, we came upon a circular clearing. We halted near the edge, still under tree cover. Twenty paces ahead, a wall of blue radiance stood about ten feet high and thirty feet wide. The surface shimmered, reflecting warped images of the forest around us.

Fallen trees littered the perimeter, their foliage green, and foot-high stumps dotted the leaf-strewn area.

"This place was cleared recently," I said. "Maybe to prevent a fire. Whatever that radiant field is, it might ignite wood."

"Let's see how big it is." Shanghai vaulted onto a nearby oak's lowest limb and scaled the tree as easily as she would a ladder. When she reached a point about thirty feet high, she stood on a branch, braced herself with a hand on the trunk, and looked toward the clearing. After scanning the area, she climbed back down and rejoined Saigon and me.

"It's a rectangular building, maybe a couple of hundred feet long. That blue energy field surrounds the whole thing."

"To keep Sing inside?" I asked.

"That's what I'm thinking." Shanghai picked up a pine cone. "Let's see if it'll keep us out." She threw the cone.

When it struck the wall, it shot back toward us, a stream of fire and smoke trailing it. The cone dropped a few paces away and burned with a crackling sizzle.

Saigon shook her head. "That's not exactly a welcome mat."

I sat on the ground and gestured for the others to join me. Once we were seated, I spoke in a low tone. "Let's assume Alex and Bartholomew are inside, and they know exactly where we are. Any ideas about how to enter without them detecting us?"

"Maybe some kind of distraction," Shanghai said. "Draw them out into the open and sneak in. Even if it doesn't work, we could fight them here where we'll have the advantage."

"Right. Instead of inside where we don't know the layout." I scanned the forest again. "We could start a fire. That pine cone proved it wouldn't be hard."

"Wait." Saigon slid a hand into her cloak pocket and withdrew the detonator she had used to blow up the bank building. "Remember what Ollie said about resetting this to control something else?"

I nodded. "I remember. He said it didn't work with Betsy's bomb."

"Right, but maybe it could control an electrified field."

"Are you saying a detonator for explosives that we found in Chicago doubles as a controller for a security field hundreds of miles away? That's really a wild stretch."

"Yeah, well think about it. When we helped Betsy, I found the fuel cell. While we were on the yacht, you found the anti-radiation pills. Both were put there to help us get to this place. But we didn't find anything at the school where Anne was."

I whispered, "Except the detonator."

"Exactly." Saigon pried the detonator box open and showed me the inside. "Which button did you press?"

I touched a button with my finger. "This one."

"Press the other one."

I complied, holding it down for a few seconds.

When I released it, Saigon snapped the box back together. "Should we try it?"

"I still say it a wild stretch."

"Someone went to a lot of trouble to make sure we got here. Whoever it was wouldn't help us come this far only to let us get stuck in the woods."

"Suppose it does work," I said. "The field goes away. Then Alex will know for sure that we're out here. We'll walk right into her clutches."

"Well, I'm betting our helper has already thought of that. He or she probably made sure we won't get caught the moment we set foot in that place."

Shanghai crossed her arms. "The stretching is getting worse."

Saigon shrugged. "I'm just guessing. If you have a better idea, spit it out."

"Let's test it," I said. "If it shuts off the field, turn it right back on. If they notice, we'll just have to deal with it."

"Will do." Saigon aimed the detonator at the wall and pushed the button with her thumb. The radiant shimmer began fading. A second later, she pushed the button again. The shimmer returned to its former brightness. "Ha! Score one for the optimists."

Shanghai grasped my wrist. "I have an idea. We'll turn the field off, send Saigon inside, and turn it back on. Then she'll go into ghost mode. I'm betting the field will keep her from flying away. She'll be invisible to everyone but Alex, so she can snoop around and see who's in there, look for Sing, or whatever. After a while, she'll return to physical form and we'll turn the field off to let her out. Then she can give us a scouting report."

"That sounds great." I looked at Saigon. "What do you think?"

She grinned. "I said I was your secret weapon. It's my turn to use my super powers."

"All right, then. Let's do it."

We rose to our feet. Shanghai withdrew Alex's watch from her belt and gave it to Saigon. I pulled Kwame's from its pouch and synchronized it with Alex's. "It's four past three," I said. "We'll turn the field off for your exit at ... let's say three fifteen."

"Three fifteen. Got it." Saigon slid the watch into her pocket, handed the detonator to me, and set her feet to run. "Ready."

"Remember, even at the risk of someone seeing you, you have to be out of ghost mode by three fifteen. If you're still a ghost when I turn the field off, you might get sucked into the sky."

"What do I do if I start getting sucked into the sky as soon as I become a ghost, even when the field is on, I mean?"

"Go straight out of ghost mode. If you succeed, you'll drop to the ground, but you'll also be stuck in there in physical form until three fifteen. Anyone will be able to see you."

"And if I don't succeed?"

I glanced toward the clear blue sky. "I suppose the next time we'll see each other will be on the other side of the Gateway."

She licked her lips and nodded. "Good incentive."

I aimed the detonator at the wall and pushed the button. When the radiance faded, a metal double door appeared at the center of a cinder-block wall. "I hope it's unlocked."

"I'll know in a minute." Saigon dashed to the warehouse, opened the door, and disappeared inside. When the door closed, I pushed the button again. The radiant field returned, hiding the inner wall from sight.

CHAPTER FIFTEEN

"OKAY," I SAID, my stare on the watch, "in ten minutes we should know a lot more."

We looked at the wall, glancing at Kwame's watch every few seconds. Time seemed to crawl at a glacial rate.

After a couple of minutes, Shanghai exhaled heavily. A pensive expression weighed down her features.

"What's wrong?" I asked.

She glanced away. "I'm not sure I should say."

"Shanghai ..." I grasped her hand. "You can tell me anything. We have to trust each other."

"Okay. Here goes." When she turned back toward me, tears pooled in her eyes. "I think Saigon's on their side."

A quick denial flashed to mind, but I swatted it down and kept my voice calm. "What makes you say that?"

"Her figuring out that we should use the detonator was way too convenient."

I nodded in a conciliatory fashion. "True, but, like she said, it was the only thing we found at the school —"

"I heard her." Shanghai's frown deepened. "There are too many coincidences going on. Like Saigon said, some-one's putting out breadcrumbs for you to follow, and she was there to make sure you found them all — the fuel cell, the pills, the detonator, and mentioning the autopilot."

"But she destroyed all those illuminaries."

"Did she? She says she did, and you heard Alex say she did, but they could have been lying."

"True, but Saigon's been risking her life to —"

"I know. And you've been risking your life for Sing and me. Like Saigon's been saying, you're a hero. Heroes do that. Risk their lives to save people, I mean. And Saigon's saying *she* wants to be a hero. She's kind of obsessed with the hero idea."

"She does seem to be hooked on it, but who is she trying to save? She's been a district hound for twenty years. Life doesn't get any lonelier than that. She doesn't have anyone in her life. Except now she has you and me."

"Well, she has latched on to you. She's been buttering you up with all that hero talk and trying to be like you."

"Are you saying she's flattering me to keep me from guessing that she's really on Alex's side?"

"Yes, that's pretty much what I'm saying." Shanghai crossed her arms. "I take it you don't agree."

"Not necessarily. Like you said, too many coincidences. But you haven't been with her as much as I have. She really was out of energy. Nearly dead. I read the meter. I know she could have staged it, but the risk would have been astronomical."

Shanghai nodded. "True, but she seems willing to take a lot of risks."

I raised a hand. "All right. I'm calling a truce. Your theory makes sense, and I can't prove it's wrong, but I'm not going to accept it just yet. After all she's gone through, that wouldn't be right. We'll just keep any new information between ourselves and watch her closely."

"Fair enough." After a long moment of silence, Shanghai touched my arm near the bullet wound. "How does it feel?"

I lifted my arm to waist level, but roaring pain forced me to let it drop. "Still pretty sore."

"Then when we go in, let me lead the way. If we run into hostiles, I'll be the first line of defense."

"No argument from me. I'll be the rear guard." I read Kwame's watch — twelve minutes past three. "Three minutes to go."

Again we stared at the shimmering wall while glancing at the watch in my palm. The three minutes seemed interminable. When the minute hand drew close to the three, I aimed the detonator at the wall, my thumb on the button. "Tell me when."

Shanghai kept her stare on the watch. "It doesn't have a second hand. I'm guessing ten seconds." She counted down one second at a time. When she reached one, she followed with, "Now."

I pressed the button. As the field dimmed, the metal door returned to view. I held my breath. The door stayed closed, no hint of movement anywhere.

Shanghai whispered in sing-song. "I don't like this."

"Me neither." I slid the watch into my pocket. "Do you think she flew into the sky?"

"Maybe we'd better —"

The door opened. Saigon slid halfway out and waved for us to join her.

I flexed to run, but Shanghai grabbed my sleeve. "Phoenix, this has ambush written all over it."

"Only if Saigon is a traitor. We have to believe in somebody."

"All right, but I'm still —"

Saigon hissed, "Get your butts in here."

We leaped into a sprint. When we reached Saigon, she grabbed us, hauled us inside, and closed the door. Her hands shaking, she latched on to my wrist and pushed the detonator button.

She looked up and stared at the low ceiling, as if able to watch the field returning. She whispered, "You see? No changes, not even a sound. You can't tell from in here if the field is up or down. Maybe no one knows we're inside."

"How's the dizziness?" Shanghai asked.

"Pretty bad." Saigon wobbled but caught herself on my good arm. "It hit me just a few seconds ago. I think a shot of adrenaline kept me going till you got here."

Shanghai flashed a skeptical frown. She had good reason. Saigon's sudden lapse into dizziness seemed too convenient. Yet, at this point, we were inside the warehouse. We had come this far. It didn't make sense to call a retreat.

I attached the detonator to my belt and scanned our surroundings. We stood in a narrow, dim corridor that led to a single wooden door about ten feet farther in. A bare bulb at the center of the ceiling provided our only light. I leaned close to Saigon and whispered, "What did you find?"

"Better to show you than to try to explain everything. Fire up your flashlight."

I detached my flashlight and turned it on. Saigon staggered to the interior door, pulled it open, and set a finger over her lips, signaling for quiet.

Shanghai and I joined her. Aiming the flashlight straight ahead, I took a few steps inside the dark chamber, halted,

and shifted the beam from left to right. Cloaked illuminaries stood motionless in a dense array on either side of
the rectangular chamber, leaving a six-foot-wide corridor
in between.

Above, parallel wooden beams ran across an unfinished ceiling as did a set of braided wires between two of
the beams. At the far end of the building, radiance outlined
another door, as if a brilliant light shone behind it and leaked
through the gaps.

I whispered again to Saigon, "Do you know what's
behind that door?"

She nodded. "I poked my head through it in ghost mode.
It's like a big closet filled with cloaks and metal gizmos, I
guess for making illuminaries. But here's the important
part. The light's coming from a cage, like a zoo cage with
vertical electric bars real close together. And guess who's
trapped inside."

"Sing?"

"Yep. The bars were glowing real bright, so they made
her look blurry, but it was her all right. She was curled on
the floor like she was unconscious or asleep. I saw a camera
near the ceiling. I guessed it could pick up my voice, so I
didn't call to her. I figured she couldn't escape, so why risk
it? Anyway, since I had some time left, I looked around to
find a switch to turn off the juice but came up empty."

Shanghai scanned the room with wary eyes that gleamed
in the flashlight's glow. "And you didn't see anyone else
around? Bartholomew? Alex? Working illuminaries?"

Saigon shook her head. "No sign of movement anywhere."

"Strange," I said. "It isn't like Alex to not know we're
here. The detonator, the fuel cell, the pills. And we crashed

into the crater like a drunken elephant falling out of the sky."

"Unless she thinks you're dead," Saigon said. "The yacht explosion was meant to kill you. And maybe Bartholomew left you the pills and stuff."

"Then where is he? Did he just want us to rescue Sing without Alex knowing?"

Saigon shrugged. "Maybe. But we're here. No one else is around. Let's finish this and try to go home without getting fried."

I looked again at the distant door. The light around the edges flickered, inflaming my desire to race to door and fling it open. But we had to be careful. This was too easy. Way too easy. As if blinking signs screamed, "Ambush!"

I listened to the dark, motionless air. All was quiet except for our respirations. I kept mine slow and steady, though my heart thudded. Shanghai and Saigon breathed at faster rates — anxious, nervous.

The silence felt eerie, a sense of doom in the midst of hundreds of lifeless death machines. Might they secretly be active? If so, they could attack whenever they wished. We would be helpless. Yet, it seemed that another danger lurked, something unseen.

I whispered, "Follow me and stay quiet."

Shanghai grabbed my belt and pulled me back. "No." Her voice was barely more than a wisp. "Are you crazy? This is the most obvious trap in history, and you want to walk right into it?"

"What are the options? Leave the warehouse and go home? Tell Sing, 'Hey, Sancta who was sent from heaven to help us, it got a little too scary so we decided to abandon you to a murderous witch'?"

"No, of course we can't abandon her." Shanghai rolled her eyes upward. "Just let me think a second." While biting her lip, she tapped her foot quietly. After several seconds, she let out a sigh. "All right. I don't see any other option. But remember, I'm the first line of defense. You're the rear guard."

I nodded. "All right. Lead the way."

Her expression turned warrior-like — narrowed eyes and tense jaw. "Lights out. Stealth procedures. No more talking unless necessary."

I flicked my flashlight off. Darkness shrouded us. The light at the door seemed brighter, but it did nothing to raise the surrounding curtain of blackness.

Lifting my good arm, I slid my hand behind Saigon's belt and hung on. Since she knew the drill, she probably did the same to Shanghai. When Saigon pulled toward the left side of the building, I walked with the tug, my eyes and ears alert to the slightest change.

We pushed into the mass of illuminaries, our shoulders brushing against them as we passed. I listened for their motors' telltale hum, but all was quiet — a good sign.

Shanghai guided us in a snaking pattern, likely trying to lose anyone who might be tracking our movements. After a minute or so, we had made our way to a point near the rear of the chamber. Shanghai gathered us into a huddle and whispered, "Saigon, did you see any wires anywhere?"

"No. It was dark except for the light at the door."

I added a whisper of my own. "I saw some on the ceiling. You might be able to find a junction box up there and pull the wires out. Maybe that'll shut down Sing's prison."

"Do you know where on the ceiling?" Shanghai asked, her voice still barely audible.

"Not exactly. Maybe a little past halfway."

"Even if you knew where they are," Saigon said. "How would you get up there?"

"Standing on shoulders. A three-person tower." Shanghai added a contemplating hum. "No. Phoenix is too injured for that."

"We'll use an illuminary at the bottom," Saigon said. "Then me on top of it, and you on me."

"It might work if the illuminary holds steady. But it's a shot in the dark if we don't know where to climb."

"I can spotlight the ceiling," I said. "But I would have to do it from a distance so anyone seeing the light won't know where you two are."

Shanghai's whisper turned sharp. "Separating is against protocol. We're deep in enemy territory. Just being here at all is crazy enough. We have to stay together."

"Agreed. But do you have a better idea?"

Silence again enveloped us. In the midst of the muffling cloaks, even our breathing raised no sounds.

"Okay," Shanghai said, "but find us again quick. We'll head to a spot right under the wires."

"Will do. Just be alert for the beam. I won't keep it on long." I weaved my way back toward where we started. When I arrived at the edge of the illuminaries, I stepped into the open area, flicked on the flashlight, and waved it across the ceiling, starting with the beams near the back.

I drew the light toward me in wide sweeps. After a few seconds, the light illuminated the braided wires I had seen earlier. Not wanting anyone watching to think that the wires were my focus, I continued the sweeps for a few more seconds before flicking the light off.

Once darkness fell again, I slid into the illuminaries and worked my way toward the area under the wires. I soon found an illuminary that shifted hard to one side. I grabbed it and held it steady. Reaper shoes moved on the robot's shoulders, barely visible though they were only inches from my eyes.

Above, the women worked in complete silence, not a grunt to be heard. As I moved my gaze upward, I imagined Saigon gripping Shanghai's ankles. Since Saigon had so recently been in ghost mode, how could she stand so steadily? If I had just returned to my physical state, there was no way I could pull off this feat so soon.

After another moment, Saigon leaped down to my side and whispered, "Shanghai lifted off my shoulders, so I guess she caught the wires. I wish I could see her work. Everyone says she's one of the best."

Saigon's unsolicited compliment seemed odd, out of character. More distracting flattery? I whispered in return, "How did you keep your balance so well? I thought you would still be dizzy."

"I don't know. More adrenaline, I guess."

Her tone sounded guarded, defensive. Continued questioning would probably be fruitless. I had to keep a close eye on her. "Come with me." I grasped her hand, led her to the edge of the illuminaries, and peeked at the door leading to Sing's prison. The light at the door's boundaries continued shining.

A flash erupted above. The light at the door blinked off. In the midst of falling sparks, Shanghai dropped to the floor. When the sparks fizzled at her feet, she faded into the darkness.

"You and Shanghai go get Sing," Saigon said. "I'll transform to ghost mode and hang back in case you need me." I kept my grip on her hand. "No. The power outage might have killed the surrounding field. Stay with me."

Leading Saigon while training my eyes on the point where Shanghai dropped, I marched ahead. Since I had only one good arm, I released Saigon and felt around for Shanghai but swiped empty air. I whispered, "Shanghai," but no one answered.

"No sign of her," Saigon said. "It's like she vanished."

"Not on her own accord. Some of these illuminaries must be active. No human is powerful enough to take her without a sound."

"Then why don't they grab all of us?"

"Maybe there's just one of them," I said, "and it hopes to pick us off one at a time."

"This is why Shanghai wanted us to stay together."

"Right. Stick close to me. Obviously our cover is blown, so I'm canceling stealth protocol.

I turned on my flashlight. With Saigon at my side, I aimed the beam into the array of illuminaries at the left edge of the corridor and searched the gaps between them as I walked closer to the rear door. I then backtracked and did the same at the corridor's right edge but found no trace of Shanghai.

When I reversed course again and neared Sing's door a second time, I shifted the light to my side, but Saigon was no longer there. I swept the beam around. I was alone.

I hissed, "Saigon!" No one answered. A shudder shook my body. The image of the supposedly lifeless illuminaries darkened my mind. Either one or more of those robots had captured Saigon, or she was a traitor, as Shanghai suspected. Either way, I might be the next victim.

I ran to Sing's prison door, threw it open, and aimed the flashlight beam inside. A cage sat on the floor directly in front of me. Thin wires twisted around the vertical bars, darkened by lack of electricity. The cage was empty.

A pile of cloaks stood in one corner of the room. Illuminary arms, legs, and torsos lay in haphazard stacks here and there, just as Saigon had described, but the empty cage meant that the entire setup was a ruse. Sing was never a prisoner here. The cage was just a prop for a light show. Saigon lied.

I turned toward the darkness and pierced it with the beam, shifting it from one motionless illuminary to another to another. Nothing moved. No sound emanated from the wall of cloaked robots.

An eerie feeling crept in again. Something dark and sinister was near. My heart thumped. My throat ran dry. I had only one hope — disguise myself as an illuminary and hide among them.

I tucked the flashlight under my wounded arm and kept the beam aimed into the darkness while I backed into the cage room and felt for an illuminary cloak. The door slammed. I grabbed the knob, but it wouldn't turn. I pulled, then shoved. The door wouldn't budge.

I shouted, "Who's out there?"

No one replied.

I turned the flashlight off and clipped it to my belt. Now in darkness, I rammed my good shoulder into the door to no avail. I slammed it with a kick. The wood rattled in the frame but held firm.

A buzz emanated from the ceiling. Seconds later, a foul odor permeated the air. Faint light appeared in the lower part of my peripheral vision. I focused on it. My left hand glowed. I looked at my right hand. It, too, glowed.

A tingling sensation crawled along my skin, starting at my feet and running up my legs to my waist. I lifted my shirt. Radiance covered my abdomen.

Something clicked. The wires on the cage bars brightened. A glow surrounded them, the light from one bar blending into the lights from those on either side, blurring the area within, just as Saigon had said.

Another click sounded. The cage's door swung open.

"Get in the cage, Phoenix," Bartholomew said from a hidden speaker.

"What do you want?" I called into the air. "Where are Shanghai and Saigon?"

"Regarding your friends, they are safe for the time being. Regarding what I want, I already told you. Get in the cage."

"And if I don't?"

"Spare me the drama, Phoenix. This isn't a theater production. I am already annoyed that I had to apprehend the females to force you to do my bidding. That's more than enough theatrics already. Now if you will just do what I ask, you have my word that I will not kill them. You can see for yourself that they are intact."

A video monitor on the wall turned on. Shanghai and Saigon appeared on the screen, each sitting in one of the Council's chairs, their wrists bound to the arms and their ankles to the legs. In the floor near their feet, the abyss swirled. Light from the energy in its depths illuminated their determined faces as they struggled to break free.

An illuminary stood guard next to Shanghai. Obviously she couldn't escape, but what about Saigon? If she really was a traitor, why was she tied up? If not, why did she say Sing was in the cage?

Bartholomew's voice returned. "Fortunately for your friends, I was able to restore the electricity without much trouble, so I resisted the urge to inflict pain on them ... until now."

The illuminary guard stepped in front of Shanghai and punched her in the face, then returned to his former position. Blood trickled from a cut under her eye, and a welt was already forming. She glared at the robot, her teeth bared and her chest heaving, but she held her tongue in check.

I shouted, "You monster!"

Bartholomew's voice sharpened. "Get in the cage."

The radiant bars illuminated the room, allowing a clearer view of everything. A camera attached to an upper corner aimed its lens straight at me. I couldn't simply pretend to enter the cage. "All right. I'm going." The moment I stepped in, the door closed and latched on its own.

"Be patient for a moment while I prepare the next step."

"What next step? And why am I glowing?"

"No more questions. Keep cooperating if you want your friends to survive."

The tingling sensation continued crawling up my skin, now at shoulder level. The bullet wound ached and sent a wave of pain to my hand, stiffening my fingers. Yet, I couldn't let pain stop me. I had to get out of here somehow.

I touched one of the bars with a fingertip. A jolt made me jerk back. There was no way out of this trap. Even though we approached with stealth, realized that we had to stay together, guessed that some of the illuminaries might be active, and assumed that our enemies knew we were here, every precaution failed. We marched forward in spite of the obvious dangers, certain that we had to help Sing, no matter what.

But Sing wasn't even here. It was all a lie. And I fell for it.

Something glimmered on the floor. I crouched and found a photo stick. After picking it up, I straightened while closing my fingers around it.

A hologram of Sing appeared above my hand. She lay on the ground, apparently asleep. Since she wore traditional Reaper garb, this photo must have been taken before she died. Someone planted it here to make someone think Sing was actually in the cage.

Yet, this wouldn't have fooled me, only someone who thought Sing might take off the red cloak. Saigon had seen Sing wearing it, but no one told her what it meant to be a Sancta, that the cloak was a sign of her office. She would never remove it.

Not only that, this hologram was semitransparent, readily identifiable as a phantasm. Saigon said that Sing looked fuzzy because of the blurring effect of the electrified bars. Was that reasonable? Or was it an excuse to dodge suspicion?

One fact remained unexplained. Although Alex suspected that I had help from a Sancta, neither she nor Bartholomew knew that Sing was the Sancta. In order for them to set up this photo-stick mirage, someone had to tell them about Sing's new role. Besides Shanghai and me, Saigon was the only person who knew. Even though Saigon appeared to be a prisoner, she had to be a traitor.

The tingling intensified. Haze appeared in the air and thickened into a smoky cloud. The odor increased along with a dry, chalky sensation in my narrowing throat.

I coughed, then swallowed saliva, but neither helped. Might Bartholomew be using the same gas that choked the life out of men, women, and children at Evan's apartment building? If so, why this kind of execution? A sonic gun blast to the head would accomplish the same goal without all the trouble.

The thought of Evan brought my ghostly passengers to mind. I whispered into my cloak, "Jasper. Vera. Can you detect the odor I'm smelling?"

"Indeed, yes," Vera said. "It's not pleasant at all."

"Is it the same gas that killed you?"

"I don't think so. That odor was more biting than this one, more choking."

The haze concentrated near the ceiling, prompting me to crouch, though the odor seemed just as strong near the floor. "Any idea what this stuff is?"

"I have an idea," Jasper said. "Ten years ago … no, eleven. In any case, I went on a journey to the great mountains on the other side of the world. I hoped to ascend one of the tallest peaks, more than five miles high. The day came for the final ascent. We were all excited, invigorated, and —"

"Skip the details," Vera said, "and get to the point. Our Reaper might be in danger."

"Yes, you're right. Well, the haze shield had shifted quite low, even below the peak. After climbing for about an hour, we began noticing this same odor, and the haze became apparent. Our radiation-detection bands climbed to eight, so we decided to return to base camp."

I looked at my wrist band's reading, also eight. "So this haze is from the shield. It's radioactive."

"That's my guess," Jasper said.

"Then I'm getting cooked. What do I do? I took one radiation-protection pill, but I don't have the bottle anymore."

"Then all you can do is use your cloak as a filter. Of course, it will only be temporary protection. You'll have to hope the radioactive haze dissipates soon."

I raised my hood and pulled the side over my nose and mouth. Breathing through the fibers blocked the odor somewhat, but it still penetrated. This gas probably came from the collection tank that once sat near the edge of the crater. Alex had used it to snuff the lives of the Resistance leaders, and now she and Bartholomew hoped to finish me off. Still, the whole scheme seemed way over complicated. It made no sense.

On the monitor, the illuminary grabbed Shanghai's hair with a gloved hand and pulled upward, stretching her face. He punched her twice more, once in the nose and once in the eye.

I lunged at the bars and grabbed two. The shock thrust me to the rear of the cage. Another jolt knifed into my back and threw me to my knees. As the haze grew thicker, my head pounded. My heart thrummed erratically. Bracing myself on all fours, I looked again at the monitor.

The illuminary released Shanghai's hair and drew back. Blood dribbled from her nose. Her eye closed, the lid swelling over it, and her head wobbled as if she were fainting. From the other chair, Saigon appeared to be screaming at the illuminary, but the sound failed to come through.

I jumped up and pulled the cloak's sleeves over my hands. Setting my feet and bending my knees, I grabbed two electrified bars on the cage's door and shook it.

Pain roared in my wounded arm. Jolts ripped through my body. The door rattled but held fast. As I shook the door harder and harder, I inhaled more and more of the radioactive haze.

My muscles flexed with power. Pain in my bullet wound eased. Setting my feet, I lunged with my legs and shoved the door. The hinges tore away. My momentum sent me tumbling out of the cage and toward the room's exit. I slammed my head against the door and collapsed.

I rolled to my back. Pain from head to toe dulled my senses as the room spun in dizzying arcs. Gasping for breath, I struggled to my feet and tried to open the door, but it was still locked.

After waiting a moment for the spinning to decrease, I looked around. The remaining electrified bars made everything easy to see, including the camera mounted in the corner. Its red light pulsed, the lens still aiming at me.

I picked up an illuminary leg, strode to the corner, and whacked the camera. It toppled from its mount and dropped to the floor. The light blinked off. Bartholomew was now blind to my actions. I could try to escape without his knowledge.

Yet, if I were to leave this room, the illuminaries would see me. Somewhere in the midst of the motionless robots, at least a few had to be active. They ambushed Shanghai and Saigon, and now they probably waited for me come out. I had to figure out a way to upset their programming. Since they were looking for a human Reaper, maybe my earlier idea to disguise myself as one of them would work.

After selecting a cloak from the pile, I put it on over my own cloak. The layers were bulky, but since illuminaries were larger than humans, the bulkiness might help me pass for one of the hooded robots.

I found several sets of gloves that the illuminaries wore to hide their metallic hands. I put on a pair. They covered my glow nicely.

Standing again in front of the room's exit, I reared back and slammed a foot against the door. The jamb shattered. Wood splinters flew. The door sprang open and thudded on the wall.

I raised both hoods and extended the outer one so that it shaded my face. As I walked out, my cloak swept the floor, hiding my feet. Hoping to mimic the gliding gait of the illuminaries, I maintained a steady rhythm and minimized any up-and-down motion.

I kept my focus on the two warehouse doors I had entered earlier, both now open to the outside. The protective shield shimmered beyond the second door. Moving slowly, I reached under the cloaks, detached the detonator, and set my thumb on the button.

Step by step, I drew closer to the doors. Allowing only my eyes to move, I glanced both right and left. About five rows ahead, the eyes of one of the illuminaries flashed red. It stepped into the open area and walked on an angled path that would intercept me in a few seconds. On the left, another illuminary's eyes turned on. It, too, walked on an intercepting trajectory. Both would join me in three ... two ... one ... zero.

They turned in the same direction I was walking and stayed abreast with me. When we reached the inner door, I walked through first and continued toward the final exit without a pause. The other two illuminaries caught up and again strode at either side. As I approached the second door, I aimed the detonator at the field, keeping it hidden under my cloak.

I pushed the button. Nothing happened. Risking exposure, I halted and extended the detonator. The illuminary on my right snatched it from my hand while the other stepped in front of the door and blocked the exit. I had no way out.

CHAPTER SIXTEEN

I PUNCHED THE CLOSER illuminary in the chest. It reeled back and slammed against the anteroom's side wall. Although my knuckles struck metal, they were strangely free of pain.

I lunged at the other illuminary and reached for the detonator. With a squeeze of its hand, it crushed the box and threw it down. It kicked me in the stomach and sent me flying toward the other side of the anteroom. I crashed into the wall and slid down to my bottom.

As I gasped for breath, the two illuminaries stalked toward me side by side. Since these robots learned new tactics as they experienced battle, this pair had already adapted to my style. Punching might no longer work.

Five more robots funneled through the interior door. I leaped up, charged toward the original two, and, leading with a shoulder, rammed into them. My legs still churning, I turned and shoved them against the newcomers and bowled all but one over.

I pivoted toward the exit and tried to run, but the still-standing illuminary lunged and grabbed my hood. It jerked me into its grasp, my back against its body. With a gloved hand, it clutched my throat. Light flashed from its cloak.

Electric shocks coursed through me, making me shake. My teeth chattered. My bones felt like they were on fire.

As the other illuminaries rose, I reached back with both hands, grabbed my captor behind its head, and threw it over my shoulder. It slammed to the floor. The throw sent horrific pain shooting through my wounded arm. My limbs trembled, and numbness deadened my hands.

The other illuminaries rushed at me. I hobbled toward the exit. Without the detonator, I had no way to deactivate the force field, but I couldn't possibly survive a battle with seven super-powered illuminaries.

I threw myself toward the field and tucked my body into a ball. The moment I hit the shimmer, electric shocks jolted my brain. I tumbled along the ground outside and rolled to a stop.

Heat radiated into my skin. A horrible stench assaulted my nose. I rolled again, shedding the cloaks while in motion. As I pulled free, I curled my fingers around a section of the inner cloak and tugged it with me. When the heat diminished, I stopped rolling and looked back.

A few feet away, the outer cloak smoked while a few embers smoldered on my Reaper cloak. If I had been wearing only my own cloak, the electric field would have made it burn like dry tinder. The illuminary's cloak must have been made of flame-retardant material. Maybe it would come in handy for getting past any other blocking fields I might encounter.

My head pounding, I lay on the ground while batting the embers away. At the warehouse, the protective field continued shimmering. The seven illuminaries, now veiled by the shimmer, were probably standing at the open door, waiting for the field to deactivate.

When I climbed to my feet, dizziness washed through my brain. I extended a foot to take a step, but I had to draw it back to keep from falling. Yet, I couldn't stay. Somehow, I had to get into hiding.

I put my cloak on, dropped to hands and knees, and, after picking up the illuminary's cloak, crawled into the woods. Once I had hidden in a dense thicket, I looked back. The field's shimmer faded. Illuminaries filed out. Again I counted seven. Apparently out of the hundreds that stood dormant in the warehouse, only these seven and perhaps a few more that had captured Shanghai and Saigon were active. Maybe Alex lacked enough soul energy to fuel the others. With her fiery rampage in Chicago, she would soon have a lot more available. Then her army would be unstoppable.

The illuminaries split up and marched into the woods in multiple directions — a search party. When one closed in on my hiding place, I ducked low. As its shuffling feet brushed undergrowth within inches of my nose, I held my breath. Worsening dizziness threatened to make me pass out, but I willed myself to stay conscious and perfectly quiet.

Soon, all seven illuminaries had moved out of sight. I found a sturdy walking stick and climbed to my feet. After putting the illuminary's cloak on again, I leaned on the stick and plodded toward the Gateway building. Since at least one of the illuminaries probably hurried there to report my escape, a surprise attack was out of the question. Alex and Bartholomew would be expecting me.

At my normal running pace, I could have made it to the building in less than ten minutes, but after multiple electric shocks and a near-lethal dose of radiation, my pace felt like a turtle's — one sliding step after another, as if I were trudging through thick mud. Fortunately, no illuminaries showed up. I could keep making slow progress without further delays.

After about half an hour, I came upon the dome room. A field of radiance surrounded the entire Gateway building, explaining the glow I had seen earlier from a distance. I gave the building a wide berth and sneaked to the west side. Now that the depot supply line was gone, maybe I could get in through the breach in the wall that the energy channel once used to deposit souls.

As I approached a tall narrow gap in the building's side wall, the dizziness and numbness eased. My arms and legs strengthened, raising questions about what I had recently done. What could have given me the strength to rip the hinges from the cage and kick open the warehouse door? Maybe seeing Shanghai getting pummeled by that illuminary injected a massive shot of adrenaline.

I stopped at the exterior wall and tried to peer into the gap, but the shimmer blurred the inside. The last time I was here, a few illuminaries were working on an assembly line of sorts, using a flywheel to pull souls from the depot stream and stuff them into a holding tank.

After checking my borrowed gloves and covering as much skin as possible with the cloaks, I held tightly to the walking stick and plunged through the gap. Again, electricity stabbed me, but this field felt weaker than the one at the warehouse.

With the field providing light, I looked around. Although the soul-collection tank was still sitting on the floor, the rest of the chamber was empty — no flywheel, no illuminaries, no souls. All was quiet. Alex leaving this entry unguarded felt like an invitation to another trap, a new web for the careless fly. Yet, I had to go on. I knew it. The spider knew it. I just had to figure out how to avoid her venomous bite.

I walked to the far end of the room. The wall here extended upward to a point about three feet from the ceiling, leaving a gap, like an open transom above a door. The top of this wall acted as a perch from which I observed the flywheel-to-tank collection process not long ago, having climbed there from the soul-drainage farm on the other side.

Somehow the illuminaries transported the collected souls from this flywheel room to the drainage farm. They couldn't have taken the collection platforms over the ledge. Another passage had to be somewhere.

To the left, the wall darkened in the shadows. I walked that way and found a door near a corner. I turned the knob and pushed the door open, revealing a dark, narrow corridor, more like the inner space between two walls than a normal hallway.

I grabbed my flashlight and turned it on. The beam sliced through the darkness. The corridor led to another door about a hundred feet away. Based on my memory of the layout, that door opened to the wide hall connecting the front of the building to the dome room.

To the right, this corridor's wall bordered the former soul-drainage farm. The wall to the left appeared to be nothing more than wooden supports with gaps between them. Maybe the gaps led to an unfinished room, but I couldn't tell from this spot.

Which move would Alex expect me to make — walk down this corridor or climb over the perch? Either path might lead to a trap. I had to do the unexpected. But what could I possibly do that Alex wouldn't expect?

"Phoenix?"

The feminine whisper came from my cloak. "Vera?"

"Yes. I didn't want to bother you earlier, but we were wondering when the ... well ... discomfort would end."

"Are you and Jasper in pain?"

"Not so much now, but earlier we felt a lot of heat and, I'm not sure how to describe it. Shock waves? We still feel heat, but it's tolerable."

"Sorry. I went through a couple of electric fields. I'll try not to let it happen again." I took off both cloaks and brushed away a few smoldering patches on mine. When I put my cloak back on, I whispered, "Is that better?"

"Yes. Much. Thank you." She laughed. "If you plan to electrocute yourself again, let us know."

I draped the illuminary's cloak over my shoulder. "I'll make a note of it."

Silence returned. In the stillness, an odor filtered in — burnt hair. For the sake of my disembodied passengers, I had to avoid fire, but might fire be exactly what I needed? If I could set the building aflame, the distraction might allow me free access anywhere. Alex wouldn't expect that. I just had to make sure I set the place on fire at the right time.

Since marble and tiles covered much of the building, it wouldn't go up in flames easily. I would have to start a fire within the walls by igniting wooden beams and supports. That would require hot-burning fuel, yet it would have to burn slowly enough to make the wood catch. Maybe a combination of something flammable and flame-retardant would work.

With my flashlight beam leading the way, I walked down the narrow corridor. The vertical support boards on each side led to a wooden strut frame above, making this an ideal place to try to start a fire.

"Well, I didn't expect to see you here, Phoenix."

I halted and shone the light around. The male voice sounded familiar, but I couldn't place it.

From a gap between two supports on the left, a man walked into the corridor. I shone the light on his face, the face of Melchizidek.

A chill ran down my spine, but when my light passed through his semitransparent body, the tension eased. He was just a ghost. "What are you doing here?" I asked.

"I was about to ask you the same thing. Since this is my place of residence, I think you should answer first." He smiled, revealing his perfect teeth. Still sporting curly black hair and wearing clean pants and a button-down shirt, he seemed relaxed and comfortable.

"Since you're Alex's ally, I'll keep my reason for being here to myself."

"Alex's ally?" He laughed. "I'm her prisoner, not her ally. She put a shield around the entire building, so I'm trapped. I decided to hide in the bowels of this place so I wouldn't have to do what she demanded."

"All right." I shifted the light away from him. "If you'll help me with something, maybe I can help you."

"Of course. I'll do what I can."

"I want to burn the building down. I need fuel."

"Burn the building?" His smile faded. "Whatever for?"

"That's my business. But it helps you because a big enough fire will destroy the shield, and you can escape."

"Escape?" He looked up. "To the Gateway, I assume."

"Is that worse than hiding from Alex like a child worried about a whipping?"

He shook a finger. "Don't patronize me, Phoenix. I won't be manipulated."

I shrugged. "Suit yourself. Help me, or don't help me. But I thought you might like to get back at Alex."

"A skilled move, Phoenix. Checkmate, so to speak." Melchizidek stared at me for a moment before continuing. "Fuel isn't a problem. But burning down a building like this? That might be harder than you think."

"Leave that to me. Are you going to help me or not?"

He nodded toward the left side of the corridor. "We used that area to store construction materials, like paint, varnish, and adhesives. We wanted to keep unsightly and smelly containers out of sight."

I aimed the beam through a gap and swept it across several sealed white buckets. I walked in and found one labeled Varnish. I popped the lid off and used the walking stick to push the illuminary's cloak into the smelly liquid. After a few seconds, I drew the dripping cloak out and returned to the corridor.

With Melchizidek looking over my shoulder, I set the cloak at the base of one of the wooden supports and used the stick to make the material twist around the board. I took the lighter from my belt, flicked its flame to life, and set it to the varnish-soaked cloak. Flames sprang to life. The cloak itself wasn't burning, but it kept the varnish in place and slowed the fire's consumption of the fuel.

As I waited for the fire to catch the wood, choking smoke filled the confines. I couldn't stay much longer. I had to rely on hope that the fire would spread and distract Alex and her forces when I needed it.

I coughed as I spoke to Melchizidek. "Thanks for the help. I guess I won't see you again."

"Not likely." The flickering fire highlighted his worried face. "I suppose when I go beyond the Gateway, I will get what I deserve."

I replied in a quiet tone. "I really don't know."

"No. Of course you don't." His smile returned, though it seemed forced. "Well, go on, Phoenix. I wish you well. Put Alex in her place once and for all."

"I'll do my best." I hurried to the far end of the corridor, opened the door a crack, and peeked through the gap. As expected, it opened to the wide hall between the anteroom and the dome room. Two illuminaries guarded the mahogany double doors that led into the dome room while a third walked from left to right toward the building's front entrance. Somehow I had to get rid of them.

I closed the door, unhooked Bartholomew's tablet, and turned it on. After touching a button to reply to Alex's most recent message, I typed, "I am too injured to continue fighting. Can we make a deal? Just set Shanghai and Saigon free, and I'll tell you everything I know about the mirror. I'll meet you in the dome room in five minutes to discuss my proposal."

I sent the message and checked the time at the corner of the screen — 4:47 p.m. I reclipped the tablet and flashlight to my belt and peeked out the door again. The third illuminary had walked out of view to my right, while the other two still stood in front of the dome room.

A minute or so later, one of the illuminaries opened the dome-room door, and they both entered, maybe summoned by Alex. When the door closed, I looked to the right. The third illuminary approached. It was probably going to continue patrolling. Only one option remained.

When it drew close enough, I flung my door open, grabbed it by the cloak, and jerked it into the narrow corridor. Before it could react, I slammed its face against the floor again and again. The power in my thrusts felt supercharged, unearthly. After several more repetitions, something popped. The illuminary's body fell limp. When I turned it over, its red eyes flickered twice and blinked off.

After looking back and seeing that Melchizidek was no longer in sight, I straightened my cloak and exited into the expansive hall. Now vacant, quiet, and lacking the portraits of Melchizidek that once decorated the walls, the chamber felt like a mausoleum. Certainly it had held many souls captive, and soon it might become my place to die.

After passing the hallway's two sets of stairs, one at each side, I stopped at the doors, grasped Bill's cross, and whispered, "Help me rescue my friends. Whether or not I survive doesn't matter so much. I just need to get my friends out of here safely."

I took a deep breath and opened the door. Beyond the abyss, Alex sat in the Council's center chair, flanked by three chairs to each side. Shanghai sat to her left and Saigon to her right, both with wrists and ankles bound.

Bartholomew stood next to the abyss, facing me with two illuminaries immediately behind him.

"Welcome, Phoenix," Alex said, the white band still around her head and her hand on a leather bag at her side. "Come. I want you to see what your actions have wrought."

I hobbled in, favoring my right leg and letting my left shoulder sag, hoping she would believe I had suffered more injuries than I actually had. As I limped closer, light from the abyss clarified Shanghai's face. Bruises marred her cheeks, her left eye was swollen shut with a purple bruise covering the lid, and blood trickled from both nostrils. Yet, her right eye sparkled with life, brimming with anger and determination. She was ready for war.

Saigon sat straight, her shoulders back. She wore no bruises, but a wet splotch on her left shoulder looked like blood, though her dark shirt made it impossible to be certain.

When I drew close to the abyss, Bartholomew held up a hand. "Stop right there."

I halted within three steps of the eight-foot-wide hole. Light energy swirled at the top, though nothing sparkled on the surface. Either no souls were trapped within, or they were too deep to reveal their presence.

Furrowing my brow to simulate pain, I said, "Let them go, and I'll be your prisoner. I'll tell you everything you want to know."

Alex hummed through a laugh. "Phoenix, we've discussed this before. My prisoners are leverage, especially Shanghai. If I were to let them go, I would be powerless. You have proven that you're willing to withstand any torture. I wouldn't be able to persuade you to do anything."

I spread out my hands. "Then what do you want me to do?"

"Tell me the secret to using the mirror. We already learned who the Sancta is, your dearly departed Singapore, but she wasn't willing to tell us anything."

I feigned surprise. "What are you talking about? Sing is dead and gone."

"Don't take me for a fool, Phoenix. You know better. And you also know that I have ways of getting the information I want."

I cast a quick glance toward Saigon. Her expression was stoic, though her eyes darted. The blood indicated a round of torture. Yet, if she was on their side, why would they abuse her?

I smiled and spoke in a condescending tone. "Let's say your insane theory is true. If you think Sing is this Sancta thing you invented, then where is she?"

Alex nodded toward the abyss. "She is swimming within the cozy confines of my little pool. It was painstakingly difficult to keep her trapped within an electrified field, especially since she stayed invisible as Sanctae are known to do, but Bartholomew lent a hand with his expertise. His research into Sanctae lore has proven invaluable."

I shook my head and let out a derisive laugh. "You and Bartholomew are crazy. You think you have an invisible prisoner."

"Is that so? Who is the crazy one? If you really think Singapore isn't here, why did you go to all the trouble to come to the Gateway? Chicago is burning. Thousands are dying. Yet, you chose to abandon them and come here instead. Did you really miss me that much?" Alex turned on a heavy sarcastic tone. "No, that couldn't be the reason. I tried to kill you by luring you into a doomed boat. That should have put a damper on our relationship."

I resisted the urge to roll my eyes. "I came here because I couldn't stop the fires by putting them out one at a time. The job was too big. I had to snuff them at the source. I came here to kill you."

She touched her chest. "Is that any way to treat your host? A woman? I thought you were the consummate gentleman."

I tensed my muscles, again forcing myself to stay calm. "Just keep mocking me, Alex. If you think a Sancta is really in the abyss, maybe she's biding her time, waiting for the perfect opportunity to come out and strike you dead."

"Really, Phoenix?" Alex called toward the abyss. "Oh, Singapore. If you plan to come out and strike me dead, you should do it now. In ten seconds, I am going to kill Saigon."

Saigon stiffened. I hid a tight swallow. Alex was not one to make idle threats.

Alex smiled. "One ... two ... three ..."

"Alex, wait." I raised a hand. "You proved your point. We both know that no Sancta is going to come out of the abyss. Let's just —"

"This isn't a bluff to rattle you, Phoenix. I am going to kill Saigon. She is of no use to me anymore. But you shouldn't shed any tears. She betrayed you. She has been part of my plan from the beginning, from the moment she set foot in your alley crying for energy sustenance. She has been my mole, so to speak, and has kept me up to date, including telling me about Singapore."

Saigon cried out, "Phoenix, I agreed to help her because she said you were the reason everything in Chicago went to hell. But when I joined you, I learned the truth. That you're good and noble. I changed my mind and joined your side. I did tell her about Sing, but that was just to keep her thinking I was on her side. I helped you rescue Anne and Betsy, didn't I? I risked my life again and again."

"Of course you did," Alex said. "You love your mother very much. It would be a shame if anything tragic happened to her."

I looked at Saigon. "Your mother?"

Saigon wept, barely able to speak. "She ... she's holding my mother hostage. But I swear I was still on your side.

I thought when we killed that witch we could rescue my mother together."

Alex's eyebrow twitched. "Is that so?"

Saigon nodded, tears trickling down her cheeks. "Every word. I swear."

"For what it's worth, I believe you." Alex withdrew a knife from her belt. "But at this point, it's worth very little." She reached over, drove the blade into Saigon's chest, and pulled it out. A new splotch grew on her shirt. Her eyes widened as she choked on blood dribbling from her mouth.

I charged ahead, skirted the abyss, and dashed to Saigon's side. My arms shaking, I caressed her cheek with a gloved hand. "Hang on. Just stay with me."

She gurgled, "I'll try."

Alex casually returned her knife to its sheath, not bothering to clean the blade. "I see that you are not as injured as you tried to appear." She signaled toward the illuminaries. "Watch him. If he does anything aggressive, restrain him."

While an illuminary approached, Alex smiled. "I will enjoy watching my army force the mirror information out of you."

"Shut up!" Shanghai shouted. "Even if there really was a Sancta, and even if Sing is the Sancta, do you really think she would help you use the mirror or do anything for someone as evil as you?"

"She would with the proper persuasion," Alex said, "which I am adept at delivering."

Shanghai answered, but I tuned her out. She was providing a temporary distraction. I had to gather my wits and use whatever time she could give me. I could either attack Alex and get into a fight to the death with the illuminaries or try to save Saigon.

I kept my voice to a whisper. "Jasper. Vera. A knife to the chest. What do I do?"

"Is the blade still embedded?" Jasper asked.

"No."

"Lay the victim down," Vera said.

"If they'll let me." I withdrew a knife from my belt. The illuminary grabbed my wrist with an iron grip and snatched the knife away. I growled, "I'm just trying to cut her loose."

Bartholomew walked closer. "Let him try to save her. I am intrigued by his misplaced loyalty to a traitor."

The illuminary sliced through Saigon's bonds. The moment I gathered her into my arms, a slapping sound caught my attention. Alex drew back a fist and shouted at Shanghai, "The next blow won't be with an open hand."

"Coward!" Shanghai spat at Alex. "Cut me loose, and we'll see how brave you are."

Trying to ignore Shanghai's taunts, I laid Saigon on the floor next to the abyss. "All right, Vera. She's down."

"Expose the wound," Vera said. "Tell us what you see."

I pulled Saigon's plackets apart. Blood oozed from a hole next to her sternum valve at the four o'clock position. "A cut in her chest about an inch long. I can't tell how deep it is."

"Can you hear the sound of air passing through the hole?" Jasper asked.

I set my ear close to the wound. While I tried to listen, Alex called out, "Restrain Phoenix. I need to teach his foolish fiancée a lesson."

I whispered into Saigon's ear, "Go to ghost mode. It's your only chance. The whole building's shielded, so you won't —"

The illuminary grabbed my hood, jerked me upright, and twisted my wounded arm behind my back. I struggled to free myself, but pain shredded my strength. "No! I have to help Saigon! She'll die!"

"That was the point of stabbing her, Phoenix." Alex shoved Saigon with a foot and rolled her into the abyss. In a splash of sparks, she plunged beneath the radiant surface and disappeared.

I swallowed hard, barely able to whisper, "She's gone. She didn't have time to shift ..." I let my words trail off.

Alex pointed at the chair Saigon had occupied. "Bind Phoenix. I want him to watch."

When the illuminary loosened its grip, I jerked free, leaped into a spin, and kicked it in the face, sending it staggering backwards. The other illuminary charged. Just as I set my stance to take it on, something jabbed my neck. Numbness shot down my spine. Bartholomew stepped out from behind me, a hypodermic needle in hand. "That should calm you down for a while."

My limbs fell limp, and I slumped to the floor. The two illuminaries picked me up, set me in the chair, and tied my wrists and ankles to it.

"Now," Alex said as she lifted the leather bag from her seat. "It's time to get the information I want." She paced in front of me with a showy strut. "It was the oddest thing. Bartholomew fashioned a portable cell, an electrified cage that we used to transport the invisible Sancta. As you might imagine, we had some reservations. Might we be wrong? Were we transporting a myth? Was the cage actually empty, and we were victims of our own wild imaginations?

"Our doubts lingered until we used an energy flush to force the contents of the cage into the abyss. Imagine my relief when ..." She withdrew the mirror from her bag and laid it on my lap. "This appeared in the cage. A marvelous stroke of luck, don't you think?"

I stared at my reflection. Alex and Bartholomew really did throw Sing into the abyss. And now I was trapped with only one way to escape — tell Alex how the mirror worked, a mirror that no longer had any powers. Even if it did, and even if I gave away its secrets, what good would that do? We would die, and Alex would rule the world.

Somehow I had to buy time — give the fire a chance to catch and spread. My only hope was to offer Alex a morsel or two. I had to feign defeat at her hands. She would never try to interrupt an ego massage.

I made my voice tremble. "All right. All right. It's true. Sing is a Sancta. She did have the mirror. But she never told me how it works. And just like you thought, I did come here to rescue her, but I also came to rescue Chicago from the fire. I love the people of my city, and I love Sing."

"Chicago doesn't love you," she said. "You're on a fool's errand."

Glaring at Alex, I sharpened my tone. "What did you expect me to do? Sit in my destroyed apartment and watch everything around me burn? My home is a blown-out shell. We found the clues Bartholomew left for us to follow so we could locate the warehouse, but now I know it was all part of your plan."

At this statement, Alex threw a split-second glance at Bartholomew. Anger flickered in her eyes. She didn't know everything Bartholomew was doing behind her back. I had found a wedge.

"And since he also killed my parents and Shanghai's," I continued, infusing my tone with grief, "Shanghai is all I have left in the world, and I'm all she has. We hope to get married when we turn seventeen."

Alex resumed her pacing, though no longer with a strut. She set a hand on her chin and stroked it. Every few seconds, I sniffed the air, hoping to detect smoke so I could end this nauseating charade, but so far, nothing.

"Just let us go," I pleaded. "You won. Chicago is yours. The world is yours. Just let us go home and live in peace."

Alex halted and set a hand on my cheek. Her piercing stare drilled into me, and her steely eyes glimmered. "Phoenix, you should know by now that no lie of yours can escape my detection."

I forced my body to tremble. "And what do you detect?"

"A strong conflict. Some of your words are true, and some are false. And some you're unsure of." She whipped out her knife and flashed its blade. "But I will soon learn what is true and what is not." She cut through Shanghai's bonds. "Get up. I will give you the fight you crave."

Shanghai rose from the chair and rubbed her wrists. She looked at me, one eye still blocked by a swollen lid. With that kind of injury, her depth perception would be hindered. Alex would surely exploit Shanghai's disadvantage.

I strained against the ropes. The stuff Bartholomew injected me with was still working. I felt as weak as a kitten.

Alex took off her weapons belt, set it next to her chair, and poised her feet and hands in battle-ready position. "Come, Shanghai. The Reaper world claims you are among the finest of fighters. Show me what you're made of."

CHAPTER SEVENTEEN

SHANGHAI UNCLASPED HER cloak and tossed it to the side. Already without her weapons belt, she copied Alex's pose. Blood smears and bruises enhanced her fierce expression as she replied with a rumbling growl. "I've been waiting a long time to smack the smugness right off your face."

Alex blew a wisp of hair to the side. "Then make your move, slant-eyed little girl. I haven't got all day."

Shanghai lunged and swung a fist. Alex dodged with a head move and swept a leg under Shanghai's. Shanghai leaped over the leg, spun on a heel, and kicked Alex broadside in the ribs. Alex caught Shanghai's foot, thrust her leg back, and sent her stumbling toward the abyss.

Shanghai intentionally collapsed to the floor and slid on her back to the pit's edge. When she stopped, her head dangled over the radiance, and her hair swirled within it.

Alex stormed toward her and raised a foot to stomp her chest. Shanghai rolled out of the way. When Alex's foot came down, Shanghai swept a leg of her own and slammed it into Alex's ankles. Alex toppled back and landed on her bottom.

Like a pouncing tiger, Shanghai threw herself on top of Alex. She punched Alex in the nose with a right fist, raising a spray of blood. Alex dodged Shanghai's left fist, making her knuckles crash against the floor.

Alex shoved Shanghai to the side. Both women leaped to their feet and regained their battle stances. Blood trickled from Alex's nose. Shanghai gasped for breath. Her hair shimmered, carrying sparks of radiance from the abyss.

While they visually measured each other, Bartholomew sidled to me, leaned close, and whispered, "The sedative I gave you is fast acting, but it also wears off quickly. You should be at full strength soon."

"What?" I whispered in return. "Why are you telling me this?"

"Didn't I say I'd help you conquer Alex? You will soon be able to attack. Since she thinks you're disabled, you can take her by surprise, which is the reason I sedated you, to make her think you're not a threat. Yet, I can't cut you loose. If she sees me do so, not only would the surprise be ruined, she would probably kill me immediately." He stepped away, folded his hands at his waist, and watched the combatants.

Alex wiped her nose with a sleeve. "I've played around with you long enough." She charged at Shanghai. The two exchanged blows at close range. The flurry of fists and feet blurred. Some punches and kicks landed, while others missed or met blocking arms.

I again strained against the ropes. The numbness had eased. My muscles flexed powerfully though still not enough to break my bonds. Bartholomew expected me to escape on my own. But how?

Alex bobbed left, then right, then left once more, lunging and backpedaling again and again, a strategy likely designed to press her eyesight advantage. Shanghai's head moved to compensate. When Alex saw an opening, she leaped ahead and landed a savage punch to Shanghai's swollen eye and another to her bruised cheek.

Shanghai reeled backwards and fell against a chair. Alex swooped close and punched Shanghai again and again with alternating fists.

I lunged against the ropes, whispering at Bartholomew, "She's not looking. Cut me loose."

He kept his stare on the battle. "If you can't break out yourself, then you're not ready. You can't win."

Alex kicked Shanghai square in the face. The blow made Shanghai's head snap back, and she fell limp. Alex grabbed a fistful of Shanghai's hair, dragged her in front of me, and released her, letting her head smack the floor. "Phoenix, tell me how the mirror works. If you don't, I will torture Shanghai."

I struggled against the ropes. My wrists bled, and my ankles ached. I shouted, "Coward! You couldn't beat her in a fair fight. And now you'd hurt her while she's out cold. While I'm tied up." I spat as I continued shouting. "You're nothing but a sick, twisted, coward!"

"No, Phoenix. I am a woman in control. I killed Misty. I forced you to kill Singapore. And now, if you don't give me what I want, I will kill Shanghai. Yet this time I will do it slowly. You have proven you can endure the sudden death of a loved one, but can you endure extended suffering?"

I stared at Alex. My mouth dropped open, unbidden. What could I say? Without a doubt, Alex would torture Shanghai, and I couldn't do anything about it. The mirror had no powers Alex wanted. I couldn't possibly do anything to prevent Shanghai's slow death. The fire was my only hope. I had to try to stall again.

"Okay. Okay. I'll tell you. Just give me a few seconds to think."

Still on my lap, the mirror faded, the reflection replaced by Sing's face. She floated in a sea of radiance, her curly hair shining like the sun. Her voice came through in a breathy whisper. "I am in the abyss, and I can't help you. But you have the strength you need to defeat Alex. Call upon it. Remember who you are. You are Phoenix. Like your namesake, you have been sown in the gloom of disaster, rooted in the shroud of death, and watered by tears of grief. Like Yeshua, when you rise from ruin and burst into the light, you will be free, energized to do what you must."

A hint of smoke tinged the air. The fire had caught. Soon it would spread. When everyone evacuated, maybe Bartholomew would cut me loose.

Alex retrieved her weapons belt, strapped it on, and withdrew her knife. "You've had your few seconds to think. Allow me to begin the persuasion process. This is merely step number one." She lifted Shanghai by the hair and plunged the knife through her swollen eyelid.

"No!" I lunged again, but the ropes held me back. A string of insults swelled in my throat, but I swallowed them down. What good would they do now?

Alex slowly withdrew the blade. Red-tinged serum oozed from the gash. "Her other eye is next, unless you reveal the mirror's secrets."

I balled my fists. "Untie me! Take me on, you coward!"

Alex shouted in return. "Don't doubt me, Phoenix! I skewered one eye! You know I won't hesitate to do the same to the other! Tell me the secrets!"

"There *are* no secrets! It's just a mirror!"

"You're lying." Alex dropped Shanghai, stomped over to me, and picked up the mirror. After glancing at it, she set it close to my face. "See? See? It's Singapore, your little half-breed lover. This is the result of your loyalty to each other. Death. Torture. The abyss. Just give me what I want, and I will set you all free. No one else needs to die."

I forced my voice to relax. Staying calm might be my only hope. "Look, suppose you're right, and the mirror has great power. Why do you need it? You have an army. They can kill people to create their own fuel. You already have everything you need to control the world."

"Not so, Phoenix. The illuminaries are powerful, but they are slow. I can't possibly control the world without quick transport, and the mirror provides —"

An illuminary burst through the entry door, squealing a series of mechanical beeps. Dense smoke followed in its wake.

"Fire!" Bartholomew said. "We'd better go before the exits are blocked."

"No!" Alex set the mirror on my lap again. "We have come too far. We won't have another opportunity like this."

"I'll get an extinguisher and check it out." Bartholomew gave the illuminary a hand signal and followed it out through a blossoming cloud of smoke.

"Shut the door!" Alex shouted. Her command fell unheeded.

After muttering an obscenity, she showed me the knife. Red liquid smeared the blade. "This carnage is what you have wrought. Will you finally give up the stubbornness that has caused the deaths of Misty, Singapore, and Saigon and now the maiming of your beloved fiancée? Will you burn with Shanghai upon a wedding pyre, forever blended in a heap of ashes? While Chicago awaits in flames, I await your answer."

Fighting down another screaming outburst, I looked straight at Alex and spoke calmly. "Listen. This is the truth. The mirror once could transport people out of danger. It was powered by a Sancta named Scarlet. She helped a pair of my ancestors save the world. When their crisis was over, the mirror lost its ability. Now it just shows images of the past, with sound, like watching a video. I don't know what happened to Scarlet, but Sing is the Sancta in charge of the mirror now, and she has no idea how to make it transport anyone."

Alex's Owl eyes shimmered again, piercing my mind. After a few seconds, she backed away a step. "You believe your words to be true. But are they?"

"Of course they're true. I told you everything I know."

"I believe you, but your explanation makes no sense. The mirror is clearly working magic of some sort, and I seriously doubt that Scarlet has lost any power. Perhaps she just needs a bit of persuasion." Alex took the mirror and set it to the side. She hoisted Shanghai onto my lap and propped the mirror in her hands so that I could see the reflection. "Since Singapore can see you, I assume Scarlet can as well. Perhaps she will rescue you."

"And if she can't?"

"I will have to assume you were right and go about my business." Alex nodded at the illuminaries. "You two stay here and guard Phoenix. Don't let him leave this room."

She walked away, skirting the abyss as she headed toward the exit. "Remember," she called, "if Scarlet rescues you, I still have Saigon's mother. If I don't find your scorched bodies among the ashes, I will assume you transported through the mirror." She stopped at the door, smoke veiling her as she turned toward me. "If you are rescued, contact me with your tablet, and we will set up a meeting. If not, Saigon's mother will die within twenty-four hours, and the entire city of Chicago will burn." She exited into the smoke and disappeared.

I shouted, "Alex!" My call ended with a hacking cough.

The illuminaries walked to my chair, one at each side, and stared at me with flashing red eyes. In the new silence, their motors hummed without a hint of worry that Alex had given them a suicide assignment. She was willing to sacrifice two of her few remaining active soldiers for a piece of glass that couldn't perform the magic she wished for.

Hoping to arouse Shanghai, I lifted a leg and prodded her with a knee. "Shanghai. Wake up. You have to untie me."

The tablet attached to my belt beeped. "Phoenix, this is Bartholomew. Can you hear me?"

I angled my head toward the tablet. "Yes. Can you hear me?"

"Barely."

"How can we talk without me manually permitting the link?"

"That's my tablet you're using. I didn't expect Saigon to steal it from me, but the outcome worked in our favor. I sent a private override code that allows me to control the unit. But no more time for that. Listen carefully. The fire will soon spread into the dome room. In order to escape, you must break the ropes that bind you."

"Don't you think I've tried? They're triple looped. It's impossible."

"It's not impossible. Any rope will snap if enough pressure is applied."

"A knife would be easier. Why don't you come back and cut me loose?"

"Because the way is blocked by flames. Not only that, it is essential that you do this yourself. I have led you through every step of the process to gain the strength you need to conquer Alex. Since the mirror is a sham, which I assumed all along, you need to —"

"Wait, wait. What do you mean you led me through? What are you talking about?"

"It's a long story, but here is a quick summary. You are a Phoenix Reaper. Exposure to radiation makes you stronger, just as it did to the first Phoenix. Saigon and I conspired to trap you in the electrified cage so I could expose you to the radiation. Her motivations were noble, but that's an unnecessary tangent.

"This is the relevant point. Watching the video of Shanghai being tortured incited you to call upon your new strength and break free. My hope was that this strength would be enough to conquer Alex, but either I miscalculated, or you have not yet been able to manifest your full potential simply because you didn't realize that it's there. You now have plenty of motivation. If you don't break free, you and Shanghai will both die. If you do, then you will have the power and confidence to face Alex again and kill her."

"So you're playing both sides," I said. "If I succeed and kill Alex, I owe it all to you. You'll be a hero. If I fail, you're Alex's number one agent and will be richly rewarded. Am I right?"

"Nonsense, Phoenix. I have always been on your side. Did you think I was blind or stupid, that I really didn't see you hiding in the corner of my office? And Saigon told me that you found the items I left for you. I trust that you also heard about Shanghai's real name etched behind the mirror in her cell. I did that to signal my alliance. Until you spilled the information about the clues, Alex knew nothing about them. The bottom line is that I'm the one who led you here to rescue Singapore. Yet, I couldn't simply tell you about my plans. You would never have agreed to my motivational tactics."

"You strapped bombs to little girls."

"I trusted your skill. No harm came of it."

"You drained Saigon of energy and tortured her. You chased her to my apartment with the threat of execution."

"To induce her to help. She became a valuable asset to a worthy cause."

A dozen insults begged to respond, but I batted them away. "Never mind. Just help me with one thing."

"What?"

"Even if I snap the ropes, Alex left two illuminaries to make sure I don't escape, the advanced ones that can break me in half."

"Yes, I heard. Incentive for Scarlet to act. Pure rubbish, if you ask me."

"Maybe so, but they're practically breathing down my neck. I might be able to handle one, but not both, especially if they attack me at the same time, or if one of them threatens Shanghai."

"A fair point. I will see if I can get a control tablet and power them down, or at least countermand Alex's directives. Maybe I can send them somewhere else."

"How long will that take?"

"Impossible to know. I have to search for the proper tablet. Just do what you must, and don't rely on my success. You have precious little time remaining."

"All right. All right. Just find the tablet. I'll keep trying to break loose."

"I wish you well, Phoenix. For both of our sakes. I fear that Alex will not take kindly to what you told her about me."

The tablet beeped again and fell silent. Flames licked the top of the exit-door frame. More smoke billowed in. I pulled and pulled against the ropes. My left arm, still stinging from the bullet wound, gave up first. I pressed my feet against the floor and tried to stand, but, as Alex had once told me, the chairs were bolted to the floor. I couldn't budge them.

I rested and let out a groan. I had set my own death trap. And Shanghai's. And Saigon's. Once again, guilt assaulted me. Every step of the way, I knew potential ambushes lay ahead, but I marched into each one, hoping I could beat the odds, avoid the snares, and somehow rescue a hostage. Bartholomew had learned well from Alex. Just bait me with a damsel in distress, and I would dive headlong into danger.

Near the door, fire crawled across the ceiling and began a slow advance up the dome. Tiles on the floor broke. Flames erupted in the gaps and crawled along the floor toward us. Smoke grew thicker, making it more and more difficult to breathe, as if a contest had commenced. Which would kill us first, fire or smoke?

I jerked against the ropes again. The scratchy fibers cut into my skin once more. Blood oozed from the wounds and moistened the fibers before trickling to the chair arms. I called out, "Sing, I don't know what to do. Is there any way you or Scarlet can help me?"

The mirror flashed. In the reflection, a young man about my age sat on the ground playing a violin in the midst of a lightning storm. Blood dripped from his hands as multicolored bolts crashed to the ground and ignited fires in surrounding buildings. A teenaged female sat between him and a red-haired young woman who held a small mirror in her lap. The girl in the middle had no eyes, just empty charred sockets.

As they sat on a pristine lawn, encircling flames drew closer and closer. Wind whipped their hair and clothes. The eyeless girl sang in spite of the storm. Intense pain twisted her face. The words squeaked out in rattled verse, laughter and sobs punctuating her song with shattered emotions.

Ascend on high, O captive ones,
And rise above the solemn sound;
Your joy will make the angels laugh
And lift your souls to higher ground.

I stared at the singer. Somehow she looked familiar, but I couldn't place her. What was the mirror trying to show me? A tragic event in the past? If so, how could this tortured girl with burned-out eyes sing such an optimistic song?

The mirror's image froze. Sing's whispered voice came from the glass, carrying words she had spoken not long ago. "More than two hundred years ago, the world was in much more danger. The tragedies of that time period would take too long to describe, but ancestors of yours did what was necessary to save the world."

My ancestors? The ones who used the mirror to transport out of danger? Then why were they stuck in this dangerous place? Why hadn't the mirror helped them escape?

As if reading my mind, Sing responded. "Escaping danger was not their goal. Saving the lives of countless innocents was their only thought, and this passion drove them to do the impossible."

I shouted, "I don't care if I escape, I just want to save Shanghai's life!"

"Then you must break your bonds," Sing said, her voice soft and calm. "There is no other way. You have new strength, and you have used it to some degree. Now you must summon it again. Reach deep within and release the fire, for only love will ignite the power you have been given."

I looked at Shanghai as she lay unconscious on my lap. Pink liquid continued oozing from her perforated eyelid and trickling down her bruised cheek. This courageous warrior had stood by my side every step of the way. When she thought I was wrong, she told me so, yet she stuck with me when my stubbornness refused to yield. Her passion for protecting the innocent, rescuing captives, and defeating evil were unequalled. She was the best person I knew, the woman who had captured my soul, not with her cloak, but with her heart, a heart of gold, a heart of compassion and truth. In the midst of sorrows, she was always there to lift me up. I needed her, without question. And now she needed me to save her life.

Only a few steps away, flames edged closer on the floor, gushing through cracks in the tiles like miniature geysers and inching around the abyss. Smoke infused every breath, making me cough and wheeze. The illuminaries still stared at me as if waiting for the slightest opportunity to pounce. They seemed not to care that in mere moments we would all perish. Their cloaks might protect them for a while, but intense heat would surely destroy their circuits.

The ropes, now lubricated by blood, allowed me to turn my arms until my gloved palms faced upward. I clenched my fists and pulled with all my might. The ropes stretched and yielded a tiny bit of slack, but not enough to slide my hands out.

Gasping for breath, I tried again. I flexed every muscle and pulled, screaming, "Shanghai, I love you! I don't want you to die!"

I strained, twisted my arms, and pulled yet again. More blood broke forth. Heat scalded my skin. Finally, my right arm ripped through the ropes. I reached over and tore away the bonds on the left. I shifted Shanghai to the floor, the mirror still in her grasp, then untied my ankles while blood dripped from my wrists and into my gloves.

When I threw the ropes to the side and rose to my feet, one of the illuminaries pushed me back down. I shoved it with both hands, sending it backpedaling. I rose again, grabbed the other illuminary, and threw it to the floor.

I scooped Shanghai into my arms and took a step toward the exit. Flames erupted just beyond the abyss. Part of the floor collapsed, revealing a blazing inferno in the sublevel. Another hole opened a few feet in front of the doorway, and a tower of flames blocked the exit. Only one escape remained — the dome over our heads. I had to get to the controlling switch on the side wall.

The illuminaries got up and charged. As smoke continued choking every breath, I ran with Shanghai toward the switch. The mirror fell to the side, but no matter. It couldn't help us now.

When I arrived at the wall, I found the toggle switch and pushed it with my nose. A grinding sound ensued. A circular gap appeared at the apex of the dome and widened quickly. Smoke poured through the hole, making it easier to breathe, though the flames continued emitting noxious fumes throughout the chamber.

One of the illuminaries snagged my hood and slung me away from the wall. Shanghai and I hit the floor and slid until we slammed into the back of a Council chair. The chair erupted in flames. I leaped to my feet and dragged Shanghai to safety a few paces away.

From the wall, the illuminaries marched toward me side by side. I grabbed a spool from my belt and threw the weighted end toward the receding ceiling. The claws caught the edge and held fast.

I picked Shanghai up and, using a bare hook on each of our belts, attached the back of hers to the front of mine, then pushed the spool's auto-reel. The motor whined. The illuminaries lunged. Grabbing the line with both gloved hands, I leaped away from their grasping fingers and climbed. As I ascended, the line swung us back toward the waiting robots.

They jumped and reached out. I lifted my feet, but one illuminary caught my cloak and jerked us to the floor, tearing my grip from the line and detaching Shanghai's belt from mine, though I managed to hang on to her with an arm. The spool slipped from my belt. Its motor engaged and sent it shooting toward the ceiling.

Lying on my right side with Shanghai, I instinctively raised my left arm just in time to block an illuminary's pounding fist. My forearm cracked. Pain roared to my neck and jolted my skull. Another fist crashed down on my shoulder near the bullet wound. A shock wave knifed into my spine.

I kicked one of the beasts in the knee. Its metallic leg snapped, and it toppled over and landed on Shanghai. I bit the end of my right glove and slipped my hand out, then dug my fingers into its eyes, latched on to the sockets, and ripped out its brain unit. Its arms fell limp, draping Shanghai with its cloak.

Expecting another blow from the remaining illuminary, I tried to raise my left arm, but it wouldn't move. The illuminary's dark fist zoomed toward me. I rolled into its legs and sent it toppling over to its back. I leaped to my feet, grabbed it by the ankle, and threw it into the surrounding fire.

The flames drew closer, now within three paces all around. After stripping off the other glove, I pushed the fallen illuminary off Shanghai, taking its cloak in the process. I wrapped her in the cloak and scooped her into my arms again, though tearing pain throttled my senses. My only hope was to dash through the flames and dodge the holes in the floor.

When I took a step, my broken forearm gave way. I caught Shanghai with my right arm and hoisted her over my shoulder. The air relatively clear because of the open dome, I took a deep breath and ran around the burning chairs.

When I passed the abyss, I slowed to a hobbled walk and looked into it. Radiance no longer spun within, its engines likely destroyed. Firelight provided a good view of emptiness all the way to the bottom. No sign of Sing or Saigon. Somehow they escaped. Maybe Saigon had transformed to ghost mode. But if so, did she rise to the Gateway? Maybe both were drawn into the sky.

With no time to ponder their fates, I ran ahead. As flaming geysers erupted from cracks in the tiles, I leaped from side to side to avoid them. About halfway to the door, the floor exploded in raging flames. The force sent me staggering in reverse. Something slammed into my spine. Shanghai flew from my shoulder, while I fell on my back. Sharp pain careened through my body, then faded to numbness.

I tried to get up. My limbs refused to help. My head moved but only side to side. I couldn't see behind me to check on Shanghai. Had I broken my back? Sprained it? Either way, I couldn't get up.

From behind me, an illuminary walked into view, its cloak smoking and its fist curled, the fist that had probably punched me in the back. It crouched over me, poised to strike again. I was helpless.

Just as its fist flew downward, it froze. Its eyes flashing like strobes, it straightened and marched into a wall of approaching flames and out the door.

I whispered, "Thanks, Bartholomew."

Again I tried to move my limbs, but they wouldn't budge. "Shanghai?" I shouted. "Can you hear me?"

Something touched my hand. "I'm here, Phoenix. Right here. Next to you. Always."

I gasped for breath. "Keep the cloak on. It's fire resistant. Maybe it'll save you. Just try to get out the best you can. I'm paralyzed, and there's no way you can carry me."

"I'll keep it on." She crawled over me chest to chest, grunting with every move. She draped the cloak over both of us, her arms spread to cover as much of me as possible. "But I'm not going anywhere without you."

In the firelight, her expression seemed at peace in spite of her horrific wounds. I breathed out, "Shanghai, I failed. Alex won."

Her lips firmed. "No. I refuse to believe that. We're going to get out of here alive, and we'll cut the head off that snake. If there is a God, I can't believe he would let it end this way. We'll survive somehow."

I tried to nod, but my head wouldn't move in that direction. "I love you, Shanghai. I love you with all my heart. But you have to get out."

"I love you, too, Phoenix. That's why I'm staying here." The encroaching flames sent scalding heat across my face. Shanghai pulled the cloak over our heads and laid her cheek on my chest. "Till death do us part."

The thick cloak allowed only the slightest glow to pass through, and the material covered my mouth, muffling my voice. "Shanghai, you can't. You have to —"

"Don't tell me what I can't do. I'm not turning tail this time." She grasped the cross as it lay on my chest. "No fear. Never again."

I opened my mouth to protest once more, but my strength had drained. I could barely breathe. With numbness dominating my body from the neck down, I couldn't feel Shanghai's weight or whether or not she had covered my legs or feet. If they burned, I wouldn't feel it.

I closed my eyes. Flames crackled closer. Heat radiated through the cloak and warmed my face. Shanghai's respiration and heart rate slowed, as if she had lost consciousness. "Shanghai?"

She continued breathing without answering, though another voice penetrated my senses. "Phoenix?"

I opened my eyes. "Vera?"

"I feel heat. And I heard you screaming. What's wrong?"

"I'm trapped in a burning building, surrounded by fire. I think I broke my back. I can't get up."

"Are all four limbs affected?"

"I think so. I can't move any of them."

"Any tingling in your toes or fingers?"

"Just my fingers. I can't feel anything past my waist."

"I will try to prod an arm through your cloak while Jasper examines your spine. Let us know what you feel."

"Can you find your way to the right places?" I asked.

"Yes. We've been exploring and figured out where everything is. A doctor's curiosity, you know." A tingle ran across my shoulder and along my arm. "Can you feel this?"

"Yes. A little."

Another tingle coursed down my back, and a slight sting prodded my spine. "How about this?" Jasper asked.

"Yes. Definitely."

"And this?"

The question came without a sting. "No. Nothing."

"Vera, it's no wonder he can't move his legs, but he should be able to move his arms."

"I agree," she said. "Phoenix, maybe you can belly crawl using just your arms."

"My left arm is broken, and I have to get Shanghai out of here. She's covering us both with a fire-resistant cloak."

"Are you lying on your back?" Jasper asked.

"Yes."

"If the fire is surrounding you, then why do I feel intense heat from below?"

"The sublevels are burning, and fire sometimes breaks through the floor, like an eruption."

"At the rate the temperature is increasing, I think you might be right over an impending eruption. The fire-resistant cloak won't help you or Shanghai."

"You need to wrap both of you in it," Vera said. "Use your arms. And hurry!"

"I told you my left arm is broken."

"Then use your right arm. If you don't, you'll both be toast. Literally."

Heat radiated into my neck, increasing rapidly. Jasper and Vera were right. Something was definitely about to blow. I slowly curled both hands into fists. A tingling sensation ran to my shoulders. Using my right arm, I pushed Shanghai off. She rolled to her back a foot away, the cloak open in front, her eyes closed.

Fire encroached from all directions, though the billowing smoke funneled up and out through the open dome, keeping the air breathable. When I lifted my left arm, pain at the break point surged. A tremor shook the floor. I had only seconds left to save Shanghai.

Shifting my body as much as possible, I reached with my right hand, drew her legs under the cloak, and closed it in front. Although pain hindered every move, I refused to let it stop me as I covered her face with the hood.

When I finished, I flopped down to my back. Heat erupted from underneath. Light flashed. New pain swallowed my head and shoulders. I was on fire. In seconds, I would be dead.

CHAPTER EIGHTEEN

COOL, SWIRLING WIND surrounded me. A bright light slowly orbited my head, but was it moving, or was I spinning? The only sensations were a gentle glow, cool air, and weightlessness — no noise or pain.

Eventually, tingles filtered to my toes. A sense of gravity pushed on my feet, as if I were standing. Music played somewhere, soft and sweet. The melody soothed my mind, like a refreshing shower during a stifling afternoon.

A familiar whisper broke in. "Phoenix, wake up."

"Sing?" I opened my eyes. I stood on my apartment's fire-escape platform. Across the alley, Sing sat on the railing, dressed in a Reaper's forest green pants and black running shoes. She no longer wore the Sancta cloak.

I looked at my apartment. The window was intact, no sign of the explosion that had destroyed my home.

I turned back to Sing. "What's going on? I thought I was in a burning ..." I let my words trail off. Was it all a dream?

"You were in a burning building, but that danger has passed." She patted the railing. "This is where we first talked. Remember?"

"But the explosion destroyed my apartment. And you were in the abyss. Trapped." I tilted my head. "Weren't you?"

"I was." She climbed to her feet and leaped over the alley gap. She landed on my platform with a soft touch and faced me. "The fire destroyed the abyss engines and the shield around the building. Since the dome was open, the Gateway drew me into the sky. I had changed to spirit form to survive the abyss, and I didn't have time to change back to a physical body. I was here before I knew it."

"Here? Where is here?"

"We are beyond the Gateway. In this realm, we can fashion any surroundings we choose. I thought a familiar place would be a comfortable setting for us to talk again."

"About what? And how can I be beyond the Gateway? Don't you have to die to get there?"

Sing nodded. "Yes, Phoenix. You are dead. And since you died in an unshielded room, you ascended to the Gateway without need of a Reaper."

I touched my chest. "I died?"

"A raging fire consumed your body, instantly expelling your soul. Since the fire also burned your cloak, the two souls you carried ascended to the Gateway as well, and they are safe. Although you are spiritual in essence, you feel as if you are in physical form, much like you felt whenever you transformed to ghost mode. Yet, here you will never feel pain or sickness. Every injury has been healed."

"What about Shanghai? Did she survive?"

"Let me show you." Sing waved a hand. The fire escape and the surrounding buildings dissolved, replaced by the dome room. Charred remains littered what was left of the floor. At least ten manhole-sized craters marked fire-eruption points.

Sing and I stood where the Council chairs had been. They were now nothing more than piles of gray ash, blown about by swirling air funneling in from the open dome.

"We are looking at a scene on earth as if we had a viewing mirror," Sing said. "Since we're beyond the Gateway, we're able to see three-dimensionally. We can watch events unfold around us and even walk close to objects to study the details."

I scanned the area where I had fallen with Shanghai. A lump of black material lay there, moving slightly. I ran toward the spot, dodging the holes in the floor.

"Phoenix," Sing called. "This is just an image. Your touch won't affect anything."

I halted next to the material — an illuminary's cloak covering what appeared to be a human body. It rose and fell in a respiration rhythm. Shanghai had to be lying within.

"What am I seeing? The present? The past?"

"This is a view of past events." Sing caught up and stood at my side. "When I returned here to look for survivors, I learned about Shanghai's condition, but I want to show you instead of telling you. Since I don't know what happened after I left, we can watch and learn together."

At the dome room's entrance, Bartholomew walked in, stepping carefully to avoid the holes. When he saw the cloak, he hurried to it, crouched, and peeked under the hood. He whispered, "She's alive."

He straightened and called out, "Phoenix? Are you here?" He hustled to the abyss. Sunlight shone from the open dome as he scanned the depths. After a few seconds, he returned to Shanghai, gathered her into his arms, and strode out with rapid steps, again careful to step on solid flooring.

When he walked out of sight, I turned to Sing. "Where did he take her?"

"I don't know. I wouldn't know where to look. Since I have been assigned to help you, it's much easier for me to open a viewer to where you are physically present, even if your presence is nothing but ashes."

"Ashes?" I crouched near the spot where Shanghai had been. A small pile of ashes lay on the floor. "Is this ... me?"

"Were you lying next to Shanghai?"

I nodded. "I think fire erupted from the floor and consumed me."

"You're probably right."

"Shouldn't the pile be a lot bigger?"

Sing squinted at the remains. "The pile *is* small. Maybe the passage of time will tell us more." She waved a hand. Night fell and flew by in seconds, replaced by daylight. Then another night ensued followed by rays of dawn. "Let's see if that's enough."

"Enough? How much time has passed since I died?"

"A few hours less than three days."

"Three days? That's strange. I couldn't guess at all. Other souls seem aware of time passage while they're wandering around as ghosts. Why the difference?"

"Yours is an unusual case. We'll discuss that soon."

Bartholomew walked in with a flashlight in hand. Although the rays of morning provided enough light to avoid the holes in the floor, he swept the beam across them slowly, as if searching for the safest spot to plant each foot.

About a minute later, Liam entered and surveyed the area. "This room is worse than the others."

"It is, indeed." Bartholomew turned and looked at him. "Did you find the box?"

Liam nodded as he drew closer. "Fully intact. The power and energy were still running, like you said."

"Hiding that from Alex was quite a chore, but I managed." Bartholomew gave him a small silvery cylinder that looked like a fuel cell. "When we finish here, put this in the box's energy input slot. That'll keep it running till we get back to Chicago."

Liam slid the cylinder into his pants pocket. "Will the box ride safely in your cargo carrier? It might stick out on the sides."

"I think so, but you can fly behind me and watch it."

Liam shifted from foot to foot. "I understand that we have to take it, but what will you do when you're finished with it?"

"Liam, don't worry. If Alex hasn't poisoned the well too thoroughly, we won't even use it, and I will provide the proper arrangements. I'm confident we'll find at least one person to volunteer."

"I would, but I have my wife and wee ones to —"

"Of course you do. No one would ever fault you for that. But we'll discuss the possibilities later." Bartholomew knelt close to my ashes and studied them. "The remains are far lower in volume than I expected."

Liam knelt with him, withdrew a whisk broom from his back pocket, and brushed the edge of the pile back. "Look. A hole."

"Let me check something." Bartholomew shifted to another hole and, lowering the flashlight below floor level, aimed the beam toward the ashes. "Just as I suspected. The tiled floor is above a concrete subfloor. The pile starts on the foundation and rises through the hole. Fire consumed Phoenix from underneath, and his ashes fell through. Looks like bone fragments are mixed in. It must have been quite a blaze to make them crumble."

"Like hell itself." Liam pulled a large plastic bag from under his jacket. "How could Shanghai have survived?"

"Hard to say," Bartholomew said as he continued looking under the floor. "Maybe Phoenix was directly over a fire eruption while she wasn't. When he started burning, she might have been unconscious from smoke inhalation and instinctively pulled the fireproof cloak around her body."

Liam nodded. "Which explains why she doesn't remember the details. Even if she did remember, I'm not sure she would tell me much. She doesn't want to talk about it.

"She probably feels guilty, but she shouldn't. I'm sure she had no chance to save him."

"Aye, but she's beside herself with guilt. Inconsolable. When she learned that the surgeon removed her damaged eye, her emotions tumbled all the more."

At this news, I stiffened. Grief swelled within. I longed to ask questions, but that was impossible.

Bartholomew flicked off his flashlight and rejoined Liam. "Has she mentioned what she plans to do now that Alex is taking control?"

"No, but I fear what she might do when she recovers her strength."

"A suicide mission to kill Alex is my guess."

Liam nodded again. "Exactly what I fear. She was able to walk last night, so she went to Phoenix's apartment to look for keepsakes, and she found her battle staff. It won't be long before she straps on a weapons belt and marches to war."

"To her death," Bartholomew said. "Alex has fueled every illuminary and moved them out of the warehouse.

Shanghai can't defeat one of those robots, much less a hundred or more. It's up to us to stop Alex, but we can't let Shanghai know what we're doing. She wouldn't like it."

"I don't like it, either, but it's the only way. I will keep the secret."

"Good." Bartholomew withdrew a spoon from his shirt pocket. "Let's get to work. If my reading of the legend is accurate, we have to be careful to collect every particle. It's an untested theory, but it's the last hope we have."

Using the spoon, Bartholomew scooped ashes into the plastic bag held by Liam. After every few scoops, Liam swept any spilled ashes back into the pile.

I turned to Sing. "What are they going to do with my ashes?"

"I don't know. I'm just learning about this now. Like I said before, I came here to look for survivors and then returned to the Gateway. But I will tell you what I saw while I was here. Shortly after the fire burned itself out, Alex came in to see who survived. She found the mirror on the floor near the remains of the Council chairs and took it. She might think the mirror transported you to safety. I'm not sure."

"Okay. Then what?"

"When she saw Shanghai on the floor, she drew a knife to finish her off. I let myself be seen and charged straight at her, screaming in Japanese. She ran like a bat out of hell."

I allowed a smile to break through in spite of my dismal mood. "Good. You saved Shanghai's life."

Sing nodded. "But I couldn't stay. Once I learned that you were dead, I had to leave. My mission on earth is over."

Her last statement felt heavy, final, and her sad expression reflected her disappointment. But there was nothing

I could do about it. I had to keep probing for information. "Liam mentioned a box he found. Any idea what it is?"

Sing shook her head. "And all of that stuff about a volunteer and Alex poisoning the well didn't make any sense."

"Whatever the box is, it needs energy." I walked around the two men as Liam collected bone fragments from the pile, using a set of small tongs. "They came prepared to take my remains. Someone must have known I burned up, or at least thought I did. Since Bartholomew called my name, he wasn't sure."

Sing tapped a finger on her chin. "The collecting of your ashes is troubling me. I should ask Scarlet about it. Although she no longer comes here, she is still the head of our order."

"Sure. Ask her. But in the meantime, what can I do to help Shanghai?"

Sing folded her hands at her waist, her expression somber. "Nothing, Phoenix. You died. You're beyond the Gateway now."

"But can you ask for an exception? You said I'm a special case. What did you mean?"

Sing wrinkled her nose. "Well, it's like this. Since fire consumed your body, your soul was, in a manner of speaking, spat out, expelled violently instead of gently removed by a Reaper or gradually separated by natural processes. Your soul was immediately swept through the Gateway in a traumatized state. That's unusual enough and explains your time disorientation, but there's more.

"When you arrived, you were not immediately sorted, that is, you didn't travel the path to peace or the path to destruction. You stayed in what we call the vestibule, which is why you didn't regain your senses for a while. The same thing happened to both my mother and me."

"And you both went back to earth," I said. "Maybe that's why I'm stuck in the vestibule. I'm supposed to return to earth."

"That thought did occur to me, but there are two big differences. One, Peter brought my mother's soul back across the Gateway, and my mother brought mine back. Only a Reaper can do that, and the Reaper has to die to make it happen. I'm sure you don't want Shanghai to sacrifice herself to pull you from beyond the Gateway."

"No, definitely not."

"And difference number two is the clincher. My body and my mother's body were kept in stasis. Your body was burned to ashes. Even if Shanghai did pull you back, you don't have a body to return to. You would be a ghost on the earth, and Shanghai would be beyond the Gateway."

I shook my head slowly. "I can't imagine asking any Reaper to die for me, especially Shanghai or Saigon."

"Phoenix ..." Sing took a deep breath. "Saigon didn't survive the abyss. The electric field was killing her. She switched to ghost mode, but it was too late. When the abyss engines stopped, she and I both ascended to the Gateway along with any souls she was carrying in her cloak."

Imagining the scene brought a new weight of guilt. I had made so many mistakes that resulted in death. If only I had killed Alex when I had the chance, Saigon might still be alive. "I assume she went to the path of peace."

"I hope so. I haven't heard."

"Any idea what happened to her mother? I mean, physically?"

"That I do know." Sing bit her lip. "She's dead."

"What? How? Why? Alex was going to use her as leverage if the mirror helped me escape."

"I suppose the fire got to her too quickly. When I went to earth to look for you, I found her scorched body, her arms still locked in chains."

My muscles tensed. No words came to mind. What could I say that would describe the darkness in Alex's heart or my crushing guilt?

"I didn't see what happened to Saigon's mother's soul," Sing continued, "but she must've gone straight to the Gateway."

"You're probably right," I whispered, my throat too tight to speak any louder.

"At least maybe Saigon and her mother are together. If they traveled the path of peace, they'll never suffer again."

I touched my chest. "Then why am *I* still suffering? I'm stuck here worried about Shanghai. The people of Chicago. The world. And I can't do anything about it."

"It's because you're in the vestibule. Once you go on to heaven, all worry will be erased."

I shouted, "But I don't *want* it to be erased! I don't want to live in a fantasy world pretending nothing's wrong. I want to help Shanghai! I want to stop Alex!"

Sing waved a hand. "Phoenix, calm down. When you get to heaven, you'll understand. There you will find peace. Misty is waiting for you, and she'll help you —"

"No! Stop it!" I clapped my hands over my ears, but Misty's name still echoed. Although the thought of her once brought delight, now it stabbed me with yet another dagger of guilt. "I can't be with Misty. And I can't be here. I have work to do on earth."

"Not anymore, Phoenix. You have to face the truth. You're dead. Your life on earth is over."

I paced the dome room floor. "I *can't* face it. It's just not right. I could never be at peace here, not when Shanghai needs me, not when Alex is about to run roughshod across the planet. Not when every man, woman, and child will suffer because of her sick, demented, evil plans. Not when my stupid decisions not to kill her gave her another chance to hatch her plans. And now, even as idiotic as I was, I can't help but think that I'm the only person who can stop her."

"Your lament makes perfect sense, Phoenix." As I continued pacing, Sing stared at me from under a tight brow. "I don't understand. Scarlet said even in the vestibule you would start becoming content with the idea of leaving earth, but you're getting more and more agitated. If only you could hear your voice. You're really getting carried away."

"Okay. Okay. I'll calm down." I halted and inhaled deeply. After letting my emotions settle, I looked again at Sing. "Where's Scarlet? Maybe I should talk to her."

"She went to discuss your case with a higher authority, to find out why you stalled here in the vestibule. Since a Sancta was in charge of your progress, it's her responsibility."

"When will she return?"

"I don't know. I have no idea how long —"

"I have returned."

The soft yet authoritative voice came from the dome room's entry doors. A red-haired girl who appeared to be no older than sixteen walked in, her gait as graceful as a waltz. Adorned in a simple red dress that buttoned high in front and dropped past her knees, she halted within reach and folded her hands at her waist.

She stared at me with piercing eyes. Her smooth skin, smallish nose, and narrow chin made her seem even younger close up. Yet, her stunning beauty gave her the appearance of an ageless goddess. "Phoenix, you look so much like my beloved Nathan. The resemblance is striking."

"Nathan?" I asked.

Scarlet's stare stayed locked on me. "Kelly's husband, the gifted one for whom I powered the mirror. Your ancestor." After a few seconds, she broke the stare and nodded. "Yes, I see that it's true."

"What's true?"

"The reason you could never be content here. The same reason you halted in the vestibule. You never completed your purpose on earth."

I nodded rapidly. "Right. It's not complete. So I have to go back."

She smiled. "As if you think I can snap my fingers and send you there. You have no body to inhabit."

"But you're powerful, right? You could transport people instantly through a mirror. Surely you can —"

"Can what? Form a new body out of ashes?" She reached for my hand and took it in hers. "First of all, Phoenix, the mirror lost its transporting ability long ago. Second, you died because of your own lack of preparation and execution. I have a full report from Singapore. She warned you repeatedly to attack and kill Alex, did she not?"

I let my shoulders droop. "She did."

"And you allowed other circumstances to stop you, exactly as you were warned against."

I gave her a resigned nod. "Guilty as charged."

Scarlet's eyes shimmered, much like Alex's, though reddish instead of silvery. "Then how can you be trusted to alter your path? What will prevent you from allowing fear to chart your course? In short, what has changed?"

"It wasn't fear that charted my course. I know it looks that way, but it wasn't."

Scarlet lifted her brow. "Oh? Then please explain."

I released her hand and pressed mine over my heart. "It was love. I love Shanghai. And Sing. And I've grown to love Saigon. I don't want them to suffer. The same with the citizens of Chicago."

"And what has been the result?"

"You already know. Complete failure. Alex is on a rampage, Saigon and her mother are dead, and Shanghai lost an eye. It's been a disaster."

Scarlet sighed. "A disaster for us as well. Singapore was thrown into the abyss and is now here, mourning over a failed mission."

I looked at Sing. She dipped her head low to avoid eye contact. Obviously my decisions had reached even into heaven and cast shadows there. Yet, couldn't I undo the damage? I needed one more chance. "Scarlet, you asked what has changed. I have. Misty once told me that I was God's instrument to heal the world. I believe that. But I'm still learning what it means."

I slid my hands into my cloak pockets. Odd that I was still wearing it, as if I still needed it for an uncompleted task. And even more odd, the journal was still in one of the pockets. "I guess I felt like I'm the only one bearing a sword, but now that I'm dead, I realize that the battle goes on without me. I'm expendable. This war isn't about me. It's so much bigger. I needed to do my part and not try to save the world by myself. My duty was to kill Alex and let

God take care of everyone else. But I still feel like I'm the best weapon against her. I just wish I could try again."

"Oh, Phoenix." Scarlet pulled me into her arms and laid her head against my chest. "You are so much like Nathan, so willing to confess your wrongs, so anxious to make them right." She pulled away and looked at me once more. "How I wish I could send you back, but, like I said, you have no body to inhabit."

"Right. And no Reaper to pull me through the Gateway."

Scarlet lifted a finger. "Actually, that part is not an issue."

"What do you mean?"

"Saigon never came through. She refused. She said she heard from you that Reapers can pull people from beyond the Gateway, and she waited at the boundary to see if you would survive. When she learned that you died, she said she would stay put until she could bring you back."

A lump swelled in my throat. "I don't know what to say. Did you tell her about my body being burned to ashes?"

Scarlet nodded. "And that her mother was already in heaven waiting for her, but she was adamant that she knew her duty, and she was bound and determined to carry it out. She said someone else could decide what to do with you once you got back to earth. So she's still waiting there."

"Well, then can I go to earth as a ghost? Maybe I could do some good."

Scarlet shook her head. "It is not natural for disembodied souls to walk the earth. It is an aberration that we cannot support by adding to their numbers. It would be a violation of a heavenly principle. I'm sure you understand."

"Trust me. I know about principles. They've always been the reason I couldn't bring myself to attack Alex, the reason I have to protect Shanghai and the others. It's part of who I am."

"Who you *were*." Scarlet lifted Bill's cross from my chest and set it on her palm. "You decided to follow Yeshua, and you did it literally, even to the point of sacrificial death. Yet, you also did so spiritually. Your old self died, and you are a new person. As you said, you no longer have fear, only love."

Scarlet stepped back and looked again at Sing, then at me. Her irises glimmered as she stared long and hard. Finally, she nodded. "Now I understand."

"Understand what?" I asked.

"Why you had to die."

CHAPTER NINETEEN

"HAD TO DIE?" I said. "What do you mean?"

"I will try to explain in a moment." Scarlet turned toward Sing. "Did you show him the story of the original Phoenix?"

Sing nodded. "He saw it."

"Then he knows his ancestor was named after the mythical resurrection bird." Scarlet looked at me again. "I gave Nathan a prophecy, a promise, actually, that one of his descendants would rise from the ashes to save the world."

"From the ashes," I repeated. "Literally?"

"At the time I spoke the prophecy, I didn't know, but now I think so." She pressed a finger against my chest. "You are the Phoenix bird. You died, and you need to be reborn. In your previous life, you brought mercy in your wings, but Alex rejected your kindness. When you rise, you will deliver wrath. This death has prepared you for your new course."

My hands trembled along with my voice. "Okay, but how do I rise?"

"I don't know, but now I am convinced that we must make it happen."

I turned to Sing. "Any ideas?"

She pursed her lips. "Well, since Bartholomew read Kelly's journal, he knows about the prophecy. That has to be why he collected your ashes."

"Where is the journal?" Scarlet asked. "Maybe we can induce someone on earth to read it."

"It was in my pocket when I burned." I withdrew it and showed it to her. "Somehow I still have it."

"That's not unusual. You have a resurrected copy much like you have a resurrected presence yourself." Scarlet took the journal and leafed through its perfectly restored pages. After nearly a minute, she stopped. "Here it is." She silently read the page and the following one. "Apparently there are several versions of the Phoenix legend, but according to the one Kelly believed, the Phoenix rises when the ashes of a person who loved him are intermixed with his in a fire. The Phoenix resurrects within the flames, immune to their influence. It seems that the sacrifice of love draws his soul to the blending."

The lump in my throat returned. "You mean someone who loves me has to die?"

Scarlet looked at me and nodded. "A willing sacrifice."

"So Bartholomew is trying to get the process started, and he needs a volunteer, but does he know everything he's supposed to do? The journal he had was badly fragmented."

"We should talk to Saigon," Sing said. "Since she and Bartholomew worked together, maybe she knows something we don't."

"Come." Scarlet extended a hand. "We'll go together."

I grasped her hand, and Sing took mine on the other side. A moment later, the dome room dissolved. A pristine meadow appeared around us — lush grass that stretched beyond the limits of sight to both sides and behind us.

Blossoming flowers dotted the greenery with vibrant blues, reds, and yellows.

Straight ahead, a black iron fence with a double gate divided the meadow from a gray expanse on the other side, ground that looked like ankle-high fog.

Saigon sat alone at the near edge of the grayness. Wearing Reaper garb with her hood pulled back revealing restored hair, she leaned sideways against one of the gate's iron bars.

I ran toward her, calling, "Saigon, it's me, Phoenix."

She grasped the bars and pulled herself to her feet. When she saw me, she set a hand on her hip and smiled. "Well, it's about time, hero boy. I asked every angel and soul who came by to go and fetch you."

Hoping to lock wrists with her, I reached between the bars, but when my hand touched the boundary, it wouldn't go through. Light sizzled at the point of contact — not painful, just impenetrable. "Sorry for the delay. I came as soon as I could."

She looked past me and whispered, "So it's all true. You're dead. I'm dead. I heard my mother is, too."

I lowered my voice as well. "That's what they told me, and the head of the Sanctae said you want to pull me back."

"Right. It's kind of like a duty, you know? I might be the only Reaper on this side of the Gateway besides Shanghai."

I glanced behind me. Sing and Scarlet stood several paces away, both reading the journal. I refocused on Saigon and pressed a hand against one of the bars. "Can you tell me more about you and Bartholomew working together?"

She heaved a sigh. "Look, I know I pulled the wool over your eyes, but it wasn't to betray you. It was to make you stronger. Bart did all this research about your ancestors. He said exposing you to radiation would kick you into high gear so you could kill Alex, but since you would never agree to getting doused by a flood of deadly gas, we had to lure you into that cage in the warehouse. He said putting Sing in there would get you to go inside for sure."

"But she wasn't in there."

Saigon narrowed her eyes. "Yes, she was. I saw her myself. The whole point was to lock you in and force you to break the cage door, you know, by being motivated to rescue her. You needed hero-type persuasion."

I shook my head. "He lied to you. What you saw was a photo-stick hologram. My motivation was watching Shanghai getting beaten up."

"What?" Saigon clutched two bars tightly. "I swear I knew nothing about that. I mean, I saw Shanghai getting beaten up, but I never agreed to it. That was the whole reason I told him Sing is the Sancta, to use her as bait and a motivator and also to give him a reason not to torture anyone."

I stared at her long and hard. Her testimony matched the facts. I had to give her the benefit of the doubt. "It's all right. I understand."

She exhaled, obviously relieved. "Anyway, Bart expected you to attack Alex and kill her, but ... well, you were there. You know what happened."

"Did he say anything about my ashes?"

Saigon blinked. "What?"

"My ashes. Did Bartholomew mention them?"

"Not that I can ..." She furrowed her brow. "No. Wait. He said something about a Plan B, kind of in passing, that if you died in a fire, then some sort of prophecy was true. He didn't use the word *ashes*, but the fire thing sounds related."

"What's Plan B, then?"

"No idea. When I asked him what he was talking about, he brushed me off, saying it was a joke." Saigon shrugged. "That's all I know."

"Then he read the prophecy in the journal. He's preparing for it."

"What are you talking about? What prophecy?"

I gave her a quick explanation and finished with, "So I'm wondering if he's planning to sacrifice a volunteer to bring me back to life. Probably Shanghai."

"Not likely, Phoenix," Sing said as she and Scarlet joined me at the gate. Sing slid the journal into my cloak pocket. "According to the Kelly, *anyone* who loves you can be the sacrifice. Bartholomew acted like he didn't want Shanghai to know what he was up to. Remember?"

That part of his conversation with Liam flowed back to mind. Sing was right. Yet, why would he bother trying to find a volunteer when Shanghai would be willing if asked?

"All right," I said, "suppose Saigon pulls me back through the Gateway now. Will I wait on that side till Bartholomew sacrifices someone?"

Scarlet nodded. "A soul and its body are brought together by a spark of life. Erin gave her spark so Tokyo could rise. You and Shanghai hoped to do the same for Singapore, though your efforts were never brought to fruition."

"Because I didn't want to return," Sing said to Scarlet. "I had terminal cancer, and I would just die a horrible death. I also wanted to be with my mother, not to mention that I didn't want anyone to give their spark of life to me."

"Yes," Scarlet said. "I heard the report."

"So is it *impossible* for someone to resurrect without a life spark?" Sing asked.

"Impossible for normal souls, but in your current Sancta form, you could resurrect to your cancer-riddled body without someone giving you a spark."

"Really?" Sing said. "I didn't see that in the journal."

"We didn't read all of it, but it could be there. It's part of Sancta lore."

Sing whispered, "Interesting."

"Interesting but not relevant." Scarlet turned toward me. "No matter what Bartholomew does with your ashes, someone will have to sacrifice his or her life to resurrect you. You will need a life spark."

At that moment, more of the conversation between Bartholomew and Liam made sense. They were saying they might not be able to find a sacrifice if Alex had poisoned the well, that is, convinced everyone that I was a villain. Also, the part about having something in a box clarified. "So Bartholomew probably got a life-spark crystal. There were a few left in the crucible. Maybe that's what's in the box Liam found. It needs energy to keep the crystals alive."

I shook my head at my own words. "No. Bartholomew made it sound like the box was a backup plan. If he gets a volunteer, he won't need whatever's in there."

"Then the box remains a mystery," Sing said. "We'll have to wait to see how events unfold."

I nodded. "I just wish I could put a stop to the whole business. I don't want anyone to die for me."

"When someone dies for another person," Scarlet said, "it is rarely the choice of the beneficiary. The benefactor is the one who chooses. You have no way to stop the sacrifice."

The truth of her statement weighed heavily. Someone on earth might soon give his or her life for mine. I felt weak, helpless, undeserving.

"Yet, you can still decide to stay here," Scarlet continued. "You don't have to accept Saigon's offer to pull you back."

I shook my head hard. "No. That's the worst possible option. If I stay, someone might sacrifice for me anyway, and then that person would die for no reason. I have to get back to earth."

"Very well," Scarlet said, "but you won't go until the life-spark crystal has done its work. Saigon can pull you to the other side of the Gateway, and you will stay on the threshold until you are drawn back by your physical body's resurrection. If that doesn't happen soon, you will have to return to this side."

"I understand. I don't want it to happen, but I understand." I turned to Saigon. "I'm ready if you are."

"Ready." She looked at Scarlet. "What do I do?"

"It's quite simple." Scarlet grasped a bar near the central latch and swung the gate open. "Just reach over, take Phoenix's hand, and pull him across while you leap in. You are able to come to this side, but he can't pass the boundary until you draw him out."

Saigon extended a hand through the opening. Sizzling sparks coated her sleeve and crawled toward her shoulder until her motion stopped. I grasped her hand. She pulled me forward and jumped into the boundary at the same time.

As I crossed, light flashed. The soft music evaporated. Perfect comfort altered to a sense of deep, bitter coldness, as if someone had stripped off my clothes and abandoned me in a snowstorm.

Shivering, I turned back. When Scarlet began closing the gate, Sing stopped her and whispered into her ear.

Scarlet dipped her brow. "Why would you want to do that?"

Sing glanced at me, then refocused on Scarlet. "I just want to know if it's an option."

Scarlet also cast a glance at me. "I understand." After firming her lips for a moment, she said, "It would work, but there are crucial consequences. I'm sure you know what I mean."

Sing lowered her head. "I do, but I don't think it will happen. It's just a precaution."

"Very well, then." Scarlet pulled the gate open again. Sing walked through with ease, not hindered by the blocking field or needing a Reaper's help. Her red cloak reappeared, covering her Reaper garb.

"What was that all about?" I asked.

"Secret Sancta business." She took my hand. "It seems that my mission is not yet finished."

"Good. I'll need all the help I can get."

The Gateway closed with a metallic clank. Smiling from the other side, Saigon said, "I hope it'll be a long time before I see you again, Phoenix. At least seventy years or so."

I reached between two bars and grasped her hand. "Thank you, Saigon. You've been a great help. And don't worry about pulling the wool over my eyes. I know you had good intentions."

"That means a lot to me. Really." She released my hand, turned, and walked away with Scarlet. Seconds later, they faded from sight.

With the music gone, all was quiet. Mist twirled slowly above the spongy ground. All we could do now was chat through the wait, however long it might take.

"So, I suppose you're able to leave without a Reaper's help because you're a Sancta."

Sing nodded. "I have a new essence, neither completely physical nor completely spiritual. As long as my mission on earth continues, I have the authority to come and go as I please."

"I wish *I* had that authority. I have to count on someone to sacrifice himself, and I don't even know who it might be. And, like I said before, I don't want anyone to die for me, but I can't stop it no matter what."

"No, you can't. But maybe I can. That's the reason I asked Scarlet if my mission could continue." Sing waved a hand as if washing a window. "I'm setting up a viewing screen. When I arrive on earth, it will expand into three dimensions in the place where your ashes reside and show present events as they happen. This way, you'll be able to follow my progress."

"All right. Good."

She grasped my hand, raised it to her lips, and kissed my knuckles. "Pray that wisdom will guide our steps." She gazed at me with tear-filled eyes until she faded and disappeared.

My hand held empty air. As I looked at my fingers, her words echoed. *Secret Sancta business.* Although I ached to know what she had in mind, obviously she wasn't ready to tell me, but at least I would soon have a chance to watch her work.

I stared at the spot where Sing had waved a hand. A pane of glass hovered in the air, reflecting my face, still smeared with ashes from forehead to chin. The visage seemed odd. I was dead, a disembodied soul. Why would I manifest in this condition?

The pane flashed. My reflection evaporated, replaced by a street scene — pavement, sidewalks, and people milling about, including at least twenty who waited in line in front of a gray metal table that sat in the middle of the street.

The scene expanded and surrounded me. I stood next to a woman at the front of the line. Smoke filled the air, casting a haze over everyone and everything. Fires blazed in several nearby buildings, maybe one in every three.

Hundreds of men, women, and children huddled in the street. Smoky skies had become their shelter, though bitter wind assaulted them as if trying to sweep them back to the infernos that had spat them from their homes.

Some wore coats and hats. Others had only pajamas or even less, forcing them to warm themselves near the very fires that had left them destitute.

The crowd appeared to be watching the people in line. Wearing a bulky coat, gloves, and a hat with earflaps, Bartholomew sat in a wooden chair at the other side of the table, his fingers near the base of a gray urn, similar to the ones the executioners shoveled ashes into after burning their prisoners. To his right, a small wicker basket sat next to a covered foundry crucible and a pair of tongs.

I eyed the crucible, the same one Erin kept the life-spark crystals in. Had they stored this crucible in the box they mentioned earlier? It seemed that the puzzle pieces might be coming together.

Bartholomew poised a pen above a sheet of paper, his hooked nose making him look like a bird of prey searching for victims. Vapor puffed from his lips as he spoke. "Name?"

The woman at the front of the line stepped closer. "Fiona Fitzpatrick," she said with a heavy Irish brogue.

I sucked in a breath and looked closer. Not only did Fiona wear a dirty, long-sleeved dress and a hat that covered her hair as well as her ears, soot smudged nearly every inch of her face. No wonder I didn't recognize her right away.

Bartholomew squinted at her. "I know that name. Don't you have two little girls?"

Fiona nodded. "Betsy and Anne plus my dear Molly in heaven. If I get picked, then it's God's will. I have someone who'll take care of my girls. I'll do anything for Phoenix. He risked his life to save my family time and time again." Tears ran down her filthy cheeks. "When I heard he was in the city savin' folks from the fires, I just had to come and help people escape; let him know he's not alone in this fight. I hoped to tell him one more time how much I love him, but then he ... he ..." She abruptly walked away, sobbing.

Bartholomew tore the portion of the sheet that held her name and palmed it as he pretended to drop it into the basket. Probably no one saw the stealthy move besides me. "Next," he called.

A hefty black woman stepped up to the table. "Georgia Taylor. Phoenix came to my house in the worst blizzard in a century to reap my little Tanya, and he was a mentor to my son, Noah. Since my husband and both of my children are in heaven, put my name in there ten times. Or a hundred. I should be the one to die for Phoenix."

"Well, you certainly qualify on the love aspect." Bartholomew wrote her name on the page and tore it off. "But just one entry. Fair is fair." He tossed the scrap into the basket, this time for real. "Next."

Iris's father stepped up. "Cyrus Biddle. Phoenix saved my wife and children." He lowered his head. "Well, all except Iris, but her ghost told me how he faced death in the fire for all of them. He's a hero, no matter what lies Alex tells. We need him to return to stop her, and if I have to die to make it happen, so be it."

"You qualify." Bartholomew wrote his name and set the scrap in the basket. "Next."

Another man stepped up and recalled a tale about me smuggling an illegal antibiotic that saved his wife from a bout of pneumonia, though she died of cancer several months later. Now alone, he wanted to be the one to sacrifice himself to bring me back from the ashes.

And so it continued. One at a time, more volunteers recounted tales about how I helped them. Some stories I remembered; others I had forgotten. Each person shivered in the cold wind with the telling, though their hearts seemed on fire as voices shattered and tears flowed.

While I watched and listened, a flash of red caught my attention. Sing walked behind Bartholomew and approached another table a few paces away. A rectangular box about six feet long lay on the table's surface. Sing looked into it as if it had a glass top, but I couldn't tell from where I stood. Might this be the box Bartholomew and Liam had talked about?

I took a step toward it, but a loud call made me stop. "Who is on Phoenix's side?"

Everyone turned toward the sound. The crowd divided, revealing Shanghai as she strode down the street, shoulders back and head erect, her battle staff in hand. Wearing a patch over her left eye and dark bruises on both cheeks, she swaggered forward, disguising a limp as her cloak flapped in the breeze.

When she arrived, those in line gave way. She stood in front of the table, her visible eye sharp and sparkling.

Bartholomew shuddered, fear in his expression. "Have you come to volunteer?"

"Volunteer for a sacrifice that you concocted?" Shanghai shook her head. "I have come to call for volunteers for a different cause. We have plenty of people who are ready to die for Phoenix, and their love is real, honest, and good. They are heroes in their own right, and I hope for their sakes that your research is correct." She withdrew a dagger from her belt. "Yet for me, a woman who loves Phoenix with all her heart, I cannot give my body over to be burned. No, not while I still have breath, not while I can set one foot in front of another and march to war. I have to avenge my beloved's death. I have to kill Alex."

Gasps rose from the crowd. While the stirring settled, I glanced at Sing. She turned semitransparent and stood motionless, still staring into the box. I edged toward her, pulled by competing forces — to see what Sing was looking at and to stay close to Shanghai.

"Who will go with me?" Shanghai continued as she lifted her staff high. "Who will help me rid the world of this devilish scourge once and for all?"

Liam stepped out of the crowd. "I will."

"That's one." Shanghai lowered her staff and scanned the people, her brow deeply furrowed. "Anyone else?"

"It's suicide," a man said, shivering as he held a little girl's hand. "They say she has hundreds of Peace Patrollers at the City Center building. It's impossible."

"Not if we counter hundreds of them with thousands of us."

He snorted. "You have two. Where are you going to get thousands?"

"Thousands always start with one or two." She scanned the crowd again, but no one else volunteered. "Very well, then, we'll settle for two." She gave the dagger to Liam and grasped his arm. "No fear?"

He clutched the hilt tightly. "No fear."

"Then let's go." They strode away side by side. Soon, smoke drew a gray curtain behind them.

Silence descended. Bartholomew rose from his chair and called out, "Since Shanghai's attack will surely incite Alex to launch her onslaught, we don't have time to take any more names. We'll pick one now and begin the ceremony." He reached into the basket, withdrew a scrap of paper, and read the name out loud. "Fiona Fitzpatrick."

CHAPTER TWENTY

I GRITTED MY TEETH. This couldn't be. Bartholomew rigged the drawing to choose Fiona. But why? She had two young daughters to care for, two precious little girls Saigon and I had saved only a few days earlier. Would they soon be without a mother?

I looked at Sing. She had to stop the sacrifice. She couldn't let Fiona die for me. It was madness.

Although Sing couldn't see me, she nodded in my direction. Her lips twitched into a weak smile, though her eyes spelled torturous pain. She climbed onto the box and passed through the top. As she sank inside, Bartholomew picked up the items on the table and set the urn and basket on the ground. Still holding the crucible and tongs, he said, "Start the fire. The table will be our altar."

While a pair of men turned the table over and piled kindling on the underside, I walked to the box. The glass top had frosted over, not allowing a view inside. I instinctively tried to open it, but my hands passed through the lid.

Moments later, a knee-high fire crackled at the table. Fiona stood on one side of the flames, Bartholomew on the other. She shed her coat and handed it to a woman standing nearby. Sobbing spasms rocked Fiona's voice as she said, "Give my love to Anne and Betsy."

I ran to her and shouted, "No! You can't do this! Don't die for me!"

My call went unheeded, unnoticed.

Bartholomew opened the crucible and used the tongs to withdraw a life-spark crystal, a shining ball the size of a fingernail with tiny pliable spikes covering the surface.

As he extended the crystal toward Fiona, his arm over the fire, she opened her mouth to receive it.

I trembled. If she swallowed that crystal, there would be no turning back. She would die in mere seconds. Why hadn't Sing put a stop to this? She just disappeared into the box for no apparent reason.

When the crystal came within inches of Fiona's mouth, Sing shouted, "Stop!"

The box lay open. Sing crawled out and down to the ground, wincing with the effort. Now dressed only in Reaper garb, she hobbled toward the fire. With every step, she grimaced. "Let me do it."

I stood motionless, paralyzed by the scene unfolding. Sing looked so different — gaunt and weak — far from the glorious Sancta she had been only moments ago.

Bartholomew drew the crystal back from Fiona. "Welcome, Singapore. I was worried you weren't going to show up."

His plan suddenly registered. The box held Sing's body in stasis. He had hidden it from Alex at the Gateway building, and I had forgotten it was still there. He intentionally chose the sacrifice volunteer most likely to make Sing act. If he had picked a single man, a widow, or someone else upon whom no one depended, maybe Sing would have let it happen. Bartholomew *wanted* Sing to be the sacrifice. He took a huge risk, a cruel risk, but it worked.

Sing halted next to him. "I wasn't going to come until I figured out your plan." Again grimacing, she laid a hand over her chest, her fingers splayed, revealing the hole where her fake valve used to be. "I forgot how much it hurts."

"The cancer?"

"Yes. It probably got worse while I was in stasis." She straightened and took on a brave face. "Let's get this over with. Regarding love for Phoenix, I assume I qualify."

"Without a doubt." He extended the crystal. "Open your mouth."

"Wait," Fiona said with a trembling voice. "Does this mean she's takin' my place?"

Bartholomew nodded. "It would require too much time to explain, but suffice it to say that Singapore is dying of cancer and wants to be the sacrifice, assuming you don't object."

"Object?" Fiona fanned her face. "I pretended to be a brave soldier, but I was shakin' in my boots. By all means, she can take my place."

Sing opened her mouth. When Bartholomew laid the crystal on her tongue, she closed her mouth and swallowed.

Bartholomew picked up the urn and set it in Sing's hands. "Do you know what to do?" he asked.

She nodded. "I read the journal." She walked into the fire to a chorus of gasps from the crowd. Holding the urn at her chest, she looked straight at me and mouthed, "I love you."

The flames caught the cloak around her legs and crawled up to her waist. She closed her eyes and grimaced once more. As the fire enveloped her, she opened the urn and poured my ashes over her head. The gray fragments and sooty powder spilled over her shoulders and into the flames.

As a spray of sparks flew into the air and swirled in the breeze, heat coursed through my body, as if generated by my ashes' contact with the fire.

A powerful force pulled me toward Sing. I gave in willingly, eagerly. I walked into the fire and wrapped my arms around her. Although I expected to feel only air, I felt her body — hot and weak. She groaned and whispered in gasping spurts. "I ... I feel you ... Phoenix. Will you ... stay with me?"

"Until the end." I hugged her close. "And forever."

"Forever?" A pain-streaked laugh followed. "Someday. But now you ... won't have to ... worry about me ... showing up uninvited. ... My Sancta days are over."

"What? That's the consequences? You can't be a Sancta?"

"It was the only way ... to come back to life ... without a crystal." She let out a loud groan. "I had to ... expend my Sancta power."

My throat narrowed. Tears flowed. My dear Sing had not only reentered her cancer-ridden body and walked straight into the gates of hell, she also gave up her greatest gift, to be a Sancta who could help me for years to come. This brave young woman was the most heroic of us all.

My words of doubt about her ongoing presence stabbed me mercilessly. I had been such a fool. But it was too late to do anything but speak the truth. "I'm sorry if it sounded like I didn't want you around. I was stupid. Forgive me."

"All is forgiven. That's what love does." She let out another groan, this one wild and uncontrolled. I drew back. Fire swept over her chest and flickered in front of her face.

Her cloak burned away, and her shirt blazed. She dropped to her knees, gasping as she spoke. "If I give my body ... to be burned ... but have not love ...what good is it?"

I dropped with her and pulled her close again. "Oh, Sing. You have love. More love than I can ever imagine having. What am I going to do without you?"

Her gasps breathed into my ear, barely discernible as whispered words. "You don't need ... a Sancta anymore. I have ... finished my course ... I have ... forged a man of iron."

I drew back again, still holding her flaming body. "You mean, me? I'm a man of iron?"

"Yes ... my beloved. ... You are ... a Reaper reborn." She took in a labored breath and exhaled once more. "Now ... go and kill Alex." She slumped in my grasp. Flames shrouded her body and sizzled across her curls.

As she shook in death throes, I whispered, "I love you, Sing, and I always will."

She looked up at me. A smile appeared. Then she let out a long sigh and closed her eyes. Flames erupted in a geyser. Her skin melted, leaving behind an eyeless skull. Her body then crumbled into scorched bones and ashes.

I looked skyward and let out a long wail. Heat plunged into every pore — scalding, torturing fire. I rose from my knees and stood upright. People gasped once more. I spread my arms and looked at my body. Flames covered every inch, though they didn't seem to be consuming my skin or cloak. With my arms spread, I really did look like a bird on fire, a flaming Phoenix. Every word of Scarlet's prophecy had come true.

Stepping high, I walked out of the blaze and shook myself, flapping my arms and stomping my feet. The flames fell and drizzled to the ground in dying embers. I wore an intact cloak as well as a weapons belt supplied with the same items it held when I died. I reached into my pocket and felt the journal — still there but once again in a tattered state.

Every pain, from my bullet wound to my broken back, had vanished. Strength coursed through my muscles. Energy spiked, as if I had been newly charged at the depot. I checked the cross, dangling at my chest as before. Sing's words returned to mind. *Following Yeshua's footsteps might mean giving your life in sacrifice, but for those who do, death always leads to resurrection. Knowing this makes us strong, courageous, able to face any evil that darkens our doors.* I whispered, "It's time to kill Alex."

I looked at the fire. Sing's ghost walked out of the flames. She gave me a sad smile and hurried away.

Just as I took a step to follow, Fiona ran to me and pulled me into her arms, then immediately pushed back. "You're hot!"

"Not as hot as about a minute ago." I gave her a polite smile. "Sorry to cut this short, but I have to do something."

I tried again to follow Sing, but Bartholomew stopped me with a gloved hand. "Welcome back, Phoenix. We have a lot to talk —"

I punched him in the face with a roundhouse right. He staggered backwards and fell to his bottom. Rubbing his cheek, he looked up at me. "I guess I deserved that, didn't I?"

"And a lot more." I looked for Sing, but she was nowhere in sight. I lost my chance to talk to her, at least for now. I grabbed Bartholomew's wrist, jerked him to his feet, and spoke with a throaty growl. "That punch was a warning.

All the scheming, tricks, and playing games are over. I came back from the dead to try to save the world, and if you're not one hundred percent on my side, you'll find yourself at the painful end of my fist again."

As he tried to maintain a calm demeanor, his chin quivered. "I understand. How may I help you?"

"I need information. I heard Alex is at the City Center, and Shanghai and Liam went to face him. Can you confirm that?"

"How did you hear —" He waved a hand. "Never mind. The answer is yes. I didn't bother to try to stop them. I got the impression that nothing could alter Shanghai's resolve."

"You're probably right." With Fiona at my side, I rotated slowly in place. The crowd had dwindled to about seventy cold Chicagoans, all staring at me as if petrified by fear. I called out, "Listen, my friends. I was able to watch many of you line up to volunteer to give your life for mine. Your love touched me deeply. I never knew how much impact I made in your lives, and for that I am forever grateful."

Cyrus stepped to the front of the crowd. "We're grateful to you, but you're wasting time. Just tell us what you need. I, for one, will do whatever you ask."

"So will I," Georgia said as she walked toward me.

I squared my shoulders, hoping to communicate confidence. "We'll march to the City Center and confront Alex and her robots. Bring any weapons you can find — knives, clubs, discarded boards, anything. I'll need you to keep her robots busy while I attack her one on one."

"They'll kill us," a man deep in the crowd called.

I nodded. "I won't lie to you. Some of you might die. Maybe most of you. I do know this, though, that there is life after death. I have been beyond the Gateway, but I also learned that there are two paths — one that leads to eternal peace and another that leads to destruction. I can't possibly know who'll go on which path. You have to judge that for yourselves. If you don't have faith that you're ready to die, then stay here with your families. I don't want anyone to come who isn't certain of where he's going to end up."

I joined hands with Fiona and Georgia. "Now, who's with me?"

Cyrus took another step forward. "I'm with you. Without question."

About twenty other men and several women joined him, all making similar declarations.

"Then gather your weapons. We leave in two minutes."

The volunteers scattered. Some hurried to nearby apartment buildings while others searched the ruins for suitable weapons.

When Fiona and Georgia tried to join the volunteers, I kept my grip on their hands. I drew them close and whispered, "Did either of you see Sing's ghost coming out of the fire?"

Georgia nodded, a serious aspect in her dark eyes. "I saw something, a glimmer of light shaped like a girl."

"I did as well," Fiona said.

"Did you see which way she went?"

Fiona shook her head. "It was just a glance. I wasn't even sure it was a ghost. After I saw her, I looked at you again."

"I kept my eye on her for a little while," Georgia said, "but with so many ghosts around, there's been a lot of appearing and disappearing, if you know what I mean."

I focused on Georgia's serious, motherly face. "You said you'll do whatever I ask, right?"

She nodded. "Get to the point, Phoenix. Time's running out."

I released her hand. "Instead of going with me to fight, find Sing."

"Is that all?" Georgia chuckled. "Glad to. I'm not much of a fighter."

"Then please hurry. She can't have gone far."

"On my way." She hustled down the street and disappeared around a corner.

I kissed Fiona's dirty cheek. "Thank you for being willing to give your life for mine. I'll never forget that. But I want you and your girls out of the city as soon as possible."

She nervously brushed soot from her dress, though her efforts did little good. "If you say so, Phoenix. Seein' that you saved both of my daughters and took Molly to heaven, I will do what you ask. Like Georgia said, I'm not much of a fighter."

"Good. Leave me a way to contact you, and I'll let you know when it's safe to return."

"I will. And I'll pray for you." After kissing my hand, she turned and walked away.

I swiveled to Bartholomew. "What are you going to do?"

He laughed under his breath. "If you're asking if I'm ready to meet my maker, then the answer is certainly no. I plan to stay far away from the illuminaries. But allow me to work behind the scenes once again. I have given you enough reason to believe that I was on your side all along, though I had to appear to be working for Alex. My methods aren't exactly orthodox, but they do, if you'll pardon the expression, reap results."

I shoved a finger into his chest. "Your methods led to Saigon's death, Shanghai's maiming, and Sing's loss of Sancta power. I don't trust you for one second."

"You need to trust me for at least a moment. I have some information that I'm sure will help you."

His sincere expression gave me pause. "All right. I'm listening."

When I drew my finger back, he stepped closer. After glancing to each side, he whispered in sharp tones. "Alex is waiting for you, expecting you."

"Why? Did you tell her about your resurrection plans?"

He scowled. "Certainly not. But she believes the mirror transported you from the fire. Her passion to learn its secrets has skyrocketed. It's a mad obsession now. You can use that against her."

"Okay. How?"

"I don't know. Just be aware of her obsession when you go to battle. You're smart. You'll think of something."

"Maybe, but she has a way of figuring out what I'm thinking. When the time comes, I'll have to blank out my mind and just act."

"Good plan. And take note that the band she wears around her head helps her control the illuminaries. Once she has given them a command, no one can counter it without a controlling tablet or that headband." His whisper dropped in volume, though no one was listening. "When you defeat her, just remember that I have been risking my life by helping you on the sly. I could have kept kissing up to Alex, and I would have been her number one officer, a far better position than a monitor at Gateway depot number three."

"Don't con me. In the end, you'll attach yourself to whoever wins. You have no loyalty to anyone but yourself. You didn't care who suffered or died while you were terrorizing an entire city with your bombs. And for what? Just to get on Alex's good side."

"Ridiculous. I hate Alex with a passion. But I had to stay close to get the information I needed to help you fight her, and the only way to do it was to take some extreme risks. Yes, a few hundred people died. Unfortunate. Tragic. But it's better than a few hundred *thousand*, maybe more."

I gave him a stare that I hoped communicated complete disgust. "Anything else?"

"One more thing. Alex knows you're a pushover if she threatens innocent lives. She'll demand that you tell her everything about the mirror, or she'll do something that will devastate Chicago."

"What? Some kind of weapon? A nuclear bomb?"

"Not a bomb, but something just as deadly. For several weeks, the Gatekeeper siphoned radioactive gas from the atmosphere and stored it in the warehouse, the same gas I used to enhance your strength. Alex brought what's left to the City Center where it will be easy to dispense across the region, perhaps through existing natural gas lines. In fact, from chatter I heard, she already tested the system to root out some Resistance leaders."

I nodded. "It's true. And it works."

"All the more reason for me to stop Alex's scheme. While she's distracted by your attack, I hope to get to the tank and figure out how to stop the deployment."

"Figure out? Won't it have a shut-off valve?"

Bartholomew snorted. "You know Alex better than that. She'll have some kind of failsafe device, a kill switch you might call it. In other words, the gas will deploy citywide unless she personally stops it, and the result will be catastrophic to everyone but you. She doesn't know that the gas makes you stronger."

"So if she sprays us with the gas, the people who go with me will die."

"Most likely, but like you said, you need them, both as a distraction and as a decoy. In other words, when she sees them, they will become her immediate target. That will clear the way for your direct attack. She'll try to harm them to bring you to your knees, because she knows you're not afraid to die." He chuckled. "Especially considering that you already have."

I growled. "Stop laughing, you disgusting rodent, or I'll —"

"What? Kill me? I'm sure you could, but that's not who you are. Your principles demand —"

I squeezed his cheeks together with my hand, silencing him. "I am sick of hearing about my principles from people who don't have any." I shoved him back. "Go ahead. Work behind the scenes. Disarm the kill switch. Just get out of my sight."

"Gladly." Bartholomew stalked away, grumbling something unintelligible.

When my volunteers reassembled, about fifteen men and three women, I spoke loudly enough for all to hear. "Listen carefully. I just learned that Alex is threatening to release a radioactive gas as a way to coerce me to reveal a secret, but the secret exists only in her mad obsessions, which means I can't give her what she's demanding even if I wanted to. Our immediate problem is that anyone who goes with me to face her will be a target. You can run from illuminaries but probably not from the gas. She'll use your vulnerability against me."

A man called, "Aren't you vulnerable?"

"No, that's why yours is the greater risk. It's not cowardly to change your mind and try to get your families out of danger. You have to do what you think is best." I scanned my little army. "Who's going with me?"

They all raised a hand. Cyrus cried out, "You saved my wife and three of my children from a fire. You killed the tyrant Gatekeeper. You even rose from the dead. Man, I'll march into hell with you."

Several in the group murmured their agreement. A few tapped rakes or boards on the street.

I waved an arm. "Let's go." I took off in a quick march, wishing I could sprint, or at least jog. Since Shanghai and Liam left a while ago, they might be at the City Center by now, especially if Liam had brought his van. But some of my band were injured or weak. They could barely walk the distance, let alone run.

Still, having courageous supporters behind me stoked an inner flame. They were willing to die alongside me. Even though they carried boards and shovels and had little to no fighting skills, I couldn't ask for a more passionate army.

I let out a long sigh. Or maybe they were just a flock of sacrificial lambs.

When we drew within sight of the City Center, I signaled a halt. A huge grass courtyard spread around the base of the complex's central ten-story building, no place to hide on approach, especially since dozens of illuminaries packed the area, probably one to every fifty square feet of turf.

At the far end of the courtyard, concrete stairs shaped in a huge semicircle rose to an expansive platform, an area directly in front of the main door that could serve as a speech or performance platform for an audience in the courtyard.

Alex stood at the center of the platform, her blonde hair discernible even from our distance of about a hundred yards. Instead of her usual black leather ensemble, she wore what appeared to be hazardous-materials coveralls that protected her body up to her neck. The uniform hung loosely, considerably too big for her. Under an arm, she held matching headgear, likely complete with a built-in gas mask.

Cyrus walked to my side. "I work part time for the gas company. One of our main pipeline network nodes is right under that building."

I nodded. "A perfect place to distribute the killer gas to the city."

Cyrus pointed toward Alex. "She's standing in front of a portable gas tank that has a diffusion valve. A tank that size can hold enough compressed gas to flood the courtyard."

"And it probably wouldn't hurt the illuminaries at all."

"Illuminaries?" Cyrus asked.

"The cloaked robots standing in the courtyard. Alex's killing machines. About two hundred of them."

Cyrus squinted. "I thought I saw them when we first got here, but I don't see them now."

"They must have shifted to invisible mode. Only Reapers can see them."

"So we normal humans have to fight invisible killing machines." He puffed out his chest. "Yeah. Sure. We'll do it. But it sounds like she's going for overkill. What does she fear? You?"

"Hard to say, but the invisibility shift means she knows we're coming." I scanned the area. Where were Shanghai and Liam? Maybe the overwhelming odds gave them reason to hide somewhere to strategize before attacking. Yet, I couldn't stand around and wait for them. We had to plan our own attack.

"We'll split up," I said to Cyrus. "You take eight with you, and I'll —"

A loud bang shook the air. Alex pointed to our left and shouted, "That van. Half of you go and subdue the driver. The other half stay on the alert." She looked around, the shimmer in her Owl eyes evident even from our vantage point.

When half of the illuminaries began hurrying from the courtyard, I pointed toward the right side of the area. "Take everyone that way. Shout. Scream. Whatever you have to do to get the illuminaries to chase you."

"You got it." Cyrus called to the others. "Follow me. Make as much noise as possible." They ran toward the courtyard, shouting and yelling. I followed in their wake. When we closed in on the edge of the grass, they veered to the right while I slowed my pace and continued straight ahead — straight toward Alex.

Alex yelled at the remaining illuminaries. "Four of you join me! The rest of you go after them!"

When the illuminaries gave chase, Alex stepped to the gas tank and set a hand on the valve. The zing of a spool line ripped from somewhere high above, making her turn. Shanghai swooped down from the right, her battle staff in hand.

CHAPTER TWENTY-ONE

ALEX DROPPED HER headgear and set herself in battle stance. Shanghai detached her spool and flew the rest of the way. When her feet touched down, she swung the staff at Alex. Alex ducked and thrust out a leg. Shanghai leaped over it, skidded to a halt, then spun back and charged. When she swung the staff again, Alex blocked it with a forearm and grabbed the end.

Locked in a tug-of-war for the staff, they glared at each other, teeth clenched as they pulled. The four remaining illuminaries rushed up the stairs, only seconds from the battle.

I broke into a sprint, but I was about a hundred fifty feet away. I couldn't possibly get there before the robots could. I shouted, "Hey! Want a piece of me?"

Alex, Shanghai, and the illuminaries looked my way. Shanghai gasped. Alex narrowed her silvery eyes. Two illuminaries peeled off toward me while the other two continued up the stairs.

I sidestepped the closer one and tried to spin past it, but its gloved hands caught my cloak. When I jerked away, I stumbled headlong toward the second one. I lowered my body and barreled into it. Pain from the collision racked my shoulder. The force of the blow made it backpedal until it could regain its balance.

At the platform, one of the illuminaries tore the staff away from Shanghai. She recoiled, then regained her ready position, glancing from Alex to me then back to Alex. Shouts and screams bounced from the surrounding buildings. My little army was probably losing their battle. I had to end this soon or we would have a bloodbath.

Behind me, the first illuminary closed in. The second did the same from the other side. I had to time this perfectly.

Just as they lunged, I ducked and thrust myself to the side. I flew about three feet before one of the robots grabbed my arm and yanked me back. It punched me in the solar plexus, knocking my breath away.

My legs buckled. I slumped to the ground, gasping. An illuminary threw a fist. Although I ducked, the hard knuckles delivered a glancing blow to the side of my head, scraping my scalp.

Another fist hurtled my way. I blocked it with a forearm, then a second fist with my other arm. I grabbed the illuminaries' cloaks and banged their heads together, but the collision didn't faze them. They latched on to my arms, one on each side, and pulled as if trying to break a wishbone.

As my arms stretched, they lifted me off the ground, facing the platform. Shanghai lay there prostrate. One of the illuminaries stood over her with a foot planted on her back. The other knelt at her legs, tying her hands behind her.

My joints popped. Pain tore through every muscle and ligament. At any second, the robots would rip my arms from my shoulders.

Something snapped. One of the illuminaries collapsed. The release sent me flying into the other one, making it topple backwards. I jerked myself free and leaped to my feet. Liam stood over the other fallen illuminary, a sledge hammer in hand.

Breathing heavily, he said, "It's visible now. I couldn't see it before, but it was easy to guess where it stood."

"Thanks." I grabbed the sledge hammer and lunged at the other illuminary as it tried to rise. With a downward swing, I slammed the hammer against its head, crushing its skull. As its body twitched, electricity arced across its silvery face.

I spun toward the platform. Alex was putting on her headgear while the other two illuminaries stood guard next to her, Shanghai kneeling between them. One clutched a fistful of her hair. She looked at me with her exposed eye, her expression despairing.

To our right, illuminaries filed into the courtyard, some dragging limp bodies — my valiant but defeated soldiers. These robotic reinforcements would arrive at the platform in less than a minute. We had only seconds to act.

I whispered to Liam, "Where are the illuminaries that chased you?"

"I led them into a warehouse and trapped them there. At least I think I did. It's hard to be sure with invisible robots."

"Let's hope you're right." I handed him the sledge hammer. "Ready to go to battle?"

He gave me a firm nod. "I am."

"Then let's go."

Just as I began jogging toward the platform with Liam, Alex set a hand on the tank's control valve and shouted through an open flap at the front of her headgear. "Stay where you are, Phoenix, or I will flood the area with radioactive gas and kill every human in a five-block radius.

Shanghai will be the first to perish." She raised the mirror with her other hand. "Just tell me how to use this, and I will set her and everyone else free."

"Keep going," I whispered as I continued my quick march. Liam matched me stride for stride, though he glanced at me nervously. Shanghai stared. Her expression seemed conflicted, torn, wanting to be rescued but not wanting me to die.

"You know I'll do it," Alex called. "Don't test me."

Staying silent, I quickened my pace. Liam did as well.

"You have sealed their fate." Alex closed the headgear flap and turned the valve. From a nozzle on the tank's side, a cloud of sparkling gas spewed and quickly shrouded the platform.

"Run!" I sprinted ahead and dashed up the stairs into the cloud. The two illuminaries stepped into my path. I barreled into them, but they each grabbed an arm and held me fast. Now in the midst of blinding smoke, I couldn't find Shanghai, Liam, or Alex. Somehow I had to get away. With more illuminaries coming, there was no time to spare.

I inhaled deeply, taking in as much of the gas as I could. The noxious fumes scraped my throat and lungs. Every breath rasped. My heart raced, and power surged through my muscles.

Letting out a guttural cry, I jerked away from the illuminaries, elbowed one in the throat and tripped both with a leg sweep. I pounced on one, tore its arm off, and used it to pummel the other in the face. As it squealed and tried to throw me off, sparks and smoke spewed from its eyes. Seconds later, its limbs flopped to the ground.

I rose and faced the spot where the gas tank had been. A cold breeze blew in and whisked much of the cloud away. Alex stood next to the tank, a step behind Shanghai. When the rest of the gas cleared, Alex tore her headgear off, dropped it, and drew a sonic gun from her belt. She set its barrel against the back of Shanghai's head.

"Is this a familiar sight, Phoenix? Your beloved dangling at the edge of death?" Alex huffed. "Apparently you think radiation poisoning won't kill her, but you know as well as I do that this gun will obliterate her brain stem. No one will repair it. No one will put her body in stasis. When I pull this trigger, Shanghai will be gone forever."

Trying to stay calm, I looked around. Liam sprawled on the platform facedown, the sledge hammer at his side. Two broken illuminaries lay nearby, apparently victims of his hammer. Active illuminaries surrounded us, some with motionless human bodies at their feet. Fortunately, the half that had chased Liam and his van were still missing.

Shanghai's head bobbed and wobbled. She looked at me with dazed eyes, still conscious, but barely. Her lips moved as if she were trying to speak, but no audible words came out.

Still holding the sonic gun, Alex picked up the mirror from the platform floor and showed it to me. "Tell me how the mirror works. I give you five seconds. You have suffered through a similar countdown before. I hope you won't wait till the last second this time."

"Don't worry. I won't wait." I charged toward them. When I collided with Alex, she pulled the trigger. As the telltale pop resounded, I bowled her over, knocking the gun away, though she hung on to the mirror, clutching it against her chest.

I sat on her stomach and threw punches at her face again and again, but she deflected the blows with lightning-fast blocks. With each block, the mirror, now lying loosely on her chest, jostled, my reflected face bouncing with it.

I caught hold of her wrists and pinned her arms down, her fists next to her ears. Our noses nearly touching, she stared at me. Her shimmering Owl eyes pierced my mind. She whispered in a soft, crooning tone. "You have already lost, Phoenix. Bartholomew and I have taken everyone you hold dear — your parents, Misty, Singapore, Shanghai. You have no one."

My muscles weakened, as if drained by her gaze. Illuminaries closed in from all around. They moved slowly, probably waiting for Alex's command to pounce.

"Even as strong as you have become," she continued, "you cannot defeat so many of my soldiers. Why not give in? Be the face of a new world order. I noticed that you brought loyal followers, and they died nobly. The people still love you, no matter how much I tried to destroy your reputation. Why not build a following of citizens who can live in your light instead of dying in your shadow? Why not share your goodness with everyone? The oppressive heel of the Gatekeeper will be gone forever, and you can be a shining light the downtrodden people need. Just tell me the mirror's secrets and all will be forgiven."

The mirror flashed. My reflection faded. Misty appeared with Alex behind her, holding the sonic gun to her head. Alex pulled the trigger. Misty's head rocked, and she closed her eyes. Then Sing appeared, kneeling in the corrections camp yard as prisoners ran for their lives. She reached back and pulled the trigger of the sonic gun in my hand. Like Misty's, her head jerked, and she slumped to the ground. Finally, Shanghai appeared, her face bruised and one black swollen eyelid drooping over an empty socket, the result of Alex's cruel stab.

In the image, Shanghai set a patch over the socket and fastened an attached elastic band around her head to hold the patch in place. Her jaw firm and a tear trickling from her good eye, she whispered, "I'm doing this for you, Phoenix. I'm going to kill that witch. I might die trying, but if I do, at least I'll be with you." She brushed a tear with a knuckle. "I love you, Phoenix, and I always will."

The mirror flashed again and returned to normal.

"You're doing it," Alex said. "I heard a voice from the mirror. Release me, and tell me what you know."

At least ten illuminaries drew within a few steps and made a half circle around us. Their bodies cast crisscrossing shadows over us. Still sitting on Alex's stomach, I released her wrists and lifted the mirror as I straightened.

I looked at Shanghai to my left. Four steps away, she lay curled on the platform, twitching. When I knocked Alex down, I probably threw off her aim, but not enough. The damage was done. Shanghai was dying, and I had no way to save her.

Alex continued, her voice alluring. "Now is the time. Tell me the secrets, and you will soon be known as the true Phoenix, the Reaper who raised the entire world from its ashes."

"All right." I licked my lips, not yet sure what I was going to say. "The mirror is a viewer. It shows events from the past, like a movie."

Alex propped herself on her elbows. "Good. Keep going."

"I know of only one power it has besides showing a reflection, maybe the most important of all."

Her brow lifted. "Excellent. I'm ready."

"So am I." I slashed the mirror's edge across her face, ripping a gash from cheek to cheek. I then pushed her to the platform floor and rammed the mirror's corner deep into her eye.

Alex screamed, her words garbled by blood. "Kill him! Kill him now!"

As Alex beat my chest with her fists, I shoved the corner deeper and penetrated her brain, turning the mirror to drill a hole. A second later, she fell limp and breathed no more.

The illuminaries closed in, their arms outstretched. I jerked the mirror out and plunged my fist into the gouged eye socket. Groping with my fingers, I found her soul, wrapped my hand around it, and shouted, "Call them off!"

Her response rode up my arm and into my mind. "Never!"

One of the illuminaries grabbed my wrist. I tossed the mirror to the side, snatched the illuminary's sleeve, and threw it over my head and into another illuminary. They both collapsed in a heap.

I reached for the band around Alex's head, my only hope to stop the attack. The moment my fingers touched it, two of the illuminaries latched on to my arms with powerful grips, one at each side.

Still clutching Alex's soul, I rose with their upward pull and jerked the shining sphere out of her head. Black tears flowed. The dark liquid from her punctured eye socket mixed with blood and dripped to the ground.

Now suspended in the air, I held Alex's soul aloft. It morphed from a sphere with broken tentacles into her distinctive form, my hand around her throat. As she kicked and thrashed, I shouted at the illuminaries, "Put me down, or I'll strangle her!"

They looked at Alex's ghost, then at her corpse. Unable to communicate through her headband or speak because of my pressure on her throat, she continued thrashing.

Bartholomew rushed out of the building and onto the platform. He tore the band from Alex's head, and slid it around his own. He eyed the two illuminaries and said, "Put Phoenix down and let him go."

They lowered me to the ground and released my arms.

"Now," Bartholomew continued, breathing heavily as he touched an illuminary's cloak, "take Alex's coveralls from her and come with me. The rest of you power down."

One by one, their eyes flickered and turned off. Except for the illuminary that was stripping Alex's body, they stood motionless, similar to the way they had been stored in the warehouse.

"I found the tank," Bartholomew said as he picked up Alex's protective headgear. "I'm taking this illuminary to help me disable the kill switch. If I survive, I'll return to help you." He took the coveralls from the illuminary, and they hurried together into the building.

My arms throbbing, I opened my cloak, pushed Alex's ghost inside, and waited for the fibers to absorb her. My mind demanded that I run to check on Shanghai, but I had to dispose of Alex. I couldn't release her foul soul to the wilds.

I glanced at her corpse. Wearing her usual leather pants and white T-shirt, she lay face up with a huge hole where her left eye used to be, the eyeball now crushed somewhere in the gap. Her right eye stayed open, staring blankly, no longer shimmering.

Her motionless aspect felt unearthly. Somehow it seemed that she ought to get up and give me another wicked stare, let out her hideous laugh, and once again intimidate me with a threat against a loved one or a prediction based on my principles. But the Owl was dead. She had no power over me anymore.

When her soul disappeared, a shimmer rode up my arm and settled at my shoulder. Instead of fading, its luster stayed vibrant. "You're trusting Bartholomew?" Alex asked from my cloak. "First you brutally killed me, and now you're an ally with a snake like him? What has become of your principles?"

"You don't deserve an answer, Alex. You lost. I finally outsmarted you. Soon I'll take you to the Gateway and send you to hell where you belong." I took off the cloak, ran to Shanghai, and knelt at her side.

After turning her face up, I checked the pulse at her throat, cold against my warm fingers. Her heartbeat thrummed, steady, though weak. From my gut, a spasm broke through, a laugh blended with a sob. She was alive but near death. The earlier twitching had to be a symptom of something terrible. A stroke? Brain damage? Both?

I wrapped my cloak around her, slid my arms under her back, and lifted her as I rose. Although she remained unconscious, she instinctively slid an arm around my neck and rested her head on my shoulder — a good sign ... I hoped.

A few steps away on the platform, Liam sat upright, propping himself with both hands on the sledge hammer handle as he looked at a fallen illuminary."

"Are you all right?" I asked.

"I am. Nearly dead is better than dead, I think." He climbed to his feet and hobbled to me, leaving the sledge hammer behind. "How is Shanghai?"

"Bad. Maybe brain damage. Definitely radiation exposure. I guess you got some, too."

"I did." He laid a hand on his chest. "My lungs are burning."

We looked at the bodies of my fallen soldiers. A few writhed and let out soft moans while others lay motionless. "I'll see about them," Liam said as he pushed a set of keys into my pocket. "My van is parked at a curb just west of here. The robots punched a few holes in it, but it I think it still runs."

"I'll try to drive it up on the courtyard."

He squinted, obviously in pain. "Try? Haven't you driven before?"

"Just motorcycles. Don't worry. I'll figure it out." With Shanghai in my arms, I walked gingerly down the steps, not wanting to jostle her fragile body. When I reached the surrounding grass, an explosion rocked the City Center building. Liam ran down the platform stairs, grabbing and dragging two bodies on the way.

The building's roof caved in. Sparkling gas shot up from the opening and into the sky. The entry door flew open. Dust poured out in spasmodic bursts, as if the collapsed structure were coughing.

In one of the bursts, a man tumbled within the debris. Wearing hazardous-materials coveralls and headgear, he rolled with the wave until he stopped at the edge of the platform, inches from the stairs.

Within seconds, a breeze swept the cloud away. The man climbed to his feet and brushed dirt from his uniform in a careful manner. He had to be Bartholomew.

He looked around. When he spotted me, he walked down the stairs, removing the headgear as he descended. "I failed to disarm the kill switch, so I redirected the flow into another container. Unfortunately, it was unable to handle the pressure and exploded." He looked down at his filthy body. "I, however, appear to be intact."

"So is the danger's over?" I asked. "The gas won't be deployed?"

"Not through the utility network." He looked up. "I'm afraid the atmosphere's radiation level will be higher for a while, so I wouldn't say that the danger is over, though it is certainly lower."

My thoughts turned thankful, but it was hard to speak them to this diabolical version of a hero. "I appreciate what you did."

"And the same to you. It seems that the entire world owes you a debt of gratitude."

I nodded toward the street. "Walk with me. I have to get Shanghai, Liam, and the others to a doctor. If I can find one."

We walked together at a brisk pace. "It's a good thing we're on tolerable terms," Bartholomew said with an air of self-importance. "I know a medical practitioner who is sure to help."

"Great. Thank you."

"And I will be thankful for your help in strategizing. Within hours, the news of your triumph will spread faster than the fires. Your fame and appeal can be used for the good of all."

"How?"

"As a catalyst for setting up an election. Since the risk of assassination is lower, I will run for Head Chair of the World Council, and now that you know I am not as selfish as you likely thought, I hope you will publicly support me."

An image of the Fitzpatrick girls strapped to bombs came to mind. I couldn't shake it away. "You're a cold, callous killer. There is no way on earth that I will ever support you. You're lucky that I don't do to you what you did to Anne and Betsy."

"Ah, yes. I thought that might be your answer. Yet, I promise you this, I won't be anything resembling a tyrant. In fact, I'll put you in charge of the illuminaries and teach you how to control them. Since you and Shanghai are probably the only Reapers left in Chicago, you'll need them to collect the ghosts and also to maintain law and order until we can establish a viable authority structure."

His mention of ghosts incited me to look around. A few level ones wandered here and there — an old man carrying a grocery bag, a woman walking with a little boy, and a teenager staring at smoke rising from a nearby building. Physical people also populated the area. A girl lay in a gutter, her dress and hair scorched. A mother knelt at her side, weeping as she gathered the limp corpse into her arms.

Despair shrouded the streets, a shadow more frightening than gas or ghosts. These people needed help. They needed healing. They needed hope and comfort, to be sure, but we had to start with down-to-earth physical help.

"Listen," I said to Bartholomew, "if you promise no more bans on medical care, I'll consider the position. Better me controlling those robots than you."

"Of course. Medical care is a must. I'm not ashamed about seeking power, but I know that the best way to keep power is to take care of the people, both the living and the dead. That includes our resident ghosts." He looked toward the sky again. "The shield is still intact, thicker than usual over this region. I will have to design a new soul-delivery system. With my ideas, it will be better than ever."

When we reached the van, Bartholomew helped me open the door and lay Shanghai on the cargo floor. Now that she was out of the cold wind, I removed my cloak from around her and wadded it in a corner, glad to separate her from Alex's soul.

I climbed into the driver's seat while Bartholomew entered on the passenger's side. "Eventually I have to go back to the Gateway and deposit Alex," I said as I closed my door. "The sooner she's gone forever, the better."

Bartholomew closed the door on his side and set his headgear on his lap. "I agree, and I can help you get there."

"Good." I inserted the key and started the engine. The usual clatter brought a sense of relief, as if an old friend had joined my efforts. "After we take care of the living."

CHAPTER TWENTY-TWO

I STOOD IN THE burned-out Gateway building where the dome room used to be, the ceiling open to the sky and my cloak draped over an arm. The air not as cold as in Chicago, I felt comfortable wearing only my normal Reaper outfit, recently laundered and mended. After washing thoroughly at Liam's home, my face and body were clean, though wounds from the final battle with the illuminaries two days ago still stung.

Standing in front of me and wearing his coat, Bartholomew held in his gloved hands a propane tank that emitted a conical blue flame from its nozzle. Since fire had ruined the equipment needed to extract souls, we had to resort to the only method remaining.

Now that my radiation-enhanced energy had faded, the cloak no longer shimmered, giving me no clue to Alex's whereabouts. Still, a few experiments had proved that I kept my ability to physically manipulate ghosts. Maybe that new gift would last for a long time to come.

I breathed on one of the sleeves, starting at the shoulder and working my way down. When I reached the elbow, the fibers sparkled. "Here she is." I extended the sleeve toward Bartholomew.

"Just a quick scorch should do it." He set the whooshing fire close. Cool wind swirled in the circular room, disturbing the flame. "Let me know when she emerges. I probably won't be able to see her."

As the flame singed the fibers, they emitted a stream of mist that formed into a head with a distorted face — Alex's. Her eyes glowed silver, pulsing in a way I had never seen in a ghost, still piercing, still haunting. Her Owl powers had survived death.

She smirked. "Phoenix, it seems that you —"

"No!" I grabbed her by the throat, jerked her out of the sleeve, and tossed the cloak to the side. As she dangled from my grip, I shook her and shouted, "You have nothing to say to me! Nothing!" I added a growl to my voice. "But I have something to say to you. You are a murderer and a coward. You used frightened men, women, and children to seize power. And you baited me into psychodrama conversations way too many times."

I took a deep breath and looked into her evil eyes. "Alex, I commit you to the path of destruction. When you get there, you won't be able to talk your way out of eternal punishment. The entire world will celebrate your condemnation to hell. Good-bye, and good riddance."

I flung her upward. The Gateway's pull caught her and sucked her toward the sky. As she flew, her face contorted into a mask of terror, shrinking in the distance until she disappeared.

Bartholomew shut the flame off. "Well, that's a relief."

"Tell me about it." I picked up my cloak and examined the damage. Not too bad. It wouldn't take long to repair. "Let's go home."

As we walked out of the charred room side by side, Bartholomew looked at me. "What is home for you, Phoenix?"

"A sofa in Liam's house, until I find a place of my own."

"I have a place in mind."

"Where?"

"I plan to take residence in the Gatekeeper's mansion just outside of Chicago. Alex was living there for a short time. Now that her ghost is gone, I have no fear that she will haunt its halls." He withdrew a key from his pocket and set it in my hand. "I am offering my house to you free of charge. It's clean, somewhat furnished, and well-maintained."

"Thank you. I accept." I slid the key into my pocket. "Since Liam's on bed rest for a while, and his wife stays up late to care for him, they're not doing much to corral their kids. When they get up in the morning, the sofa transforms into a bounce-on-Phoenix playground."

We both laughed. My laugh sounded strange — carefree, alive. Purging Alex's soul did more than send her to destruction; it liberated my own soul.

"Speaking of sofas," Bartholomew said, "mine is comfortable. When Shanghai is released from the hospital, she could move in with you, take my bed while you take the sofa. I'm assuming your principles would demand a separate sleeping arrangement."

For some reason, his mention of my principles didn't bother me this time, as if no one could ever wound me with that knife again. "That's probably what we'll do. Thanks."

"Good. Good. Just be sure to feed a stray cat that comes by every couple of days. He was nothing but skin and bones when I started feeding him. He's doing much better now."

I halted and faced him. My newfound joy seemed to melt away. "Wait a minute. Since when do you care about a life besides your own?" Anger rising, I spat out my words. "You killed my parents. You killed Shanghai's parents. And now you're worried about a cat? Listen, you freakish —"

"Whoa, tiger. Whoa. Don't fly into a rage. There's a lot you don't know."

Simmering fury bubbled in my gut, ready to explode, but I kept it in check. "All right. Spill it. I heard you tell Alex that there's more to the story, the whole truth, something about you keeping that sword in its sheath till later."

"All right. The whole truth, if you care to believe it." Bartholomew cleared his throat. "Your father helped me gather information about Reapers and their ancestors. He was my right-hand man. In fact, it was his idea to eliminate rebellious Reapers along with their parents, and he carried out several of the executions himself, including Shanghai's parents. You survived because of your relationship with him and Alex's desire to use you for her own goals."

Bartholomew's claims sizzled in my ears. While he paused, my father's words returned to mind, words I had mentally replayed a hundred times. *I asked Bartholomew to keep an eye on you. He thinks you have a special talent that will make you a target, so he'll give you advice when you need it.*

It was all true. I did have a special talent. I was a target — Alex's, Bartholomew's, and potentially even my own father's, but I escaped summary execution because I was his son.

"Your father planned to kill me to take over the operation," Bartholomew continued. "In fact, he came to Chicago to do just that, though your poor mother knew nothing about his plan. Fortunately for me, my assassin killed him first, though unfortunately for you, he killed your mother to eliminate any witnesses. I'm sure you don't approve of such gangster-style assassinations, but you don't live in my world. It's an ugly business, and now I have a chance to clean it up."

I couldn't take it anymore. My emotions exploded. "Clean it up? You? How can filthy, blood-covered hands clean anything up, hands that haven't lifted a finger to help anyone but himself? And now you want the Council's Head Chair? A person who knows nothing about the desperate strife in our city or any city?"

"Wait a minute, Phoenix. Listen to —"

"No! You listen to me! You want to rule the world, but you're ignorant about its despair. Have you walked our dark streets? Have you held a dying little girl in your arms, her spindly limbs consumed by cancerous lesions? Have you bandaged those sores while bloody pus oozes, reeking with the stench of infection while she cries in pain? Have you brought a potato to an emaciated teenager who kissed you for supplying her first meal in a week? Have you splinted the femur of a brittle, gray-haired widow who wondered what happened to the promise of protection that heartless bureaucrats couldn't possibly deliver?"

I heaved in a breath and continued. "Well, I have, Bartholomew. I dipped my hands in the filth. I smelled the stench. I tasted the acidic bile that erupted when I rolled a corpse out of a pool of vomit. Where were you for these people? When they cried out for help, who answered? All they heard from government types like you was silence, or maybe a slap in the face, or the pop of a sonic gun pressed against their skulls, or even the vacuum sound of a soul getting sucked into oblivion by a self-important depot clerk punishing an innocent Reaper who had only one more cycle before he could retire in peace."

I stabbed a finger at him. "You need a wake-up call. You need to listen to the people. We live on the dark side of the street, and it's ugly. It's painful. It's suffocating. And most of all, it's lonely. Why? Because when we're suffering, no one in power cares. Rulers in high places can't gain anything from a sick, dying nobody. They just turn and walk away, especially arrogant, power-hungry little men like you."

As I breathed heavily, I glared at him, my neck hot in spite of the cool air. He stood quietly with his hands folded at his waist, his expression stoic, though his face had paled.

After several seconds, he spoke calmly. "Phoenix, your evaluation of my on-the-street experience is accurate and well-stated. I do lack sympathy, which is why I will seek counsel from, as you put it, *the people*. I hope you will consider an advisory post, though I would understand if you decline. I can imagine how awkward it might be to offer counsel to the man who arranged your parents' deaths."

I stared at him, dumbfounded. He had to be the most clueless, hypocritical man I had ever met, a murderer who killed Mex and my parents and claimed the right to do so. Yet, the news that my own father was the same kind of man raised no anger, only deep sadness.

As I tried to regain my composure, I fought back tears. This was not the time to grieve. I just wanted to fly home and check on Shanghai. "Let's go."

As we continued walking, Bartholomew said, "Do you think you would want an advisory position?"

I focused straight ahead as we descended the remains of the building's front stairs. "Either shut up or change the subject."

"All right. I won't press it. I feel fortunate that you haven't yet broken every bone in my body." He cleared his throat again. "On to another subject. Have you looked for the mirror at the City Center?"

"I scoured the place. No sign of it. I guess it must be gone forever."

"Well, that could be good or bad. Time will tell." Bartholomew patted me on the back. I resisted the urge to dodge his touch. "I need to say this in no uncertain terms, Phoenix. You really are a hero, a much better man than I am. I know you probably don't want me harping again about your principles, but I will keep them in mind as we work together to forge a new society. The worst is over. Better days lie ahead."

"If you say so." When we stopped at his air-transport vehicle, I looked him in the eye. "Just keep your promises, and we'll get along. Step out of line, and I'm coming after you. Mark my words."

"Indeed I will." Bartholomew gave me a genial nod. "We'll fly home at top speed. I'm sure you want to visit Shanghai again."

"I do. And I'm still looking for Sing's ghost. No one's seen her anywhere." We climbed into the vehicle and began the journey home. As we ascended, I looked at the burned-out building that once housed the great mysteries that I had pondered and feared for so long. Now it was just a harmless, broken shell. Like Alex's corpse, it no longer held power over me. The evil within had been purged, and another haunting ghost had fled my mind and taken its enslaving chains with it.

As Saigon had said recently, it felt good. Real good. Righteous.

More thoughts of Saigon seeped in, her courage, her passion for life, and the torture she endured. Then Sing's final sacrifice came to mind, her loving expression as she burned in my embrace, loyal and selfless to the end.

While my emotions floundered, my mind wandered through other fields of sorrow — Misty's murder, Dad's treachery, Mom's tragic death. Where were they now? Eternal peace? For Mom and Misty, that path was likely. But for Dad?

Like a flood, bitter sadness overwhelmed me. I wept, not bothering to conceal my grief. To his credit, Bartholomew said nothing, and we flew the rest of the way to Chicago in silence.

CHAPTER TWENTY-THREE

I ENTERED THE ROW house that once belonged to Bartholomew and closed the front door quietly. As I approached the bedroom, I grasped the cross at the end of my necklace and whispered, "Give me the right words to say. She's hurting so much."

After taking a deep breath, I walked in. Shanghai sat on the side of the double bed, her socked feet dangling inches above the floor and her battle staff lying on the mattress. Dressed in Reaper garb, she looked at me, blinking her good eye, the other one covered by a black patch.

In a corner to the bed's right, Georgia sat in a plush armchair, knitting a purple shawl for Shanghai. With winter upon us and snow paying an occasional visit, she would need it.

"Good," I said. "You're both awake." I shed my Reaper cloak, repaired since its brief encounter with the propane flame, and laid it on the bed over the staff. "Why are you wearing your Reaper clothes?"

Shanghai swallowed hard and spoke slowly, straining to push out every syllable. "I'm … feeling better."

"I helped her get dressed," Georgia said as she rose from the chair. "Helped her shower, too. She's moving around real well. Pretty soon she'll be doing everything by herself."

"Any problems since I've been gone?" I asked.

Georgia set her knitting on the seat. "Just a nightmare last night, but only one. Much better than usual. At least she didn't roll over and punch me in her sleep like she did a week ago."

I smiled. "That's good. I need you to stick around. I couldn't ask for a better caregiver."

"Oh, I think you won't need me much longer." She winked. "When's the big day?"

Shanghai wrinkled her brow. "The big day?"

Georgia tensed. "Oh. Well, I think I'll give you two a bit of privacy." She bustled past me. "I'll be in the kitchen. Give a yell if you need me."

Although I knew exactly what Georgia meant, I brushed it off with a laugh. "She's such a godsend, isn't she?"

Shanghai nodded and looked at me with a hopeful expression. "Any news? ... You've been gone ... for three days."

I shook my head. "No sign of Sing. I asked everyone, even the ghosts I rounded up. I'm wondering if she took the train to the Gateway or maybe walked there."

Shanghai's countenance wilted, her gloomy aspect silently asking the question she had repeated several times before. Why wouldn't Sing want to see us again? I had an answer, but I hated it with a passion and couldn't bear to tell Shanghai about Sing's dying words. *You won't have to worry about me showing up uninvited.*

I had already shouted to the heavens a dozen times asking Sing to forgive me for my foolishness, but silence was the only answer. Although she said she forgave me as we stood together in the fire, her long absence made me wonder if she had changed her mind.

My emotions surged, threatening a fresh round of tears. I had to change the subject. "Let me have a look at you." I set a hand under Shanghai's chin. The bruises on her face had faded, but the burns on the side of her neck looked as painful as ever. While she was unconscious, the doctor had shown me equally nasty burns on one leg and down the side of her back. Although the pain would eventually ease and maybe disappear, the scars were permanent.

"You're healing fast." I moved the cloak, uncovering the staff. "I see you're still keeping your staff close by. Are you going to try to walk soon?"

She grinned. "I'm keeping it … as a weapon."

"In case I get out of line?"

"Maybe. … Just behave yourself."

"Me?" I winked. "You're the one who charged into battle against Alex and dozens of high-powered robots."

Her grin wilted into a frown. "Well … no worries … about that anymore."

"Oh, you'll be back in battle shape in no time." I sat next to her. "I talked to the doctor this morning. The test results came in. He said the radiation-inhibitor shot you took a few months ago helped you survive, but your recovery is still nothing short of a miracle. The poisoning is already out of your system."

She lifted her brow. "And Liam?"

"Pretty much the same. His company provided the same shot just a couple of weeks before we met him, so he's doing well. Needs a cane to walk, but he's getting stronger. Anyway, we just have to monitor you for damage symptoms, including cancer, but that chance is remote. Also, your brain scan is clear, and you scored off-the-charts on the intelligence test. You just have a disconnect to your speech motor. The doctor thinks it'll improve over time, but he's not sure how much." I massaged her shoulder, one of her few uninjured spots. "Everything's going to be fine. You'll see."

Shanghai shifted her gaze straight ahead and nodded, saying nothing.

I turned her face toward me. In spite of the eye patch, bruises, burns, and a sad frown, light shone from deep within and dressed her lovely face in an ethereal glow. "Shanghai," I said softly, "we did it. Alex is dead. The Gatekeeper, too. We toppled their empire. It's true that we lost some friends. Sing, Colm, Saigon, and ..."

A tear tracked down Shanghai's cheek. I brushed the tear away. The list of heroic sacrifices was far too long. So many had died, including thirteen of the brave volunteers who distracted Alex's illuminaries, though Cyrus survived. I was glad of that, especially for the sake of his wife and children. In any case, I had to get off the death topic.

I forced a cheery smile. "More good news. Medicines are being distributed freely. New elections are next month. Liam is running for one of the Council seats. Word got around about his role in getting rid of Alex, so he's expected to win by a landslide. We'll need him there to keep an eye on Bartholomew." I pointed at her. "This is all because of your courage and sacrifice."

She offered the slightest of nods. "And yours."

"Okay. Right. But my point is that everything is on the upswing." I patted her knee. "I'm telling you all this to cheer you up."

"I know ... all those things ... are good."

"Then what's wrong? Why are you looking so glum?"

"I'm ..." She inhaled deeply and looked at me. "I'm broken ... scarred ... ugly."

"No, you're not. You're —"

She set a finger on my lips. "Let me finish."

When I nodded, she lowered her hand and gazed at me, her eye sparkling. "I know you say ... I'm not ugly. You're so sweet ... but ..." She bit her lip. "I need to believe ... you really think so ... that you're not ... just being nice ... to make me feel better."

I tilted my head. "What have I ever done to give you the idea that I think you're ugly?"

"Not ugly ... I guess ... just not as important ... as before."

"Not as important? How could that be? You're everything to me."

"No ... I'm not." She covered her face and broke into sobs. "Phoenix ... I'm so terrible ... even thinking like this. ... You don't deserve ... a selfish girl ... a vain ... selfish ... crippled ... brat like me."

"What? How can you say that? You risked your life so many times. You saved countless people."

Letting her hands drop to her lap, she looked at me. "I risked mine ... but you *gave* yours. ... You died ... and after that ... you changed. When you saw me ... I mean."

"How? How did I change?"

"You attacked Alex ... and she shot me. ... You never would have ... done that before." Her sobs renewed. "You see? ... I'm so selfish. ... I wanted you ... to protect me ... instead of the whole world. ... And I'm stupid enough ... to think it's ... because I'm ugly now." She covered her face again. "I'm so sorry ... to feel like this. ... But I can't help it. ... I'm just not ... good enough for you."

I rubbed her back and let her cry, whispering, "I understand. Trust me. I really do." As she wept, conflicting thoughts battled in my mind. I followed Sing's advice. Ignoring the risk to others, I attacked Alex and killed her. I saved the world. But I wounded the soul of the person I loved the most. Shanghai suffered because of my decision and would likely continue to suffer for a long time to come.

Without a doubt, if given the option, she would have shouted at me to forsake her safety and attack Alex, but I did the forsaking without her consent. And that made all the difference in the world. To her, it seemed like I no longer cared as much about her as I did about killing Alex.

"Shanghai," I said as I continued rubbing her back, "you have a deep wound, a feeling that makes perfect sense. I made a choice, and you didn't come first. Maybe I was wrong. Maybe I wasn't. I don't know. I don't know if I'll *ever* know. At the time, I thought my choice was right, because Sing kept telling me to charge in and kill Alex, but it still doesn't *feel* right.

"Anyway, I'll tell you this. I didn't make the choice because you're any different than you were before. In my eyes, you're just as wonderful as ever. Smart. Courageous. Loyal. Generous. And beautiful. There's not an inch of you that's ugly. Every bruise, every scar, even a missing eye reminds me of your love and sacrifice. They shout heroism to me, and that makes me think you're all the more beautiful."

She sniffed and brushed a tear from her cheek. "Then what ... what changed?"

"Like you said, *I* changed. My perspective, I mean. If I wanted to protect you, Sing, Saigon, the whole world, I had to destroy the evil that threatened you. If I put you in a locked box and merely fended off the attacks, the attacks would just keep coming. Besides, you're a warrior, not a helpless little maid who can't fight for herself. To treat you like a weak kitten who needs my constant protection would be disrespectful, untruthful, wrong. You're every bit as able to stand and fight evil as I am."

She nodded. "Thank you ... for saying that."

"We both know you weren't Alex's only target. She killed so many others. As long as I let her live, no one would be safe. I had to attack."

She spoke through stifled sobs. "So ... to protect the world ... you had to ... risk my life."

"That sounds pretty terrible, but ... yes. I just wish I had a chance to ask for your ... your blessing, I suppose. Your approval."

"You didn't have time." She took a deep breath. After settling herself, she leaned close and kissed my cheek. "You have my blessing ... after the fact."

I smiled. "So you're all right? You don't feel ugly?"

She laughed under her breath. "It's not that easy. ... Like you said ... it's a deep wound. ... But I'll heal."

Now that she had more peace of mind, it seemed like a good chance to move on to a surprise I had planned, the "big day" Georgia had let slip. "Maybe we can do something that will make your wound heal faster."

She shrugged, wincing at the effort. "I'm not sure ... how you could do that."

"I might have a way."

She tilted her head. "What?"

"Have you kept track of the days, I mean, how long it's been since we defeated Alex?"

"No. How long?"

"Five weeks. Today is your birthday."

"Oh." She averted her gaze. "Well ... happy birthday to me."

"Yes, happy birthday to you." I slid my hand into hers. "I arranged a surprise. Maybe it'll cheer you up."

"I doubt it ... but you can try."

I reached into my cloak's pocket and withdrew a large envelope. From inside, I pulled out a sheet of paper and showed it to her.

As she read it, I said, "It's a marriage license with our names on it."

Her mouth dropped open. She stared at me, a new tear trickling, but she said nothing.

I knelt at the side of the bed and held her hand. "You asked me to marry you when you turned seventeen, when we're both legal. And I said yes. But I'm switching the question around to make sure." I ran my thumb along her knuckles. "Shanghai, will you marry me?"

Her lips quivered. "You ... you still want to?"

"With all my heart." I rose and sat next to her again. "I hope you haven't changed your mind."

"Never!" She threw her arms around my neck and pulled me close. "Oh, Phoenix ... I love you ... so much!"

"I love you, too, Shanghai." When we separated, I showed her a series of blank lines on the license. "All we have to do is sign it with a couple of witnesses. We can do that at the city clerk's office. I'm sure Georgia and Fiona will go with us. Maybe Liam if he feels up to it."

Shanghai caressed my cheek. "Phoenix ... it's wonderful ... but what about vows?"

"The law says we don't need them, but if you'd like to say —"

"I would." Shanghai bit her lip before continuing. "I mean ... I really want to ... but I can't."

"I understand. It's too hard. Don't worry about it."

"No. ... I have to. ... And I will." She slid a hand into her pants pocket and withdrew a photo stick. "Remember I said ... I would show you?"

"Right. The reason you used my camera."

"I was practicing." She closed her hand around the photo stick. "Listen ... to my vows."

A glow ascended from her hand and formed into a miniature image of herself, dressed in Reaper garb, as usual. Her expression serious and her hands folded at her waist, she spoke with passion. "Phoenix, I am Shanghai, a Reaper who has loved you from afar ever since we first bruised each other in training when our ages were but single digits. Now we are close, and my love has come to full blossom, publicly acknowledged, fully confessed, and ready to be taken into your forever embrace."

Shanghai and her image inhaled at the same time, and the real Shanghai moved her lips to match the words as she gazed into my eyes. "As long as I have breath, I will speak kindness and courage to your heart. As long as I have strength, I will support you with every fiber of my being, whether I pull you from a pit of darkness, bandage your wounded body, or provide the pleasures of married love. And as long as I have love, I will pour its ointment over you and massage it into your soul with affirmations, encouragement, and kindness. I will be your lover in every way — body, mind and spirit. Till death do us part, God as my witness."

The image faded and disappeared.

Shanghai exhaled as if she had spoken the vows live, then took my hand and whispered, "Your turn."

I bit my lip, trying not to cry. Her words were so beautiful, so perfect. How could I possibly say what was on my heart so eloquently?

"Phoenix?" She grinned. "I'm waiting."

"All right, I'll try, but I never had a chance to practice." I cleared my throat. As I looked at her radiant, loving face — her battered, noble face — I knew I couldn't possibly make it through the vows without breaking down.

I silently begged for the right words to come. Hundreds of lonely nights had enabled me to become eloquent in my ruminations, but speaking my thoughts might prove to be a lot harder.

Taking both of her hands in mine, I spoke with a soft voice. "Shanghai, I have fought many battles, suffered many wounds, and spilled blood on many a path. I suffered for the sake of the poor, the sick, the hurting, and the oppressed. I have even killed so that these downtrodden people could be set free from tyranny."

Shanghai nodded along with each phrase, as if anticipating the next and expecting a climactic peak, though I had no idea if one was coming. Then, as if whispered in the wind, the words breezed to mind.

"Yet, there is one thing I never did for them. I never died for their sakes. A wise person once told me that if I give my body to be burned but have no love, what good is it? Such ashes are just ashes. They are swept away in the wind, debris that no one regards.

"But I did die for someone ... for you, Shanghai. In the dome room, I wrapped you in the fireproof cloak to keep you safe and gave my body to be burned."

Her mouth dropped open. She whispered, "I didn't know. ... Nobody told me."

I let out a shushing sound and continued. "Don't fret. I did it gladly. Why, you might ask? Because I love you. While it's true that I risked your life to kill Alex, even if time proves that I made the wrong choice, love was my motivation. And love will continue to be the principle that guides every thought, word, and action. If the need comes, I will die for you again, even if I can't rise from the ashes a second time. Knowing that you're alive and safe will make my sacrifice a life well spent."

Shanghai wept as I went on, my own tears welling. "I will stay with you no matter what tries to separate us. We are Reapers, to be sure, and we will share that crucial duty together, but we will be husband and wife first, holding to each other whether healthy or sick, whether happy or sad, and whether or not we *feel* in love. We will always *show* love, and we will never part while we walk this soil. God as my witness."

"Oh, Phoenix." She pulled me into a tight embrace. "I'm sorry ... I ever doubted you."

"And I'm sorry I gave you reason to."

"That was so beautiful!" Georgia walked in, brushing tears from her eyes. "So, so beautiful."

I drew back from Shanghai and wiped my own tears on a sleeve. "You heard us?"

"Every word, Phoenix. I guess I'm an incurable snoop."

"I heard you as well." Liam limped into the room, supporting himself with a cane. "I hope you don't mind that I let myself in."

I smiled, glad to see him up and around. "Not at all. But why did you come?"

"A certain little squirrel told me I needed to be here."

I sucked in a breath. "Sing? You saw her?"

"Saw her?" He nodded toward the bedroom door. "I *brought* her."

Sing walked in, her phantom hands folded at her semi-transparent waist and her signature curly hair shining. Instead of Reaper garb, she wore a white calf-length dress trimmed with lace. Her expression stoic, she said, "Hello, Phoenix."

I rose from the bed and stared, unsure of what to do. I tried to speak, but her sudden presence strangled every thought.

Sing smiled and spread her arms. "Don't I get a hug?"

I walked into her embrace, able to feel her nebulous body, strong and tender as always, though her warmth had fled. Our points of contact tingled, as they did with every ghost I touched. Even after several weeks of rounding up souls, I hadn't yet adapted to this new and odd sensation.

Sing stepped back, her radiant smile unabated. "I needed some time alone. You know, to think about things. I hope you understand."

"Um … yeah. Sure. But why are you here? I mean, I'm glad you're here. I'll never say otherwise again, but —"

Sing laughed. "Oh, Phoenix, you're such a kind soul. Don't worry about hurting my feelings. I heard your cry for forgiveness, and even though I already told you, I'll say it again. I forgive you without question."

"Thank you. That's a huge relief." I cocked my head. "So why did you decide to come?"

"I followed you to the city clerk's office, and I guessed what you were doing. I knew Georgia was already here." She nodded toward Liam. "I thought you might want a second witness. Fiona and her girls went to stay with Colleen for a while, so I decided to ask our kindhearted van driver."

Liam reached into his pants pocket. "And she also asked me to make this for you." He withdrew a leather boot string with a wooden cross dangling at the center. "She guessed you couldn't afford rings, so maybe your cross and this one will do."

I took the necklace from Liam and, after untying mine and taking it off, sat next to Shanghai again. Lifting the ends of the new one, I said, "May I?"

She smiled. "You may."

I reached the ends around her head and tied them at the back of her neck. She took the older necklace and did the same to me. When she finished, she touched her cross, a sleeker one than mine. "Now we'll … follow him … together." She looked at me and grinned. "But … no more dying … all right?"

Everyone laughed. The lightheartedness felt so good, so liberating.

When the laughter quieted, Sing said, "Well, we all heard your lovely vows and witnessed the exchange of gifts. I think we should get in Liam's van and drive to the office. Make everything official." She looked down at her dress. "That's why I'm wearing this."

I turned to Shanghai. "Do you feel up to it?"

She nodded. "I'll manage."

"Great. All we need to do is sign the license. After that, we can come straight home."

"We should … finish here first."

"Finish? What do you mean?"

She spoke with a serious tone. "You have to … kiss your bride … of course."

Warmth flooded my cheeks. "Um … Right. Of course."

"Wait." Shanghai slid off the bed and pressed her feet on the floor "For this … I'm going to stand."

"Let me help you." I held her shoulders as she stood in front of me. "Are you okay?"

"No dizziness so far." She wrinkled her nose, a new grin emerging. "I said … when this is all over … I'm giving you … the biggest kiss in history." She laid a palm on my cheek. "Now, my hero … make me dizzy."

I pulled her close and pressed our lips together — softly, warmly, passionately. She slid an arm around my shoulder and returned the passion. Tingles ran along my skin. Heat caressed my heart. Love poured anointing refreshment over my soul, just as she had vowed.

How long our kiss lasted, I don't know, but it was wonderful. The biggest kiss in history? Well, it certainly was for me. When we parted, I ran gentle fingers along her cheek and whispered, "What God has joined together, let nothing on earth separate."

Georgia clapped while Liam let out a sharp whistle. Sing stood quietly and smiled, her eyes sparkling. The moment felt surreal, a dream come true. The long nightmare was finally over.

As planned, we went to the clerk's office, signed the license, and hurried home. The trip, even as short as it was, wearied Shanghai. I helped her lie down, though she stayed awake. We bade Liam and Georgia good-bye, once again thanking them for their help.

When they left, I sat on the bed and looked at Sing. Now wearing Reaper garb, she stood only a step away, a grim expression on her face. "Phoenix," she said with a somber tone, "I can go to the Gateway, or I can stay here. Either choice is fine with me. One will send me to eternal peace and happiness with my parents. The other will keep me here with my dearest friends, you and Shanghai, for as long as you need me, though I won't be a Sancta, just a ghost who'll try to help you in any way I can."

"So you're saying whether or not you stay here is up to us?"

Sing nodded. "No pressure, I hope."

I reached out and grasped her hand. "Then stay. Please. You're welcome here anytime."

"Yes," Shanghai said. "Please stay."

Sing's smile seemed to brighten the room. "Thank you." She stepped back, her eyes sparkling. "But this is your wedding night. Don't expect to see me for a few days. And I'll figure out a way to let you know I'm coming for a visit."

Tears again welled in my eyes. "That's perfect, Sing. Thank you."

Shanghai waved. "We'll see you soon … my friend."

When Sing turned and walked out, it seemed that the light in the room dimmed, though a warm sensation took its place. Was it the closeness of friendship? The joy of camaraderie? Whatever it was, I hoped for much more to come.

I kicked off my shoes and settled in bed next to Shanghai, our backs propped by pillows. As I looked at her, new thoughts streamed, wonderful thoughts I never really believed would come true, at least not for a long time.

This woman was now my wife, and I loved her more than anything in the world.

I combed my fingers through her silky hair and luxuriated in the warmth of her loving glow. "It's been a long journey," I whispered.

She nodded. "And a ... strange one."

"Strange is a good word. I expected things to be so different. The victors are supposed to live happily ever after. But you're still suffering from terrible wounds. And so many people died. My parents. Your parents. Sing. Kwame. Saigon. Colm. Countless innocent people. The city's still a disaster zone. Another murderer is going to be elected as the world leader. Liam's still sick. Fiona's a widow. Her daughters are fatherless. The list goes on and on. We should be celebrating with our friends, but instead it's just you and me, weeping over what we've lost."

She laid her head on my shoulder. "Life isn't ... like storybooks, Phoenix. ... Good people suffer. ... Heroes die. The nights are ... dark and gloomy. ... And it's still night ... for most people."

"But, you know, somehow it feels like dawn is coming. Like it's a lot closer than before. We can have hope."

"I do have hope." She looked me in the eye and smiled. "I'm married to you."

"And you give *me* hope." I caressed her cheek with a thumb, inches from a burn scar that ran from near her ear lobe down to her neck. To me, it was another sign of her sacrificial love. I whispered, "You are so beautiful."

"I believe you think so ... but just to be sure ..." She slid her eye patch off, revealing the empty socket and its surrounding dark, ravaged skin — more reminders of her heroism. "What about now?"

"Still beautiful." I kissed her. "And you always will be."

"Thank you." She smiled with tight lips. "I'm going to ... bounce back soon. ... You'll see."

"I'm sure of that. And I'll be with you every step of the way. Together we'll help all of Chicago bounce back. We'll do whatever it takes, including training other Reapers to collect souls without the energy. That's when you're fully healed, of course."

"The city ... can't wait that long. ... We'll get started right away." Her mouth stretched into a wide yawn. "Well, maybe tomorrow. ... Let's have one ... good night's sleep together ... then I'll tackle anything."

"That sounds perfect." I interlocked thumbs with her. "Tomorrow, we start healing Chicago."

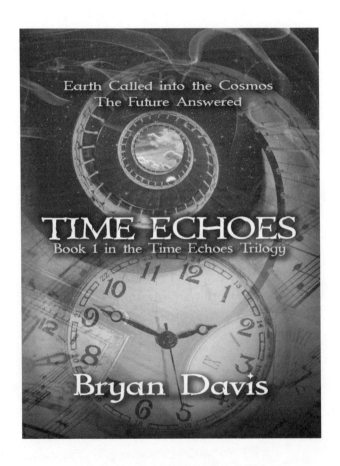

Earth Called into the Cosmos
The Future Answered

TIME ECHOES
Book 1 in the Time Echoes Trilogy

Bryan Davis

The Time Echoes Trilogy
The prequel series to the Reapers Trilogy